# The Next Thing You Know

## Also by Jessica Strawser

*A Million Reasons Why*
*Forget You Know Me*
*Not That I Could Tell*
*Almost Missed You*

# The Next Thing You Know

## Jessica Strawser

ST. MARTIN'S PRESS
NEW YORK

First published in the United States by St. Martin's Press, an imprint of St. Martin's Publishing Group

THE NEXT THING YOU KNOW. Copyright © 2022 by Jessica Strawser. All rights reserved. Printed in the United States of America. For information, address St. Martin's Publishing Group, 120 Broadway, New York, NY 10271.

www.stmartins.com

Designed by Devan Norman

Library of Congress Cataloging-in-Publication Data

Names: Strawser, Jessica, author.
Title: The next thing you know / Jessica Strawser.
Description: First Edition. | New York : St. Martin's Press, 2022.
Identifiers: LCCN 2021048594 | ISBN 9781250241641 (hardcover) | ISBN 9781250241658 (ebook)
Classification: LCC PS3619.T7437 N49 2022 | DDC 813/.6–dc23
LC record available at https://lccn.loc.gov/2021048594

Our books may be purchased in bulk for promotional, educational, or business use. Please contact your local bookseller or the Macmillan Corporate and Premium Sales Department at 1-800-221-7945, extension 5442, or by email at MacmillanSpecialMarkets@macmillan.com.

First Edition: 2022

10   9   8   7   6   5   4   3   2   1

*For artists everywhere,*

*and for people who do the hardest jobs (including the unpaid ones)—*

*and always, always, for J. and Boop*

*Tell me, what is it you plan to do*
*with your one wild and precious life?*

—MARY OLIVER, "THE SUMMER DAY"

# The
# Next Thing
# You
# Know

# 1

## *Mason*

THEN

Mason had already promised himself he wouldn't make any decisions today.

He scuffed his Vans on the side porch of the old house, facing the office entrance, and told himself again: He was here only for the free consult. He didn't *need* this. He'd been the one to make the call, and at any point he could unmake it. Bypass this extra step—no explanation necessary. A no-risk proposition.

Which left him no real reason not to go in and see what this so-called expert had to say.

This seemed a nice enough place. The porch was swept clean, its paint bright white even now, when the rest of Cincinnati had reached the gray-brown *sludge* stage of late February. A pink kid's bike lay in the driveway, helmet discarded in the grass. The cold air carried faint hints of some pleasantly herbal smell awaiting him inside.

Signs of life.

He just couldn't take his eyes off the actual sign. Hand-painted on wood, swinging slightly on its hinges. PARTING YOUR WAY, it read. END-OF-LIFE DOULAS.

He'd been doing a lot of pretending lately, but even he drew the line at acting nonchalant about walking through a door labeled END-OF-LIFE.

*What's wrong with you?* he asked himself. *This is literally what you came to do.* He kept waiting to feel more ready even as he suspected that no one ever did, and hell if that didn't sum up the problem exactly.

Maybe he would have turned around, driven home wondering why he'd ever thought this would work. But the door swung open, and a woman in a long paisley dress filled the doorway.

"Mr. Shaylor?" she asked, smiling. He looked around for some feasible way to act lost, but he clearly wasn't. He was right on time for his appointment.

"Mason," he said quickly. More formality was the last thing this moment needed. "You're . . . the death doula?"

She nodded, eyes flicking sideways to her sign, then back at him. Ah. She preferred *end-of-life doula,* but was too polite to say so. "Kelly Monroe." She extended a hand, and he moved close enough for a brief shake.

He watched as she looked him over, her smile unwavering. He hadn't bothered to clean himself up, seeing no point. But facing this bright-eyed woman, he had the belated decency to hope the smell of wood-smoke clinging to his down vest was enough to cover the stale beer and general misery permeating from the rest of him. He caught his reflection in the white-curtained office window: puffy eyes, sallow cheeks, ghost of a beard. He was thirty-six, but she'd easily guess him ten years older in this state.

Well, so what. Surely most people with reason to come here were at least this deprived of sleep and nutrition and especially luxuries. Like hope.

"Welcome. Shall we?" She stepped aside and gestured for him to come in.

He hesitated. At this angle, she blocked his view of the sign. Not that he could forget where he was, but he appreciated the symbolism being dialed down.

With a shrug, he stepped through.

Kelly's office was large and warmly lit, the walls themselves seeming to glow. Her desk was tidy but not clinical: cozy, but not in a grandmotherly way. A contemporary quilt hung on the wall—simple patterns, subdued hues. French doors opened to a sitting area that bore more semblance to a living room than a waiting room, though it was clearly arranged for families needing a private word. On the far side of the suite, a pocket door stood open to a nook containing a daybed and rolls of yoga mats.

He turned to find Kelly beaming behind her violet cat-eye glasses. Clearly this was when visitors remarked on how lovely the space was, how positively full service.

He flopped into a leather armchair opposite the desk before he could lose his nerve.

Full service wasn't what he was looking for.

"Coffee?" she asked.

Then again, maybe it was. He offered a sheepish smile. "Please? Black is fine."

Kelly chose a gray-blue mug from the corner kitchenette and filled it from the carafe, which smelled fresh, even midafternoon. He accepted it wordlessly as she slid behind her desk.

"So," she said. She folded her hands and inhaled slowly, making a point—or a show—of centering her attention on him. "What can you tell me about the situation you're facing?"

Mason gestured toward the business cards arranged in a glazed clay dish. She'd named this place like a promise: Parting Your Way. "Isn't everyone here kind of facing the same one?"

She exhaled, nodding calmly. "Yes and no. I've yet to encounter two that *feel* the same."

There was that expectant look again. He took a long sip of the coffee, though it was piping hot, to keep from rolling his eyes.

"I was thinking more of timeline, prognosis," she elaborated. "The immediate needs that bring you in. Whose behalf are you here for today?"

Now there was a question. *Everyone's,* he wanted to say.

"I guess I looked at this consult as more informational. I don't want to waste your time with my story if I'm not . . ." He cleared his throat. "Can we start with an overview? What exactly you do here?"

"No one is ever wasting my time with their story. But certainly." She leaned back into her seat. "Would hospice be involved from the start?"

"No, not . . ." He cleared his throat again. "No."

She nodded, pushing her eyeglasses higher onto her nose. "We can work collaboratively with them, of course, if and when the time comes. But for starters, then, my role would be as the client's advocate and your family's support as together you put a plan in place for a peaceful end-of-life transition. Families often come here overwhelmed with shock, sadness, fear, all of the above. My first step is to help stabilize that whirlwind of emotion."

"How exactly?" He held the mug to his chin, hiding behind the steam.

"We doulas operate on the philosophy that there are five general aspects to achieving peace of mind as end of life nears. One, the physical: Beginning with a plan for where the client would like to be cared for and what would make that possible, all the way through to their bodily wishes for after they're gone. The caveats here are that we do *not* provide medical care—legally, we can't administer medication or anything of that nature—and we do not take the place of licensed funeral directors in any way. But preceding, during, and sometimes after death, we can be present and hands-on in other support roles tailored to the family's needs—whether you need a shoulder to cry on or a spokesperson or an advocate. Make sense?"

He nodded. "Two," she moved on, "financial: I can assist with getting any outstanding paperwork in order, everything from recording internet passwords to designating beneficiaries."

"Isn't that stuff you'd go to a lawyer for?"

She seemed to sense his skepticism, cocking her head to discern whether he really wanted to know or was playing devil's advocate. Valid question: Even Mason wasn't sure.

"To the extent that you require or prefer that expertise, absolutely. I can act as a liaison with professionals of your choosing or refer you to trusted providers. To be honest, thanks to the internet, you can take care of a lot without any professional at all. Many families find it helpful, though, to have an experienced point person who can help emotionally and logistically carry the burden, so you may be as fully present as possible for your loved one's remaining days."

"A point person," he repeated. He couldn't help but wonder at the sort of client who'd buy into this completely. He imagined she'd look a lot like Kelly herself.

"Well, aside from the overwhelm of filing legal paperwork and medical directives, these can be hot-button issues for families. What the client wants for themselves does not always align with what their loved ones want."

Mason sat straighter. He and his family had never *aligned*. But they did seem to have reached a tipping point. Kelly picked up on his cue.

"Even with one another's best interests at heart, people can find themselves butting heads at the time they most want to get along," she said gently. "Emotions run hot. That's where an objective third party familiar with this terrain can prove useful."

She bit her lip, like she wanted to say more but thought it best to quit while ahead.

He had to admit, her instincts were pretty good.

"And you can do that?"

She nodded. "Even when caregivers and patients are on the same page, the situation can get away from them. For example, the lion's share of terminally ill people say they want to die at home, but the stats on what actually happens don't reflect that. Most take their last breaths in a hospital. It's not always enough to proactively say what you want. Once enough doctors are involved . . . Sometimes you need to dig in your heels." She smiled. "We doulas are good at that."

"So when you say you can work with traditional providers, you mean you can be a thorn in their sides?"

"Who, me?" She grinned, then pulled a folder from a stack on the shelf behind her and offered it across the desk. He flipped it open and scanned the pamphlets inside.

*A Caregiver's Guide to Being a Patient Advocate. Having a Positive Hospice Experience. Estate Planning Made Easy. Caregiver Checklists & FAQs.*

"I know it's a lot—we'd go over the enclosed forms at our first meetings, get everything completed and witnessed, and discuss who should have copies of advance directives and so on. But this gives you an idea of where we can start, what we can cover."

He flopped it closed. "You said five areas? Physical, financial . . ."

"And the big three: mental, emotional, spiritual. Letting go of pain, accepting the outcome they're facing, seeking forgiveness—many people have unresolved feelings and regrets they need to address before they can come to terms. We have ways to move them forward, and again mediate if necessary."

*We have ways to move them forward.*

The idea of hiring someone else to do this thing Mason could not do . . . this was what had sparked his curiosity, lured him here. Because it sounded too good to be true.

He needed to know if it was.

"What qualifies you to do all this?"

Kelly pulled a face. "I have to hand it to you for skipping the platitudes. I'm no stranger to skeptics, but usually they precede those questions with *No offense, but . . .* or, *Don't take this the wrong way . . .*"

He winced. "Sorry?" Bullshitting had never been his style.

"Don't be. It's refreshing, actually. Plus, what qualifies me is a fair question." This was the most genuine her smile had looked. "On paper, I've completed the leading nationally recognized training and certification program for end-of-life doulas, and attend annual trade conferences for continuing ed. For about ten years prior, I worked as a caregiver and companion in senior nursing facilities, and saw vast room for improvement in what our final years look like. Since opening Parting Your Way five years ago, I've shepherded more than a hundred clients and their families through positive transitions. Their testimonials say more than I could."

He'd seen the testimonials. Mason had done plenty of things on a whim, but this wasn't . . . Well, actually, this was one of them. But not *such* a whim that he hadn't looked at the website.

"You honestly think peace of mind is possible?" If he'd been antagonizing her, he wasn't anymore. In fact, he could have saved them both this whole awkward exchange if he'd worked out a way to call and ask just this. But that had seemed abrupt.

Kelly paused, considering the question. Mason felt an unexpected trust warming in the center of his chest.

She took this too seriously to overpromise. Whatever she said would be the truth.

"Some clients have real emotional work to do for that to happen," she granted. "Time isn't always on our side, but we try to get it there. One recent client was with me for only a week—but seeing her last wishes honored was enough for her to declare herself ready. She had five children and thirteen grown grandchildren: classic case of too many cooks in the kitchen. They hired me to ensure everyone had a chance to say goodbye the way she and they wanted."

"What might that look like?" This seemed a more reasonable question than *what if I'm tapped out on emotional work? What if I just want you to tell me what to do?*

"Well, it might look a lot like love. The smell of apple crisp baking in the oven. The sound of grandkids' laughter drifting up the stairs. A special song, maybe, for old time's sake."

He examined his lap. He'd never bothered to remove his vest, and beneath it several strings had come loose from his flannel and splayed across his denim-clad thigh like fireworks.

"What if someone doesn't want to say goodbye? They just want to . . ." His hand raked the patchy new growth of his beard, searching for words that wouldn't come. It had been itching all week, but he'd neglected to shave it.

"The client is always in the driver's seat, even when there are eighteen other willing caregivers right there in the room." Mason could have sworn Kelly's eyes went wet, thinking of that sweet grandmother—but in the next blink, they were clear.

"The five areas we cover are a menu, not a roster. The whole point is for this experience not to be clinical. Some end-of-life doulas are former lawyers and can cut out the middleman for legal concerns. Others are former nurses and appeal to clients undergoing complicated treatment plans. Others are reverends or rabbis whose clients prioritize spirituality. My background is in eldercare, period. I focus my energy where the client wants me to. I simply listen and help as best I can."

Mason let his eyes travel the room, from a bookcase labeled WELL-NESS LIBRARY, where a clipboard for signing out titles dangled by a length of twine, to the wood-grain essential oil diffuser humming on the shelf behind her.

"What's in there?" he asked, pointing. This was definitely the source of the smell he'd first detected outside—inviting but not overpowering.

"My custom blend. Lavender, ylang-ylang, and wild orange. It's meant to facilitate an uplifting, positive sense of calm."

"Huh." Maybe it wasn't genuine trust he was feeling, then—but it sure felt close to it. If he did want a doula, why not one who seemed to have thought of everything? He liked that she wasn't fazed by his questions. She wasn't less hippy-dippy than he'd expected, but she was more methodical—a reassuring combination. And yet.

"What qualifies anyone to do this?" she asked suddenly. "I can't say I haven't asked myself the same thing." Only in repeating his earlier question did she look unnerved by it. She gestured broadly, as if to encompass not the room but the universe. Et al.

"Death is a one hundred percent certainty for all of us, but nobody wants to talk about it. Even when someone does, people aren't receptive—as if it's morbid rather than smart to prepare. The result is that we're all equally unqualified when the time comes. Having walked that path with so many people gives me a breadth of experience that I hope makes me a well-suited companion in those uncertain moments. But that choice is up to every client. It's a big decision, a big responsibility, and certainly not one I take lightly."

"Okay." Mason deposited the mug on her desk with a *thunk*.

"Okay?" She looked unsure of the word's meaning. "If you'd like to talk it over with your loved ones, my tiered pricing is in the folder . . ."

He waved her away.

"Let's do this. I told myself I wouldn't decide on the spot, but to hell with it."

"Well." She smiled, still off guard. "I'd be honored. I mean, I am honored. We can onboard you right now, if you've time to walk through best practices, fill out some forms?"

He spread his arms wide, the universal sign for *at your service*. Though at this moment, it felt more like, *at your mercy*.

"Tell me about your family's situation."

He swallowed hard. He hadn't meant to mislead her to assume he was here for a parent or a grandparent—but it had been easier that way.

"My situation. I'm here for myself."

"For yourself?" She blinked.

"Look, cutting to the chase is more my style. I'm not saying I don't need *any* help in all five areas, but this acceptance stuff—it's the biggest leap. And you seem like . . . well, I had my doubts, but . . ." He stopped, seeing how her head shook. Fast and hard, as if motorized.

"There's been a misunderstanding." Her fingers drummed nervously on the polished wood between them. "As I said, I'm an eldercare specialist."

"You said every client is different."

Her cheeks flushed. "Even so, I don't accept clients below age sixty. Personal policy."

Something about the look on her face made him recall the child's bike in the driveway. Right. Of course. She was raising a kid in the home on the other side of these walls. There was no nice way of saying: *Look, what you're going through is natural. But you can't pay me enough to go through it with you*. Mason got it, though. In fact, he found himself more amused than offended. They'd called each other's bluffs—he deserved this probably.

"If you're saying I'm too young to die, I agree."

"I'm sorry," she said. She curled her hands into fists and lifted them to her forehead. "I'm not supposed to say that," she whispered, more to herself than to him. Her hands dropped to her lap. "Sorry," she said again, automatically.

He raised an eyebrow.

"I'm simply not the right person to do this for you."

He stood. She looked more defeated than he felt. She'd clearly had higher hopes for this whole arrangement than he'd dared to venture. He wanted to tell her no worries, he was a lost cause anyway. But he knew saying that would only make her feel worse.

Kelly rose from her chair, too, and he swore she seemed shorter than when he'd arrived. He bet if he looked beneath her desk, he'd find her shoes kicked off, so at home was she in this place, with this work. Such an odd path for her to have chosen, to devote her career to walking people through this door of hers, to creating for them this safe, sacred space inside. He should be ashamed of himself, taking up this woman's time, flustering her so clearly out of character.

But it had been a long time since he'd been able to summon the energy required for shame. Or virtually any other emotion born from human connection.

"I don't suppose," he said, trying for a joke, "you have a premature death specialist on staff?"

To his surprise, she laughed, relief jingling out of her like sleigh bells. And he saw then she wasn't going anywhere. That she'd risen not to see him out, but to stop him.

"As a matter of fact," she said, "we do."

# 2

## *Nova*

### THEN

I lean with the motorbike, sharp left around this curve, hard right around the next, reveling in the speed, the warmth of the leather seat, my grip on the vibrating throttle—firm yet precarious, too. I could let go, skid the shine right off this silver Yamaha, disappear into the brush. It's a classic beginner cruiser; no one would be all that surprised to see me lose control.

Least of all me.

Maybe I always feel this way when I leave a client—I guess I do. Like I need to reset, refuel with some exhilaration on their behalf. The barren February wind batters my face, drying the tears before they can leave my eyes, pulling strands loose from my long braid. I breathe it in, greedily—not air, but wind, hyperaware of the difference, willing it to pass through me.

It wouldn't be right, wouldn't be human, for anyone to simply *swallow* the wind.

Would it?

I like the idea of energy unbound to the laws of physics, finding some way through.

Here on Cincinnati's far east side, these forested roads with their scattered, set-back houses give way to suburbs without warning. Our neighborhood is tucked behind a worn business district, but I hit every green light, getting lucky. When I turn into the driveway, I see them: Kelly and some scruffy guy, on the platform atop the stairs leading to Parting Your Way's annex over the detached garage: my studio door. She's resting one arm on the railing, hand talking with the other—likely explaining something about us, or me. He's nodding without much interest, hands thrust into his puffy vest pockets.

I roar to a stop beneath them, my boot meeting the kickstand with practiced efficiency.

"Helmet," she calls over the railing, sternly. Her mom voice. I pat the bag fastened to the back of my seat, yanking the zipper so she can see the gleam of the visor inside.

"Doesn't do you any good if it isn't on your head."

She's wrong. I carry it in on my visits to Mr. Whitehall. He sees it under my arm and gets a gleam in his eye, starts chatting about what a crisp day it is for a ride, and then he's back in the seat of one of his stories, and I am, too: The time he rode alone all the way to the Rockies, or almost married a bikini model at Daytona Bike Week. His hearing isn't good—he always seems surprised when I ring the doorbell, no matter how loud I rev the engine on arrival—and he rarely steps foot outside anymore. If I didn't have the helmet, he'd never share the stories. He might not have even hired me, come to think of it.

But that doesn't mean I have to wear the thing.

Two pairs of shoes tap down the stairs, and then they're standing in front of me. Up close the scruffy guy is even scruffier, though not in an unappealing way. Slimly built, a few inches taller than my own five-foot-six. His eyes are intense, his features roughly cut, like a sculpture that isn't quite finished.

Something about him seems familiar.

"Nova Huston, this is Mason Shaylor." Kelly gestures needlessly, almost like she's nervous. "Sorry to catch you on your way in, but he's a prospective client, if you have any time?" Her eyes are pleading— *I'll owe you one*—and I don't need to ask why she's casting him off on me.

When I came on as partner, cast-off duty was kind of in my job description.

Mason is looking from my bike to me and back again, as if trying to join two things that don't fit. Square peg, round hole. Plain Jane, death on wheels. I wonder if he knows this model is called a V Star, and thinks I'm the type to force a match based on something as superficial as a name. I'm not, by the way. I like its low center of gravity, comfortable seat, modest size, and right price. Even if I didn't exactly think through *all* the implications of trading in my car.

I can't afford both, and can't trade back now. My parents would be way too glad.

Then Mason smiles at me, like maybe I said that out loud. Or more like I didn't have to, because I'm somehow familiar to him, too.

"My next appointment isn't for thirty minutes," I say, smoothing my flyaways. Kelly excuses herself, but neither Mason nor I make a move to go inside. To be honest, I make a better first impression on the go. My office upstairs is nothing like hers, but merely a tiny, minimalist room that came as sparsely furnished as the efficiency apartment beyond: desk, chairs, lamp, potted palm. I've added only a bookcase to display my mishmash of secondhand frames, photos of the places I've stayed longer than a week or two. St. Augustine. Savannah. St. Simons. Weaverville. Cumberland Falls.

If I ever print a picture of this place, that'll make thirteen. An unlucky number.

"She says you can help me make peace with the inevitable," Mason says drily, one unconvinced eyebrow raised. Hmm. I'm no stranger to this look. I ignore it all the time in polite conversation with strangers and see more than my share in medical professionals, too. Kelly has coached me to quietly sidestep until it subsides—when they see just how pathological we are about giving their patients the benefit of the doubt. But on a client?

This is new.

"How often do we need to meet," Mason asks, "to make that happen?"

My attempt at a grin comes out sideways. "Usually people want to talk with a doula first. See if they dovetail." My practical side gives my inner customer service rep a kick. Unlike Kelly, who can survive on referrals alone, I could use the work. But Mason only gestures toward my bike.

"I dovetail," he says. "So, how often?"

Here's the thing about the benefit of the doubt. It might not sound like a radical concept, but in the most difficult times of their lives, people get prickly. Carving out a sacred space around them, protecting it? That's where we pick up the slack for the overwhelmed and underprepared. And it's not just important. It's everything.

So this time I smile for real. "You tell me."

"Twice a week? Three times?" He glances at his watch, so I take the cue. We set his first appointment, and he uses one thigh as a table while he scrawls a check for his deposit.

"Enrollment fee plus the first month, right?" He rips it off and hands it over, and my conscience twinges again as I fully take in the smell of a campfire, the slept-in look of his clothes—of his entire body, really.

"If it's a hardship, we can work out a payment plan? Or break down the commitment differently." I'm not the stickler Kelly is, and she has yet to call me out on my more creative accounting. But Mason surprises me with a scoff.

"This?" he says, gesturing around us—the billowy sky, the row of evergreens lining the property line, the cardinals chirping—"is not a hardship."

Then, he strides to the dusty blue Jeep parked on the street and pulls away without so much as a wave, while I stand there thinking maybe he gets it already. The meaning of things, the scale. Maybe he doesn't need me at all.

Later, Kelly fills me in, after I've joined her and Willow for our weekly spaghetti dinner: squash-based pasta, gluten-free garlic bread, Caesar salad, a recap of the goings on in fifth grade. Kelly is the mama bear breed of single mom, and she's adamant about not talking shop in front of her daughter, which is fine with me—if she didn't force the break, I'm not sure we'd ever take one. Over a sink of dishwater, once Willow is out of earshot in front of the TV, Kelly recaps how Mason's consult threw off her game, how she hadn't realized how rusty she'd gotten with walk-ins and cold calls. I can see what she means: Most of Kelly's clients arrive bursting to unload the burden they've been carrying alone for too long. *I can't believe how quickly it spread . . . I knew we'd be here eventually . . . Sandra said how much you helped Gary . . .* Mason, she explained, had been so tight-lipped that she'd ended up trying too hard to win him over and then feeling mortified and graceless in realizing her mistake. When it came to her elderly clients, I had yet to see her flustered. Mason was a special case.

If she'd had the slightest idea just how special, she'd have escorted him straight past my annex and back to his Jeep never mentioning him to me. But she didn't.

Which, I suppose, is the extent of the blame she shares in everything that came after.

# 3

*Nova*

NOW

I promised myself I wouldn't watch this video again—at least, not to-day. I've already hit my self-imposed limit, and if there's one thing I have left to hold onto, it's my convictions. Lose them, and I officially won't know who I am anymore.

But this is my favorite of all the footage I've found of Mason, and that's saying something.

I had to rationalize my internet sleuthing at first. He was so withdrawn—what choice did I have, if I truly wanted to counsel him? He ostensibly wanted that, too, after all. I never gave up hope that I'd spot some crease in the picture that I'd overlooked, something I could smooth out to reveal the answer we were both looking for. And I thought I'd found it in this video.

Watching it again won't change the fact that I was wrong.

Still, this three minute and twenty-one second clip is the only one anyone would need to really see him. As he was before, I mean—the only way, in his own mind, he was meant to be. So I cue it up again, not bothering to lie to myself that it's the last time, and curl tighter in my swivel chair, hugging my loose-knit cardigan like a protective fur.

In a window on my laptop, Mason perches on a barstool on the smallest stage you've ever seen, little more than an egg crate in the corner of one of those likeably paradoxical places that doubles as a coffee house and a bar. It's dark, without proper lighting for the performance, and the picture goes pixilated as the camera lens tries to cling to the image. He's wearing that same flannel he wore that first day in the driveway, but it's newer, brighter even in the dim, and unbuttoned halfway down his chest the way only a musician can pull off. He strums his acoustic once, dances his fingers along the frets, and then . . .

The crowd loses its ever-loving mind.

The roar is too large for the coffee shop slash bar slash concert hall, and the image shakes with the force of it. Mason goes still. You can see the instant it registers on his face:

That *he* is too large for this coffee shop slash bar slash concert hall.

That he has outgrown this egg crate of a stage, by a whole stack of them and then some. By a truckload. By a mountain.

That he is going places. And these people, these true fans who recognize this song that he started out with back when no one was watching, are going to follow him.

But first, he's going to give them the show of their lives.

He starts to sing, and a chorus of voices joins him in the opening line, but then these people crammed into this too small space to see this too big artist collectively pull back, hush down. Because they're not here to sing along, not if it means drowning him out. They're here to listen. And they don't want to miss another second of this. A constellation of lighters flickers and sways to the harmony, and then the chorus comes along, and everyone is singing again—they can't help it, it's contagious, and anyone can see it's feeding him, amplifying the vibe, enlarging the pumping heart of it all. Mason is smiling in a way he rarely has in the three months I've known him. Like there's something he can't wait to tell you, if you'll stick around for the next set, the next show, the next album. The next plateau.

And then the screen goes black, and a Play Again icon appears in the center, an arrow twisted into a circle, daring me.

I wonder if Mason ever watches this anymore.

I wonder if he stares at these two little words, hating them.

Before I can click, my phone breaks the cruel silence. It's Kelly's ringtone, a series of wind chimes. Glad to be saved from myself, I pick up right away.

"Nova." Her voice sounds funny. Formal. "Am I catching you in the office?"

"Yeah, what's up?" She knows I'm here. We ate lunch on the porch a bit ago, admired how big the annuals had already grown—it's only the day after Memorial Day—synced our afternoon schedules.

Rather, she ate lunch. I pushed my salad around my plate until she finished.

"Your client, Mason Shaylor?" My alarm system engages. We're on a first-name basis about all our long-term clients, would be even without our weekly check-ins. Never mind that I haven't worked up to telling Kelly that Mason isn't my client anymore. "Could you please check his file and see if he authorized us to discuss with his mother? Bonnie Shaylor."

I freeze. Kelly has schooled me to know this sort of thing off the top of my head. Checking files for basic info is for medical personnel, not for holistic partners. And definitely not for Parting Your Way. She's tipping me off with wording that sounds natural to anyone but me.

The someone with her *is* Mason's mother.

Our privacy policy is clear. Communications with health providers comply with the federal and state laws to which they are held. Beyond that, our code of ethics pledges confidentiality, and clients complete a form granting consent for Kelly and me to discuss their care among ourselves (in the rare event that I need to fill in for Kelly, or vice versa) and stipulated family members and caregivers. Clients sometimes designate degrees of disclosure: *basics only* or *full proxy* or even listing relatives who they do not, under any circumstances, want involved.

When I declined to let Mason omit this form entirely, he wrote *emergencies only* next to his mother's name. From the overall sparse nature of his file, you'd never guess I've spent far more time with him than my average client. Bonnie Shaylor is his sole emergency contact, as well as his beneficiary on his insurance policies, his long-drained investment accounts—everywhere but his creative assets. This is exactly the snub it looks like: He owes her, for raising him and his brother alone and well. But he can't trust her not to undervalue or even discard his legacy. And I'd estimate that's representative of about 90 percent of their relationship.

"On a limited basis," I tell Kelly, wondering whether Mason's definition of *emergency* would gel with his mother's or even with mine. I doubt it's possible to make Mason any more upset with me than he already is. I haven't been relegated to videos for nothing. In fact, I've been steeling myself against the possibility that I'll never see him again.

The impossibility, is more like it. That's how unbearable the idea is.

But I expected to see his mom even less.

"In that case, are you able to come down to my studio? Mrs. Shaylor is here with some questions for us both." I'm already on my feet when she adds, "It's important."

In this business, *important* is rarely good news.

I'm halfway down the exterior stairs before I see the station wagon parked out front. It's an unassuming vehicle—a decades-old model complete with faux wood paneling—except for the minor detail that it's parked catawampus across the driveway, as if the driver arrived in the kind of hurry typically reserved for a mad dash to the hospital with a laboring woman, or a desperate airport run to keep one's true love from departing for another life.

I skim the yard and porch for some hint of explanation, but all is quiet.

In the absence of any commotion, it looks an awful lot like the driver, or at least the parker, wanted to stop anyone else from coming in. Or out.

And suddenly I really, really want out.

Kelly isn't at her desk, but in the sitting room beyond. She's visible through the doorway, occupying half the love seat, and relief crosses her face as she gestures me in. The woman sitting across from her turns her wide, gray eyes on me, and I stop midstep—because it's Mason. If I take away all the beige—her short-sleeved cable-knit, capris, espadrilles—and if I unclip the surprisingly large gold hoop earrings and brush back the thick, box-dyed auburn hair, her face is Mason plus twenty years of weary life experience, Mason having walked the slow march of maternal heartbreak, Mason at his most curious and accusatory and confused. It's Mason at his worst, the way he hated to be, and so much makes sense then that I wish he'd introduced us earlier.

"I'm Nova," I say, recovering, uncertain whether to shake hands. She neither smiles nor stands, so I settle onto the couch next to Kelly. Now that I'm closer, I'm not sure I've ever seen Kelly sit so stiffly, and though she'd seemed glad of my arrival, she isn't looking at me now.

"Your colleague was trying to explain what you do here," Bonnie says by way of greeting. Her tone signals *what we do here* sounds like bunk to her, but we're used to it.

Plus, that's Mason, too.

"Mrs. Shaylor was not aware Mason had signed on as a client," Kelly explains, her eyes fixed on the wall straight ahead. "She came across his calendar and was surprised to see so many appointments with you."

I bite my lip, uneasy.

"I still don't understand what exactly you've been *doing*," Bonnie snaps, and I feel for her. Only an explanation from Mason himself would be sufficient. Then again, it's off-putting, a grown man's mother going behind his back. Before I can answer, she thrusts a wall calendar at me, its pages flapping like wings. "Sometimes four days a week? Five?"

It lands in my lap, and I flip it open to last month for lack of another way to respond. It's a cheap dollar store number with oversaturated pictures of American landscapes, and across the top of May, a glacier gleams nearly neon in the Alaskan sun. Mason told me how he'd disabled his cell phone calendar after his last tour was canceled, and sure enough, his messy handwriting has marked our meetings with my name and the time. I page back to April and see that a few note a place when we met off-site, but there's nothing to indicate who I am or anything about Parting Your Way. I flip to March, then February, where his first consult is written with the business name and address, and an arrow drawn to his second visit and the first jaggedy *Nova*.

"Have you asked Mason about his experience here?" My days of being spoken to like I'm a petulant child are long over.

"Notice anything else strange about that calendar?" she asks, like I haven't spoken.

I look at the pages again, each numbered square a step in our progress. Many of them tied to a memory—so tightly I almost wish I could keep this. Add it, nonsensically, to his file.

That's when I realize what she's getting at.

There's nothing else on them at all. Only me. I flip to June, and the whole month is blank. I suppose because our last meeting was just over three weeks ago.

"Not once has he mentioned you. Yet none of the places he's told me he was off to are here." Her eyes are hard, as if I might have lured him here against his will, forged this schedule myself, and coerced him into keeping it from her.

"I'm not sure what's led you to check up on him, but—"

"Don't you say that like it's a bad thing," she seethes. "You have *no idea* how badly I wish I'd been checking up on him all along."

This seems disproportionately dramatic, but I lift my hands, capitulating. "I'm sorry you're upset. I was only about to suggest you ask Mason about his experience here first."

"You're sorry I'm *upset*?" She's talking like she parked the station wagon now, slashing through everything I've said or am about to say.

"Maybe you could come back together—"

"I can't!" she yells. "We can't! This is all I have! This and *you*!" Lunging from her chair, she snatches the calendar from my lap and hurls it across the room with an animalistic roar. Then, she breaks down in sobs, collapsing into her seat, utterly defeated.

And I know.

Behind all this baffled hostility . . . I don't know how I didn't see it first thing.

*Don't say it,* I beg silently.

If she doesn't say it, maybe it's not true.

"Mason's Jeep." She sniffs. "There was a crash."

*No.*

"Saturday. Late."

*Please, no.*

"He didn't . . ." I don't know if she actually says the word *survive,* or if my brain fills in the blank. White noise pounds in my ears. The room is tilting, the blood rushing to my head, until I'm upside down, helpless. Hopeless.

*He can't be dead,* I think, irrationally. *I was just watching him sing—* never mind that the video is years old. Denial chokes me as I try to make my brain stop its whirling horror.

No more Mason.

I bow my head, covering my face with my hands, summoning strength to hold it together. I can't fall apart in front of Bonnie the way I want to, the way I need to. It *has* to wait.

I'm the professional.

Kelly's gentle hand finds the center of my back. "I'm so sorry for your loss," she says—to us both—and her hand moves in slow circles. *I've got you.* "Nova was—is—especially fond of Mason. Do they know what happened? Bad weather? Or another car involved?"

I flail through the fog of my memory, looking for Saturday. Three agonizingly long, ignorant days ago. A Memorial Day weekend I'd pledged to spend uneventfully here, working just enough to keep my mind off having no place else to be. But then Kelly and Willow had that big fight—typical mother-daughter stuff heightened by this last week of school approaching, plus tech rehearsals for Willow's year-end play. I'd ended up making myself scarce. Was Saturday when those thunderstorms came through? What time had the accident been? What had I been doing? How did I not sense his absence somehow, then or since?

It's my *job* to keep tabs on death. I've had it on a tight leash for years. Bonnie takes a shuddering breath and grabs noisily at the tissue box beside her.

"He went off an overpass. Killed on impact."

Bile rises in my throat.

I shut my eyes tighter, trying not to cry out. I'd do anything to drown out the imagined sound of crashing metal. Mason's big talent on that small stage, spinning through the dark night.

"What a terrible accident." Kelly breathes, shaken. "He still had so much life in him."

That's when the full horror of it hits me:

Mason isn't here to explain.

"The police," Bonnie says, so quietly I have to strain to hear. Kelly slips me a tissue. Parting Your Way doesn't skimp on grieving supplies, and it's soft as I press it to my eyes, hiding from whatever this older, grief-stricken Mason is about to say. I'd rather picture him as before. Unmarred by . . .

By this.

"They're saying it might not have been an accident."

"What do you mean?" Kelly asks, automatically, even as I think, *My God.* Even as I feel Kelly stiffen, thinking the same thing.

Bonnie sniffs. "They found a note. In his glove box. Saying . . . goodbye."

I hear Kelly's sharp intake of breath.

"I don't believe . . . I never imagined . . ." Bonnie's tears well up again, and I just want her to turn around and take her questions out that door, never looking back.

But when she clears her throat and tosses her hair behind her shoulders, I can tell that's the last thing she'd do. "You say your job is to see patients who are on their way out."

Kelly winces. "Terminally ill," she says for me. "Yes."

My face burns. I'm staring intently at my lap, but there's no mistaking the focus of Bonnie's enraged energy. "You're used to clients dying then, Nova. But you seem upset."

The room turns again on its axis, emptying the air from my lungs.

"We care about our clients, Mrs. Shaylor." Kelly sounds hurt that this isn't obvious.

"Then answer this, Nova." She keeps saying my name like it's some overrated new product she's prepared to hate. "Did he give you any indication of plans to end things?"

I look up at her, tears clouding my vision as I swallow hard and will my voice to come. "Mason wasn't forthcoming about his plans for anything," I manage. "I don't think he found what he was looking for here. He stopped seeing me a few weeks ago."

Kelly's head swivels toward me, and my shame burns even hotter.

"That matches the calendar," Bonnie says. "What reason did he give?"

I shake my head. "He just stopped."

"And that didn't give you cause for concern? To check on him maybe?"

I can't answer. I *did* call the house. Bonnie herself picked up. But when she said he couldn't talk, I made the mistake of not leaving a message.

"We never want our clients to make this choice, Mrs. Shaylor. If Nova had had an inkling of any suicidal ideation . . ." Kelly's voice cracks. She's struggling with this, too, and I know it's not only the emotions.

It's the implications.

We're in the business of death, but not this kind.

"She'd have taken appropriate measures," Kelly finishes, finally, sounding so sure of herself—of me—I have to turn away.

Of course we *never want our clients to make this choice.* Least of all, in my case, Mason.

Kelly puts an arm around me, for comfort or protection I'm not sure. I need both, but in Bonnie's eyes it's plain to see I deserve neither.

"But none of this is 'appropriate.' That's what I don't understand," Bonnie says. She takes a deep, long breath and looks straight at me. Waiting. "Mason was never terminally ill."

# 4

## *Mason*

Mason looked across the desk at Nova's expectant face and reminded himself he'd paid handsomely for his seat in this shell of an office— which had been left off the initial tour for glaringly obvious reasons. He'd give her this: The fact that she'd made little effort to extend Kelly's warm, Zen-like quality to this afterthought annex over the garage made him feel a certain kinship to her. Even if the rest of this meeting did not.

She'd spread between them all the forms from Kelly's "onboarding" folder—the one he'd promptly thrown in his back seat and forgotten— for them to begin this process by addressing it together. His eyes leapt from one page to another—the health care proxy, power of attorney, emergency medical checklist, and, most dauntingly, a thick packet titled New Client Overview and Future Care Plan. This one, Nova had explained, was mostly for her own reference. Which should have been a comfort. But what jumped out at him was a guilt trip.

*Had he thought about where he'd like to die, and who he'd like there with him? Had he told his family the specifics of his condition? Had he been honest with them about his wishes?*

He'd hoped to bypass his family by being here with Nova. But now he saw this might not be that simple. The blank lines taunted him. Wasn't this what he'd wanted? For her to tell him what to think about, what to do next? To offer a system to make sense of it all?

Well, he'd been mistaken. Clearly this was one of those things that seemed better in theory than practice. All he could think was, *I didn't sign up for this*—even though he had. All he could think was, *Mason Fucking Shaylor does not spend his days sitting at dreaded desks filling out dreaded forms*—even though he hated the sound of his own laughably misplaced arrogance. Even though the things Mason Shaylor damn well did do had ceased being damn well doable.

The doula was staring at him. He had no idea what she'd said, but it seemed his turn to speak.

"Is this really necessary?" When in doubt, hedge. "I mean, my reading skills remain intact." He tried to smile. "Can't I do these on my own at home?"

Nova cocked her head, and the fringe on her dress—an improbable lavender suede number that was part cowgirl, part flapper—swayed with her. She'd coiled her long, brown hair behind one ear, and though she was attentive, she looked like someone who surely had someplace more interesting to be. Who might be headed there, right after this.

"You could. But part of my role as your doula is to be intimately familiar with your wishes and reasoning behind them. These are good tools for bringing me up to speed."

He crossed his arms over his chest. All he'd done, since he'd rolled back into town, was bring people up to speed. He wasn't sure what he hated more: The way his throat would wad into a ball over the truth he still couldn't believe himself, or the looks of pity that followed. The assurances that people he'd scarcely seen in years were *there for him, whatever he needed.*

They had no idea what he needed. And if they did?

They'd run—sprint—the other way.

"In my experience," Nova went on, "talking through your responses, starting with the prognosis and timeline, is much more helpful to both of us than me reading over your answers. Plus, you'll likely have questions—there's some jargon here."

"Am I required to get into these specifics, if I'm more interested in the psychological side of this? Kelly mentioned five areas, but said this arrangement was flexible."

Nova looked taken aback. "I'm not big on requirements. But this is a pretty key frame of reference." Her eyes bore into his: *How am I supposed to help you if you don't tell me what's going on with you?*

What had he expected: To come in, remain virtually anonymous, and get catchall-sized advice that actually fit? At the consult, Kelly made it sound within reach—but he hadn't thought enough about what it would be like to do the actual reaching. He should leave.

Instead, he picked up a form headed *Letter of Instructions.* "I can't be the only one who finds this overwhelming," he ventured. "People really rush in and make spot decisions on how they define quality of life? Plans for organ donation? Who should get their pets?"

Nova held his gaze. "They often have no choice but to rush."

If this was meant to make him feel lucky, it didn't work. Stupid—that, he felt.

"You have a pet?" She was reaching for a bright spot. Or, she was seeing through him.

"No." A complaint could be both hypothetical and valid, couldn't it? He expected a rebuke, but she smiled.

"That's an easy one then." She wrote *None* on the corresponding line.

"One down, nine hundred forty-seven to go," he said drily.

"Look, this packet is designed to put you in control, and help us form a plan together." Nova spoke with the exaggerated patience of someone whose frustration is about to breach her dam. "Kelly likes us to have all the paperwork on file in the first week or so—for your own sake. But I understand not feeling ready to think about these things."

"It's not that." Maybe it was that. "But I need time. Putting these answers in writing seems so . . . final. Especially under the circumstances."

Her expression reminded him he had yet to tell her the circumstances. She was looking him top to bottom, no doubt wondering what was wrong. Was it his brain? His heart? An army of cellular invaders in his bloodstream? A vital organ breaking down? In what way, precisely, was he fucked?

If he picked up the pen, she would start to see.

Then again, if he picked up the pen, she'd have a stronger argument for doing this together, here and now.

"Would it make you feel better to know that even perfectly healthy people should fill most of this stuff out? To answer your earlier question, of course it's natural to find these overwhelming. That's why we do a dozen appointments a week with one-off clients just for this, despite a lot of these forms being searchable online. With terminal clients, my philosophy is to meet you wherever you are with this. I can only do that if you share with me where you are."

No person would want to meet him here. He'd hoped she'd lead him somewhere else.

"Let me ask you this," he said, abruptly and to his own annoyance. This was his manager's most overused and worst line. Mason liked Dex—hell, he even missed him—but Dex's padding of cringe-inducing requests left something to be desired. *Let me ask you this, Shaylor: I know we talked about Miami, but ever been to Omaha? Great steaks! Let me ask you this: Thoughts on sharing top billing with a pop artist? Chicks go crazy for boy bands! Let me ask you this: Could we drop the album earlier if we did only eight tracks? Has a retro ring to it!*

Mason didn't bother padding his own. "Why in God's name would you want to be an actual premature death specialist?"

Nova laughed—not uncomfortably, but with sincere mirth, her surprised giggle exploding into something fuller. "No such thing. Who gave you that idea?"

"Kelly."

"Somehow I can't picture Kelly using those words."

"Well. They might have been my words." He tried to look charmingly caught. "But she explained you're the only one who takes nonelderly clients."

"So? I take elderly clients, too."

"Business would be pretty slow otherwise, wouldn't it?"

"You'd be surprised." She wasn't smiling anymore.

"I guess I'm wondering if the difference says more about Kelly, or about you."

She thought about it. These doulas sure were comfortable with long pauses. "Both," she said finally. "What about you? What should it tell me about you that you're here?"

"Besides the fact that life as I know it is over?"

"Not besides that. That exactly. What you're feeling about it, what your support network feels about it, what you want to do about it—or not do about it—how I can help."

He took a deep breath. He had to give this a fair shot if he wanted to keep coming here. Which he wasn't sure he did.

But where else would he go?

"I know you're right," he said, "about the importance of paperwork when the clock is ticking. But at the moment, I have nothing but time. I mean, until it runs out."

She nodded, slowly. "Have you had to make changes in how you spend your days?"

"To put it mildly."

She appraised him. "I've heard it said that doulas are essentially agents of change. You'll be facing some big ones, but . . ." She drifted off, then started again. "Some people try to change too much, too fast. For instance, once you've been diagnosed, it might seem pointless to keep going to work. Like, who wants to spend their borrowed time *working*? But sometimes people end up missing the purpose it brings to their days."

"I do," he said, flatly.

"You do what?"

"Want to spend my borrowed time working. But I can't."

"Because you're physically unable, or because well-meaning people pressured you to stop?"

"Yes."

"May I ask what you do for a living?"

He was simultaneously grateful and angry she did not say *did*. "I'm a musician."

"What kind?"

"Guitarist. Singer-songwriter."

"With a band?"

"Sometimes."

"Locally, or—?"

"All over."

"So, when you say you're physically unable, does that have to do with needing to stay close to your doctors? Or with physical limitations?"

He flexed his hands in his lap, where she couldn't see, then curled them back into fists. It was fitting this had become his most comfortable resting position. Anger seemed to be his all-around default.

"It has to do with being physically unable," he mumbled.

She didn't look frustrated anymore. Only sad. "And when you say you've been pressured to stop by well-meaning people, would that be your family or your manager or—?"

"Yep."

She pursed her lips. "I imagine it's culture shock to give up that lifestyle. When people get bad news, some freeze in denial, but others overcorrect. I'm just wondering if there's a way you could scale back rather than going cold turkey."

*Gee, why didn't I think of that,* he wanted to snap, even as her words pulled him by the wrist. Because beneath the maddening nature of the question was this startling fact:

Nova understood. Culture shock, she'd called it.

No one else had.

It was one of his life's great ironies that he'd gotten more sympathy about being on the road than about leaving it. How tiring, people would say, to always be on the go. To wake up disoriented, having to recall what city he was in. To exist without the familiarity of his own bed, the ease of a well-stocked fridge, the comfort of routine. The road, in their view, was a thing to be endured, the dues paid along the way to greatness, the necessary evil, the nature of the beast, and a bunch of other silver-lined clichés.

Not once had it occurred to those people that he might find these selling points rather than caveats. That the first seconds he spent awake in a hotel bed, or on a random couch, or in the back of his Jeep, before his memory kicked in made the most exhilarating start to a day. They didn't know the lovesick joy of waking with a smile spread-eagle on your face and not even consciously knowing yet why. They didn't fathom that things they found comforting—the Sunday pot roast at Mom's or the weekly trivia night at the pub—struck him as stifling. He didn't think less of anyone who wanted those things; sometimes he envied them. But he recoiled from any suggestion that he simply learn to like being one of them now.

The only place he found his feelings reflected—as was often the case—was in song. Willie Nelson strummed about it as *the life I love.* John Mayer philosophized *it doesn't matter where you roam.* Sturgill Simpson wisecracked: *Tell 'em I'm somewhere looking for the end of that long white line.*

That one was an inside joke. The whole point was that there was no end.

But Mason had found it anyway. Back where he started, in a town where there was no one who thought the slightest bit like him.

There was, however, apparently, Nova.

"Okay," she said suddenly, thumping her open palms onto the forms in front of her. "We can do these at your own pace."

"You won't get in trouble with your boss?"

She raised an eyebrow. "I'd like to give you a tool to use when you feel overwhelmed. Whether it's by these well-meaning questions or those well-meaning people. Okay? Repeat after me: Right now I'm okay because . . ."

She waited. He remained silent.

"The idea," she coaxed him, "is to set aside worry about tomorrow or yesterday and ground ourselves in gratitude for something in the moment. Even if only that the sun is shining, or your shower is hot. Right now I'm okay because Kelly is more of a partner than my boss, and she knows I do things my way."

Again, she looked at him expectantly.

"Right now I'm okay . . ." No. He couldn't. He hadn't come here and paid good money to lie. "Because nothing. I wouldn't be here if I was in any way okay."

There was something in Nova's smile, as she let him off the hook. A secret.

Though maybe not an entirely happy one.

"Let's walk through these as I put them back in your folder, so you know what to mull in the back of your mind, okay? Not line by line. I'll sum up, you don't have to say a word."

She was right to press him. He hadn't come here for a free pass.

But he wouldn't need half of these forms anyway. And she couldn't know how complicated these questions really were in his case.

Because how much time he had left was entirely up to him.

# 5

## *Nova*

### THEN

Glenna has been standing with her hand on the doorknob for a full five minutes, engaged in a proper Midwestern goodbye with the hospice worker. Step one: Nod wistfully when your guest announces it's time to go, thanking her profusely for coming. Step two: Make your way slowly to the exit, taking every opportunity to detour or stall, all the while trading reminders about when you'll see each other again. Step three: Hug farewell, then think of something you forgot to say earlier and launch right in. Step four: Resume small talk as if your guest is arriving rather than leaving (if only!), your hand on the knob the only sign that the latter is true. Soon this will continue in the open doorway, where you'll discuss the weather, then conclude with a second hug before moving out to the driveway. There, Glenna will at last stand, appraise the curb appeal of her modest two-story Tudor, and wave.

Personally, I adore Glenna's prolonged goodbyes. Now that Wendell is confined to bed, where he spends more time out of consciousness than in it, I've built them into our schedule, never wanting to rush her. But as I watch from the kitchen island, where I'm prepping a small pot of tea to her specs—because sometimes, offering support boils down to securing loose leaf in the basket strainer and setting the timer for a three-and-a-half-minute steep—I can tell the hospice worker is growing impatient. It's midafternoon, but she has a half-dozen appointments left before she can call it a day.

The door opens and closes behind them at last, and I glance at the clock on the wall, an oversized cat face with a swinging tail in lieu of a second hand. Kelly is counting on me to get Willow from play practice today, so I can't cut this close. The swooshing tail is oddly soothing: back and forth. Steady. At one point in my life, any hint of ticking could raise my anxiety level—better hurry—but I've become mindful of how amazing it is that anything can remain so carefully measured, so constant.

It's why I keep a Steven Wright quote written on a Post-it on my desk: *Everywhere is within walking distance if you have the time.*

Glenna swoops back in, one hand on the pink headscarf that does little to hide the effects of endless chemotherapy, the other reaching toward me. I meet her hug with a tight squeeze.

"Thank God you were here," she says. "I'm such a dimwit."

The timer dings, and I push the teapot toward her. "Stop. How would you have known?"

"You came right in and recognized the change in his presentation. The second she adjusted his position and upped the oxygen, his hands warmed up, his color improved . . ." She pours a half-cup of tea and holds it in a trembling hand.

"I'm trained to recognize those changes. And you," I say, steadying her grip with my own, "are doing your best."

She lets me help her raise it to her lips and takes a tentative sip. She smiles sadly. "When you hear *hospice,* you think round-the-clock care, but don't realize it'll come from you. No one mentions the nurse will only be there one hour every five days, until you're already signed up."

Frankly, Glenna has so much medical information coming at her any given day, it's a wonder she can process any of it. Ten years ago, she sent her breast cancer running into remission, like the boss she is. When it returned, six short months ago, she was already reeling from her husband's diagnosis of late-stage lung cancer.

Glenna elected an aggressive treatment course with the sole aim of keeping herself functional enough to care for Wendell—which, back then, consisted of a fifty-fifty split between canoodling and arguing that he hadn't given up his pipe tobacco. "That's like insisting on condoms *after* we've gone and gotten pregnant," Wendell scoffed. "Why ruin what's left of the fun?" They had no children and would need help at odd and long hours surrounding Glenna's treatments, making them tough candidates for a single mom like Kelly. Over the past few months, I've spent many nights wearing a path between Glenna, sweating on the bathroom floor, and Wendell, rasping in their bed. They'd whisper messages for me to volley back and forth, inside jokes that went over my head but would never fail to make the other smile.

"We do everything together," Glenna joked, sadly, the first time I met them. They weren't sure yet which would go downhill fastest.

I can't decide if it's noble or unfair that Wendell is going first.

"You just saved him nearly a week of suffering," she frets. "Hell, he might not have survived the week."

He still might not, but I'm pretty sure Glenna knows.

"What else can I do for you?" I ask, gently. Hospice is making Wendell a priority—they'll be back in the morning—so Glenna will be mine.

She stares stoically at the prescription bottles lined up like soldiers on the counter. "There's no end to the irony of this whole mess," she mutters. "Do you know I've waited my whole life for cannabis to be legalized? Now I finally have a prescription, but am stuck smoking it alone." Her eyes twinkle, for the first time all day. "What fun is that?"

I grin. Having seen Glenna and Wendell's old photo albums, I have a pretty good guess they didn't exactly wait for a doctor's note. "Can't be that hard to find takers. You're the hookup. How about the biddies down the street?"

This is what Glenna calls the white-haired sisters who bring her a casserole every other Friday, each one demurely clutching a white toy poodle as a handy excuse not to come in. Glenna claims each dish is more inedible than the one before but doesn't have the heart to throw them away. The chest freezer in the basement is full of them.

She looks at me sharply. "Can you honestly picture them scarfing Doritos with me and giggling at *Golden Girls* reruns? Even Rose Nylund could run circles around those two."

True. I reach for my coat. "Nacho or Cool Ranch Doritos?"

"Oh my God," she says, hand on my arm. "Would you really?" Her eyes hold so much hope, I burst out laughing again. The poor woman needs a break. "I don't want to get you fired," she worries.

"Then don't fire me."

She throws her arms around me, and I hug her back tight.

It won't be the first time I leave the best part of my week out of the consult with Kelly.

I consider this on the short motorcycle ride to Willow's school: the kind of client I want to spend my days with. Not everyone is as downright likable as Glenna, obviously. I'm not scared off by someone who doesn't know yet what they want or need—we can both find meaning in figuring it out together. Most people who pursue this transition from *patient* to *client* have been caught up in a litany of medical drama for so long that it's more about paring back details than prying them out. I don't need to know about the scare that turned out to be heartburn or the time they had that allergic reaction or the reasons their once-helpful brother-in-law has become a narcissistic prick. But if they want to tell me, I do need to listen, for listening's sake.

Anger does unflattering things to people, even when the anger is justified. But the thing about me is, I don't have to toe any company line. "Wow," I can agree, "that *is* bullshit." Bullshit that the prescription made them worse, bullshit that the doctor didn't explain better, bullshit that they're going to die. And they blink at me, surprised by how rare it is to have the person sitting with them act like a human being and treat them like one, too.

Kelly waxes poetic about how nice it is to be free of the regulations that tied her hands at the nursing home, but she still operates within a cautious standard. She'd draw the line at smoking weed with a cancer sufferer, even off the clock, even if the client begged. But I've had enough nonstarter careers to have it drilled into my head: The customer is always right.

It's been three days since my first real sit-down with Mason, though, and I can't get him out of my mind. Because *he* could be wrong. I've turned down clients who weren't a good fit, but always at the initial consult, and usually mutually. The fact that Kelly and Mason's first meeting bypassed me puts me in an awkward spot.

Clearly someone talked him into this; it's strange he didn't bring them along. He's not my first client my own age, or the first who's proven hard to get to know, but something about the way he looked at me made me uncomfortable.

Like he might be holding back because he could see more of me than I wanted to show.

Heads turn as I pull up outside the auditorium, and I want to tell everyone to chill. I'd never put Willow on this bike. We'll walk the half-mile home and I'll double back for it later. It's a nice day for it, the winter chill lifted enough with the start of March that I can unzip my heavy coat once I dismount.

Inside, the kids are finishing up rehearsal. It's *The Wizard of Oz,* and Willow is Dorothy. What I wouldn't have given for her guts at that age. I was the kid in the back row mouthing the words, an understudy no one had enlisted. I'd stayed after school on audition day but ended up hiding in a bathroom stall, listening to the puzzled echo of my name being called down the empty hallway. No one had discouraged me; I'd had no embarrassing fail. I'd dreamed of my turn onstage, practiced, signed up. But when the moment came, I just . . . couldn't. Instead, I'd gone home, performed "Somewhere Over the Rainbow" perfectly for my empty living room, and followed the yellow brick road straight upstairs, refusing to come down.

My parents assumed I'd bombed. They were so incredulous that I hadn't even been cast as a Munchkin, I was terrified they'd call the school and complain. To their credit, though, they were always big on letting me stand on my own feet.

Here's what's maddening: When I was finally ready to step out was the first time they ever tried to stop me. And they haven't let up since.

People talk about audacity like it's a bad thing, but the truth is, you need some.

"Nova!" Willow skips down the aisle toward me, practicing her "We're Off to See the Wizard" dance. "Did you see us? The Tin Man is totally going to be your favorite. When we oil him unstuck, he does this, like, break dance. It's bonkers cool."

"I already have a favorite." She rewards me with a wide grin as we head out the double doors and down the sidewalk. I'm a fast walker, but Willow's shorter legs bolt out ahead of me like she's on a perpetual rescue mission.

"But, Nova? The lines at the end are kinda . . ." She wrinkles her nose, pulling a face. "It's like Dorothy gets scared back into this little box. *And I'm not going to leave here ever, ever again, because I love you all!*"

She gestures theatrically at the street, as if this block of shoddily maintained Cape Cods illustrates how ludicrous the point. The newly remodeled school may be the nicest thing about the neighborhood, but it's a functional mishmash. Blocks ahead and around the bend, Kelly's older, larger Queen Anne sits back from the road, dividing this residential district from what was once a quainter main street: a bank, library branch, convenience stores, cafes. It's no Oz, but it's no sepia Kansas, either.

"It makes no sense. She was a total badass in her dream," Willow insists.

"Language." I issue the warning on Kelly's behalf even though Willow will ignore it, like usual, because I'm terrible at hiding that I get a kick out of her.

"I get being homesick," she grumbles. "I just don't see what's so never-leave superior about Tornado Alley."

I nod. The three of us watched the Judy Garland film when Willow was cast—firing up the air popper again and again, until our stomachs ached—and it had been fascinating to see how little I retained from my own childhood screenings. The Kansas versions of the Oz characters were a delightful surprise. But the line she's citing bugged me, too.

"Do you know what it means if I say something *holds up?*"

"Like, it doesn't fall apart in the wash?"

I laugh. "Yeah. It withstands wear and tear, and time. If we're talking about a story instead of a sweater, that means it stays relevant long after it was created. *The Wizard of Oz* does a decent job, but that line might conjure dated perceptions of a girl's place in the world."

"So, do I tell the director I don't think it holds up?"

I consider this. "Maybe. But try to focus on the stuff that does hold up. The bigger themes."

"There's no place like home, as in the people you love," she says dully.

"Also: Everything they needed was within them all along. I mean, you can tell from Scarecrow's first scene that he has a brain. And you said yourself, Dorothy was pretty badass."

"Language!" She grins again, and this time, it sticks.

We walk on in companionable silence. One of the biggest surprises of linking up with Kelly has been how much I love talking to Willow. I can never be sure what she'll say next, which is a way better look on her than on me. Perspectives that seem different can be refreshing coming from a kid but strange or jaded from an adult.

Which begrudgingly reminds me of Mason. He'd take issue with the same line Willow did. For him, coming home clearly felt like punishment or failure, maybe both.

"That's what you do for people," Willow says out of nowhere, like we're still talking.

"What's what I do?"

"Help them see what's been inside them all along. Like, I wouldn't've auditioned for the play if you hadn't pulled that flyer from my backpack. And Mom's much happier since you came. She talks all the time about how you've freed her up to focus on stuff she couldn't before."

I blink at her, touched. "That's a nice thing to say."

In one short, long year, Willow and Kelly have become a surrogate family to me, but my real family would call this compliment more generous than accurate. They think I'm bent on doing pretty much anything but staying in my own lane. But maybe I just remember what it's like to have everything you need for an audition except the guts.

Maybe I can even spot a glimmer of that feeling in a guy who gets as far as my office and then freezes up cold.

If anyone needs to find hidden strength already inside them, I'm pretty sure it's Mason.

And if Willow thinks I'm equipped to help, I owe it to him to try.

# 6

*Kelly*

NOW

If Kelly had doubted how Nova had come to feel about Mason, there was no question anymore. Her colleague had gone from initial shock at the news of his death to a state that was closer to catatonic.

*Mason was never terminally ill.*

The words lingered terribly in the air, draining the color from Nova's skin, her eyes, even her hair, if that was possible. Nova had turned the same shade of gray as her cardigan, as if she herself were composed of thread, spun into strands that hung knotted together, one snip away from coming to shreds.

"Not everybody shares their diagnosis with their family straight away," Kelly told Mason's mother as gently as she could.

Kelly found herself staring through her open office door at the chair where Mason sat so restlessly that first day. She could usually tell instantly when a client felt they belonged here. Mason had all the hallmarks of *resenting* belonging here: bouncing knees, averted gaze, twitching jaw. Most gruff facades, she'd learned, hid the tender bruises of a rough internal struggle. It wasn't hard to imagine him not being forthcoming. With anyone.

"When I saw he'd been coming here, I thought I'd have to accept that, too," Bonnie said. "But there's no record. I know what doctors he's seen for his arms. I drove him to the surgeries. I'm a proxy in his patient portal, because he couldn't type for so long. I've been through the invoices mailed to the house, called everyone I can think of. There's no sign of him being treated for anything else."

"Not finding a record could simply mean he didn't want you to find a record," Kelly began, but Bonnie held up a hand.

"Mason's health insurance lapsed when he had to leave the musicians guild. I highly doubt he's been secretly seeing some other specialist out of pocket. Plus, he lives with me. If he were on his deathbed, don't you think I'd know?"

Kelly didn't want to add to this woman's pain by pointing out that not all seriously ill people sought treatment, especially if it would bankrupt their families. What a lot to swallow: that her son had hidden an illness, one that had driven him to take matters into his own hands sooner than tell. Why point out the obvious questions they may never get answers to? Why point out that evidently plenty had escaped Bonnie—suicidal thoughts included?

From what Kelly knew of Mason's case, he'd gone from being set on going through this alone to eventually leaning on Nova—a meaningful step for client and doula both. Nova didn't deserve to have that undone by this hostile third degree, but the shock seemed to have rendered her incapable of responding.

"I'm so sorry you're in this position," Kelly told Bonnie. "We encourage clients to involve their families in everything they come here to do. But ultimately, it's up to them. We can only support them in what they decide."

"Like in deciding to die?" The words cut so quickly, they must be the ones she'd sharpened before she'd come.

Kelly shrunk into the upholstery. "Of course not. Absolutely not."

"Seems to me that's what he was doing, not being terminal and all. Coming to an end-of-life doula so he could end his life."

"That's—" Kelly turned again to her slack-jawed partner. There was no way around speaking up now—but Nova remained frozen. A statue where Nova used to be.

"That is unequivocally not what we do here," Kelly finished, as firmly as she could.

"Let her answer," Bonnie said, tossing her head in Nova's direction like an angry mare. "I came to see *you*, Nova Huston, not your handler. Did he ever give any indication he might do something like this?"

At this, Nova's tears began streaming down her face. Kelly looked futilely at the script letters she'd mounted on the wall—B.R.E.A.T.H.E. She'd designed this as a safe space for clients and their families—for hard conversations, too.

But not this conversation. Not this—unimaginable.

Bonnie got to her feet, stepping to the love seat where both doulas sat. "Did my son tell you he wanted to do this? Did you help him 'make peace with it'?" Her hands flung into air quotes, so close to Nova's face even Kelly flinched. "What did he say? How could you let him?" Bonnie was half sobbing now, and at last a defiant flush of pink returned to Nova's cheekbones.

"I didn't," Nova whispered.

Kelly exhaled the breath she'd been holding. "We take claims of that nature very seriously, Bon—Mrs. Shaylor. We have protocol—"

"I'm not asking *you*," Bonnie cried, "unless you overheard him with *her*!" At this, Nova straightened and finally looked Mason's mother square in the eye.

"I did not," she said, low but clear, "have conversations of that nature with your son." It was the gray Nova talking, but at least her voice belonged to her full-color self. In control.

If Kelly had to describe Nova in two words, those would be it. Nova might be the less experienced partner, but throw her on a high wire and she'd still look steadier than Kelly ever felt on solid ground. Eyes straight ahead.

"What exactly did he tell you was wrong with him?" Bonnie stood, hands on hips, and Kelly tried to pretend she wasn't as curious to hear Nova's answer.

Because when it came to Mason, the only thing Kelly felt sure of was that she'd never known the whole story. She hadn't needed to. Maybe hadn't even wanted to. But now . . .

"Those surgeries you mentioned," Nova ventured, "did not end well."

Bonnie turned her eyes heavenward, bracing for an unholy blow. "Are you saying they found something else, something worse, while trying to repair his damage?"

Nova's gaze ran an exhausted lap around the suite, as if searching out someplace to crawl and hide—not to get away, Kelly saw, but to grieve.

"I'm saying," Nova said, "I think the problems with his arms were indicative of something more catastrophic than you realized. And I wish Mason had discussed that with you. But as I said, he didn't want me involved anymore, either. I can't speak for him, and especially not for the last few weeks."

It nagged at Kelly that Nova hadn't mentioned Mason deciding not to continue. True, they'd been skipping their weeklies; Kelly was inundated with Willow's end-of-school-year activities: the choral concert, zoo field trip, summer camp signups, teacher appreciation lunches, field day, all on top of amped-up play rehearsals. Not to mention Willow's first bout with preteen trouble: getting caught sneaking out—*sneaking out!*—forcing Kelly to ground her. Maybe Nova *had* seemed preoccupied, but so was Kelly. She wouldn't press Nova in front of Bonnie, though. Nova had called the mother's permissions *limited*, and Mason's death didn't change that.

"Mrs. Shaylor," Kelly said, switching to her voice of reason. "This has come at you fast. I understand why you're here, but have you had the time yet to compare notes with other family members? It's never ideal to have to puzzle something like this together, but it's possible Mason left different pieces of the whole picture with different people he cared about."

"His brother doesn't know anything more. And when he finds out about this . . ." She shook her head. "I hoped not to tell him until I figured out what the hell had been going on."

"Is there anyone else? Old bandmates?"

"We've been treating this as a private family matter." Kelly saw it then: shame, disbelief, all the things a family should never have to feel in the wake of suicide, but usually does anyway.

"Are the police certain?" Nova asked. "That the car accident *wasn't* an accident?"

Bonnie sighed. "Ostensibly, they're investigating. That's why I've been waiting, to . . ." She cleared her throat, then switched to a flat recitation of the police report. "They can't locate any surveillance video of the crash. No witnesses have come forward, and it's likely there were none, given the time. No one knows where he was going at that hour. The reconstruction indicates he wasn't speeding, but he'd accelerated, then swerved for no apparent reason, and made no discernible moves to course correct the vehicle."

"All of that could potentially be explained away," Kelly mused. Unwise to play devil's advocate, perhaps—beside her, Nova had gone pale and limp again. But her mind spun out ahead of her mouth. A deer in the roadway, maybe some kind of medical event—a seizure, or—

"Except for the suicide note. How do you explain that?"

How indeed. Kelly wanted so badly to know what it said, how they knew for sure it wasn't, say, a different kind of goodbye letter, maybe even one Nova had encouraged him to write for when the time came. Was it possible it had mentioned Nova, leading Bonnie here?

This did not seem the moment to dare ask.

Bonnie pressed a fistful of tissues to her face. When she pulled them away, her determination seemed to have shifted into the rigid set of her jaw.

Ready to bite.

"What regulatory board oversees end-of-life doulas? Who licenses you?"

"No board." Kelly knew it sounded bad in this context, though she'd always viewed that freedom as something to celebrate. There was certainly no shortage of red tape elsewhere. "We're certified. But there's no license."

Bonnie barked a laugh, somewhere between *of course not* and *I should have known.*

"So what recourse do I have to file a claim or complaint? The Better Business Bureau?"

Kelly wasn't about to give the woman instructions.

"And then what?" Bonnie went on. "A lawsuit won't bring Mason back. It won't keep anyone else from coming here and ending up dead for the wrong reasons."

Kelly's gut roiled. She wasn't naïve—she knew how susceptible a business like hers could be. That's why she was so careful. The slightest hint of suspicion could do her in. But suspicion involving Mason Shaylor, of all people?

It had been a shock to realize, midway through his tenure, the extent to which he was Parting Your Way's most high-profile client.

Under no circumstances could Kelly allow this to be their highest-profile death.

"Mrs. Shaylor, let's take a minute. Those are serious allegations."

"You're damn right. And if you want this place to survive, I suggest you prepare serious explanations. I didn't come here to get you all tongue tied. I want the truth."

Nova got shakily to her feet and stood facing Mrs. Shaylor, eye to eye.

"The truth is," Nova said, "you have a very wrong idea of what went on here. I can understand wanting someone to blame, something to explain this. But this isn't right."

Mason's mother stared back. Hard. "We can agree on that. I shouldn't have come here. I should have gone straight to the police. This is beyond. I can't."

*To the police.* Kelly's breath went out of her. Before she knew what was happening, the woman had snatched her purse off the chair and bolted for the door.

"Mrs. Shaylor, wait." Kelly scrambled off the love seat after her. Nova was one step ahead, catching the door before it slammed. They rounded the bend in the wrap-around porch before Nova was close enough to reach the woman's shoulder.

"Please, Mrs. Shaylor."

Bonnie whirled around, eyes wild.

"You shouldn't drive in this state." Nova's concern was genuine, Kelly could see. This was Mason's *mom,* after all. "Why don't you let us call someone for you."

Why *had* she come alone? She'd made it clear that there was no Mr. Shaylor, that she wasn't keen to involve her other son, but wasn't anyone sitting with her? Three days on, had she already buried Mason? Wouldn't Kelly and Nova have seen something in the news?

"Don't give me any more of this compassionate care crap." She pointed her finger at Nova, then turned on Kelly. "You coax people into this place, and cozy them up on your couch, and you get them feeling all warm and fuzzy that you'll be with them when they die." Her voice broke with such ferociously raw emotion that Kelly stumbled backward. "Where were you when my son's body was incinerated behind the wheel? I learned a long time ago—when my husband was blown to dust in his government-issued uniform, with those service stripes he was so proud of on his sleeve—dying is something you do alone. Anyone who claims otherwise is no one I want following me around, trying to apologize for things they can't undo."

Kelly was trembling, all over. "Mrs. Shaylor, from one single mom to another, Nova is a good person. I assure you she is not responsible for what happened to your son. I trust her with my own young daughter. She's the *only* person I trust with my daughter."

Bonnie had already turned to go, but she paused to look back and meet Kelly's eyes.

"I'd rethink that if I were you."

Then she was gone.

# 7

## *Nova*

### THEN

Mason has a cut on his hand. A bad one, from the looks of the blood-stained bandage mummy-wrapped around his fingers. I eye it as he settles into my visitor chair, noting the tremor in his movement. Slight, but detectible.

Is it Parkinson's, then—young onset? Or perhaps worse, ALS?

He volunteers nothing as we stare blankly at each other across the desk. At this rate, the hour ahead will crawl by. Again. Clearly it's up to me to say something, ask him something.

But I have the strong feeling whatever I pick will be wrong.

"Would you believe I've never ridden in a Jeep?" I don't so much ask this as announce it. Awkwardly. He looks startled, then incredulous.

"You prefer transportation with a higher mortality rate?"

I feign offense. "Surely the man who prefers life on the road isn't afraid of a motorcycle."

"Where would I stash my gear, or sleep? I need a back seat."

"Hmm. Remind me to call shotgun, then. I try to stay out of my clients' beds."

At the first hint of his smile, I stand. "Should we get out of here, then?"

He blinks. "Seriously?"

"I don't think either of us wants a repeat of last week, do we?"

If I'm not mistaken, there's relief in the surprise passing across his face. He gets to his feet, careful to keep his arm out of sight, and with his good hand tosses me his keys.

I hadn't meant I wanted to drive—but then again, gripping the wheel through that bandage can't feel good. At the curb, the top is already off, which I take as a good sign: Even Mason is not immune to the open-arms feeling that comes with the first taste of spring. The sky is clear blue, the air warmer than it's been since last fall. Not *that* warm, though. I zip my coat tight.

"Where to?" I ask. "Any favorite spots for a drive?" He pulls a face conveying that we can't possibly get far enough away. I consider the options. He's my last appointment of the afternoon, and I'm off Willow duty today. "Got somewhere to be after this?"

He laughs, as if the question couldn't be more ridiculous.

So, I head for the interstate. South. Midafternoon on a weekday, it's mostly truckers on this route over the Ohio River, rumbling by at a deafening volume that's part nuisance, part exhilaration. I've driven clients' cars to help with errands or appointments, but mostly locally, slowly and carefully. As we sail across the bridge—a mess of construction hanging above water too brown to look inviting—I feel unexpectedly light. The odometer is creeping toward two hundred thousand miles, but the ride is sturdier than my Yamaha, more fun than a car.

Even on a route so *Ohio* I can practically feel Mason rolling his eyes, I get the appeal.

I'm shivering in my jacket by the time we take the first exit across the Kentucky state line, but it's easier going here, and the sun stays bright. We ride in silence through the first several miles of the stop-and-go state route, past strip malls, big box stores, and enough chain restaurants to feed everyone in the state. Then, things open up.

Or, rather, they narrow down. On these country roads, you have to draw your own lane, and even then you're playing chicken. I keep my grip on the wheel relaxed, my eyes always on the next curve as Mason's head swivels to take in the crumbling homesteads and farmland around us. I see no speed limit sign, so I guess on the high side.

"Pretty out here," he begrudges, and I nod. It really is worth the forty-five-minute drive.

The state park looks overdeveloped at first, I know: the groomed hills of the golf course giving way to the recreation buildings, the public access parking, the empty rectangle of the pool waiting for summer. But I stay the course, and then we're pulling up to the entry gate at the campground, staring down a surprising number of RVs—the diehards who "camp" all four seasons thanks to the wonders of electric generators. The camp host leaps from the closest camper and runs across the road to the registration hut.

"Nova?" She squints at me, grinning. Since I saw her last, Carrie has trimmed her blond dreadlocks ultrashort into a sort of frizzy pinwheel. I dig it, and her Dolly Parton sweatshirt is on point. "New wheels?" she asks, then looks twice at the Jeep. "I mean, new old wheels?"

"Loaner wheels. Carrie, meet Mason." I glance at the passenger seat and find his expression as polite as I've ever seen it. Carrie has that effect on people—like you can so instantly tell she'd let you get away with some shit, you don't want to take advantage.

Unless you're me.

"So hey, is that site open, down by the water?"

Carrie frowns, glancing into the back seat. It's obvious we're not here to camp.

"You know we're not supposed to allow day use. There are a few access spots across the lake—I'll give you a map."

"But those aren't as good."

She looks again at Mason and then back to me, a question uneasy in her eyes, and I give the slightest nod, hoping he doesn't see. *Yes, he's a client. Please?*

She lowers her voice. "Look, I left some of my gear down there . . ."

"Even better. Hey, I'll owe you a shift as camp host. Next time a pack of shower hogs runs you out of hot water, we can trade digs."

"Overnight," she bargains. "Hot shower, real bed, and you order me a pizza."

"Done. And I won't let anyone steal the firewood this time."

She glances over her shoulder toward the lackluster bathhouse. On cue, a teenager strolls out pinching a dirty diaper and hurls it, unbagged, into the dumpster out front.

"Two hours. Be gone by the ranger's next rounds." The gate lifts, and I blow her a kiss and hang a sharp left downhill to the primitive sites. No one has ever bothered to bring out a Bobcat and level the things, which make for an off-kilter night's sleep. This time of year, midweek, hardly anyone is chancing the overnight lows in a tent, and we roll by rows of unoccupied fire rings and picnic tables sloping down to the lake, to the best sites you can fish from, paddle from, even swim from if you ignore the warnings of toxic algal blooms. A few brave canvas pop-ups dot the prime loop, but beyond them, it's as I'd hoped when I chose this destination: no one. I beeline for the far side of the cove, where two nylon hammocks are strung near the water's edge and a pair of kayaks sits on the bank. The gear Carrie referred to. I skid to a stop on the gravel pad, triumphant.

"If this is how you drive other people's vehicles, I don't want to see you drive your own," Mason quips, as I yank the parking brake.

"Hey," I tease, "the doula relationship needs to be built on trust."

"I *trust* you have the Jeep checked off your bucket list now, and I can drive us home."

The thuds of our doors interrupt the scutter and birdsong of the forest, and we stand surveying the scene.

"Any interest?" I nod toward the kayaks. Mason holds up his bandaged hand.

"Oh, right. What happened, anyway?"

"I cut myself." There's really no word for him other than maddening. I shake one of the hammocks to dislodge any insects, and as he follows suit toward the other one, I'm stricken by how listless his stride is. I can't tell if he just doesn't care whether he ever reaches the hammock, or if it's taking untoward physical effort to drag his legs beneath him.

We put our feet up, ankles crossed, and from this position we can look over the water and into the treetops as easily. The branches are bare now, but not for long.

"This is nicer," I say, "than staring at each other across the desk, I think."

I choose to take his silence as agreement. Then, he asks: "Why this place?"

I keep my eyes on the skeletal canopy above. "I spent time living near the Gulf, then the Atlantic. I miss the water. I've moved back to Ohio recently myself, and when I start feeling claustrophobic, it helps to get somewhere I feel less landlocked."

Mason looks out at the lake, and I can guess at what he's thinking: This sedentary puddle in Kentucky can compensate for the wide kinetic motion of the open sea?

It's nothing I haven't thought myself.

But if I brought him at sunrise, he'd see how the fog hovers over the water, how the blue herons glide through it, all prehistoric and regal, how when the boats aren't out yet, you can hear the fish jump. How in that moment you're not sure if you'd rather be the fog or the heron, but at least being among them takes your mind off of being you.

"How do you know Carrie?"

He thinks he's changing the subject.

"Through her younger sister."

It's not wrong to imply Emma was my friend—even though I'd also been her doula for a month before Carrie asked me to help plan Emma's last birthday party. I'd dare anyone to share an evening in a private karaoke room at Tokyo Kitty and *not* leave bonded for life. If the song selection doesn't bring you together, the robotic drink service from the ceiling will.

When a bacterial infection whisked Emma away soon after, it was Carrie I worried most about. Carrie, who wasn't ready to say goodbye, who took Emma's whole group under her wing and back to Tokyo Kitty, gathering us onstage to sing "We Are Family" in tribute. Who spent the whole night trying to do "big sister" things for the others until they shied uncomfortably away.

I call in the occasional favor not because I can't find some other lake, but to let her flex that coping mechanism. She may be surrounded by people out here, but she still seems alone.

A breeze rustles the brush around us into a hushed chorus, and I close my eyes, listening. I might be in over my head with Mason. But right now I'm okay because it feels good to be alive: sun on my face, fresh air in my lungs, music in my ears.

"What have you been up to since I saw you last?" I ask. It would be more to the point to press him on his health again. Or to ask about his family, how they're taking things. But I'm hoping a less intrusive approach might get us there naturally.

"Literally nothing."

I wait for him to elaborate, but he does not.

"What's your typical day look like?"

"Don't remind me," he grumbles.

The patience of a saint is not an attribute I bring to this job. He is paying for my time, and I presume he could find other people who'd hang with him in sullen silence for free.

"How long do you expect we might be seeing each other?" This kind of unfiltered question will set off a sensitive client, but I'm done tiptoeing. Though doctors' guesses can be wildly inaccurate, they're the only guideline we have, and there's a big difference in my approach to someone I'll be seeing for weeks versus months versus a year.

"The jury is still kind of out," he says.

Maybe it is. We're always telling people doulas don't have to be a last resort—there's more we can do if they don't wait until the finale to bring us in. Still.

"It would be helpful for me to know," I say, "what led you to seek out a doula in the first place. Or how you ended up at Parting Your Way. We have to start somewhere." Still nothing. "If you don't want to tell me, tell the lake, the sky. I'll just listen."

He rolls his eyes. But he lays his head back until it's hidden in the hammock folds. I wait.

"Ever have one of those nights," he says finally, "when everything takes on this heightened significance? The certain kind of rain, the bartender's name, the time stuck on the clock that's out of batteries. Every damn song that comes on the radio . . . Do you know that kind of night?"

I close my eyes, knowing well the only type of night that registers details like those. A crossroads. A point of no return. The restlessness of a big decision looming. My microwave blinking in a dark apartment kitchen: HIT START TO RESUME COOKING. The clouds parting to show Venus, and only Venus. Even a wrong number calling at the right time.

Is there such a thing as reading too much into a moment like that?

If there is, it's better I don't know.

"I do."

"Well, on a night like that, I was minding my own business, trying to ignore all those signs. I'd gotten bad news that day, and all I wanted was quality time with Jack Daniel's, alone on a stool. But there was this conversation behind me—going on and on about some *Death Doula* podcast, like it was life changing. Or I guess, death changing. Anyway, I listened to a few episodes when I got home, and I thought, why the hell not."

Even with all the wrong details included, I can see myself there, with Mason and Mr. Daniel's. The story isn't exactly helpful, but I like the way he tells it.

"You mentioned bucket lists earlier," I venture. I'd noticed because

I'd never actually said that driving a Jeep was on mine—only that I'd never done it. "Do you have one?"

"Do I seem like that big of a cliché?"

I won't tell him everyone becomes a cliché when staring down their own mortality. Thanks to Tim McGraw, living like you're dying is itself a cliché.

"I have an unpopular opinion on bucket lists, is all," I say instead. Out on the water, a metal dinghy is gliding past on the purr of a trolling motor, two fishing lines hanging off the back. "There's nothing wrong with them in theory. But I've seen people give them too much weight. Like they think they can ward off death by adding more things they haven't checked off yet. And if they can't get through them all, they struggle to accept it's beyond their control. Some people use those lists to put off thinking about what comes at the end."

"So you think: If you won't be able to check everything off, you shouldn't bother to check anything off?"

"No, the opposite: That it's more important to focus on what you can fit in the bucket today, rather than pining for things you hope to cram in later."

He frowns, lifting his head to look at me across the dappled shade.

"Do you know I was today years old when I realized the connection between the terms *bucket list* and *kick the bucket*?"

I twist my wrist to pantomime taking a bow. "Premature death specialist, at your service."

The silence falls between us again, and I let it rest for a moment before I speak.

"Want to tell me what's in your bucket today?"

"Seems to me," he scoffs—and I can taste the bitterness from here—"anything small enough to fit isn't worth the space."

"Maybe there's something we can make fit."

He drops his leg over the hammock's side. "You say being stuck in Ohio makes you want to center yourself in your calm, but it has the opposite effect on me. Makes me want to do something incredibly stupid and risky."

I know that look on his face. So uncomfortable in his skin, what he really wants is to rip it off.

"Incredibly stupid and risky like putting your life savings on a horse with thirteen to one odds? Or incredibly stupid and risky like diving from the St. Augustine Beach pier at high tide?"

"Those are . . . very specific examples."

"Stupid and risky is kind of my specialty." I grin. "You've seen me drive."

He picks a twig off the trunk above his head and starts to rip it into confetti. "I'm confused. I thought you weren't in favor of the bucket list. Now you're upset I don't have one."

"I'm not upset," I insist, though suddenly I sort of am. "Believe it or not, there's science to this transition phase. An interesting bit of which is that we tend to judge experiences by how they end. Ever notice how you can date someone for two fantastic years, but if the breakup gets ugly, that's what sticks with you?"

I'm creeping up on things I don't like to leave unsaid. That this is why I'm intent on helping people have a positive end-of-life experience. That those who can find even small, memorable happiness under the worst circumstances often feel triumphant, like they've risen to the occasion. And if a bucket list helps them achieve that, great. But if it hinders them from staying present in those moments, rushing or frustrating them when something slips out of reach, then we should do without.

But his face shuts down so abruptly, it's like I've hit an off switch.

"That's scientific fact, huh?"

He plants his feet on the ground, sitting rigidly in the center of the hammock. Straining the fabric.

"They've done studies . . ." I begin, but he stands and resumes that listless stride back to the Jeep.

"That," he says, almost to himself, "is incredibly bad news for me."

# 8

## *Nova*

Numb. That's how so many of my clients describe it—how they feel, what it's like, getting the worst news they can imagine.

I'm fond of assuring them numbness is *not* the absence of feeling. Rather, it's often overload, too many emotions coming at you at once.

Maybe it's knowing this that lays me bare in the wake of Bonnie Shaylor and all the things I wish like hell she did not say. Wish like hell were not true.

Even numb, I feel it all: everything and nothing. Alone and surrounded. Overflowing and empty. Hidden and exposed.

It's been a few hours since she left. I stood on the porch and watched her speed away, Kelly stoic at my side while I shook with sobs and that old enemy I thought I'd vanquished: fear. Kelly placed a gentle hand on my arm, not saying all the things she'd been trained to not say.

"Time," I'd managed. "I need a little time."

She'd nodded, and though we both knew we'd need to talk this over sooner than later, she let me go. I managed to wait until she was back inside before running to retch in the bushes alongside the driveway, then dragged myself, hand over hand, up the stairs by the railing.

I'm still lying where I fell, on my made bed, curled around a pillow. I've cried out my reserves, and I should stand, wash my face, and force myself to go looking for Kelly, explain what I can, put up safeguards together. But I can't stop looking at the door. I can't wrap my brain around the fact that Mason will never walk through it again.

I can't make sense of any of this.

If Mrs. Shaylor made good on her threats and the police barged in right now, all bright lights and third degrees, I'd almost welcome them. I want to know every detail—of the accident, the last three weeks, even the note. End-of-life clients are encouraged to put lots of things in writing: Might the officers at the scene have happened upon a mere exercise and mistaken it for a message? I want to hear every theory, no matter how far-fetched. Maybe they wouldn't tell me, but I don't know who else I'd ask.

He's already been gone a few days, and even if I haven't missed the funeral or memorial service—though she made no mention of one— I'm clearly not welcome.

Besides. The person I want to ask isn't there.

I shouldn't have hidden this way. I could have leaned into Kelly, and not merely as the living soul who, at this moment, knows me best. Any doula worth her salt has at least one mentor, someone who's had influence on her philosophy, on directly or indirectly getting her practice where it is today. Someone she can still turn to when things with a client get tough—which they will, because that's the nature of this line we tend between life and death. Our profession is new enough that I'm one of the lucky few who apprenticed with a doula in her own right, one I get to work alongside every day. For Kelly, her mentor is her yoga instructor Maggie Neatley, who is a part of the monthly consultation group we host. It's an eclectic but like-minded team of advisers: one hospice supervisor, one Reiki healer, two therapists, one chaplain.

None of us ever discuss specific cases by name, but we help each other not to miss the forest for the trees, so to speak. Maggie brings the most seniority as a small business owner, and closes our meetings by leading us in intention setting and mindful meditation.

In fact, I'd be willing to bet Maggie's fielding a distress call from Kelly now, if not already sitting at her kitchen table, fifty yards from where I lay. Kelly might be too loyal to wonder yet how much I might have—or should have—suspected about Mason before today. On her own, I doubt she'd jump straight to speculation about his physical condition, his state of mind. She'd hear me out before questioning my judgment.

But Maggie is another story. Maggie is deeply practical for someone people label "alternative" by trade. And if Kelly did indeed call her, Maggie is at this moment viewing me as a liability and instructing Kelly to batten down the hatches.

The truth is, I'm afraid to talk to Kelly. I'm afraid to talk to *anyone* right now. Because I don't know what to say. All the questions they're asking about me, I'm holed up in this tiny garage studio asking myself.

Late last year, a compelling TED talk by an organizational psychologist moved me to create a doula manual for my clients, filled with instructions on how they might use me. I am, in simple terms, a new product, and it makes sense to highlight my settings. This is one thing that sets my practice apart from Kelly's: She relies on checklists, on thorough rows of boxes and blank lines waiting to be marked off and filled in. My approach is more open-ended, intuitive, and yes, experimental, but I've had good results so far, and even better feedback.

Still, my manual issues no warnings to test my services on a small, out-of-the-way spot first. No one who comes to me has time for that. People jump in, skipping the step by step, picking and choosing what they want, what they need, from my menu.

*I can share stories that might help you move past shock to acceptance.*

*I can help you find the areas of greatest meaning in your life and focus your energies there.*

*I can mediate difficult discussions with your family.*

*I can help you seek—and offer—forgiveness.*

*If you'd like assistance getting your financial and legal affairs in order, refer to the troubleshooting guide. Please read carefully.*

I never pressure anyone to use me for anything they don't want to. To share anything they don't volunteer. The way I see it, the last thing people need, as they near the end stage, is to feel like they're accumulating more responsibility. So I don't push.

Nor have I ever stood in anyone's way.

If Mason chose not to *use as directed,* or even to bypass the operating instructions entirely, how could anyone put that on me? I was always clear about which one of us was leading on the dance floor.

It was never supposed to be me.

Of course, that's assuming I'd followed by own damn manual.

A brisk knock on the door startles me—though I've been staring it down for so long, it's as much an answered prayer as an interruption. On seniority alone, Kelly understands more than I ever will about grief; she is an uncommon expert at navigating this overlap between longing for support and needing to be left alone. Fresh tears of gratitude prick my eyes. Of course Kelly did not wait for me to come to her. Of course Kelly won't go cold over something like this, no matter how tenuous, no matter how concerned she or Maggie or even Bonnie is right to be.

But when I swing open the door into the fading daylight, it's not Kelly on the other side.

It's my mom.

Out of the air-conditioning, the warm air dries my eyes and sweeps over the contours of my swollen face, wrecked from crying.

She blinks at me, trying to mask her reaction, but it's evident I look like hell.

"Nova. What—did something happen?" She glances over her shoulder, and I follow her gaze to the car running in the driveway. I make out Dad's silhouette, leaning over the steering wheel, waving in greeting.

I lick my lips, which have gone as dry as my eyes. "I lost a client," I say, bowing my head. When I lift it, she looks relieved, that that's all it is. Also: annoyed.

"Does it sound crass to ask if that wasn't expected?"

Any question about my job sounds crass coming from her, and not because I'm oversensitive—debatable though that may be. My family is baffled that I of all people would want to do this work. Mom takes every opportunity to remind me how much they hope this is a phase that will pass quickly, so I can get back to living my life. Willfully ignoring the fact that I'm already doing it.

"He was young," I say, "close to my age." It's not an answer, but I know this will soften her. And even as it does, I regret saying it—because I'm proving her favorite point to make. No matter how miserable I look, she won't be able to resist making it again.

"I'm sorry, honey. That is hard." Her fingers play at the collar of her blouse. "Wouldn't you be happier doing work that doesn't always end in a funeral?"

There it is.

I clear my throat, commanding myself to pull it together. "I'm not usually affected this way," I mumble. "This is different. Usually it's . . ." I can't think of how to finish.

"Happier?" She raises an eyebrow.

Even if I were in any shape to cycle through this argument again, it would end back here, in a futile loop. "What are you doing here?" I ask instead, and her eyes widen.

"Have you forgotten Dad's birthday? Our dinner reservation?" She throws a distasteful glance at my motorcycle, as if to remind me why the ride to the restaurant is required. *Shit.* I had indeed thoroughly, regrettably forgotten.

"Oh, no. I'm so sorry. I'm really not up to it. I'll make it up to him—"

"Nonsense. You already missed the real party." She means their long weekend at my sister's, barbecuing and walking the shores of Lake Michigan. It's not that I wasn't invited—or wouldn't have enjoyed seeing my niece and nephews. It's just that it involved sharing confined space with my parents for twelve hours round trip. "I won't leave you here to wallow. Wash your face and change clothes. We'll wait. A good meal will do you wonders."

Mom knows I gave up red meat years ago, rendering the steakhouse of Dad's choice a dinner I'll endure rather than enjoy even on a good day. But today . . . I still taste the sick from earlier. The idea of swallowing *any* food right now, let alone polite conversation, is repellant.

"I don't feel well. It's not a good idea."

She cocks her head. "To recap: You're telling me your workday is making you physically ill, to the extent that you can't manage to let Dad treat *you* for *his* birthday. Yet in the same breath, you expect us to be supportive of this lifestyle. We shouldn't dare question these choices you've been making, ever since."

She doesn't need to say ever since *what. Ever since* flies solo in our family, like a secret handshake. And it marks the moment my parents started questioning *all* of my choices, long before my decision to become a doula. That's just their new least favorite.

I close my eyes. If Mason could see me now . . . If his mother watched me calmly indulge in fine dining with my parents, like today never happened . . . I wouldn't blame either of them for hating me as much as I hate myself right now.

Then again, Bonnie would give anything for the chance to sit across the table from her son again. It's my own mom standing in front of me now. And though I've tried to convince myself I don't owe her or my dad anything, that will never be true.

It's the nature of parents and children.

It's the nature of *ever since.*

"Fine," I say tersely. "Give me five." Then I close the door and lean against it, trying not to panic at the notion of an evening in public.

If anyone knows how to go through the motions of normal when everything is on the line—when you want to scream at everyone around that they have no clue how precious life is—it should be me.

That's a dangerous word though: *should.* Mom knows that as well as I do.

Mason knew it, too.

# 9

## *Kelly*

NOW

"Mom?"

Kelly's head jerked up from the kitchen table. She must have drifted off, waiting for Nova to come back. She'd called, texted, and knocked on the annex door—before dinner, ramen bowl in hand, then again after—all with no response. She felt awful about intruding on her friend's grief, but had the uncomfortable feeling they needed to get their stories straight. She'd never lie, not even to protect Nova. Still, she needed to know more about what they were up against with Bonnie Shaylor's claims—especially if morning could bring police to their door. She'd already scoured the internet for any mention of Mason's death but found none.

"Willow, love." She straightened her eyeglasses. "What are you doing up?"

Her daughter padded across the kitchen in her nightgown and polka-dotted socks. Normally, she might've come to lay her head on

Kelly's shoulder. But things between them hadn't quite receded from their weekend blowout. Willow had never tested limits this way before—neither of them were used to it. So she stood apart, looking part sullen preteen, part kid who needed a hug.

"I got up to use the bathroom and saw the lights on."

The clock over the stove blinked 2:51 a.m. Well, Kelly had missed Nova then, by hours. She pushed aside a stab of hurt that her partner could have turned in knowing Kelly would be waiting, wringing her hands.

"I guess I fell asleep," she said. "Let's get you back to bed."

"Mom, did something bad happen? Nova seemed upset earlier."

"You talked to Nova?"

Willow shook her head. "I only saw her leave with her parents. But her face . . ." *Leave? But why—oh no, the birthday.* Kelly's annoyance faded into compassion. This was exactly the kind of thing Maggie missed when she judged Nova by her devil-may-care bravado. That beneath it was a woman who didn't have the heart to disappoint people she loved, even when follow-through came at her own expense. "Plus, you don't look so happy yourself."

No denying that.

"We got bad news about one of Nova's clients today."

Willow chewed a piece of her hair, a nervous habit, and Kelly fought the urge to bat it away. "Not Mr. Whitehall?"

Kelly frowned. How on earth did Willow know about Mr. Whitehall? The side entrance to Parting Your Way wasn't just for clients: Even Kelly avoided accessing the suite from the house. There was nothing *side* about the business: She'd spent years throwing everything she had into establishing herself as a doula. It hadn't been easy, convincing old colleagues to take a chance on her in such a new, untested field. Building that referral network, moving into this house with just the right zoning overlap for the office, expanding to take on Nova. She'd finally reached balance: enough income not to worry about the bills, enough time for Willow's increasing load of academics and activities and friends, enough help to ease the challenges of single motherhood at last.

But one thing would never ease: the messy worries that came with raising Willow in the midst of it all. Every boundary Kelly had drawn around the business was drawn with Willow in mind. Nova knew this.

Nova knew better.

"Not Mr. Whitehall." Kelly took a deep breath. "Mason."

Willow's jaw dropped. "Mason was a *client*? I thought he was her boy-friend."

The confusion was understandable. For a number of reasons.

"He was a client," she said plainly. Carefully.

"But he's not old."

"Unfortunately, love, not everyone gets to grow old before they die."

Her daughter looked hard at the wall, processing. She was old enough to know this to be true, of course. But experiencing it was another level. This was exactly why Kelly kept her own client load more straightforward. She'd thought having Nova's practice detached from hers—in almost every sense of the word—would keep it separate enough.

But nothing about Nova had stayed separate. Mostly, that had been a good thing.

Mostly.

"He was sick?" Willow released the hair and it fell to her shoulder, matted and wet.

"He was. But he had a car accident."

Willow looked suddenly terrified, as if the vehicle might come plowing into the kitchen any moment. "What *kind* of accident?" she demanded.

"A bad one. He just . . . didn't make it."

"Did it have to do with him being sick?"

That was one way to put it. "No one really knows."

"He had the coolest car." Horrified tears came to Willow's eyes. "What a dumb thing to say. Gosh, I'm sorry." Her face crumpled and she started to cry, full on.

"Don't be sorry." Kelly gathered her daughter in her arms. "We all have those random thoughts when we lose someone. It's human. It's

not easy to absorb, even for people like me, who've seen it happen a lot."
This was absolutely true. The thing was, Kelly advocated—officially, as
in, with PowerPoint slideshows—that people should talk more openly
about death, at all phases of their lives. That American culture's avoid-
ance of the topic was unhealthy and left people unprepared in the worst
of ways. But somehow, this belief did not extend to conversations with
her own daughter.

She knew this was a fault: *Do as I say, not as I do.* Still, surely she
thought about it more than enough for both of them.

"Your clients are different. They've been old for, like, a while. Not
that it isn't sad, but Mason . . . It isn't fair."

Was there any reason to pontificate on the ways death did not play
fair?

"Sure doesn't seem like it," Kelly agreed.

Willow wiped at her face with her nightgown. "I bet Nova's really
sad. Is that why you're still down here?"

"That's part of why." It would take Kelly forever to fall back to sleep
with all this churning in her mind. She almost might as well stay up.
Nova would be awake at daybreak anyway, mere hours from now.

Kelly hadn't even known the sunrise had its own twilight until she
met Nova. She'd thought twilight was just for sunsets, for dimming the
light on a goodbye. They'd known each other only weeks before Nova
coaxed her out of bed an hour before dawn, pulled her to the far corner of the backyard, with its sliver of river valley view, and showed her
how the day came in stages. First: astronomical twilight, when the sky
shifts a shade brighter than absolute dark. It still looks like night, but
if you tune in, you sense change coming. Next: nautical dawn, when
sailors at sea might make out distant shadows of other vessels on the
horizon. Birds begin chirping then, the air growing slowly alive with
anticipation. Then—about twenty-five minutes before the sun's debut:
civil twilight, brightest of all. When you wouldn't need a flashlight to
find your way up a hilltop to see the main event.

Kelly had used Nova's lesson. She'd told her clients how easy it was
to overlook civil twilight, and what a shame—that the moments before

the sun broached the horizon seemed to hold more meaning than the rising itself, which only seemed to fast-forward the morning.

But she knew Nova preferred the grand finale.

Willow crossed to the kitchen door and pulled the curtain aside. Beyond the glass pane, their square half acre glowed in the bright spotlights Kelly had installed for families coming and going at all hours.

"Mom?" Her daughter's voice held no more tears—only alarm. "Is that Nova? On the roof?"

Kelly sprung to Willow's side. Indeed, a figure perched hugging her bent knees on the shingled peak atop the detached garage. The wind gusted, and the figure's hair flowed behind it, loose and wild. It could only be Nova.

Kelly grabbed her hoodie from the hook by the door. "You go back to bed. School day tomorrow."

"Oh my *God,* Mom. Have you ever seen her up there before?"

*"Gosh,"* she corrected, automatically. Then: "This is a first." Normally, she'd say this with fondness. Nova had a way of chasing firsts—sometimes, Kelly suspected, for the sake of saying she'd done it. Not that there was anything wrong with that. But this . . .

"She's not going to—to jump?"

"Of course not," Kelly said quickly. She gave Willow a squeeze, hoping that her fears really were unwarranted—that she could spare the extra seconds to do so. "But I bet she'll be happy to know she's not the only one awake. Up to bed, okay? I won't be far behind."

Kelly flew out the door, then caught herself and slowed at the driveway's edge. The last thing she wanted was to startle Nova's precarious balance.

"Nova?" she called softly. Nova didn't seem to hear, and Kelly stood inhaling the night air, still more spring than summer, acclimating to the dewy silence. High above the spotlights' glow, her partner looked like a bird, an ancient descendant poised for flight.

"Nova?" she tried again, and this time, Nova turned her head. Kelly's eyes strained but couldn't make out her face. "What are you doing up there?"

"I'm . . ." In silhouette, her head moved to pan the roof around her, as if only now realizing where she was. "Looking at the stars," she finished.

Kelly glanced skyward, in spite of herself. "Aren't you afraid you'll fall?" She cringed at how parental she sounded. Still, it was better than actually yelling, *Are you nuts?*

"No," Nova said, not unkindly—she was blunt, but Kelly had never heard her be unkind. Yet even across the expanse of open air, Nova's tone seemed to convey that this was the key difference between them. Nova was, for better or worse, not afraid—not of losing her footing up high, not of following a client out on a dangerous limb, not of raising Willow wrong, or failing at her business, or any of the things that terrified Kelly, as far as Kelly could tell.

Kelly had wished she herself were as brave.

Still, on this day, maybe Nova had cause to be a little bit afraid, of a lot of things.

Kelly tried to laugh. "I guess that should have been obvious." She hugged her hoodie tighter. "Want to come down? Have some tea?"

For a moment, Nova didn't answer. Then: "You'd feel better if I did." That kindness again. That difference again. *One of them* would feel better.

"I would."

Nova dropped so suddenly down the slope of the roof that Kelly let out a yelp. But Nova was in control. She swung in one agile movement over the edge and landed neatly on the staircase platform. Kelly clapped a hand over her racing heart as Nova descended the stairs, still looking somehow birdlike. Like if she tested her wings, she might flutter away.

Back inside, Kelly took a cursory look to make sure Willow wasn't lingering to listen in. She made quick work of the tea, a Sleepytime blend not likely to be strong enough for either of them. Nova sat at the table, looking paradoxically less steady than her silhouette had up there on that peak. The light painted her in subdued shades.

Kelly plunked the mugs in front of her partner and settled across from her. They regarded each other in silence, breathing the steam, biding time until someone got brave and sipped first.

"I can't stop thinking about you," Kelly began, carefully. "How are you holding up?"

Nova smiled weakly. "I could have done without the family dinner. My mom would not take no for an answer."

"I'm so terribly sorry, Nova. This is awful."

"I know. It is. Thanks."

"I hate to have to talk details from a client perspective right now, but . . ."

"We don't have much choice. It's okay."

Nova nodded politely, as if she'd been summoned there for an interview. Her grief was unmistakable, threatening to swallow her, maybe, or to drag her back atop the roof if that's what it took to feel closer to Mason. Kelly had seen them together—from the first day he'd peered down those stairs at Nova, she'd seen. They'd exchange a look or walk by—so in sync—and Kelly would get a sense like being in another country: the feeling they both understood some language she did not. But here was the same Nova being clinical and calm, presumably for Kelly's sake. Or at least, for Parting Your Way.

So why did Kelly feel hurt? That Nova wasn't, what, lying in her lap sobbing, bearing her soul? Clearly Nova was already doing a better job than Kelly of grasping what Maggie had said earlier: *I know she's your friend, Kel, but this is your business. This is your life.*

First things first, then. "Do you have anything that proves, for an indisputable fact, that Mason was terminally ill? A copy of test results? A contact at a doctor's office?"

Nova bit her lip. "You know requiring proof has never been an issue. Sort of a given."

Kelly did know. Just as she'd known that if Nova had proof, she'd have already said so to Bonnie. "And I guess he wasn't ill enough yet for you to think it odd he hadn't put you in touch with a care team?"

"Exactly."

"What happened with him withdrawing a few weeks ago? I had no idea."

Nova's voice held steady. "He made it clear we'd never see eye to eye on his path forward."

Kelly was afraid to ask, but she had to. "What did he see as his path forward?"

"He never said. He only rejected my suggestions."

This wouldn't exactly be mystifying to anyone who'd met Mason. Still, things between him and Nova had seemed different. Better. "Why didn't you tell me?"

Nova shrugged. "I guess I was embarrassed. Waiting to see if he'd change his mind."

"Fair enough. What did Mason tell you about his relationship with his mother?"

"She was glad to have him home."

"Most mothers would be," Kelly agreed.

Nova fixed her eyes on Kelly to make it clear she'd missed her meaning. "She was glad," she repeated.

Oh.

Kelly recalled that first afternoon, when she'd so easily taken Mason for someone worn down from the round-the-clock toll of caring for a dying loved one. That was not the face of a man who was comforted to be home.

"It's complicated, right?" Kelly ventured. "When Willow is hurting, that's when I most want to keep her close. It's instinct."

Nova opened her mouth, then closed it again. "My mother would agree," she conceded.

"Okay, look. I'm hoping Bonnie won't follow through on her threats, but I think we need to be smart in case she does." Kelly cleared her throat. "Let's break this down. Start by telling me what you *thought* you knew for a fact about what Mason was facing, health wise. Physically, mentally, the whole picture."

Kelly wasn't trying to condescend, asking Nova to reduce him to a bulleted list. Families loved lists. So did hospice workers. It stood to reason anyone who came to investigate would, too. But Nova's expression looked pained.

"I knew for a fact," Nova said quietly, "that there are lots of reasons someone might see an end-of-life doula even if they're not clinically classified as terminal. I knew for a fact that we walk a dozen forward-thinking, nonterminal clients through end-of-life planning every week."

Kelly lifted her shoulders. This was no list—this was a talking point. "We do. But they don't lead us to believe they have an immediate need that isn't present."

"Don't they? When something has shaken a client to send them running in here—whether it's a tragedy involving a loved one, or a scare of their own—you don't sense an urgency that's heightened by emotion? You don't pick up on desperation that they're so far from where they want to be? That they're relying on you to reassure them they can get there?"

It was Kelly's turn to fall silent.

"I know for a fact that sometimes looking someone in the eye and truly listening to them is the best medicine we can give," Nova went on. "I know for a fact that there's more than one way to think of ourselves as dying. We say goodbye forever to parts of ourselves every time we close an important chapter in our lives. I know for a fact that the emotional turmoil of facing death can be worse than the physical pain. And I know that a prognosis from a whole team of top doctors can occasionally be flat wrong, because nobody is ever as certain about anything as we'd like to believe."

Every word landed with conviction and respect and heartbreak. And yet not a one referenced Mason in specific terms. Kelly wasn't sure whether to feel proud or fed up that Nova clearly wasn't going to.

After all, she'd taught Nova these principles herself.

"I know for a fact," Nova continued, calmly, "these are the reasons our tenets do not include demanding proof of any condition—or stage of that condition—before administering to a client who wants our support. I know for a fact we cannot call ourselves non-medical caregivers while allowing ourselves to be questioned on medical prerequisites for care. We cannot preach building relationships on mutual trust without trust itself being our default setting."

Nova crossed her arms and sat back, her point clear: She wasn't laying out her feelings on what had happened, or what might have gone wrong. She was laying out their defense.

And she was fully capable of doing it without outing Mason's private turmoil along the way. She wouldn't dignify Bonnie's accusations with that kind of response.

Not even, apparently, to Kelly.

"So we're going to fall on the sword of our principles here?"

Kelly couldn't help but protest, even as she saw the wisdom in the plan. The nature of their partnership made it impossible not to discuss clients with each other, but they aimed to be respectful in how they did so. Only, always, with the clients' best interests in mind, not breaching privacy more than necessary. Kelly didn't play her seniority card much—in fact, she turned to Nova for advice often enough. But in a hot seat neither of them could have ever imagined, didn't Nova owe her more accountability, transparency?

Then again, maybe Kelly was hiding behind the professional excuse. Maybe what she really felt was a schoolgirl urge for her friend to tell her everything about what had gone down with this dreamy, off-limits boy. Even if it was better she didn't know.

"Nobody's falling on any sword," Nova assured her. "And I want to show compassion to the Shaylors. But if we turn ourselves into the willing middleman here, repeating everything Mason told us under the good-faith umbrella of having nothing to hide, we're going to open ourselves to layers of scrutiny that are not in our best interest, or our clients' best interest."

*Don't play any kind of game,* Kelly's dad used to say, *when there can be no winner.* Bonnie Shaylor had an awful lot of anguish and anger she needed to direct somewhere. Kelly's typical approach would be to try again with Bonnie once the heat of their exchange had cooled. But Bonnie hadn't minced words: *Don't give me any of that compassionate care crap.* If Nova and Kelly did not engage on the level she wanted them to, maybe she'd direct that energy elsewhere.

"I'll be honest," Kelly said. "I'm trying to keep it together here. I know someone you cared a lot about is gone, and of course Mrs. Shaylor is hurting, and everyone wants answers. But in all my years, I've never had a client or caregiver come at me like what happened today. The fact that this has anything to do with us . . . It freaks me out. You know what this place means to me. You know how easy it would be to make us look bad."

"I do know. That's why I'm trying to think ahead this way. I don't know what else to do. I'm sorry, Kel."

"As bad as today felt for me, I can't imagine what you're going through. Don't you want to—I mean—even if it stays between us . . ."

"If there's something else you need to ask me," Nova said, "go ahead."

Kelly thought about what she stood to gain by soliciting the play-by-play.

And what she stood to lose by skipping it.

"Willow said she thought Mason was your boyfriend," she said at last. It wasn't really a question, except that it was. A loaded one, if you read their code of conduct.

Everyone knew that was mostly for the doula's protection though. She'd never heard of a violation. Most pervy old men retired the act before they made it this far.

Nova didn't outwardly react—no flush of embarrassment, nothing to confirm or deny. Kelly couldn't decide if she was relieved or disappointed.

"Willow picks up on a lot, you know," Nova said finally. "We need to be careful what we sugarcoat for her."

She'd said *we,* at least. That's how they'd been, this last, tight-knit year.

Up until today.

# 10

## *Mason*

Mason knew plenty of musicians who'd wake up with a song in their head, on the regular. Usually the one they were sick of playing—he had a friend who claimed that of any superpower, he'd choose *earworm immunity* over invisibility or flight. They all preferred to wake up humming an old melody they hadn't performed in a while. They'd take it as a sign—a whispered tip from the gods—and add it to that night's set list. Bring the house down, or at least scratch the itch.

None of that ever happened to Mason, though.

He'd wake up with a song in his *fingers*.

When it came to his own music, he never so much heard it as felt it. Which made scratching that itch all the more satisfying, all the more literal.

Right up until he couldn't.

*Leave me alone,* he growled at the old riffs, even at the wisps of unwritten lyrics begging for a pen. *Go bother someone who can play you.* And for the most part, they stayed away, tucking back into their own pockets of despair.

Until this morning. He woke up twitching. His fingertips curling around the D minor chord that opened "Sunbeams and Moonshine." Not just curling but craving. An involuntary call and response.

He'd written that song about a day like today. Through the open window of this cluttered teenage relic of a bedroom—peeling posters, fraying quilt, cloudy dresser mirror—the sky shone like polished turquoise, the unfiltered sun disregarding his permanent bad mood. He'd fallen asleep with the screens open to the cold night, curtains pulled aside so he could stare into the stars, longing to be as far from here as they were. Now, the goddamn birds were chirping so merrily, he half expected one to land on the windowsill and bid him good morning, Disney movie style. He rolled to the far edge of his bed, pulling the mess of covers with him, but there was no escaping the unrelenting glow. It fell on his Gibson Montana Hummingbird, resting in its stand in the corner, and the guitar's sunburst gleamed golden, beckoning him.

Maybe today.

A week had passed since he'd last touched the strings. Another week of what people referred to as "time" and "rest" and "healing" and "you never know" while Mason could only call it what it was: nothing.

He'd started keeping his most prized instrument where he could see it, though he was usually maniacal about storing it with the humidifier. The neck of the Gibson had a slightly smaller radius than the dreadnought, his usual go-to offstage. Practicing with the dreadnought's extra millimeters had always made the showtime switch to the Gibson sweeter: on would come the spotlight, and his hands would feel nimble, at their best. The Gibson was too good for this room, but it stood to reason it would be kinder to his surgical scars—more persuasive, too.

Who could walk away from a guitar like that? He'd saved for years, playing through exhaustion and pain, making every mistake in the book to earn that sweet reward.

Beneath the blankets at his side, his fingers traced their airy path through the song intro. If he tried even basic fretting and strumming today, less than what "Sunbeams and Moonshine" required, and if he failed, he'd have to wait another week to try again. His self-imposed rule for maintaining sanity in exile. The doctors had finally told him not to bother with rules or pacing, not to hinge hopes on a fancy custom guitar neck radius, not to torture himself trying at all. But hearing the truth of their words wasn't the same as feeling it. And he'd never operated by theory rather than feel. Never would.

The song wasn't about him. He'd been on tour alone, up early, finishing an omelet in the front window of a nowhere diner when he'd watched the drunk stumble from behind the gas station on the corner, one arm shielding his eyes from the sun. The bedraggled man had staggered into the street, glared up at the cloudless sky, and angrily bellowed, "What'd I tell ya?" Then again, slower but no less incensed: "Whaaaaaat'd I tellllll yaaaaaaa?" Mason had looked on, fascinated, as the man pulled a flask from his jeans pocket, took a swig, and transformed into a different person entirely. One who seemed to have decided to embrace this day, right then, with the exuberance of Jimmy Stewart on his post-Clarence Christmas Eve. He strode toward the diner, shouting hello to a couple on the sidewalk, bursting through the door, clapping the hostess good-naturedly on the back.

"Gooooood mornin', sunshine!" At the counter, he ordered a coffee to go, with a wink. "Don't top it off. Leave pouring room for somethin' extra, you dig?"

When Mason got up to pay his check, he chanced a grin in the man's direction. "Could've sworn you looked like you were having a bad day a minute ago."

The man nodded gravely. "It did start that way. But long as I got my moonshine, I won't disrespect these goddamn beautiful rays of sun, know what I'm saying?" He opened his arms wide, grinning ear to ear. "Sons of bitches got me!"

Heads had turned in distaste, but Mason found himself moved by the man's 180, moonshine or no moonshine. He began to imagine a score that opened like that hungover stagger, syncopated and uncertain, then picked up rhythmic energy. He had a six-hour drive ahead of him, from Mobile to Memphis, and as he started out, the lyrical wordplay began overlaying this new soundtrack: sunlight, sunshine. Moonbeams, moonlight. His fingers worked out the chords on the steering wheel, picked the strings on the gear shift, on the windowsill, on the leather of the seat next to him. By the time he pulled into his motel, he practically ran to the front desk for his key, then straight up to his second-floor room, not bothering to go back for his suitcase. He needed to try the real thing aloud, bend it around his vision. His brain could get him most of the way, but only his guitar could entirely convert a work from idea to *song*.

He brought the more or less finished "Sunbeams and Moonshine" to the stage that same night—as luck of the calendar had it, to a venue with actual seats and tickets. When he finished and the crowd erupted in approval, he found himself yelling into the mic, "Sons of bitches got me!"

Which no one—Mason included—understood, but everyone took to mean they should cheer louder. So they did, that night and every performance thereafter.

The song might not have been about him then, but it sure as hell felt like it now.

He slipped from the bed and got to his knees beside the Gibson, shivering in the frosty room.

*Please,* he begged, silently. *Please.*

Ducking his head beneath the strap, he moved his arms into position, breathed deep, and began to play.

The twinge shot through his right elbow before he was through the first progression.

He wanted to ignore it. To play on. But the burning sensation traveled into his ring finger and pinky, begging them to stop, and when he didn't, the tingling took command of his whole hand. No matter how many second and third and fourth opinions he sought, he'd been told:

On a lucky day, his hands would obey his brain's commands for a song or two. On the left, he could play through the discomfort, but it was no longer an option on the right. He'd drop the pick, miss a string, fall sluggish in the rhythm. No amount of therapy or strengthening or medical intervention could fix his clumsy new grip, restore the speed or style the dysfunction had stolen.

He stopped cold, staring down at the guitar. The flawless $3,800 guitar with incomparable sonics and years of history. The back panel had been kissed—literally, physically kissed—by a select handful of his idols.

The ones he'd opened for.

The ones he'd known wouldn't laugh when he asked them to do it.

Then, he was on his feet, swinging that gorgeous creature through the air, cutting the streaming sunlight like a knife, smashing into the old wooden dresser so hard he heard the instrument crack, felt the vibration travel up his arm and dislodge his muscles from the nerve signals entirely. The airborne Hummingbird flew over his shoulder, landing on the unmade bed, and he pounced, taking it between his hands again and bringing it down onto the mattress, once, twice, but it stopped being satisfying. Even when he tried to lose himself in anger—in any pure, uncomplicated emotion—he couldn't escape the depressing truth.

He'd even lost the ability to *get* lost.

Chest heaving, he dropped the instrument and sank to the floor. The strap dangled over the edge of the quilt, as if he'd relinquished the bed to the Gibson after a lover's quarrel. Fitting: Music *was* the only mistress he'd ever been a gentleman to. And in the midst of his devotion, he'd neglected subtle warnings that all was not well between them. Now, she'd slipped away, no way to get her back. He let the sobs overcome him; his mother would have left for work by now, no one left to hear. Not even the fat old house cat, who'd finally died as soon as he moved home. It figured—though he'd never liked that cat anyway. He'd considered getting a dog—the one creature comfort he'd longed for on the road—but it seemed unfair to the poor animal.

Stuck as he may seem, one way or another, he was determined not to be here long.

The tapping at the door came hesitantly at first, then louder. Mason raised his face, wet with tears, to glare in confusion across the room. Whoever it was had foregone the front doorbell to knock at the entrance directly to this back bedroom. Before Mason's family came along, this had been a low-budget mother-in-law suite. The previous owners, still grieving their matriarch, had taken pity on the widow with young boys and accepted her offer below asking price. Seven-year-old Mason had protested taking the bedroom of "some old dead lady," but as a teen he'd come around to the advantages—and finally understood why his older brother, Bo, had been denied the room in the first place.

The knocking continued. Then: "Mason? You in there?"

Nova.

His self-pity-party had blown right through his appointment time, but what did it matter? He'd figured she wouldn't be too surprised when he of all people didn't show.

"Go away," he called.

The knocking stopped, but he knew she was still there.

"I don't feel well," he elaborated. "I'll call to reschedule."

"Sorry to hear," she called back. "I'd still love for you to open the door for a minute?"

It was his turn to answer with silence.

"One minute," she repeated.

"I'd rather not." He wiped his sleeve across his cheeks and looked down at his hand, which was on fire from his asinine outburst. It had curved itself protectively into a claw, visual proof that he'd undone the hard work of resting the nerves and then some.

All he'd wanted was to play "Sunbeams and Moonshine."

Even just to the bridge, two-thirds of the way through.

That was his favorite part.

"Thing is," Nova persisted, her voice annoyingly unmuffled thanks to the open window, "in my business, when a client ghosts, that advances to a level of seriousness. So. Quick welfare check, okay?"

*Ha,* he thought. *When a client ghosts, they might have become an actual ghost.* He could have retorted that ghosts can't yell through doors, but really how did he know? Plus, he was tired of yelling—like he'd *become* that man from the corner parking lot, waking up barely lucid enough to grab for something that might turn the day around.

Or, he supposed, someone.

He cracked open the door and leaned against the frame, peering out. Nova stood a few paces away, hands in her pockets, looking admirably unbothered to have had to come here. She did not comment that he looked more like a toddler completing a tantrum than a sick patient. She did not react that he'd clearly been in the midst of an emotional breakdown until she arrived.

"How did you know to use the side door?" he grumbled.

"I followed the bread crumb trail." She gestured wryly to an empty beer can crumpled against the wall. He knew it had a few friends on the bumper of his Jeep, possibly around the backyard fire ring, too. Mom had been on him to clean up after himself, stop embarrassing her, what must the neighbors think? Every day he'd agree. But every night he'd remember how small potatoes that was in the scheme of things. Small, rotten, gnarled potatoes.

Nova's eyes flicked over him for a beat, then past him.

"This is where you're staying?" she asked. "Permanently?"

He let the door fall open and turned to look at what she saw. Not the cracked guitar on the bed, not the fresh gashes in the varnished dresser top—marks of the shame he supposed he should feel right now. She'd asked about the room.

His mother had let the room be all these years—as more of a neglected storage unit than any kind of doting shrine. The wall décor was a timestamp to the late nineties, early aughts: Though he'd taught himself to play here, his musical tastes were unoriginal back then. The mountains of ticket stubs and concert programs he'd amassed weren't artfully arranged on some inspiration board, but thrown in shoeboxes, which sagged in lopsided piles atop his chest of drawers. The closet was missing a door, exposing the missing-button flannels and other discards hanging inside—his current clothes were either thrown into the suitcase open on the floor, or heaped on the desk chair. The closet's bottom held a mishmash of worn boots, dusty ball caps, and other stuff that might have been donated before the soles became unglued or the brims yellowed. Almost none of this was any use to anyone now. Least of all him.

"I don't know what permanent means anymore," he said.

She nodded. "Well, some people find it comforting to be among their old things."

He thought of Nova's stark office, and the equally sparse apartment he'd glimpsed through the adjoining door. Surrounded by all this detritus he found neither nostalgic nor homey, he understood the appeal of going minimalist.

"Are you one of them?" she persisted.

He laughed. He hadn't thought twice, ever, about heading out on the road with only what fit in the Jeep. Or with less, when he was hitching rides on the summer festival circuit.

But maybe *not* looking over his shoulder was part of the problem. He'd always known the baggage would literally be waiting for him if ever he turned back, yet he'd never taken the initiative to haul this junk to the curb. Or even to hint that he wouldn't mind if his mother did, for all the good that would've done. Maybe he'd let her preserve this museum as a mental trick, to keep himself hungry, to ensure he'd never get too comfortable on visits home for Christmas.

Or—was it possible he hadn't really wanted to let it go?

Either way, the joke was on him.

"*No,*" he told Nova, dragging out the word for maximum emphasis.

Obviously, she couldn't read his whole angsty backstory from a sardonic laugh and a one-word answer. But the way she was looking at him, he halfway suspected she could.

"Want a hand cleaning it out? Doesn't have to be now, but—?"

His eyes narrowed. Was this some handy excuse to start digging around his stuff, filling in the blanks in what he'd told her?

"I don't want you judging me on my junior prom cummerbund. I was ill advised to match my date's dress."

"Must have been some dress. And I don't judge. I help."

She was so quick with her answer, hell if he didn't believe her.

Mason had been standing here trying to look at the scene through her eyes: pathetic, tired, sad. Nova, though, had already been seeing it through his. Painful, inescapable, stifling. And she'd seen a way to ease that. One he'd been staring sullenly at for months, without considering it once.

"I'd say I can handle it myself," he said. "But I'm not sure I can." Before he could think it through, he held up his ugly claw. "They tell me pretty soon this is likely to be stuck this way. So much for teaching myself to play left-handed."

He dropped it behind his back, as tears again stung his eyes. Damn. He never let anyone see—not the hand, not the tears, certainly not the room. He'd been almost certain he'd rather die before anyone saw the truth of what had become of him. Was his brain assigning different rules to Nova, by virtue of their relationship?

She was appraising the ruined Gibson now, but had the sense to look meek doing it. For the first time, he saw a fleeting resemblance to the old professional headshot that dominated the search results when he'd googled her. It was stunning how transformed she was—the absence of that old pasted-on smile, nondescript outfit, flat-ironed hair, all of it replaced with something more authentic, naturally wavy, less designed to impress. No one would ever make the mistake of thinking Nova had stopped trying, let herself go. The difference was in her eyes, her expression, her posture. Like her soul had become more at home in her body. Knew what to do with it now.

As they both looked in despair at his ruined pride and joy, he knew he couldn't hang any more last hopes on this guitar. No matter how much he wanted to.

All he had left to hang them on was Nova.

"It has to be when my mother's not here," he said. *I don't want to have to explain who you are.* "She's more attached to this stuff than I am."

Nova reached out, and before Mason knew it, had his clawed hand between her own. He stared down at her soft fingers in surprise. At their presence. At their comfort.

At how foreign it was to be touched at all, with no wince or flinch or pity.

"Well," she said, "guess we'd better get started soon."

He still wasn't sure whether this doula idea was worth his time. But three weeks in, he had to admit she was holding his interest—sparking something in a way no one else had since he'd come home. Maybe even longer. To start, the concept of a death doula had seemed a faceless thing. But it had already become synonymous with Nova specifically. It would be Nova, or nothing.

Nothing was always an option.

# 11

## *Nova*

**THEN**

For two weeks, Mason and I clean out his room. We scratch our appointment times and find blocks of hours here and there instead:
a late morning, a long afternoon. We fill oversized trash bags with
clothes, paperbacks, and CDs for Goodwill. We vacuum thick layers of
dust, sponge mold from the windowsills, tear every last item from the
yellowing walls, spackle the nail holes. His arms clearly aren't up to the
repainting, so I offer to do that, too.

"I appreciate it," he says, "but I don't want to blow through your
whole fee on this."

"Don't worry about it." I wave him away. "Some of this . . . Consider
it my own time."

He blinks at me. "Surely you have things you'd rather do?"

I could point out that plenty of people put in extra work on special
cases without overtime pay—teachers, writers, trainers, cops. I could

admit I'm hoping he'll warm to this arrangement if we take the pressure off our time together. Or that, frankly, rolling eggshell onto his walls seems vastly easier than anything else in my doula manual.

But I'm not sure this will fly with Mason, who seems to have phrased this question just so. Uncomfortably so. Maybe I don't have things I'd rather do. When it comes to my own time, maybe this doula work *is* filling a gap that I won't have to see if I keep busy with it.

"I like the fumes," I deadpan, and he actually laughs. A win.

While I work, he sits atop crinkly plastic drop cloths, riffling through old photos. With his flannel traded for a T-shirt, surgical scars show on both elbows, and his right forearm and wrist, too. They're hard to look at, and my eyes keep drifting in search of smoother edges—the set of his jaw, the tilt of his head.

We don't talk much. Still, there's an intimacy, getting comfortable together in silence. Now and then, we laugh over bands we once liked, people we once dated. We find common ground over things we used to think mattered. And little by little, I learn just enough about Mason to feel like I'm achieving more than a fresh white ceiling.

His dad was killed during Desert Storm, and his mom never remarried. Whether he's protecting her or resenting her, he makes it clear he wants her left out of all matters at hand for as long as possible. Likewise, he and his brother were closer in childhood than in recent years, and that's all Mason has to say about it. There's no mistaking the air of disapproval regarding his family's take on his music career. He actually laughs when I ask if they might want any of this memorabilia he's dumping into the trash without a second glance: newspaper clippings, posters, at least one full box of misprinted T-shirts bearing his off-centered name. It's just as clear he doesn't want me to get a good look at any of it, so I resist the urge to rephrase with what I really mean: whether Mason himself might regret doing this so hastily.

By the time we've succeeded in making his room look as if *no one* lives there, I can't help but feel we're getting somewhere. He's even looked me square in the eye while refusing to unpack his suitcase, which has at least moved from spread eagle in the middle of the floor to spread eagle in the bottom of the closet. As we set a time for our next meeting back at my office, at last I know how I'll start, what I'll say.

But then, I'm the one who cancels.

❖

*We do everything together,* Glenna had told me of her and Wendell.

She held his hand when he had to go; I held hers.

It might be bad for business to admit it, but I don't like funerals. I'm more comfortable grieving things that haven't happened yet. By the end of four long days in Glenna's sad shadow, I'm ready to shift back to regular doula work—until Mason walks in, looking almost happy to see me.

"One less client to worry about, huh?" he says by way of greeting, plopping down across from my desk.

I glare at him until he realizes the folly of his words. It's almost funny, how shocked he looks at himself, and at me. As if I've established such a sunny *life goes on* vibe, he's just realizing I'm not immune to the tragedies that have brought us both to this room.

"Sorry," he says. "Crude attempt at a joke."

I take a turn at being the one to answer in silence. I can see why he finds it so satisfying.

"Ever know you're being an asshole, but you can't seem to stop?" he asks. He runs a hand through his beard, which has filled in quite a bit from its patchy start. Not that it looks much better. "I never realized how rare it is to just sit with someone who's there to . . ." He searches for the words, and I wait. "Who's just there. No agenda. I'm not sure anyone else really listens much when anybody talks, you know? It's taking some getting used to. But when we missed our last appointment? I *actually* missed it. So, I think I really do want to."

My anger fades. This is the most self-aware I've seen Mason. He's not right that we don't have *any* agenda, but I know what he means, in a vague sense.

"You think you want to . . . stop being an asshole?"

He smiles. "Only to you. Let's not get carried away."

He's no more of an asshole than I am. He's scared, and lonely, and angry, with good reasons to be. Even if he hasn't shared them yet. "Baby steps," I agree.

"About that." He gestures around us. "Offices don't exactly bring out the best in me. Historically, I haven't been in them for great reasons. So, if it's cool to keep hanging out other places—I wouldn't be the only one who asks that?"

"Not at all. In fact, I'm hanging with the widow I mentioned again this week, and all she wants to do is sit on her couch together and watch TV."

Poor Glenna keeps assuring me she's relieved Wendell's suffering is over. That they've been saying goodbye all year, and now she's lonely but managing, free to cancel chemo and live her final days feeling as good as she can. With his burial behind her, she wants to honor her own final chapter her own way: by sharing the only part of her therapy she's ever liked.

The Doritos are against my diet. They're also already in my car.

"Can I come?" We both do a double take at Mason's question. He seems both surprised and embarrassed to have spoken. "Sorry, I'm sure that's not appropriate."

It's not appropriate. There are several reasons bringing Mason along is a horrible idea, top of the list being that I'm not sure I trust him. The last thing I need is some Yelp review claiming that if you're looking for a doula to smoke your medicinal weed, I'm your gal. Also, my main duty in this moment is to Glenna. I might be loosey-goosey with certain rules, but ethically speaking, I've never mixed client company— not on purpose. I do my best to avoid conflicts of interest for my clients *and* myself.

The fact that he's asking, though, is tough to resist. If Mason saw the bond I have off the clock with another client, maybe he'd open up. If he saw what Glenna's up against and how her attitude shines in spite of it, maybe she'd inspire him in a way I have yet to. Frankly, I don't have any better ideas.

I can call and ask how Glenna would feel about me bringing a friend who could use a night in with company. But I already know what her response will be.

"Before you say yes," I say, "there is *one* action item you should be aware of."

✳

As soon as Glenna opens the door, I'm engulfed in a hug so tight a goofy smile spreads across my face, in spite of how thin she feels beneath her rose-embroidered sweatshirt. The silk headscarf hiding her bare scalp is a green vine pattern that doesn't quite match. Behind her, every light in the house seems to be on. How strange it must feel to be living alone for the first time in—if I'm not mistaken—her entire life.

"Do me one favor," she says, before I can ask how she's holding up. She keeps hold of me, speaking into my ear. "Let's pretend Wendell has just turned in early, okay? I know it sounds silly, but if we talk it out, I'll get weepy. I need a night off."

Oh, Glenna. Before I can answer, she bursts into giggles.

I pull back to look at her.

"I *might* already be a teensy bit high," she whispers. She pulls a mischievous face, and behind me, I hear an unfamiliar sound.

Mason has begun to laugh. With actual delight.

Glenna tilts to look around me. "You must be Mason."

"Thanks for letting me bring a friend," I say quickly. Like many doulas, I follow the rule therapists do when they run into clients socially, leaving it up to him whether to disclose the nature of our relationship. He meets my eye, getting it.

"Pleased to meet you." He holds up our canvas bag of snacks like an admission ticket.

"Pleased to meet *you*," she agrees, snatching the Doritos from the tote. She tears the package open right there in the doorway and pops a chip into her mouth, closing her eyes as she chews. "Oh, heavens. It's been so long." I'm shaking my head, still grinning like an idiot, and when I look over at Mason, he is, too.

"You two," she announces, "need to catch up."

Inside on the coffee table, Glenna has snack bowls and rocks glasses waiting, and we unload all the things she's mentioned craving in her months of being too ravaged by chemo to enjoy food: fun-sized candy bars, movie theater butter popcorn, good bourbon. I've added a few healthier picks—salted almonds, edamame—because you can take the mind-body-spirit out of the doula, but you can't . . . well, you actually just can't.

"You look familiar," Glenna says, watching Mason from where she's perched on the arm of the couch, still scarfing the corn chips. "Is there somewhere I'd know you from?"

He shakes his head—too quickly for someone who grew up in this town, full of places they might have crossed paths. "No, ma'am."

But I'm thinking of Glenna's albums of concert ticket stubs and photos. The well-kept equivalent of all Mason's torn-up boxes. Wendell and Glenna were music buffs—"snobs," she'd told me, hilariously, as if there was anything snooty about a retiree buying a three-day festival ticket to stand in a hot field with thousands of college students.

As a policy, I don't look up my clients online—I limit my knowledge to what they want to disclose. I haven't exactly assumed Mason was a no-name, but it's never occurred to me he might have been a big enough deal that she'd seen him play.

"One of those faces, I guess," she says. "So, young ones: Since we've never done this together before, I'd like to know what I'm getting into. What kind of stoned people are you?"

We "young ones" exchange a questioning look.

"You know: Do you get paranoid, silly, quiet, zoned out . . ." She's ticking the options off her fingers. "Contemplative of the meaning of life?"

Mason laughs again, and it's a pretty great sound, gravelly and warm. If his singing voice has the same quality, I'd for sure stand in a hot field to see that.

"Raunchy," I answer. "Consider yourself warned."

Abruptly, Glenna drops the Doritos and runs from the room. Mason raises an eyebrow, and I spread my arms innocently. "I was kidding!"

But she strides right back in, adjusting a triple strand of pearls around her neck. They look comically fancy next to the sweatshirt, jeans, house slippers, and Dorito dust.

"So I can clutch them," she explains, winking. "Bring it on."

We're halfway through the night when Mason tells her I'm his doula, too.

If we're talking "types" of high people, Mason has been quiet, but not in his usual brooding way—he genuinely seems to be enjoying the company. Maybe because Glenna is the hilarious type, charmingly uninhibited. We're a couple hours into rummy 500, and she's been heckling us to the point that we've started taunting her back, though I'm pretty sure we're both rooting for her to win. By the time I cry uncle and excuse myself for a bathroom break, my sensations are pleasantly heightened, my head buzzing with good feelings toward—well, everything. The idea of feeling so at home in someone else's house, the timeless camaraderie of shuffling and dealing, the acquired taste of bourbon on ice. I'm thinking of an article I read once, about solid friendships that can form between people of different ages, and how not enough people give them a shake.

It's even feeling like less of an exaggeration having told Glenna that Mason was my friend. I'd been questioning my own judgment ever since agreeing to bring him here, but it's not a disaster. I can almost forget my reservations.

I'm heading back to the living room when Glenna's cell phone chimes, and I hear her murmur softly in response.

"Does your phone give you these 'memories' reminders?" she asks Mason. "Where it sucker-punches you with photos of what you were doing last year at this time?"

"I shut those off," he says, and I slow to a stop shy of the doorway.

"Maybe you could show me how?"

"Can I see the memory?" Mason asks, surprising me. Not avoiding her grief; meeting it.

Hugging the hallway wall, I inch forward to see the back of the couch, where she's slipped into my seat next to Mason and they hunch, heads together, over her screen.

"Neither of us knew we were sick," she says, "Isn't it strange? These are photos of two people who are dying but don't know it yet."

"Do you know how to pull up your settings? There's a default we can change."

She hesitates. "Next year at this time, I'll be gone, too, and no one will be left to get these notifications. Do you think that means I owe it to Wendell to look at them now? To take them as reminders to be grateful for every day I'm here to remember him?"

"That would be," Mason says slowly, "an amazing attitude."

Glenna sighs. "Well. I owe a lot of that to Nova." This is overly generous. Her determination was well intact before we met. Either she's feeling as love-everything-and-everyone as I am, or she's gotten the wrong idea about me bringing Mason and is endorsing me as a girlfriend candidate. Before I can decide which, she smacks her forehead. "Blast! I broke my rule. Wendell is supposed to be sleeping in the other room."

Maybe Mason doesn't know what to say—attempt a joke, or express condolences?—or maybe he picked up on her Nova plug and wants to set the record straight. Regardless, what comes out is: "Nova is my doula, too." I brace my palm against the textured wallpaper, unsure how she'll react. Not wanting the dynamics of the night to change.

"Oh," Glenna says softly. That's it at first: just *oh*. She brushes her fingers across his cheek, a grandmotherly gesture. *My God,* she's probably thinking. *This nice young guy. Why you, too?* I halfway hope she'll ask him for specifics. If he won't tell me, maybe he'll tell her.

"God love her," she murmurs finally, and surprise flickers across his face. He clearly expected her to say not *her* but *you*, as did I—but rather than take offense, he softens, too.

"We could have her take our picture," he says. "Next year, this time? She'd remember."

"That she would." Again, there's that grandmotherly tone: *You do as Nova says, if you know what's good for you.* "But I'm sorry to hear you need her."

I expect he'll shut it down there, change the topic. Instead, he says: "I'm not used to needing people."

Glenna pats his shoulder. "Don't worry too much about that. Make no mistake: She needs you, too. She needs all of us."

A hollow of loneliness deepens in my chest, like a time-lapsed sinkhole. There's nothing but admiration in Glenna's tone—enough to bring tears to my eyes.

But imagine her being right. Imagine needing people who have no choice but to leave you.

"What does the sign say on an out-of-business whorehouse?" I blurt out, breezing in. I don't wait for a response. "Beat it, we're closed!"

Mason clutches Glenna's pearls, and they laugh. Seeing them together is fun, but I have to draw the line somewhere.

Raunchy jokes for the save.

※

Glenna is down by ten. I tuck a blanket around her on the couch, and Mason rinses her glass and fills it with water, setting it on a coaster within reach.

"I never said it would be a *late* night," I whisper, as we stand looking down at her.

"She's had a helluva week," he says. "Think she's just beat? Or should we stay, make sure she's not going to be sick?"

I hesitate. My risk tolerance doesn't extend to my clients. "Maybe just awhile? To be safe?"

"And to finish the roach in the ashtray?"

"So as not to disappoint Glenna," I clarify.

"For Glenna," he agrees.

The back porch is a jungle of hanging flowerpots holding the brown, dried remnants of last year's blooms. In their midst, a smooth metal bench glider. The night air has turned the vinyl cushions cold and dewy, so I grab stadium blankets from the mudroom and Mason and I settle in side by side. The swing creaks under our weight, then settles into a slow rhythm, back and forth. He puffs what's left of the joint to light it, then passes it over. Wispy clouds move across the full moon like an old, silent film reel, and I watch, mesmerized, as I inhale deeply, then pass it back.

"Do you believe in God?" I ask suddenly.

He doesn't answer right away. "Best I can say is I want to. You?"

"That's . . . a pretty good way of putting it." He's looking at me like he's expecting this to go somewhere, so I shrug. "I just realized I was supposed to know what you thought."

He shakes his head. "You," he says, "are not what I was expecting."

I can't tell if he's building up to a compliment, but I'm embarrassed by how much I suddenly want him to be. "What were you expecting?"

"I have no idea. Not an energy healer, exactly. Not a new age guru . . ."

"Someone more like . . . Kelly?" I tease.

"Kelly on steroids *is* closer to what I was picturing."

"Kelly would never take steroids. Kelly on beetroot powder is what you mean."

He laughs. "I guess that's it. Kelly on beetroot powder."

"Kelly is on beetroot powder."

He turns his eyes to the sky. "You know what I mean."

"I do." I still can't tell if this is a compliment. "I'm not that kind of doula."

For a minute, I think he'll leave it at that. But when he speaks again, his voice is serious, low. "You're the kind who loads your bathroom shelves with more vitamins and supplements than a GNC, waters down your bourbon, and sticks to unsalted almonds during a munchie fest, but will smoke the hell out of a joint. Who will hurl yourself around at deadly speeds while you carry a helmet just for show"—I open my mouth to object, but nothing comes out—"but won't share my pizza after cleaning all day, because I didn't think to order vegetarian."

His tone is more curious than judgmental, but I'm not sure how to feel about the fact that he's been keeping tabs. I'm the one who's supposed to be doing that.

Not that he's pointing out things I don't know. It hasn't escaped me that I became way more vigilant about what went *in* my body at exactly the same time I vowed to be way less careful about what I did *with* it. Which is far from the only thing that makes me a walking contradiction.

When you follow your intuition, the results aren't always logical.

"I really need to invest in a cabinet if I'm going to let clients use my bathroom," I gripe good-naturedly. "But I'll have you know, weed can be considered both a vegetable and an herbal supplement. So you're actually making me sound kind of on-brand."

I fold my legs under me, leaving it to Mason to push the glider. The motion is a soothing muscle memory; if I close my eyes, it would lull me to sleep.

"Is your brand of death doula allowed to tell me what's wrong with Glenna?"

She's open about it. "Breast cancer."

"She seems pretty sure it's not going away."

"It's not."

He nods. "The one major treatment I tried made me worse." A rare disclosure. I wait, hoping he'll say more, but his mind is clearly still on Glenna. "So that's it?"

"There are always options outside of Western medicine, but she's not interested."

"Will you try to change her mind?"

I shake my head. "That's not what she hired me to do."

"And she doesn't have family giving her a hard time?"

"Only oncologists giving her a hard time. But this isn't Glenna's first cancer rodeo: She's done the try-everything approach before. Doctors sometimes forget their patients are grown-ass adults capable of their own decisions. So I try to remember that."

"As far as grown-ass adults go, she's pretty cool."

I drop the roach into the ashtray. At risk of ruining the moment, maybe he'll take a cue: "You now know more about Glenna's case than I do about yours."

"Bet you wish all your clients were more like her," he says, not biting.

"How so?"

"How not so? She's sweet, endearing, funny . . . Seems like the ideal client."

"No such thing."

"Are you telling me *I'm* a model client?" These last hits are thickening my brain fog; I'll never find my way back to any professional headspace. What I do is start to giggle. Nervously at first, then harder. Pretty soon we're both doubled over, tears rolling down our cheeks.

"Come on!" He gasps for breath. "I'm not that bad." That sets us off again. We laugh so hard the glider rocks itself. So hard the awkwardness is forgotten. So hard it almost doesn't bother me that this night is changing everything and nothing between us at the same time.

"You really want to know?" I say, when we're wiping our cheeks, back to smiling up at the moon. "She is ideal. But not for the reasons you listed." I'm not in any shape to deliver a speech, but this one I could do in my sleep.

"It's the way she took control," I tell him. "From the day of her diagnosis—and Wendell's. A client who takes control might seem uncooperative to their doctor, or their family—people who want you to take your meds, follow instructions, be good. But the patients who are not passive about their end-of-life experience fare the best."

I make sure he's looking at me, because I'll take only one shot at this.

"Some people kid themselves that by hiring me, they are taking control. But hiring me is only the first step. I wish I could do the rest for you, but that's not how it works."

He's quiet for a long minute, surely about to call me a buzzkill. I don't think he realizes he's rubbing his elbow—protectively, almost apologetically. His eyes are watering, but not from laughter anymore. Feeling helpless is a hell of a thing. I want to hug him, reassure him of how far he's capable of coming in a short time—look at tonight. But I don't want to weird him out.

"I'm not sure I know how," he admits.

"I have ideas," I venture. "Whenever you're ready."

At last, he grins at me sideways. "I might seem like a walking contradiction at first."

"Takes one to know one," I say.

Finally, we have something in common after all.

# 12

*Nova*

NOW

My obsession with the sunrise started kind of by accident.

I wasn't up early, but rather still up, on the vapor trail end of one of those meandering nights I didn't want to see go. I'd been waitressing at a little dive on the beach in Gulf Shores, and after closing, a bunch of us employees rolled a nearly skunked keg to the outdoor seating area. Picture the end of a landlocked pier, elevated on the sand by wooden stilts, the perfect spot for dancing in the moonlight. I liked this crowd—how everyone was always invited, but no one made a fuss about whether you came or how long you stayed or how much you did or in my case didn't drink—and eventually I'd agreed to a walk down the water line with one of the guys. We'd ended up in a lifeguard chair, angled so no one could tell his hand was up my skirt, and to someone like me—with my loose string of boring attainable boyfriends since high school—giving into lust like that was nothing to be embarrassed about come morning.

It was freedom.

By the time I wandered back alone, my coworkers had gone. Every evening, that place would pack with sunburnt tourists and locals alike, with strollers and sandy feet and bar lines and laughter; we never didn't go on a two-hour wait for a table. Our food was too good, our beer too cheap, our view too inviting. Having the place to myself was a novelty, so I stayed.

I've heard it said that nothing good happens after 3 a.m. That you should go on home. I disagree. Some of the best hours of my life have occurred after 3 a.m. It wasn't the sky that mesmerized me that dawn, but the water. The moving surface of the gulf looked purple-gray in the dark, and as I watched, a switch flipped to deep turquoise green, reflecting some light that was not yet visible up above. By the time I had the sense to turn and look east, the whole beach to my left lay waiting beneath a glowing orange-pink sky, painted with silhouetted clouds.

The thought that filled my head was so simple and yet so welcome: *I'm alive.* I made it one more day. Gratitude washed over me right there on the public beach, in wonder and relief that I didn't need some mountaintop temple in Tibet to connect with the meaning of this day—every day—from the start. I could do it anywhere. Another visit from the sun was a gift: What kind of hostess wouldn't meet it at the door?

I can count on one hand the number of sunrises I've missed since, and I've had good reasons for them all.

The first morning without Mason, though, I flounder. I want to skip my ritual on principle. But though I've been awake most of the night, my body's alarm clock rings anyway. I peer through the gray light at the ceiling, despair churning in my gut. Not the dull ache I've woken with for the past few weeks, that Mason is mad at me, done with me. This is irreversibly worse. A leaden weight pins me to the mattress, re-playing everything wrong about yesterday: Bonnie's rage and my shock and my parents' disapproval and Kelly's worry. Somehow, I'd held my-self together, mostly. I suppose the shock helped.

But it's worn off enough that I can't imagine how I'll get through the day ahead.

I pull my duck boots over my cotton pajama pants and tromp out to the corner of the backyard where the trees open to that first glimpse of daybreak. Often, in the final moments before the world wakes, I spend quiet time here on yoga or meditation—but not today.

Today I simply glare at the sun, waiting for it to clear the horizon— because even now, I can't seem to cheat and settle for a sliver or a semi-circle. I hug my T-shirt impatiently as the orb of the oversized star rises the way it always does, with efficient speed.

Then, I bark the message I've been waiting to deliver, the only co-herent words I can think of for this world that pushes ahead, no matter who or what it leaves behind.

*"Fuck. You."*

The sun—which no longer seems a harbinger of good faith, only a mindless lemming of time—merely shines in response, and I say it again, louder, meaning it again, louder. Then, I turn my back on the sky, on the day, on the stupid rituals that have carried me this far. Fuck it all.

I'm not even back to my door yet when the police cruiser pulls up.

"What exactly did he tell you, about his condition?" Officer Dover didn't mince words about why he was here. But my heartbeat regained its steady rhythm as I took him in: tall, fit, blond, young, handshake that bounced my nervous energy right back at me. They'd sent the rookie. How serious could they be?

"He told me life as he knew it was over." It's surreal to see this uni-formed officer standing beside the very chair where Mason sat when he said that. I'm standing, too, at my desk. Sitting seems too comfort-able, I guess.

"In those exact words?"

"Those exact words. He couldn't work anymore, couldn't play mu-sic. He was restless."

"Sad? Angry?"

I nod. "Pretty much everyone who comes here is."

"Lots of—what, cancer patients?"

"All types."

"Most of 'em been pretty sick for a while?"

"Sometimes people get hit with a bad prognosis out of nowhere. But yes, usually if they're here, they've been through the ringer. It's not responding to chemo, or they're not fit to undergo surgery."

"And what did you understand to be wrong with Mason?"

I purse my lips, unsure how much detail I can comfortably volunteer. I've never had occasion to verify exactly where law enforcement falls on our confidentiality line. Most likely, the fact that we're not held to the regulatory standards of licensed professionals also means we're not protected by those same standards, but I'm not sure there's a precedent for this.

And I don't want to *become* the precedent for this.

"That life as he knew it was over."

I want to stick to the plan Kelly and I discussed last night. But now that the police are actually here, scrutinizing my bare walls, being elusive isn't so easy. I'm nervous. And awfully tired.

"Right. How did you respond?"

"Mostly? We just spent time together. Talked through things. I tried to point out ways he could still find purpose and meaning."

"Was he receptive?"

"Not at first. But . . . Once we got to know each other, we actually had a lot of enjoyable days together." This answer is clearly inadequate, given what the officer believes the end result to be. But it's true.

"Doing what?"

"Whatever he wanted. I helped him clean up the room where he was staying, we went for drives, went for coffee. He was lonely."

"Kind of rare, I'm guessing, for you to see someone who's in pretty good shape."

"Only in the rare best-case scenario."

"Why best?"

This seems obvious, but I humor him. "Preparing for the transition isn't just paperwork and goodbyes. The more time clients have, the better."

"More time to pay you for your services?"

I glare at him. "More time to *live*."

He concedes the point. "And that's what you believed—that he had time? He never told you in so many words that he was thinking of harming himself?"

I shake my head.

"Looking back in hindsight, are there maybe red flags in things he was doing or saying?"

Red flags. My mind reverses to the QPR intervention training Kelly required when I first joined her practice: Question, Persuade, Refer. Ironically, she didn't recommend it because of devastated young clients like Mason. The aging population was much higher risk for death by suicide.

"People come here already in crisis as a matter of course," I explain. He stares at me blankly. It's probably best I don't point out how many textbook suicide warning signs are so endemic to our clientele it's hard to distinguish them as true warnings: making arrangements for end of life, feeling like a burden on loved ones, speaking of wanting to join a spouse who's passed on . . . "I've completed an advanced QPR program—are you familiar?"

I recall there being specialized certificates for first responders, and sure enough, he nods.

"So, I'm trained to intervene in a suicidal crisis if necessary. But to my mind, every client who comes to a doula when faced with devastating news is recognizing they need help and aiming to get it. I'd be much more concerned about someone who's dealt a tough diagnosis without anyone to walk that path with them. Which is what I do: I walk with them. I listen to them, however they're feeling. I'm not here to police my clients' responses to their challenges." I flush, realizing I've used his profession as a verb. An undesirable one. "Sorry," I add, lamely.

"How would you characterize his state of mind the last time you saw him?"

The last time I saw him. His eyes, his body language, the things he said—all of it telegraphed the same thing: longing.

I'd felt it, too, so strongly. I still do.

"Frustrated."

"About?"

"The same things frustrating him the first time I saw him. His loss of motor function, the pain in his right arm and hand especially, his inability to play. Like I said, aside from companionship, I'm afraid we didn't make much headway."

"And what reason did he give for discontinuing your services?"

"We don't hassle withdrawal requests. He just said to cross him off my books, and I did."

"You didn't take that as a sign that he got what he came for, and was ready to die now?"

The words are a sucker punch. I swallow hard against the tears threatening to overtake me. "Definitely not."

"More like he wasn't going to waste any more time with you?"

He throws a mean left hook. "I guess that's . . . closer."

"But you said you had enjoyable days together. You must have thought you were making *some* headway."

An uppercut, to finish me off. "Not enough."

"Okay." The officer seems almost bored, and though I suppose that should be good news, it's rubbing me the wrong way. Next to actual felonies, I guess it wouldn't seem like a crime that someone so talented, so passionate, can no longer do the only thing he saw as worth living for.

Still, if he'd met Mason, he'd understand.

"Is there any chance I could have a look at what you all took to be a suicide note?" I ask. "I'd given Mason some checklists and worksheets that can sometimes help clients work through what they're facing. I can't help thinking what you found might have been some notes in response to something there?"

"I'm afraid I can't share that. But as far as I'm concerned, the intent was crystal clear." He gets to his feet, and I do, too, swallowing my disappointment. I'm not ready to let go of any chance to disprove this theory—but if I'm honest, I think Mason's last words would be too painful for me to read. Officer Dover smiles stiffly. "I'd love to see copies of those checklists, though, just in case. Also, your communications with him—texts, emails, anything you have."

I freeze. In my hours of reeling, the possibility of this request had not yet occurred to me. I haven't even had the presence of mind to look back at these things myself. Early on, Mason and I rarely communicated between appointments, but eventually we developed little ways of maintaining contact. I can't recall anything there to take issue with, except maybe—*maybe*—the frequency?

I'd sure like a refresher, though, on what exactly Officer Dover is asking to see. Even if the idea of reliving it all seems like torture.

"I'm not sure about that. We promise clients confidentiality."

He nods like this is understandable, and for a few seconds I dare to hope he'll say, *Just thought I'd ask,* or, *Let me know if you come across anything that might be helpful.*

"Thing is," he says, "there are a few outside possibilities we need to rule out. If you don't want to cooperate, I'll come back with a court order."

Outside possibilities?

"Hang on a second," I say. "People in care positions treat people they don't recognize as suicidal all the time. Psychologists, prison guards, even parents—no one is holding them responsible for missing signs. At least, not officially."

If this officer did the same QPR training, he already knows my entire client base checks at least one risk factor box: terminal illness. He's heard the facilitator caution that even doctors and nurses have a hard time asking patients if they've contemplated suicide. The importance of asking the question was the main takeaway. Which aligned with my thinking, in that headspace of addressing our cultural conversations surrounding death, that our whole support system for patients—at least in terms of what insurance covered—fell short in too many ways.

"Officially," he says evenly, "those providers are licensed. An alternative operation like this? I doubt your confidentiality clause will hold much water in front of a judge. Do you really want to call more attention to that flimsiness by making me find out?"

If he's bluffing, he's pretty good at it.

"Besides," he adds. "Mrs. Shaylor isn't alleging you failed to recognize signs. She's alleging you may have *helped* her son prepare to do what he did. Maybe even helped him reach the decision."

Hearing it in so many words—that's the knockout punch.

"That's ridiculous."

"You don't have to be a death doula to influence this kind of thing. I don't suppose you heard about the woman convicted of talking her boyfriend into suicide over text message?"

He can't be serious. The texts published online were so vile I couldn't even read to the end. I truly thought that woman deserved the manslaughter charge that came down on her.

And I've truly underestimated this rookie and his intentions.

"Please tell me you don't think anything remotely close to that took place here. Mason never threatened to take his own life—and if he had, I certainly wouldn't have encouraged him."

I'd anticipated, worst case, I could find myself up against a malpractice claim. But manslaughter? Of anyone, let alone Mason?

Officer Dover looks like he wants to believe me. But suddenly the crevasse seems wide between wanting to believe me and actually doing it. "Even so," he says, "perhaps something you did discuss affirmed his belief that what he eventually chose was for the best?"

"That's—" What? A deeply offensive suggestion? A possibility that will haunt me forever? Tears blur my vision. "Officer Dover, I sincerely want to believe his death was an accident."

I realize too late that I'm staring down the same crevasse. Not *I sincerely believe,* but, *I sincerely want to believe.*

He nods. "Our only aim is to conclude our cause of death investigation, set his mother's mind at ease. Let us take a look through everything you've got, and if what you say is true, we can all move on."

I nod, numbly. But Kelly . . . She was up all night worrying about some variation of this, and this isn't how we talked about handling it. We should have worked out more possibilities. If it were up to Kelly, we would have. I've been so naïve; suddenly everything feels like my fault.

"Let me clear it with my partner—it's her company, so I guess a request like this is ultimately her say."

"I'll walk over to the house with you. She was my next stop anyway."

Maybe, when she confirms I was the only one treating Mason, he'll keep her out of the hot seat, stick to getting her permission for me to cooperate. It seems the best I can hope for. As far as I can tell, we have little choice but to comply.

Even if I am afraid of what he may find.

# 13

## *Nova*

### THEN

"You really did the questionnaire?" I can't bring myself to care that I'm grinning at Mason like such an idiot, I'm bound to make him wish he hadn't.

"I did *some* of the questionnaire." Mason drops into the booth across from me, a window seat in the cafe a few blocks from my annex. I wasn't sure what to suggest for this first visit since his change of venue request—the night at Glenna's last weekend aside—but this seems to suit him fine. He's clutching his coffee order, a skyscraper cup that casts a long shadow over my herbal tea, and with the other hand waves a paperclipped stack as if it's bound to disappoint me.

"Up late doing it?" I nod at his cup.

"It's impossible to sleep in these torture devices I'm supposed to wear." He holds out his arms like a robot. "They keep my elbows from bending."

"What happens if you don't wear them?"

"I wake up in the middle of the night and can't feel my hands."

This would annoy anyone. But a musician, tied back from *every* comfort he's used to, even at rest? I'm starting to understand why his mood is always so . . . well, Mason. "Skipping questions is fine," I assure him, trying to steer us both back on track. Hell, the first time I offered him this client introduction form in his onboarding materials, he skipped the whole thing. "Want to hang onto it? Tell me the parts that spoke to you?"

He shakes his head and hands it across the table. It doesn't take long to see why. There are far more non-responses than responses. And the blanks he filled are . . . still pretty blank.

They're not nothing, though. So. Progress?

"Let's forget the questionnaire," I say, surprising us both. It's noisy here, lots of foot traffic and to-go orders, but we're far enough from the queue for anyone to overhear. I extract a sheet of paper and pen from my messenger bag, and he takes them with a shrug. I'm learning this is about as close to game as Mason gets, unless good bourbon is involved.

"I want you to write two names, okay? One person who you need to seek forgiveness from. And one person who you need to grant forgiveness to."

He tosses the pen, sending it skittering into our table's caddy of sugar packets. "Pass. Again. That was already on the questionnaire."

"All those at once can be overwhelming. Let's start here."

"Hard pass."

I pull a face. "If we're going for the most bang for your buck, this one is key. You might not even realize the suppressed—"

"It's not suppressed," he interrupts. "I acknowledge it."

He looks too miserable for me not to back off. "Okay. But you know, acknowledging old hurts or resentments isn't enough to keep them from eating at you. Letting them go usually boils down to forgiveness."

"Who said they were old?"

We stare at each other for a disheartened minute. I've studied some therapy techniques, but we both know I'm no therapist. Finally, he reaches out and taps a finger on the packet.

"I wanted to try. I did." He says this the way he said he wanted to believe in God. Or maybe I'm just still thinking of that swing in the moonlight. How we stayed there feeling warm long after the air around us turned uncomfortably cold. I don't think I'm imagining that we connected—I believe he wants to try. Even if I don't buy that he's tried very hard. "What do other people put in response to this stuff? I mean, things that lead somewhere. Can you give examples?"

I scrunch my forehead. "I don't want to influence you. Everyone is different."

"I credit my entire career in music to influences. Anyone who doesn't is lying."

I pick up the packet and skim again for the bits he's completed, sipping my tea while he gulps his coffee like it's fuel.

*If you were to divide your life into three categories—physical, mental/ emotional, and spiritual—what are some aspects of each that you think could use some improvement?*

When I went over this with Mr. Whitehall, still the only client who can motivate me to drag my helmet around, he talked about how he'd never pursued golf the way he'd wanted to. How he'd spent plenty of evenings at the driving range—"buckets of balls, buckets of beers"— but never had the discipline for the course. Whenever he woke to a perfect weather day, he'd think fleetingly of booking a tee time, then hop on his Harley instead. Now, it was too late: He could no longer manage the greens, even if he splurged on a cart and caddy. I admitted I'd never pegged him as a golfer, thinking it more of a business-class sport, and he'd replied: "That's just it! Those yuppies ain't seen nothin' till they seen me hit a double eagle in my leather pants." Within a week I had him set up with virtual reality golf right in his living room, complete with simulations of real courses he'd watched the pros play on TV.

It's clear Mason isn't going to be so easy. Under *physical*, he's written *arm* in uneven letters that put me in mind of Willow's handwriting. The work of someone who's still mastering fine motor control—or, I realize with a pang, losing it. Under *mental/emotional,* he's written *live,* in homage to the performance-driven lifestyle he's had to leave behind. Under *spiritual,* he wrote *songs.* Put together, they indicate the kind of wishful thinking that won't get us anywhere. Farther down, my eyes alight on:

*Make a list of your most emotional moments.*

He's scrawled the same three things. *Arm. Live. Songs.* Nothing new to work with there. I look instead to my long-standing favorites of the fields he's left blank.

*What are you afraid of that you've never said out loud before?*

*What is one thing you could do that might strengthen your support network?*

*How might your life change if you reduced each day's to-do list to two items: to give love, and to receive love? Could you accomplish them? How would that feel?*

*What would you do if you won a million dollars?*

My eyes stop their scroll. I can vividly imagine Mason's lifestyle flipped: him the rock star in a palatial home, his mother freeloading in the guest suite. Both of them happier that way.

Somehow this picture does not seem entirely unrelated to the forgiveness question. Which I already know is the one he really needs to answer.

Otherwise, he wouldn't be so resistant to it.

"Let's see," I begin. "I don't want to make assumptions based on your living situation, but would you say your financials have become a little . . ."

"Dependent?" Mason half-laughs. "Well, my idea of splashing out used to be a hotel upgrade to a better view. Now the only 'extra' I can justify is hiring you."

My cheeks flush, self-conscious. "If you did come into some money, how might it change things for you?"

"Besides stopping my humiliating backslide into begging my mom to buy name-brand cereal?"

I laugh. "Well, maybe that exactly. Would you just enjoy the freedom of not having to ask for things you want? Or would you blow the whole wad on . . ." I motion that the floor is his, and somehow we both end up staring at the HELP WANTED easel by the register.

"Please tell me you're not trying to make a part-time barista out of me. They have enough failed guitarists in their employ."

"Failed writers, too." I raise my hand. "Former barista here. Full-time."

"You don't say."

"In my defense, I hosted the monthly book club *and* the weekly poetry night. Which totally counted as having a job that put my English degree to use."

"Well, you did eventually though, right?" His eyes search mine, and the instant I sense what he's about to say, my heart sinks. "Seems like newspaper stringer counts."

I sigh. "You googled me." My old bylines are not exactly a point of pride. More a portfolio of failure. The best I can say is that at least it's small.

"Oh, like you haven't googled me." I shake my head. "Seriously?"

"It's best practice for me to keep our relationship based on what you choose to say or do in our time together." I don't mean this as judgment of *his* actions—vetting someone you intend to hire is reasonable, even expected—but it sort of comes out that way.

"Huh." He sounds unconvinced, and I get it. Performers must be used to scrutiny.

"Also," I add, "my taste in music is pretty basic. Just, you know, what's on the radio."

His eyes flare, but quickly dim, like I've challenged him to a fight he doesn't have the energy for. Actually, I've conveyed disinterest I don't really feel. I love music—the full-spectrum sensory experience of it, the way it vibrates in your core, wraps itself around memories. I love seeing it performed live, love turning it up loud, love building the right playlist for the right road trip. But there's nothing unique about the *way* I love it—content with classic rock, never much into the indie scene.

"Well, don't worry," he assures me. "None of your search results made sense anyway." He makes a head-to-toe sort of gesture across the booth at me, and weirdly, I know what he means. You don't have to look too closely to see I was an entirely different person then.

"What Google left out," I say good-naturedly, "is that I wasted four whole years behind the coffee bar before moving on to waste more of my life at the paper. So no, I'm not trying to make a barista out of you. But weren't we talking about you? What you'd do if money was no object? Why do I feel like you're dodging the question?"

The way he's looking at me . . . all I can see is the shame of the years I wasted, the same years Mason spent being too tenacious for any soulless job. I don't get the vibe he's holding it against me, though. He just seems interested, and for a moment, I'm terrified he's going to say, *Because I'd rather talk about you.*

"Because I don't know the answer," he says instead. "I always thought the fun of a windfall was *not* having a plan for it, you know? Whenever a gig paid out better than expected, the best was just to not have already spent it on some total drag expense, like new brake pads. I had this little ritual of treating, but otherwise . . ." He shrugs.

"What was the ritual?"

"Kind of a sharing the love thing. I'd treat the crew or merch guys, or the opener if I had one. Get drinks or a late dinner or, I don't know, Skywheel tickets. If I was the opener, sometimes I'd treat up, even though the money meant more to me than to those guys. One of my road rules, I guess: Generosity is never bad business."

I flip the packet facedown. "Maybe that's exactly what we need. The perfect next step."

"For me to pick up your drink tab?"

I grin. "This *is* top-shelf tea. But no. A ritual."

"Seems a little early in the process for human sacrifice."

"You'd be surprised."

He laughs. "Okay, I'll bite. What kind of rituals might a doula do?"

"Well, forgiveness is the big one . . ."

"Next."

I knew I was pressing my luck, but had to try.

"There's also closure, turning a page. All that stuff we cleaned out of your room—it's still boxed up in the Jeep?"

"I haven't gotten around to donating it yet."

"Maybe there's a reason for that. Maybe a drop box is too . . . unceremonious."

"Getting rid of old stuff doesn't require a ceremony."

"There's old stuff, and then there's meaningful old stuff. Maybe we should back up and set some intentions as far as what relics of your career you might keep, and which ones you're truly ready to let go. Maybe there's a symbolic moment where you thank the relics for your time together and say goodbye."

"Or maybe you should ease up on the beetroot powder."

I laugh. "Maybe. But look. People talk so much about how material possessions don't matter. I think it's helpful to acknowledge that sometimes they do matter. You're closing the door on a big part of your life, but you don't have to slam it. We can find a balance between holding on and letting go." I gesture to the abandoned packet. "Think about the few things you jotted down. Answers alluding to things you can't or won't go back and do are not going to move us forward. Maybe writing them out is important for you—maybe you should write more about them, on your own. But here, together, we need to find some real changes we could make in your way of coping, your quality of life."

"The Gibson," he says suddenly.

"The what?"

"The guitar that I—that was damaged. It's fixable. I could sell it for a pretty penny, even now." His eyes brighten. "Two birds, one stone: the goodbye ritual, and some mad money."

I frown. He's using the word *ritual*, but what he's describing is—not. "Okay, if a ritual seems hokey, I get it. But surely there's middle ground between that and pawning your guitar." I'd seen the instrument only that once, freshly smashed on his bed, but in that moment regret had cascaded from Mason's body in waves.

"There's no middle ground. Ask anyone, and they'll tell you that guitar represents the only thing I've given a shit about for the last twenty years." He's looking at me, but his mind seems elsewhere. "I don't know why I didn't think of it myself. You're pretty good at this."

This is getting away from me. "I can dig deeper," I offer. I still don't like the idea of sharing client examples, but I need to show I'm willing to speak his language. "For influences." I think fast. "I had an eighty-six-year-old decide to track down his one that got away. She was alive. Her daughter drove her two hours to come see him."

"What did they say to each other?"

"I have no idea. I waited with her daughter, outside. But the looks on their faces when they said goodbye . . . Something special and necessary happened between them. Her daughter actually called later to say thank you."

"Well, I don't have a one that got away. Unless you count my guitar."

And here we are again.

I wonder if Mason really has always been this one-track, this obsessed, or if it's a function of his grim prognosis: *You don't know what you've got till it's gone.* Or maybe of realizing too late that you've put all your eggs in one basket and doubling down: *But it was worth it.* I'm not sure if it's a sign that he had what it takes, or if it's just sad.

This much is becoming clear: When he said *life as I know it is over,* what he meant is that everything he lived for is over. Already. At thirty-six.

And he's ended up here, with me. A person who, the only time life as I knew it was over, had the audacity to find joy in it. Even when it hurt the people I loved.

A person who has since learned how it feels to know, in your marrow, that you're really only good at one thing. The thing you were put on this planet to do.

Mason's right about this, too: that I happen to be doing it, right now.

"There's no reason for me not to sell it, Nova. Come with me? Next appointment?"

I have to admit, it's the surest I've heard him sound. He stands to go, shoving his hands into the pockets of his vest, and tosses me an odd smile. One that's somehow sad and reassuring at the same time.

"It's not just in my head," he says, "that it's the most valuable thing I have."

# 14

## *Willow*

Willow slumped down in the hallway window seat until she was flat on the hardwood bench, knees bent, ear to the mesh of the screen. Mom and Maggie were in heated conversation on the porch below, and from this angle she could hear better through the cracked open window. The old frame was so warped and creaky, opening it farther might give her away.

"I don't like this," Maggie was saying. "Not one bit."

"I was hoping you'd tell me I'm overreacting." Mom's even-handed words did nothing to disguise the stress that pulled the strings of her voice too tight. A police officer had been at the door yesterday, Nova with him, right when Willow was leaving for school. She'd wanted to stay, find out what was going on, but Mom assured her this was "routine follow-up" and shooed her away. But how could it be "routine" when she'd never seen the police here before?

Plus, Mom had let Willow walk to school by herself—a first. A weirdly timed first, as they were on day three of Mom's lecture series on how Willow had "violated her trust."

"What bothers me," Mom kept ranting, "is that I can tell you're not really sorry about sneaking out on Saturday. You're mainly sorry you got caught."

Well, she was right. *And I can tell,* Willow wanted to say, *that you're not really mad about the sneaking out. You're mainly mad I won't say where I was going.*

But why should she tell? What difference would it make, other than to get her friends—who had managed *not* to get caught—in trouble? It seemed unfair to say Willow had violated Mom's trust when Mom hadn't trusted her in the first place. Walking to school was a perfect example. Willow had listed plenty of solid reasons she should be allowed: it was a few lousy blocks, she was a responsible kid, and before helicopter parenting was a thing, this was the norm. *It's a different time,* Mom said. *It's not done anymore.* Not that Willow wasn't capable, not that Mom truly thought it dangerous, but that neighbors might disapprove. What kind of crap was that, from the woman who constantly preached to Willow not to worry what other kids thought—about her never-met-him dad, the constant stream of dying people coming and going from her house, her hippy-dippy name, or any of the other weirdness Mom was quick to explain away?

That's why Willow liked Nova so much. Other people's opinions rolled off Nova like sheets of water. And this business inspired *lots* of opinions. Nova was the smooth stone holding steady beneath all that weight and motion, not merely acting like it didn't bother her, but really living it. Without Nova's example, Willow would never have finally found her scene through the drama club—the one place where pretending to be someone else actually freed her to be herself. The one group of friends who considered different cool, whose parents didn't say, "You want to go to Willow's house? Why don't you invite her over here instead?"

Nova hadn't looked smooth or steady with the officer though. Willow tried to see her after rehearsal yesterday, wanting to say sorry about Mason, to see if she was okay, but Nova hadn't answered her door. And this morning? Mom let Willow walk herself to school *again*. She'd barely even looked up from her overnight oats.

"Look, you knew how I felt about Nova before." Maggie sounded smug. She always did. "But now there's no way around viewing her as a liability. Considering she's turned over her files, I don't think it's over-reacting to be worried. You can't assume no news is good news from that officer. You have to prepare."

Willow made a mental note to look up *liability* in the dictionary, but could guess the gist.

On the record, Maggie had said from the start she thought Nova was too "unorthodox" to make a smart partner for Mom—which was one big eye roll, considering the source. There was nothing ortho-dox about Maggie heating her yoga studio to 105 degrees so she could overcharge Karens for the privilege of doing something *mindful* with their lululemon before driving their gas-guzzling luxury SUVs home to their McMansions. Maggie's argument, as a "fellow holistic profes-sional" who never tired of reminding Mom how much more experi-enced she was at "big small-business decisions," was that end-of-life doulas were new and misunderstood enough that the better strategy was to play against new age stereotype. Stick with colleagues who looked and acted like the nurses or lawyers they'd originally been, and not this go-where-the-wind-takes-me free spirit who'd gotten certified on some whim.

Fortunately, Mom's own vision had been clear enough to see through that. Because off the record, Maggie was clearly jealous of Nova's fast and easy friendship with Mom.

"I did invest in that professional liability insurance you recom-mended last year," Mom said now. There was that word again. "Would that cover us, do you think?"

On the ceiling above Willow, a large water spot was overtaking the corner, the paint beginning to crack across the stain. Mom's office suite was meticulously maintained, but up here, they did "the best they could," which probably wouldn't pass Maggie's test, either. Nova didn't throw around judgment that way. Nova was the first to laugh it off when they spent a week on a thousand-piece puzzle that turned out to have three pieces missing. Or when Mom roasted their dinner vegetables to oblivion. Or even the night she slept in the house when Mom got called away by hospice and Willow had, embarrassingly, wet the bed during a terrifying dream. Maggie was Mom's friend, but Nova was family.

"For negligence and small malpractice claims, hopefully. But this is bigger, right? The cops aren't usually involved in stuff like that."

Willow bit her lip. She'd known there was nothing routine about that officer. Then again, as far as Willow knew, people who came to Parting Your Way all died in their beds or in hospitals, the way other old people did. Not in Jeep crashes at half that age. She shuddered, hating to think of Mason that way. Wondering what his last thought had been.

Mom groaned. "I've been trying not to sound insensitive—a life has been lost, and of course it matters what happened, of course I care. But selfishly? I just want this to go away. Is it naïve to hope it will? The officer barely asked me anything, and was much less accusatory than the client's mother. Nova cooperated. Maybe when they don't find anything out of line, that'll be the end of it."

Willow had never thought about Mason having a mother. He seemed so . . . lone. Still, what could she, or anyone, have to accuse Nova of?

Maggie made a doubtful clucking noise. "Don't hate me for asking, Kel. But are you sure they won't find anything out of line?"

"Am I sure?" Mom sounded hurt. Also, unsure. "This business is my life. I mean, look around, Mags, I don't just work here, I live here! This, and Willow—it's all I have, and I've worked damn hard for it. Do you think I would have hired a partner I couldn't implicitly trust?"

"I'm looking out for you, not questioning your judgment. You know I'm loyal to a fault."

Willow snorted. This from a woman who used to coax Kelly to hire a babysitter for their girls' nights because having a kid around would "bend the energy field."

"You said yourself," Maggie added, "Nova got a little dodgy on the subject."

"I know." Mom sighed heavily. "But who wouldn't, right? Can you imagine coming under that kind of scrutiny at all, let alone when you're dealing with a loss yourself? She cared about this client a lot, maybe too much. When she first said she wasn't his doula anymore, that was my first guess as to why. But regardless of whether she did everything by the book, or made mistakes, she never would have wanted to fail him. Especially not like this."

A gentle sniffling mingled with Maggie's gentle *hey, hey,* and Willow realized Mom was crying.

There was nothing routine about that either. Mom was officially freaking out.

She thought of Nova's lonely silhouette on the roof the other night. The first time Nova introduced Mason to Willow, Willow had been glad Nova had some friend in the world besides her and Mom. As Mason came and went more often, she assumed they'd become more. Willow knew the look people got when they had a crush: Her whole lunch table was full of it.

Nova and Mason both had that look. And then some.

"I feel for Nova, too," Maggie said, but even from this distance, it didn't sound sincere. She said something else, but a dog nearby started barking its head off, drowning her out. *We're not in Kansas anymore,* Willow thought. Opening night was eight days away, and at this rate, she'd be lucky to remember Dorothy's lines. Maybe it was for the best that she was stuck with a dumb stuffed dog for Toto. At least she couldn't mess up its cues.

Then again, the whole cast was jittery this week. Willow would have welcomed the extra-long rehearsals if Mom wasn't there the second they ended, waiting to haul her back into captivity.

"I won't do or say anything to make her think I'd hang her out to dry," she heard Mom say as the barking faded, and Willow softened in spite of herself. Though Mom's very many principles drove Willow crazy, they were admirably strong. Even under the pressure of being up all night and fending off police and staring down Maggie's mean-girl front.

"Nobody's hanging anybody out to dry." The sharp edges of Maggie's words had eroded a little. "Let's reframe this discussion, okay? What we want is to shore you up against any other unpleasant surprises."

"Okay." Willow heard the muffled sound of Mom blowing her nose. "I *cannot* let any of this blow back on Parting Your Way."

"Defense." Maggie agreed. "Let's say you're right, and the police are satisfied by whatever records Nova turned over. What happens if that doesn't satisfy Mason's mother?"

"She files a negligence or malpractice suit," Mom said robotically. "Which my insurance should help cover, hopefully."

"Hopefully. You might also need to lawyer up."

"How much would that cost, do you think?"

"No clue, but you could ask around at the next group consult. Someone might have a referral."

"Okay . . ." Mom sounded reluctant.

"How are your optics online? This might be a smart time to nudge past clients to post good reviews, if they haven't already. That way if Mason's mother starts in with some buyer bewares, it looks like one alarmist with an ax to grind in a sea of happy customers."

"Right," Mom said flatly. "Just some random, outlier alarmist whose son's Jeep went off a bridge Saturday night."

Saturday night? Nobody had mentioned this happened way back on Saturday night.

Nobody had mentioned a bridge.

Willow's gut twisted. Mom was always going on about following gut feelings, how your body has a "second brain" in there. Supposedly, not only could your actual, literal gut feel emotions like the brain in your head, but sometimes the gut kicks in when the other brain does not. According to Mom, that's intuition, and people ignore it all the time when they shouldn't, because they're too removed from their primitive selves to recognize how smart it is.

But if intuition was real, how could Mason have been gone since *Saturday* without them knowing?

Mom had Maggie, and Nova had—well, Nova didn't seem to need anybody. But Willow felt she would burst up here alone, without someone to talk to. Her mind reeled, trying to make sense of it all. If Mom and Nova might be in trouble because of what happened to Mason . . . why? And what exactly *had* happened to Mason? Did anyone actually know?

Willow needed to know.

Before Mom could answer, she was cut off by the sound of a car pulling into the driveway. Willow sat up in time to see a sleek emerald two-door slow to a stop, and a tall, slender woman step out. Her fine dark hair bore a thick streak of royal blue, and she wore a smart black sleeveless jumpsuit that tapered above the ankle straps of her gold sandals. She headed for the porch in long strides, and Willow slid farther down the bench to hear better, but caught the side of her head against the windowsill. Hard. She closed her eyes against the sharp pain, knowing it probably served her right for eavesdropping. But she could hardly stop now.

"I'm looking for the owner of Parting Your Way?"

"And you are?" Maggie asked, over Mom's pleasant, "That's me."

"Asha Park. Journalist with the *Cincinnati Business Courier* and other local outlets. I'm following up on a lead submitted by a Bonnie Shaylor. I want to ask about your connection to a recent death that's under investigation?"

Through the pain still pounding in her ears, Willow heard loud and clear the silence that fell over the porch.

# 15

## *Nova*

### THEN

Mason unzips the leather gig bag and peels back the cover. We peer into the open trunk—or hatch, or whatever the back of a Jeep is called—on the side of a busy street, where we've parallel parked next to a digital parking meter blinking EXPIRED.

I know nothing about guitars, but anyone could see this one is the kind of high-end people whistle at. We stand in silence for a moment, hugging our jackets closed, regarding it with reverence. Then, he lifts it by the neck and rotates the body so I can see the extent of the damage: A thin crack down the side spans a third of its length. Another tilt reveals angry wolverine-like scratches across the back.

*Yikes.*

He glances sideways at me, like he's daring me to react.

"Cool guitar," I say.

He zips the gig bag closed.

"This will need no introduction to the guys in there. It's a Gibson

Montana Hummingbird. Vintage classic, serious custom upgrades, so even with repairs needed, I don't think you should take less than half retail value."

"You mean *we*."

"I mean you. I'm not going in." He rubs his elbow, like just looking at the guitar made it hurt. I feel for him. And yet.

"This is *your* symbolic goodbye."

"Which is why I can't do it in there."

"But you can do it out here?" I skim the storefronts around us, though on a weekday morning, more people are driving past than pulling in. Cupcake shops, bridal wear, stationery, a florist. Seems like a kind of wedding row. No wonder I'm unfamiliar with this part of town.

"As good a place as any. The music store's around the corner. I just— can't watch some guy scrutinizing the Gibson, surrounded by instruments that aren't half as good."

It does sound rough. But if we're going through with this, we need to do it right. Otherwise, at best, there's no point. And at worst?

It could backfire. Give Mason more to regret. More to resent. Including the doula who may be roundabout responsible for this idea.

"So, the concept of a goodbye *ritual* is that you release your attachment to this item and transfer it to a memory, or something significant about this moment. Not to"—I gesture around us—"street traffic and scrounging for coins if you see a meter maid." Even the sky is clouded over, though the sun is launching an attempt to burn through.

"I'm releasing. And I'm transferring it to you."

That's what I'm afraid of, in myriad ways. This is not at all what I had in mind. It's not supposed to be about me, but . . . Well, that's just it.

"Mason, I can't go it alone in a music store. I don't even know what half the value is."

"Haggle for nineteen hundred. It was impeccably maintained before its recent run-in."

I cross my arms, unconvinced.

"Nova?" Mason's face turns serious, and he reaches out and touches my sleeve. "Right now I'm okay because for the first time in a year, I'm not facing something this hard alone. Or with no one who understands that it *is* hard. Right now I'm okay because of you."

My mouth actually falls open. The guy who mocked the *right now I'm okay* exercise is doing it. Of his own volition. Looking like he means it.

"Besides," he adds, "rituals aside, your manual says you can help lessen my burden."

"True, but . . ." I stop short. "You read my manual?"

"There was nothing good on TV."

I bite down on my grin. "And you found it to be . . . ?"

"Excellent. Full of loopholes." He gives the guitar case a pat. "Goodbye, burden." He climbs back into the driver's seat and sits, staring straight ahead.

Goodbye indeed.

Inside the music shop, I'm the only customer. Beyond the front showroom—which conveys at a glance that only serious professionals need inquire here—an expansive collection of preowned merchandise is arranged on the back wall. A lone employee flips through a catalog at the service counter. He's maybe my dad's age, but tanner and fitter than I've ever seen my dad, with long locks loose around his face.

"Hey there," he says, closing the book as I approach.

"Hey there." The counter seems small for what I'm holding, so I undo the case on the ground at my feet and lift the instrument for him to see. His eyes light up even as the agony of the wounded guitar hits him.

"Zoiks," he says, placing a sympathetic finger in the crack. "Now that's a damn shame."

I nod, and though a few guitars in the window looked almost as pricey, his words feel true. This guitar must be special, if Mason considers it so worthy of both reverence and ire. "Fixable though, right?"

He clucks his tongue. "It'll cost you."

"I'm not here for a repair. I'm here to sell."

"You're kidding. Like this?"

"Just deduct the repair costs from what you would have offered, right?"

"I don't know, hon." He looks wistfully at the black curtain hung across the back doorway, where an EMPLOYEES ONLY sign dangles from a thin chain. "Our tech isn't here today. Maybe come back tomorrow."

I could take the out—an enforced waiting period. It hasn't been forty-eight hours since Mason landed on this idea. But I'm the one who waxed poetic about not interfering with grown-ass adult decisions. Even if this is impulsive, maybe that's what Mason needs right now. When I left him, on the other side of this brick wall I'm facing, Mason looked like a man determined to get this over with. And if I'm honest, that's the first real purpose I've seen in him.

I toe the gig bag at my feet, but make no move to put the instrument back inside. Instead, I run a finger admiringly down the frets.

"It's a Mason Shaylor, you know."

Who knows what possessed me to say it. An instinct to test the waters, nagging at me since that fleeting moment when Glenna found him familiar? Or a grasp at straws? It doesn't matter—because in the next blink, everything changes.

"A Mason Shaylor," he repeats, slowly. *Holy shit. He knows who Mason is.* "As in, Mason Shaylor customized the design? Or Mason Shaylor owned the guitar?"

"Both," I say smugly. As if I'm not just realizing *Mason Shaylor* is a name that means something impressive to somebody who knows what he's talking about. To probably a lot of somebodies, unless this encounter is the world's biggest coincidence.

"Well, that's a whole 'nother can of butter beans. Shit, I *recognize* this now. The last time I saw it, he was—" He shakes his head abruptly, like he's been doused with cold water. "What the hell *happened*?"

I shrug, like none of this is any big deal. "It was impeccably maintained," I recite, "until this recent . . . injury."

"Not to the guitar. To Mason. Do you know where he is? What he's up to?"

I hesitate. If I'm too vague, he might think I'm hocking stolen merchandise.

"He didn't authorize me to say. Only to handle this sale."

He sighs—like he figured as much, but had to try—and turns his attention back to the claw marks marring the wood. "Don't tell me it was some drunken hotel room brawl."

"Nothing as mundane as that."

This answer satisfies him. "Well, wow. Too bad he didn't sign it."

Too bad indeed. "You could resell it for more if he did? Despite its . . . condition?"

"If I were fool enough to resell it at all. Which I wouldn't be." He shakes his head. "My bandmates don't agree on jack shit, except this: Mason Shaylor is the most underrated musician alive. I mean, yeah, we're biased since he's from here, but c'mon. Unparalleled guitar skill, lyrical poetry, flying under the radar for years, quietly commanding respect from ev-er-y-bo-dy he shares the stage with"—it's like he's adding syllables for emphasis here—"and you feel lucky watching him light it up, because you *know* his day's gonna come. Then he finally signs with a big label, and poof. No one knows if he choked, or what. Word is he's done." He's baiting me, to see if I'll jump to Mason's defense and let the whole story slip.

Of course, that would involve knowing the whole story. Which I clearly do not.

I bend, sliding the guitar back into the case. "Could you excuse me for a minute?"

He looks confused—and sorry, too, like maybe he's said too much. But I don't let him explain, nor do I attempt to myself. "One minute," I call again over my shoulder, then push open the door and jog around the corner to the Jeep.

"They wouldn't buy it?" Mason slides to the passenger seat and hangs out over the sidewalk, looking perplexed.

I thrust the case into his arms. "You need to sign it."

"What?"

"The guy said it's worth more with your autograph." I dig in my purse and find a thin marker I use to notate on laminated charts for hospice. Mason accepts it, disbelieving.

"How did he even know . . . ?" At least he's not asking how *I* even knew to tell him. I was truthful in our talk about who had and had not googled who, but I doubt he'd believe this was a lucky guess. I'll need some time myself, to process what I've just learned—what it means.

"Let me take your picture doing it, okay? He'll think I'm the world's dumbest forger."

"Not okay. No way." He rubs his temples, and it's jarring, how purple his fingers look next to the skin of his face. Like the circulation isn't reaching them. "I didn't want anyone knowing I was in town."

"He wasn't too forgiving of the damage. You want the money or not?"

Back inside the shop, the employee's jaw drops wide.

"Wait. Mason Shaylor is *out there?*"

I flash the picture on my phone. "Just passing through on a quick visit. Like I said, I'm helping him out."

"I'll need that photo. No photo, and the autograph didn't happen."

"It'll cost you. But no social media—not a word that he's in town, or no sale. And he'll make sure no self-respecting musician shops here again."

He holds up his hands, flashing that *can't blame a guy for trying* smile again.

I smile back. "How much now?"

Back in the car, I hand Mason close to a thousand dollars more than he'd expected.

He barely even looks at it before he peels away from the curb, letting out a whoop for good measure. But I know better.

I see the shop manager in the side-view mirror, camera phone in hand. And I see the moisture in Mason's eyes, threatening to spill over.

I turn my gaze out the window, knowing what Mason meant when he said he couldn't look.

# 16

## *Kelly*

### NOW

Asha Park, journalist with the *Cincinnati Business Courier* and *other local outlets.* A vague bluff to puff up her résumé, probably.

Unless there really were too many to name.

"You should go," Kelly told Maggie quickly. "I'll handle this, call you later."

"There's nothing to handle besides saying, *No comment.*"

Maggie folded her arms, glaring at Asha—and Kelly, too—as if no one with sense would defy her. Maggie meant well. Kelly appreciated her sharp, exacting eye when it was looking at a problem *with* her, but looking *at* her? Even in the safe circle of their consult group, Kelly stumbled over words, forgot important points. She knew that Nova had noticed, and that this was part of the reason Nova never warmed to Maggie. Kelly could accept that admiration and intimidation sometimes overlapped. It was how she felt about all her mentors, about her daughter sometimes, even about death itself. But Nova didn't indulge intimidation, in any form.

Which was, ironically, another quality Kelly found intimidating, if she dwelled on it.

"Look, all I want to do is talk, ask a few questions. I'm not saying there's a story here, or what that story would be," Asha said smoothly. Though she was on the older end of the millennial scale, she had the styled look of a social media influencer, like she was somehow wearing the photo filter. "If you refuse me, I'll have nothing to go on other than Bonnie Shaylor's account. I'm guessing you don't want that."

"I certainly don't," Kelly said. "But if you were a client here, I doubt you'd want us discussing you with a newspaper."

"Bonnie Shaylor doesn't have an *account*," Maggie scoffed. "She has secondhand assumptions. The *Courier* would never print just her story, and you know it."

"Do I?" Asha said coolly. "Disdain for the client's family noted."

Maggie's face reddened, but Kelly put out a hand to still her. "Maggie is not affiliated with Parting Your Way," Kelly said. "So, no reason to note that. And she was just leaving."

Maggie opened her mouth, then closed it. She wasn't used to being told what to do, but even she could see that she wasn't helping here. She pulled Kelly into a hug goodbye and whispered, "Say as little as possible. Don't let her bait you."

Kelly nodded, and stood silently with Asha as they watched her go.

"To be honest, your friend isn't totally wrong about Bonnie Shaylor." Asha's tone softened with Maggie out of earshot. "She cold-called the newsroom so persistently when my colleagues blew her off that eventually she landed with me. I figured if I looked into it a little, she'd leave us alone."

It was obvious Asha was purposely being disarming. But Kelly could be, too.

"What happened with her son is a tragedy, and it's understandable she'd look to us for answers," she said. "But there's no story here. Mason was seeing one of our doulas, but he was not forthcoming with that doula about the specifics of his situation. Our job is not to fact-check our clients' medical records. It's to offer non-medical support they're not getting elsewhere. We stand by the fact that his doula did that job to the best of her ability. Full stop."

"Can you understand why the family would be reluctant to accept that, given the nature of your business and the facts of Mason's case?"

"I'm a parent myself, and when I think of losing a child, at any age—I don't think *reluctant* touches the way Bonnie must feel. But my partner and I have cooperated with the investigation, and as far as we've heard, they've found no fault with Parting Your Way. For that matter, we have no reason to think they've found anything here to further their investigation into his cause of death." Technically speaking, this was all true. Never mind that they hadn't made any judgments yet. "We're as baffled as anyone else, if not more so."

Asha frowned. "I confess, I'm curious to learn more about what you do here. A lot of people seem to think you're meeting a real need in the community."

The tension that had gripped Kelly by the throat loosened its grasp a little. "We are. Do you know twenty percent of baby boomers don't have children? And one in five people in the U.S. will soon be over sixty-four years old? Companion care under the traditional system is not financially tenable for all those people, even if those facilities had the capacity to meet demand—which they don't." Kelly could never go back to working in that system, knowing what she did now about how deep its inadequacies lie. "But we also understand that end-of-life doulas embody an unfamiliar concept for many people. There's confusion about what we do. You reporting on the Mason Shaylor situation—which is truly an anomaly—could perpetuate those misconceptions. Furthermore, it's immoral. His mother may be comfortable with his struggles being public, but as I hinted at earlier, we honor our clients' privacy."

"You're the good guys," Asha offered.

"Parting Your Way is a good place." Kelly gestured for Asha to take in the fragrant herb garden, the homey porch, the calm, natural aesthetic, and draw the obvious conclusions.

"It's certainly an interesting place." Asha looked thoughtful.

Kelly had the distinct impression denying Asha would only stoke the reporter's interest. If she played along a little, maybe she could take control of the narrative, and leave Mason completely out of it. As he should have been all along.

She wished she could be 100 percent certain Nova had nothing to hide. But she did have total faith that her partner followed their creed to do no harm.

"When it comes to Mason, I'm telling you," she repeated, "there's no story. But we've had the privilege of being a part of many other families' journeys, and made a real difference."

"I'll be up front that I never make promises what the scope of a piece will or will not include. But if you look up my bylines, you'll see I write a mean small-business profile."

Maggie's warning nagged her. But Asha was going to write *something,* Kelly could tell. Being proactive was the lifeblood of Kelly's business. Running scared was not. At least, it wasn't supposed to be.

"How about some coffee?" She smiled at Asha. "Or tea? All fair trade, of course."

"Tea would be lovely."

Kelly led the way to the sanctuary that never failed to impress, her mind running out ahead of her. She would show Asha the memory boards of notes and pictures from past clients—and their mothers, too. She'd put her in touch with those who'd consented to being referrals: All would give glowing accounts. She'd give her the behind-the-scenes tour, not just of her space but her philosophies. And Asha would see. How could she not?

"And would you introduce me to Nova Huston, too?"

Kelly did not allow her smile to falter as she held the door open for Asha to enter. Had she said Nova's name earlier? Had Bonnie given it to her?

"Absolutely."

"I used to have a colleague named Nova Huston," Asha said chattily, breezing through the door. "Oh! What a nice space. Good energy. Anyway, it's been years and we'd lost touch, but—she must be the same one, don't you think? Such an unusual name."

How had Kelly not thought of this possibility? Nova didn't like to talk about that part of her life, but she *had* been a fledgling journalist, a stringer who could never get off a beat she loathed. Petty crimes and court cases: Kelly honestly couldn't picture it.

"Must be." Kelly agreed, pouring spring water into the electric kettle. "You were at the *Enquirer*, too, then? Did you know she'd come back to town?"

"No. I never dreamed she would."

Even Nova still seemed surprised she'd come back. Wanderlust was a strong calling. But this work was stronger.

Kelly handed Asha the basket of assorted tea bags and dropped amicably into her chair. "She's lived all over," she agreed.

But Asha stayed standing, a packet of lemon zinger plucked between her fingers.

"As far as I knew," she said evenly, "she was dead."

# 17

*Nova*

THEN

"If I didn't know better, I'd think you were nervous," Mason teases. "Were you not the one who mentioned horse racing in the first place?"

Before us, Belterra Park looms at sharp angles. What was once, when I left Cincinnati years ago, a tired riverside racetrack is now part of a sprawling gaming complex, complete with casino, live entertainment, and dining. Mason had his pick of spots in the mostly empty lot, but he's taken one far enough away to sit and take in the enormity of the place. The sign at the entrance advertises Horse Racing Season Now Open! but this must be a slow Thursday. Either that, or they'll never pay off this remodel.

"I believe we were discussing stupid risks at the time," I point out.

"Stupid risks you'd taken. And lived to tell."

When it comes to my gambles—which are usually figurative, by the way—minor pitfalls like not knowing a damn thing about horse racing never stopped me if I had my eye on the prize or the thrill. But I can only imagine what it took for Mason to trade in that guitar, damaged or otherwise. *Especially* knowing what I do now about how far that instrument took him. What kind of doula would I be to let that turn out to be for nothing? Especially under my influence?

"Yeah, but I was in an all-or-nothing financial situation to begin with." That was no small bet: win, keep doing things my way; lose, go home. My palms still clam up thinking of it, that too-late panic of *what the hell am I doing?* In that moment, I changed my mind: No one knew about the deal I'd made with myself. Which meant I didn't have to keep it.

I wasn't going home no matter what.

Lucky for me, my horse won.

But I don't want to talk about that now.

"You already have enough for all the Cocoa Puffs you could eat," I persist. "And whatever else you want to do."

"This is what I want to do." The well of emotion I glimpsed in him earlier has subsided, and I have to admit he doesn't look to be wrestling with this. "Thirteen-to-one odds, wasn't it? I remember, because it sounded like an unlucky bet."

"Luck was a big factor. I've never even been here before. Only to Churchill Downs."

"Home of the Derby? Well, that's bigger-time than this." He pops the door and climbs out. When I still don't move, he walks around the hood until he's standing at my open window. "Look," he says. "Until recently, you wouldn't have caught me dead here. Throwing around my hard-earned cash, like I'm crazy enough not to care if I lose it?" He laughs like he still considers this crazy, and somehow, it's reassuring. "You wouldn't have caught me dead," he repeats.

"What's so different now?" It's the same hard-earned cash, after all.

He shrugs. "You've already caught me dead. Just about."

His expression is so warm—no, so *fun*—I'm thrown. This isn't the Mason I first met, as he bluntly pointed out, but it's not the one I've come to know over the past month, either.

I don't know who this is.

"Come on. Wouldn't it be a terrific story if I won big on some horse named, I don't know, Acoustic Hookah?"

"It would be a terrifically sad story if you lost."

"I'd only be back where I started."

"Minus a very valuable guitar."

"Look, I have way too much respect for that instrument to let it turn into home décor. Letting it go made sense, like righting something that's beyond just me: It's meant to be played." I guess we're ignoring the fact that he might have thought of that before he beat the shine off it. "If it makes you feel better, it's not my only guitar. I have others."

"That's not the only issue with this fantasy. Choosing horses based on their names is like choosing wine for a cool label. Looks chic, tastes like a moldy basement."

"Suit yourself. We'll choose your way. And no matter what happens, I promise not to hold it against you," he coaxes. "As long as you show me exactly what you did last time."

I've walked into this—and see no way out. Arguing with Mason feels too much like debating myself.

Inside, we head toward the track side of the complex. The high-roller club is members only, so in to the bar & grill we go. A few groups are scattered at tables with burgers and pints, but the barstools are all empty, the bartender "busy" wiping counters that already look clean. We approach and Mason orders two mint juleps: a drink that says, *When in Rome!* even though the Romans are all sipping beer.

Good thing my strategy doesn't involve pretending I belong.

"Who here," I ask the bartender conspiratorially, as he scoops ice into two tall, slender glasses, "is really smart about racing?" I gesture to the tables around us. "Who's the guy who didn't come here on a whim—who actually knows which horses have a chance?"

He stops midscoop and feigns amazement. "You want the guy who knows which horses are going to win? Gosh, why didn't I think of finding that guy?"

Mason laughs. I shoot him a look: *Whose side are you on?*

"No," I say. "I want the guy who knows which horse everyone else is underestimating. And I don't care if it wins. I'll settle for place or show."

He rolls his eyes, but Mason goes quiet. Like *I* am the horse he's been underestimating.

The bartender points a sprig of mint at a corner table, where a man with tufts of salt-and-pepper hair sits alone, hunched over a newspaper with a highlighter.

"That one thinks he's smarter than everyone else," he mutters, sliding our cocktails over. "You two should get along great. Want to start a tab?"

Mason pulls out a twenty. I can tell he's thinking we should trade up for a bartender with less of an attitude, but I got what I came for.

"Hey," I ask, "do bands ever come here, before or after Riverbend?" Next to this gaming complex is the city's main outdoor concert venue, known for its sloping Astroturf lawn, and I've hit on the right topic. With newfound enthusiasm, the bartender launches into a story about Bret Michaels flirting with some high roller's wife, and without excusing myself I simply walk away, leaving Mason stuck listening, shooting daggers at me across the bar.

Not much of a Poison fan, I guess.

But Mason won't like my approach, so it's better to get this done without him. In my defense, he's the one who said to do what I did last time.

My new friend's annoyance at my interruption is short lived. One look at my business card, one sad nod in Mason's direction, and he's happy to help me honor a dying man's wish. He walks me through the rosters, sharing a tip on the champion jockey who's quietly testing out Barn Bachelor, and another one on Buttercup, the mare whose odds inexplicably don't reflect her last three victories—different species, same old patriarchy. In thanks, I give him my untouched mint julep. That's what's known as a win-win.

I just really hope, for Mason's sake, we don't lose.

I'm not sure where the term *grandstanding* comes from, but this track does less of it—or has less of it—than Churchill Downs. We forgo the bleachers to stand near the railing at race level. The weather has improved, and I'm glad I cleared my schedule for this client, this day: On this stretch of concrete overlooking the dirt arena, the afternoon sun—overtaking those morning clouds at last—is warm, and Mason downs his julep and hits up a vendor selling light beer. This diet cheat I can do: My nerves won't withstand this sober. I order one, too.

"What bets did you place?" I'd relayed the votes of confidence for Buttercup, in the first heat, and Barn Bachelor, who doesn't run until later, but hung back while Mason queued at the window to make his wagers. I draw the line at weighing in on how much he should risk.

"What kind of name is Buttercup?" he muses, dodging the question. "I enjoy a *Princess Bride* reference, but for speed over beauty, wouldn't Dread Pirate Roberts be better?"

"Dread Pirate Roberts was a male."

"Dread Pirate Roberts was an alias, handed down. Who's to say there was never a female?"

I grin. "That's actually a great idea for a sequel."

"The Princess Pirate!"

"Yes! But, it's still unfair to judge horses by their names. I mean, do people expect you to build stone walls?"

"All the time. But it's not the name, it's these giant arm muscles. Do people expect you to be explosive and sparkly?"

"Are you saying I'm not?"

"I'm—no. Do you want to be?"

"I've been known to earn a few supernova jokes." I don't mention that some supernovas *implode* before they burst. I lean over the railing, straining for a better look at the jockeys leading the horses onto the track. "I don't love attention, though. So only a little bit sparkly, maybe."

"Little Bit Sparkly isn't a bad horse name. But I like Supernova." He cups his hands around his mouth. "Supernova's leading the charge around the curve! Little Bit Sparkly is closing the gap, but no! Not sparkly enough! Supernova takes the inside! Holy space balls, Supernova's got it!"

I bow.

The horses come into the gates for the first heat. Mason drapes over the railing alongside me, and when our elbows touch, he doesn't move away. It's been a long time since I've felt this unexpected, adolescent charge—the brush of a hand or a knee that leaves you wondering if it was accidental, wanting to do it again to find out. Man, did I love where that led with Andy on that hike outside of Knoxville, and Ryan in the kitchen in St. Augustine, and Dave at the bike shop in Savannah, and *why* have I not indulged since moving home, and no *wonder* I've been so restless ever since switching to the career that's supposed to be my calling.

Clients are off-limits though. The reasons are many and obvious and besides, Mason barely looks at me. If he did, I wouldn't have so many chances to catch myself studying his face, wondering how I ever didn't find it this distractingly attractive.

And reminding myself Mason cannot stay.

The race caller—who doesn't have quite the same gusto Mason did—starts introducing the lineup over the loudspeaker, and I clear my throat. "Okay, seriously, what did you bet? Who are we cheering for?"

"Seriously," he says, "thank you for coming with me today. And I don't just mean here."

"Don't thank me yet," I joke.

"I mean it, Nova." This time, he stares right at me, his eyes so sincere everything seems to slow down. My intake of air, the beads of condensation dripping from our cups, the murmur of the sparse crowd behind us.

I inch my arm away, and the time lapse is restored. Mostly. "You're welcome."

The starting pistol pops. Our heads snap around in unison. The horses are running, and he never even said—

"Buttercup's out in front!" he hollers.

"Get it, Buttercup!" I echo. The spectators are making up for their low numbers with volume, yelling their heads off, and the excitement spreads, contagious. By the time the hooves pound past us, we're jumping up and down, beers splashing.

Buttercup—who really is a beauty, with long strides and a shining, golden hide—lags a little, at the end. The horse alongside her does not.

Buttercup comes in second.

I turn breathlessly to Mason, "Please tell me you wagered across the board." Across the board means second and third place pay out, too. Across the board means he isn't cursing me and my highlighter-wielding source right now. Across the board means he hasn't lost the only part of that Gibson he has left.

"I wagered to win."

I squeeze my eyes shut. The minimum bet is two dollars. Maybe he didn't bet more than that. Maybe he dodged my questions because he didn't want to admit he chickened out.

"How much?" I can't look. There's signage everywhere warning, like a parental lecture, that no one should place a bet if their housing, clothing, and food are not taken care of. Mason barely qualifies—rendering this ludicrous, and not the fun kind of risky, unless you win.

"All of it."

Damn, damn, damn it.

"But not on Buttercup."

My eyes fly open. "What?"

"I was on board with your strategy till I got to the window and saw the lineup myself."

"And the judge signals," the announcer bellows, "these placings are official!"

Mason points at the leaderboard, and I train my eyes on the first-place slot.

Hummingbird.

As in, Gibson Montana Hummingbird.

I look to him in amazement. That's not picking by any old name. "You believe in signs."

"Always have. I hired you based on a night I took as a sign, remember? Also, I didn't want you to feel responsible for my choice if things went south."

I still can't believe it. "But you cheered for Buttercup."

"Well, I put two dollars on Buttercup for you. So, sorry about that."

Relief bubbles out of me in laughter. "This is amazing! You *won*."

"Don't get too excited. Hummingbird was a favorite, so the odds are nothing to brag about." But his smile is stretching ear to ear, and we're aglow in the sunshine, breathing in that victorious dust, and I haven't let Mason down.

But only because he didn't let me.

"Come on," he says, "let's cash out and put money on Barn Bachelor."

"Not all of it," I say. The thing about luck is, you don't push it.

"Not all of it," he agrees.

Hummingbird's three-to-five odds were nothing to brag about on a $2 bet, but with $2,800 down? Mason banks $1,764. We designate the $64 to get us through the rest of the afternoon, and find seats in a quiet spot to the side. We settle into the companionable silence that's becoming familiar between us, breaking it only to cheer for the next heat. The winning thoroughbred—not one either of us picked—doesn't want to calm down when it's over, and the jockey looks caught between affection and annoyance as he tries to steady the animal.

"You know," Mason says, "when these horses get hurt, they just put them down." I can't tell if he thinks this is a blessing or a shame, but the comment doesn't seem offhand.

"Depends on the injury," I say, hedging. "Broken legs, yeah. But not because they don't want to bother repairing them. Because they *can't*. Isn't it something to do with fragile bones? They're such heavy animals."

"Still, people consider that humane. When these creatures can't physically do what they've been trained to do, what they've been born to do, no one pretends they're not done for. No one expects them to lie around a pasture without even being able to stand. No one says, *well, at least they can enjoy the view.* What makes humans think we're above that? Or beneath it?"

"Well, we sort of are. None of us is a one-trick pony."

I wait for him to groan at my pun, but he doesn't break.

I won't belittle Mason's pain and frustration by telling him I've seen exactly how deep quality of life can sink, and he has a long, long way to go before he's there. Intellectually, he already knows there are worse things in the world than losing the ability to handle his guitar. And depending on how his condition progresses, he might face those things. But he might also be right that the hardest goodbye he ever says is the one he's grappling with now.

"Seeing as how you believe in signs," I counter, "what do you think it means that when you finally decided to take a big part of your old life and have me unceremoniously trade it for cash, the universe didn't let you? Any rando could have been working at that shop today, but we got someone who knew exactly what he was getting. Who wouldn't let that part of you fade into anonymity, even if you thought that's what you wanted."

"That guy will hock it on eBay if he can't find a local buyer who's a big enough sucker."

"No way. He didn't buy it to resell. He couldn't believe his luck. Almost makes you wonder what else you're ready to retire that might still have more value than you think." I'm not talking about possessions anymore, and he knows it.

Mason goes quiet. "We should get something straight," he says. "And I'm not saying this to be a pain in the ass. I'm saying it 'cause I like you. I respect what you're trying to do for me."

I glance in his direction, but Mason is looking away. His cheeks are flushed from the sun, or the excitement. If I didn't know better, I'd think he was blushing.

What comes to mind is: *I like you, too.* What comes to mind—again—is that my heart rate is supposed to remain stable when a client, of all people, benignly, even reluctantly, says he likes me. Like he didn't plan to. Like he doesn't know what to do about it.

For once, I think I know how he feels.

"Okay," I say carefully.

He takes a deep breath. "If you think I'm that guy who just needs an attitude adjustment, and then I'll become some inspirational success story? Some motivational speaker at school assemblies?" He shakes his head. "Trust me: I'm not that guy. And I don't want to be."

I have a big problem with the phrase *false hope*—I've seen too much evidence that no hope is ever false. Yet I also understand why people are leery of it. Because hope, with or without science or rationale behind it, might be the most powerful force there is.

"There are major league baseball pitchers," Mason continues, "whose arms are torn to shreds, pretty much everything between the skin and the bone, and yet specialists can patch them back together, pump in pain meds, and send them onto the mound. There are NFL players who spend Monday through Saturday packed in ice so they can take the field on Sunday. There are singers who rest their vocal cords between concerts, who can't even whisper to their wives when they're offstage. But all those people still find a way to do what they're here to do. If they want it bad enough—and they do—there *is* a way." He bears down on the words. "And then there's me."

His fingers flex, and I watch them curl back into their distorted resting position—like his grip is spring-loaded with resistance bands instead of tendons.

"There's no such thing as sucking it up and doing a set. Pain has nothing on me—and on my left side, I *can* play through it. But there's no amount of physical therapy or vitamin B or compression sleeves or electrical stimulation or ice or heat or massage that can make anything below my right shoulder do what my brain tells it to." He laughs, a hollow echo of irony. "They thought surgery could buy me time, but all they did was botch it, hurry me to this point."

"Did they know that was a risk?"

"The fine print acknowledged the very small chance, but they acted like the procedure was such a no brainer, it wasn't worth discussing. They said doing nothing would guarantee a premature end to my career, but surgical intervention could prolong the inevitable. We could hope for the best—people defied the odds all the time. Even after it failed and they scheduled the revision surgery, they kept saying the same thing." He coughs. "I defied the odds, all right."

"But yours isn't a simple overuse injury," I venture. "Those linebackers and pitchers are not battling a degenerative condition, a progressive disease beyond their control." Though he still hasn't labeled his diagnosis, all signs point here, and when he doesn't correct me, I'm satisfied that I've drawn the right conclusion. "It's not fair to compare yourself to them. Besides, they're wrecking their bodies, wearing them out all the way. They might be jogging onto the field once a week now, but they'll be hobbling up and down stairs for the rest of their lives."

"That's their choice, though. To decide if it's worth it."

I catch his eye again and hold it. "How do you know they don't regret it later? All any of us can do is make choices based on the information we have available. It's harsh on ourselves to look back and say that if we'd known what would happen, we'd have chosen differently."

*Even if other people think the outcome seems worth it.*

He slaps his knees. "I appreciate what you're trying to say. And yeah, it's easier to be mad at the stupid surgeon, but I need to own my choices. Which means I have no one to blame but myself."

It's strange, but—our afternoon isn't wrecked. This conversation is overdue.

"Blame won't help no matter who it's directed at. That's a perfect example of why forgiveness—"

"Stop. I've met my ritual quota for this term."

I sigh. "Back to my original point: Your career was all-consuming, and it was wonderful. But that doesn't mean you can't find purpose without it."

"It's been my life." Four words have never conveyed such despair.

And I know they're true, at least to some extent. I also know it's my job to convince him this doesn't have to stay true. In fact, it can't stay true. Because then what?

"Ever heard of Kirlian photography?" He shakes his head. "Some holistic practitioners point to Kirlian photography as affirmation that auras are real. There was this series of imaging experiments where they applied electromagnetic discharges to objects and then took these trippy photos that show the energy of the thing. So, if you take a Kirlian photo of a leaf, what you see is this bright outline of the leaf and all its veins, on a pitch-black background, and this hazy glow around the whole object."

"The aura?"

"Possibly. What turned heads were these phantom leaf experiments, where they'd tear off part of the leaf, photograph it again, and see a faint glow where the torn part used to be."

He's looking at me like I'm a street magician reading his mind. "Like the aura knows it's supposed to be whole."

"Well, that's what they thought. Later, it appeared to be debunked when researchers tried cleaning the imaging surface after tearing the leaf. Their theory was that cellular debris caused the glow, and when the second photo was taken on a clean background, it did reflect the new, torn shape."

Plenty of people ignore this reversal. Maggie mentioned phantom leaf auras in our group consult once, talking about an amputee enrolled at her yoga studio, and no one corrected her, though everyone should have known better. I was the newbie, but when I pulled Kelly aside later and asked whether Maggie didn't know or just didn't like that it had been disproven, she shrugged and pointed out Maggie had brought comfort and confidence to the amputee, who was thriving in class.

But it wasn't Maggie's misinformation that bugged me. It was her students missing the deeper lesson.

"So auras and energy fields aren't real?" Mason asks.

"I didn't say that. What I think is that our energy is more pliable than we know. We might need to clean away the remnants of what's been lost to see the new shape of things clearly. But that picture still looks like pure energy when it glows."

Around us, the stands erupt into groans—a long-shot horse has taken the win. I hear one lone whoop, and see my friend from the corner table waving his newspaper in a flutter of glee.

"How's that for an energy field," I say to Mason, laughing.

"Phantom Leaf," he says, shaking his head, "would be a badass name for a horse."

# 18

*Nova*

NOW

Mr. Whitehall's daughter, Quinn, is on the phone from Santa Fe, giving me the flight information for her visit tomorrow, when I spot Willow through the window. She's crouched near the sill pointing urgently at the door, like the world's most obvious spy. I motion for her to come in.

"You sure you don't mind picking me up?" Quinn asks as Willow slinks in and rushes to the window, as if she fears she's been followed. She's picking up quite the flair for drama at play practice. "These red-eyes land inhumanly early. I could Uber."

"Inhumanly early happens to be my specialty. As long as you don't have reservations about me driving your dad's truck." He's asked me to, of course: It's what Quinn will be using while she's in town—his vision is declining fast, and soon his virtual golf games will be going the way of his driver's license. But all I have otherwise is my bike.

"Of course I don't," she says. "You're family. I honestly don't know what any of us would do without you. Is there anything else I should know about what I'm in for?"

I cringe at her phrasing. She means *in for* with her dad, of course. She couldn't know—doesn't need to know—that his doula may be in dire straits, too. That it feels uncomfortable and wrong to talk business as usual while my own is under investigation. Dragging myself out of bed to face this day, I'd longed to take bereavement leave. But I'd worried how it would look. Death doulas, by definition, do their mourning on the clock.

Besides, what difference would a day off make? No amount of time would ever be enough.

It's comforting, though, hearing Quinn call me family the way so many other clients have, and I cling to this like a shield that might protect me from Mrs. Shaylor. At least, I'm *trying* to stay focused on Quinn and her warm, grateful energy. Willow has bounced into my guest chair, where she is now fidgeting and widening her eyes in that universal sign for *hurry up!*

I shoot her a look meant to convey that she's too mature to be this rude and swivel my chair away to brief Mr. Whitehall's daughter on his frail appearance and low appetite. "There's one thing he never passes up: Holtman's Donuts. He says they're your favorites."

"Oh, Dad." She sounds teary. "I wish I could manage more than four days—it's never long enough."

"We're both really looking forward to seeing you."

When I hang up, Willow runs over and throws her arms around me. She smells of Jolly Ranchers and Aussie shampoo, young and sugar sweet, and my annoyance fades. "Nova, I'm so sorry about Mason. I've kept trying to come find you, but Mom said to give you space."

I blink back tears. I had no idea, until this second, how much I wanted to see Willow. Open-book-hearted, uncomplicated, unjudgmental Willow. And how much I needed a hug. "I'm sorry, too," I manage. She steps back to look at me, that manic look returning.

"I sneaked out here to warn you—"

A brisk knock on the door cuts her off, and Willow smacks her forehead.

"There's a reporter here," she hisses. "With Mom."

Panic rushes me. A reporter? Who Kelly is actually giving the time of day?

"Nova?" Kelly's voice calls through the door. "Got a minute?"

I meet Willow's eyes, my instinct to reassure her that everything is fine, we have nothing to hide. But Willow has this way of seeing through me, knocking my defenses down. Which is exactly why I can't have Willow and a reporter anywhere near me at the same time.

She clutches my arm. "Nova, I need to ask about Saturday night."

Before I can answer, the knock comes again, and the door swings open. "Oh good," Kelly says with exaggerated cheer. "You're here." She frowns when her eyes fall on Willow, who looks exactly the way I feel—like a kid irritated that her mom hadn't bothered to wait for an answer to her knock. But then Kelly steps in, the person behind her filling the doorway.

And I can't look at Willow anymore.

Ever see an old classmate or coworker, and all at once, the relationship floods your memory with the place, the time, the group dynamics of it all: tapping your pens through all those harried meetings, queuing for snacks at the half-broken vending machines, combating the daily crises—a downed server, an unhappy advertiser, a layoff rumor?

That's what it's like seeing Asha step into my office, only without any sense of camaraderie. Like I'm way back where I started, in all the ways I didn't want to be. That unshakable power shift: me, the late start who never managed to convey I had my act together. Asha, the head start who cared more about her power trip than her stories—and who had no patience for anyone in her way. It hits me like a kick when I'm down: the reminder that no one can *really* put the past behind them.

I had a pretty basic reason to want to, though. I disliked that phase of my life. And one of the things I most disliked about it was working with Asha.

"It really is you," she says by way of greeting. "Holy hell."

"Hello," I venture, taking in everything I can tell at a glance is different—notably the style upgrade—and everything I can tell at a glance is not. "What a . . . surprise." Asha is best regarded with a begrudging respect that might border on envy, were it not offset by a guttural wariness that can only be earned.

But Kelly smiles at Asha like it's they who are old acquaintances, then turns her gaze to me, full of empty reassurance.

"I told Asha to give up waiting and come back, but she was so eager."

*Eager.* Oh God. How much have they already said to one another? They're both in professional overdrive—equal parts formal and phony—and there's no way I can summon the same right now. I deeply admire good journalists: When you look at history, they can be downright heroic. It's why I used to want to be one. But given our situation—which we don't *want* to make history—the presence of any reporter cannot be good news. Especially this one.

"This neighborhood's a bit out of my way." Asha's voice is all honeyed apology, the way she says *this neighborhood* conjuring an image of what her own must be in contrast: some sleek high-rise of condos downtown, full of empty-nester execs and season ticket holders. Someplace where blue hair actually turns heads. That's the only reason the Asha I know would have dyed it.

"Kelly, we should talk privately," I begin, but she's shaking her head, like everything's under control.

"We're a contender for a small-business profile in the *Courier.* I was explaining to Asha the broad reach of the important work we do and setting her up with client referrals. The Murray family, the Swanigans, the Dunbars . . . anyone from your list we should add?"

I bite my lip in confusion. A profile? No way. The timing is too uncanny.

"Mom, come on," Willow interjects. I'd almost forgotten she was still there. "Like this isn't about—"

"She started out following up on a lead that turned out to be nothing,"

Kelly interrupts tightly. "But she was so fascinated by our practice, she saw no reason to leave empty-handed."

"Didn't she." Asha doesn't flinch under my cool gaze. Not that I expected her to.

"It's been a fascinating couple hours shadowing your partner," Asha gushes. "Kelly speaks so highly of your role here, I didn't want to leave your perspective out of my piece."

*Couple hours.* The panic I've been trying to quell swirls faster inside me. I want to pull Kelly aside and ask if she's out of her mind thinking she can trust Asha to write things the way she wants her to. At the *Enquirer,* Asha didn't elbow into the feature writer job by luck or skill alone. Any interview Asha does on the record should come with a waiting period for the source's own good—much like drunken Vegas weddings, assault-rifle sales, and social media rants.

But when Kelly's eyes turn wary, they're not directed at Asha, but at me.

And I know. Before she can speak, my defenses bubble up: *I can explain* and *it's not what you think* and even to me, the *Jeopardy!* category sounds way too much like *things guilty people say.*

"Asha tells me you used to work together," Kelly says, the words measured. Unnaturally even. "You'll have to fill me in later."

A thousand unasked questions hang on that last word, and damn it, I want to feel angry with Asha but I can't. Asking after me might have been the only innocent part of her visit.

"Willow, I need your help at the house." Kelly's voice is a warning—to both of us. There will be no stopping this train to debrief now. She's bought our tickets, and I'd better get on board. Because if anyone here is untrustworthy?

It's me.

Willow mouths *I tried* as the door shuts behind them.

*Thanks anyway,* I want to say. Also, preemptively: *I'm sorry.*

Asha looks around as if she can hardly believe any of this is real. "I have to tell you I thought maybe someone had stolen your name. Like, ripped it off an old byline and run with it. When you left, your reasons why—was that a ruse? I mean, you could've just quit."

"It was true."

"But I thought—" Even Asha, the queen of smooth, is having a hard time wording this graciously. "I thought it was a question of when, not if."

I nod. "I can assure you it still is. For you, too."

Her face darkens. "Does Drew know you're back?"

I shrug, lowering into my desk chair and gesturing for her to sit opposite me. At least this way, I have the allusion of the upper hand. "We fell out of touch. He still at the *Enquirer*?"

"I think so? I'm barely there myself—I'm kind of everywhere now." She hesitates. "Last time I saw him was an engagement party for, um, him and Marissa."

"Good for them." I hold my gaze steady so she can see that I mean this. She looks right back so I can see that she's relieved—she wasn't being cruel.

Not about Drew.

"Well, wow," she says. "That's the real story here, isn't it? You?"

"Definitely not. I want nothing else to do with headline news." I fold my hands on the desk, not liking the sound of her being *everywhere*—in print or otherwise. "Nothing," I repeat.

"I'm surprised you didn't get back to journalism once you had the chance," she observes. "I thought you were hell-bent on finding the better stories."

She is using my exact word: *better.* The last time I said it to her—on my way out the door—I wasn't splitting hairs. I was *done.* I'll never forget the indignity of begging my editor for one last byline, one I could be proud of. And of Asha refusing to cede the assignment "just because someone played the pity card."

I smile. "I am."

Asha looks confused. "Are you ghostwriting these people's memoirs?" She brightens. "Is there a Mason Shaylor manuscript in the works?"

I don't even flinch. Of course she's here about Mason.

"There's more than one way to tell a worthwhile story," I say calmly. "I decided the most meaningful way was to help people live them."

"As a *death* doula?"

"I don't know if you've heard, but a lot of people think your industry is dying, too."

"Low blow, Huston. You know as well as I do that those of us hearty enough to stick around the newsroom are fighting the good fight."

Asha's lips curl in mockery just thinking of my old un-hearty bylines. For a brief, hallucinatory period, I'd actually thought the police blotter might turn out to be exciting. Like I'd have a first look at the action, sussing out signs of a big story about to break—and being the one to break it. In reality, of course, the tenured reporters already had heads-ups on anything of real interest. And though my beat extended to the courthouse—arraignments, indictments, even trials—the same was true there. What fell to me was the rest.

If you'd done something stupid that could ruin your job prospects? If you were caught squatting in your foreclosure, hanging on by a thread until you could overcome your addiction or fix things with your wife? If you were in a trailer park brawl so inbred that middle initials and suffixes would be necessary to distinguish one defendant from another in our coverage? There I was, feeding it to our copy desk for their schadenfreude field day. Their quest to out–*New York Post* each other's headlines was the only pleasure anyone got from my beat.

Still, I gritted my teeth and put in my time, waiting to be assigned less soul-sucking work, until it became clear I couldn't stay on any career path that would take years to get me where I'd wanted to start in the first place.

"Seriously though, a death doula—someone must have had an impact on you, made you want to do the same?"

I shake my head, and I'm not being coy. I made up my mind to have an impact on myself. But it's not a story I'm willing to share. Least of all with Asha.

It's not a story I'm about to let her ruin the ending of now, either.

"Asha, I don't know what you're after, but Kelly is a good, solid person. A single mom who put everything she has into doing good, solid work. Her business doesn't deserve even a hint of negative attention. It's too easy to misconstrue what we do—it could be really damaging."

She nods. "Funny, though, that she seemed to have a *misconstrued* idea of her partner's history."

"With due respect, you have no idea what you're talking about. I haven't misconstrued anything that matters. Not to Kelly, not to you, not to any of my clients."

"Look. If you want professional courtesy, take my word for it that you'll be better off answering a few questions. Fair enough? Then, I'll go."

She flips open a prim perfect-bound notebook and cocks her pen expectantly. I'm willing to bet her phone is set to record, too.

"Not about Mason Shaylor."

"Imagine my surprise when I took that phone call and heard your name. Those were the first words of Bonnie Shaylor's rant I even understood. To think I'd been trying to politely get rid of her."

"Why do I doubt you were being polite?"

"I'm being polite now. All of my questions relate to procedural things. Cross my heart."

I fold my arms. "You said you wanted my perspective. Let's cut to that, okay?"

"With pleasure." She smiles thinly. "Say a client or prospective client expressed suicidal thoughts. What would you do?"

My teeth clamp tight, as if that might keep my fury from escaping.

"Better off answering," she repeats.

"Better off avoiding Mason Shaylor," I echo. "Whose death has not been ruled suicide."

"Just covering the bases—hypothetically. Unless you have car accident protocol I should also be asking about?"

I roll my eyes.

"Great. So, Kelly said that you, or at least that she, would follow protocol from the suicide intervention training all doulas are recommended to complete. Can you explain that protocol? To be sure I have it right."

Kelly has never been able to resist defending her business, but I can't believe she answered this. Still, if this story goes south, it can't be because of me. If she's asking standard questions, I'll give standard answers.

"Well, we're not mental health professionals, so the first step would be to urge them to see someone who is."

"And if they weren't receptive to going?"

"They don't necessarily need to *go* anywhere. We could get someone on the phone, to start. We could even call together."

"A crisis hotline?"

"And/or their hospice team or emergency contacts."

"Say they're not receptive to any intervention."

"If they had the means to act right then—say, they had a gun—I'd call 911. And remove the means if possible. In a suicidal crisis without imminent risk, I'd monitor the situation, offering support while making welfare calls aimed at connecting them to a mental health professional. Statistics show most suicides are not spontaneous but planned. There's usually time to go through appropriate channels."

"And do most of your clients have caregivers you could notify?"

"Most do, yes. And I would, yes."

"That's not breaching confidentiality?"

"Most terminal patients designate their caregivers as proxies. For obvious reasons."

Asha jots this down, which has the instant effect of making me regret saying it. "Speaking of obvious reasons: What would you say to someone who points out they're dying anyway?"

"Asha, we're done here." I cross to the door, fire in my step, and fling it open—if Asha won't get out, I sure as hell will. Instead, I nearly crash into Kelly.

"Oh! Sorry! Willow forgot her—" She stops. "What's wrong?"

I fling my arm toward Asha, who is standing now, with the kind of exaggerated calm that the most maddening people summon when someone is justifiably upset. The obvious purpose being to escalate their opponent's anger to the point of acting crazy. "I'm not comfortable with her questions, and you wouldn't be, either."

"I just want clarification on where you stand," Asha persists. "I understand state laws vary on whether a terminal patient can opt for assistance in ending their life."

Kelly's hand flies to her chest in alarm, and it's all I can do not to yell, *seriously, what did you expect?* "That is not something we get into at Parting Your Way," she says sharply.

"What about other death doulas?"

"I can only speak for myself and Nova. But let's not distort the mission of our profession."

"The mission being, to make end of life as positive and comfortable as possible? That doesn't sound unrelated to assisted suicide to me."

"That's an outdated term," I interject. "What you're referring to is physician-assisted death, and death with dignity acts, which are distinguishable from *suicide* for a reason."

"Still doesn't sound unrelated."

"Well," Kelly huffs, "it's unrelated at Parting Your Way, and unlawful in Ohio. Even if it weren't, we are not physicians. We would not be a fit for a client who meets that description, and we reserve the right to refuse any client, for any reason. Why are you harping on this?"

"She implied these hypotheticals relate to Mason Shaylor's situation," I say. "Which they don't."

"Because he wasn't terminal?" Asha asks.

In spite of my best efforts, this conversation has been greased until no amount of mental acrobatics would help me keep hold of it.

"Because there's *no* story here involving Mason Shaylor." Kelly sounds genuinely shocked this has come up again, and I'd feel sorrier for her if I wasn't so scared.

"I understand it's an uncomfortable topic," Asha says, hands up. "I just have a hard time believing this doesn't come up when you devote your careers to talking to people about death."

My cell phone rings loudly on the desktop, and all three of our heads turn toward it. I rush across the room to silence the call, and freeze when I see EASTERN TOWNSHIP POLICE on the screen.

I need Asha out of here. Now.

"I think we've gotten off point," I say, squaring my shoulders. I haven't done anything wrong. And I am not the same Nova who once let Asha make her feel so small. "By and large, what we do is comfort people who don't *want* to die. If they come around to acceptance, that's only a good thing because they have no choice in the outcome."

"Hmm," she says. "People who do want to die don't really need comfort, I suppose."

"I didn't say that."

This hints at exactly the kind of technical debate—between the legal and the moral and the procedural—that I've been terrified would surface. Asha is twisting this corkscrew in ways even Officer Dover didn't think to. At least, not yet. Should the investigation turn down this narrow path, whether through law enforcement, a jury of our professional peers, or the court of public opinion, Kelly and I would find ourselves in unchartered territory. There is no telling what standards we might be held to, or what we might be accused of.

"That's interesting, though. I could see a segment of people who'd argue: You know what, if a suicidal person wants to hire a death doula, why not? That's their right. Suicide is not a crime, and if it's going to happen regardless, why *not* bring them as much comfort as possible?"

Kelly bites hard on the bait before I have the wherewithal to stop her.

"Look," she snaps. "In that highly unlikely scenario, even if the doula was oblivious to the client's intent, that situation would not play out the way you're thinking."

"Even if Nova was oblivious," Asha repeats, like she's trying to make sense of this. Like I'm not right there, even as my name goads me into silence. "Why not?"

Kelly's eyes are bright with alarm, but also passion—still thinking this is some misunderstanding. Still thinking she can make Asha see. "Because what would happen in that sacred client/doula time together would be a journey toward redemption and appreciation of the gift of life. Just by doing her job, she'd change the client's mind."

My phone starts ringing again, and I don't dare look. I can guess at who's trying twice.

Asha nods, then shrugs. "Unless she didn't do her job." She slides the notepad into her jacket pocket. "Thanks again for your time. I'll be in touch if I need anything else."

With that, she strides out, taking what's left of our confidence with her.

# 19

## *Mason*

Mason swore up and down that on some base level he'd known, from the very start, that the surgery had gone wrong. The surgeon would call this impossible, saying Mason's initial post-op complaints had been indistinguishable from the most successful patient's recovery. Dr. Smugface would stroll into the exam room week after week with his crisp white lab coat undone—the hands-on work behind him—and insist the only "significant" difference with Mason was that "wait and see" results failed to materialize: No one had expected his functionality to return overnight, but it *was* supposed to improve, a slow but sure progression that turned out to be not so sure after all.

When it did not, the revision procedure was supposed to fix that.

Instead, it rendered his ulnar nerve—through the elbow, down the wrist—beyond repair.

Mason kept trying, of course, long after they advised him to stop. What the hell else would he do? But he'd been contending with the truth for longer than he wanted to admit, plagued day and night by urges and sensations he could no longer act upon. Even his doctors seemed to misunderstand the infuriating nature of *phantom limb syndrome*: The person suffering isn't under some delusion he'll wake up one day to find the limb restored. He's well aware—hyperaware—that he's living with a whole lot of nothing where something important should be.

Mason was not delusional. Mason just could not live like this.

His inability to let it rest had gotten him into this mess in the first place. How many times had Dex told him to take a breather, get that pain checked out, and how many times had he shrugged it off, unable to stop chasing the next gig? If he'd seen a doctor sooner, interventions might have been more successful. Nova had assumed the condition was by nature degenerative, and he'd let it ride because by now, it was. How could he tell her it didn't have to be this way? He'd been so proud of his long game, yet so shortsighted.

The instant he'd met Nova, though, he'd had that same certainty from the recovery room:

That he'd walked into something he could never undo.

Nova seemed to have some sort of read on him, though he was positive he'd shown her the bare minimum. She was turning out to be infuriatingly persistent, if a little ridiculous at times, the kind of audacious that people fancy themselves but rarely actually are. He liked that she'd never suggest anything she wouldn't do herself. But he couldn't figure out why she seemed so unmoored—a grounded sort of person who seemed entirely without actual ground of her own.

He also, more to the point, couldn't stop *trying* to figure her out. When the last thing Mason had wanted was someone else on his mind, there she was.

And then along came her phantom leaf story, full of hope and compassion and beauty. Full of Nova herself. Making him wonder, for the first time. What if?

Two words had never held so much possibility.

If he'd met Nova years ago, he'd have written a song for her. To capture her spirit, the closest thing he'd encountered to music in human form. Composed of restrained emotion and power and crescendos and yes, even rests where you least expected them. He'd have stayed up all night, maybe two, maybe a week straight, unable to sleep in anything but fits and starts until he had it down. When it was done, it would have the feel of a song he surely must have always known, always loved, though of course he couldn't have, because he'd never heard it until now.

He didn't let himself imagine the way the notes might arrange themselves to begin, but he knew the *type* of song exactly. The type he wouldn't let come easily, even if it tried. The type where he'd push himself to elevate some new combination of chords, some unexplored riff, that was worthy of its muse, that no one had ever played before—though of course everything had been played before. But not by him. Not the way he could. In his hands, it would be different.

This was the best way he knew, the only way he knew, to get some-one out of his system: To acknowledge a connection, turn it into some-thing he could wrap his soul around. And then, to set it free so that it wouldn't belong to him anymore, but to everyone who would sing along and ascribe their own meaning and memories until the song became bigger, beyond what he could have imagined.

He'd done it with friends who'd died too young—in his business, not the rarity it should be—and with lovers who'd never belonged to him at all, and with every woman he'd ever thought he loved. Done it back in col-lege, with the "barometer girlfriend" who came to all his shows—her no-bullshit facial expressions his first reliable measure of how a set was going. Done it ten years back, with the shy beauty who walked and talked with him all night, moonlight shining on the lake, and who he thought—right or wrong—he owed it to them both to leave behind. Done it with the sexy bassist whose path crossed his every few months on tour, stealing nights together until she took a bigger chance on some other guy. He'd done it with the whole notion of romance, and with other dreams too little to get traction alongside the big ones. And it had worked, every time.

A song like that, he couldn't write for someone else to play.

He *had* to play it himself.

No point in writing it then. No matter how much he itched to.

When he'd told Kelly and Nova he was looking to make peace with things, he'd meant it. What he hadn't explained was what peace looked like when he closed his eyes and visualized an end goal:

It looked like *permission to let go.*

That was what he'd come for. A deliverable he aimed to check off his list—the very end of his list—as efficiently as possible. Which—fine, looking back, that had been unrealistic. Had he been thinking clearly, he'd have anticipated this whole process would require more buy-in than he bargained for. Still, in no universe had he come here for something new to look forward to. Certainly not for this strange, stunning woman who made him feel he'd won some prize every time he made her smile.

He wasn't supposed to be making people smile. He was supposed to be making peace. She was supposed to be showing him how. Surely these weren't all parts of the same thing?

They literally could not be.

No one, nothing, had ever made him consider changing course once he'd set his mind to something.

Until now.

Nova wasn't afraid to look ahead with him to the end, to fill the space between then and now with moments that had meaning. She'd dared suggest that, though these lost areas glowing on the lens of his life were nothing more magical than cellular debris, maybe they could still justify believing in magic.

What he found himself thinking about when they were apart wasn't so much what she'd said, though.

It was Nova herself. The way she watched him even though she thought he wasn't looking, the way she talked even though she thought he wasn't listening.

The way their fleeting moments together had started to feel—and this still seemed impossible—*lucky.*

Maybe you had to be on the receiving end to see she wasn't just doing this for her clients. It seemed plain that she was secretly looking for the same thing he was.

And that she hadn't found it yet, either.

He couldn't help but wonder if that meant it didn't exist.

# 20

*Nova*

NOW

I used to spend a lot of time at a police station like this. None of the familiar sights or smells—impatient typing, stale coffee—conjure happy memories. If you ever want to know just how petty and pointless and nonetheless life-ruining run-ins with the law can be, try working the police blotter for a city paper.

Then again, the bigger joke may be that I used to wish I were doing the investigative stuff—like Asha—instead. In real life, I was a paid town crier, but in my fantasies, I was on a first-name basis with cops like Dover, calling him up to say things like, "Hey, Johnny, what've you got for me?" And, "Damn it, man, I need the exclusive, give me twenty-four hours!"

Back then, I had an easier time denying that how you're spending your days is, in fact, how you're spending your life. It's no accident that I'm now spending mine helping people put their mistakes behind them, privately, on their own terms.

But it's doubly surreal that somehow, that's landed me back here. Like one of those *how it started/how it's going* memes.

"Again, we appreciate you cooperating," Officer Dover says now. He couldn't find us an available conference room, so I'm in a wobbly wooden chair next to his desk, in the open-floor-plan chaos without so much as a privacy wall. "This is a difficult time for the family, and it's easier when we work together to get the answers we all want."

Is that what we're doing? I don't feel *together* with anyone. As Asha strode out of my office, I'd answered the phone, grabbing at a desperate, delusional hope that Eastern Township Police was calling to end things right here. New evidence, they'd say, pointed conclusively to an accident. Sorry for the trouble. Sorry for your loss.

Instead, they asked me to come in. Now. To "clarify" some things.

Kelly wasn't having it. "First, can you *clarify* why that woman thought you were dead?"

"She said that?" I could only stare as Kelly nodded, her eyes nearly unrecognizable. This was new, this distance between us. For two people who worked in crisis management, we were not handling this one well.

"Well," I'd tried to laugh—*clearly not dead!*—but it came out stifled and strange. "You can see why Asha and I were never friends. Let me clear my head from whatever they want down at the station first. Then, of course I can explain. I'll tell you the whole, long story."

No way around it anymore.

"First I should ask," Officer Dover continues now, "if you're sure this is everything."

Yesterday before he left my office, I'd turned over Mason's paper file and a flash drive of all the exported *Mason Shaylor* search results from my email and hard drive. Officer Dover had a cable that did the same from my phone. It was the compromise we agreed on, with Kelly's blessing, to protect the privacy of my other clients, though I didn't like the way he said that would suffice *for now*.

"I'm sure. That's all."

He sniffed. "Given the length and nature of his time on your roster,

I'm surprised there isn't more written communication. No emails to or from a different address, even your own chicken-scratched notes?"

How to explain? "Clients dictate their communication preferences."

"Hmm. So it was Mason who preferred . . . emojis?" He double clicks something on his laptop and turns the screen so I can see. At the top of the window is the first text message Mason ever sent me: a string of emojis arranged in an equation. Horse plus bird plus trophy plus a bag of money equals fingers flashing the thumbs-up sign. I took it as his tongue-in-cheek version of my *right now I'm okay* exercise, in spite of the serious turn our conversation took at the track. His way of saying thank you. So, I texted back a horse plus a princess equals a dollar bill flying away on wings plus a shrug. That elicited a greater-than sign, a clover, and an arrow pointing to a clock. It took me all night to translate: *Better luck next time.*

We texted nearly every day after that. But never in words.

"Yes. Mostly he'd recap something funny that happened. I always took it as a positive sign, that he was still thinking about our time together."

"Was this him being cute, or having a hard time physically typing on the screen?"

"I assumed both."

"None of these make sense to me. Roller coasters, a moon . . . You *never* used words?"

"Mason and I had a more in-person kind of relationship."

"Face-to-face."

"Exactly."

"Pretty rare these days."

Is it worth pointing out this is a sign of how authentic things were between us? This officer has nothing to go on but my word, and if he was eager to take it, I wouldn't be here. "Not as rare in my line of work," I say. "Plenty of older clients aren't too big on computers and smart phones, or by the time they hire me they're not up to communicating much. So I'm pretty used to operating that way."

"All right." He opens the manila file on the edge of the desk between us. On top is Mason's questionnaire. The only one from his new client folder that he halfway tried to do. "You said nothing in particular gave you reason to think Mason was contemplating taking his life."

"Correct."

He flips the first couple pages, and stops on the third, where Mason's handwriting breaks the empty silence.

"Here," he points, to the question about identifying areas for improvement in your life. Physical, mental/emotional, spiritual. "Can you explain why you didn't see this as a flag?"

I look, though I already know what it says. I can hear the clatter of the cafe, see Mason slouched in the booth as I take in those three one-syllable words: *Arm, live, songs.*

"Okay." I swallow hard. "First, I should note we didn't spend much time analyzing these responses. You can see how little effort he put in."

"For some people, I'd imagine it takes effort to write even this much."

"True. But these responses were more about his past than his present and future, which was not the assignment."

"How is this about his past? It says to identify areas he wants to improve."

"Exactly. But he wrote things it wasn't possible to improve. His physical problems with his arm, and his resulting inability to perform his songs live."

"Live," he echoes back to me.

I nod. I honestly have no idea what he's getting at.

"See, now I read *live,* as in, *to live.* Gotta say, coming in cold, it looks like he wrote down, right here, that he needed to improve his will to live."

I open my mouth, then close it again. "The word isn't out of context. It's right here next to his guitar *arm* and *songs.* This is clearly as in, performing live onstage."

"I'm not sure it's as clear as you think."

I blink. "I suppose you can take it any way you want in hindsight. But you asked why it didn't raise a red flag, and I'm telling you: Because

I took it as a clear-cut, *three*-word reference to the career he desperately did not want to end. You can also see we didn't move ahead with completing the worksheet. Not every tool works for every client, and he wasn't feeling this one. We only used it one day, as a jumping-off point for a conversation."

"Noted, Ms. Huston. Also note someone else could reasonably come in and think this should never have been a jumping-off point for anything. Because though he didn't spend much time on this, he spent enough to write down a cry for help."

I slide to the front edge of my seat. "There's no exact science to this stuff, but it's ridiculous to argue that because of one debatable word on a half-assed questionnaire, I should've known Mason might drive his Jeep off a bridge."

"Warning signs can be subtle," he says, unmoved.

I pick up the pages and wave them, their mostly blank surfaces fluttering like a surrender flag. "If this is evidence of anything, it's that my client was a tough nut to crack. Do you really think this is a man being forthcoming, giving me something to work with?"

I'm trembling, but not for the reason Officer Dover probably thinks. Not from terror that the police will pursue this and come after me.

What if *living* was exactly what Mason meant to imply?

What if I really did miss it?

"When did you become aware Mr. Shaylor was a musician of some notoriety?"

"Gradually."

He nods, like he can relate. "You know, I'm still not sure his mother even realizes the extent. I gather she disapproved, but I'm not sure anyone is *that* modest."

It seems best not to weigh in on that. "I knew for sure the day we sold one of his guitars to a collector."

He slides me a pen and notepad. "Mind writing down where you sold it?" I scrawl *music shop on Benson Street* and slide it back, though I can't imagine how this would be helpful. "You know," he says, and it's not a question this time, "giving away prized possessions is another textbook warning sign."

"With due respect, all my clients give away prized possessions."

"I guess they do." He gives a conciliatory nod. "Look, we need to be prepared for these questions to be raised. We've kept this quiet—I don't want to deal with a social media firestorm any more than you do. But when word of his death gets around . . . I guess we'll find out how many real fans he had."

*When word gets around.* My mind flies uneasily to Asha, and I realize I have no idea if the name *Mason Shaylor* meant much to her. She seemed focused on me. But she's not one to shoddily research her stories. Selectively, yes. Shoddily, no.

"You said this was about whether I knowingly encouraged or aided Mason, but that's not what it feels like. This seems more about holding me responsible to a standard you wouldn't hold a traditional practitioner to. Like I've opened myself up to this just by doing my job. Even the act of preparing a will is listed as a suicide warning sign. Are estate attorneys accused of helping people feel *too* ready to die?"

"That's . . . quite a point, Ms. Huston." Officer Dover stands, and he looks like he wants to apologize. Like he knew this was playing dirty but had to try. "Thanks again for coming in. If we have further questions, we'll let you know."

But my own list of questions is only growing. I'd come to think that Mason—in all his poetic lyricism—had sought out Parting Your Way when he did for metaphorical reasons. He had never minced words about believing life as he knew it was over, knowing I'd take them at face value. Even as things with Mason muddied, then became more clear, I always believed we both wanted the same thing: to help him learn to let go of that life and embrace a new one. Regardless of how much he had left of it.

Since the day I met Bonnie, I've struggled with the idea of far worse suspicions being true—that ending his life really might have been an option for Mason all along.

But what if it wasn't just an option, but a plan? The *reason* he came to me at all?

I let myself care about him, deeply. He seemed to let himself care back.

It wasn't enough to change his mind.

Officer Dover offers his hand, and I see it, feel it, the moment he decides to believe my side of the story.

Just when I've stopped believing it myself.

# 21

*Willow*

THEN

"He's a dead ringer!"

"He's a doppelgänger!"

"A *dog*-elgänger!"

Willow dropped to her knees in the patchy brown-green grass, laughing, and the terrier ran into her lap, snuffling and trembling with overexcitement. Travis, the Tin Man, had invited them over after play practice to meet the new rescue his family was fostering, and they couldn't believe their luck. The dog really did look exactly like Toto.

Maya—who was such a good Scarecrow, Willow could no longer imagine a boy in the role—bounced a tennis ball across the front lawn toward Nolan, their Cowardly Lion, and Toto scrambled after it. "The fab four gets a mascot." Maya giggled, and Willow looked around at the circle of them and felt she might burst with happiness. It wasn't just the spring bulbs pushing through the flower beds at last, or the tangle of coats they'd flung in the driveway—*we don't need you anymore!*

She'd been bit by the theater bug, hard—not by acting itself, but the shared experience of it all. She hadn't known it was possible to get so tight with new friends so fast. As soon as the final bell rang on practice days, they'd meet at the vending machine and pool their change to share cans of cherry Pepsi (Mom would flip) and bags of cheddar popcorn. They were onstage a lot, but when the director pivoted to the Munchkins or flying monkeys, they'd run lines, tag-team homework, split earbuds and lip sync to Taylor Swift. They had so many inside jokes, the rest of the cast called them the Funny Four. You had to be in the four to call it fab.

Even in the excitement for the show's three-night run, Willow didn't want this to end. She guessed she was a little scared it would. Summer would come, and then what? Would they all go back to what she thought of as their "original friends"? The next auditions weren't until fall, with no guarantee they'd all get cast so well again. Nothing could ever duplicate these magic months. She wanted to hang onto them, stretch them out.

"Mascots are cool," Nolan agreed, "but I'd still rather become the fab five."

"I'm telling you, I think my mom is going to let us adopt." Travis scooped up the dog and cradled it like a baby. "Who could turn this guy over to someone else?"

"Mrs. Oden, apparently." Maya scowled. "I can't believe she won't even let us try."

"I'll get you, my pretty!" called a witchy voice from the road behind them. "And your little dog, too!" Willow whipped around to find Nova grinning at her from the sidewalk. That Jeep Willow had seen in their driveway was parked at the curb, and Willow took her first good look at the guy who owned it. He was hanging back, looking around at the neighborhood, which Willow's mom said had been *all the rage in the eighties.* Willow loved visiting friends in this subdivision. The split-level houses had easy access to basement fridges stocked with Popsicles, all the overgrown shrubs made for killer hide-and-seek, and most driveways had basketball hoops. Who cared if half of them were rusted out?

The guy looked a bit like a rusty hoop himself. His right wrist was in some brace, and he seemed to be having some twitchy issue with his eyes—even through his sunglasses, she could see him squeezing them shut, then opening wide. Still, he was cute. Willow had never seen Nova with a guy before, and didn't really know what she'd expected. But . . . There was a kind of coolness factor, the best kind, that you couldn't imitate or manufacture or even define. You either had it or you didn't. And this guy had it.

Which seemed right. Nova had it, too.

"Isn't he perfect?" Willow skipped down the sloped yard to Nova's side. "But Mrs. Oden said *no* real dog. She doesn't even want to meet him!" She couldn't contain the whine in her voice. "She's not the one who has to throw a stuffed animal through Oz's curtain. Honestly, I look ridiculous. People are going to laugh."

"They'll get that it's a prop. No one's going to accuse Dorothy of launching Toto at Oz."

Willow huffed, blowing her wispy bangs from her forehead. She turned to the cool guy. "Don't you think our director is being lame?"

He considered this with sincerity, taking in her rainbow-striped Girl Boss tee. The whole fab four tried to wear rainbow colors on rehearsal days. Another one of their things. "I think," he said, "anyone who's looking too closely at the dog while you're lighting up the stage is missing out." Willow felt herself blush. "I'm Mason, by the way."

"I'm Willow."

"Mason and I ran an errand earlier, and then he realized this new medication for his hand was making it unsafe for him to drive." Nova waved at the air like this was no big deal, but Willow saw concern in her eyes. "I didn't have time to drop him at home before picking you up, so he's riding with us. Hope that's okay."

"In the Jeep?" Talk about cool. "Can we take the top off?"

Nova looked at Mason, and he nodded.

"Sucks about your hand," Willow said. "What's the medicine?"

"Neuro—ah, neuro-something. The only part of the labels I read anymore is the side effects. Because I get them every time." He brightened.

"But I'm glad for the chance to tag along and meet the dog who will sadly *not* be cast as Toto. What's his real name?"

"*Her* name is Honey. But she's only had it for a few days, so we're trying to get her to answer to Toto." At the top of the slope, Travis was attempting to coax the terrier into an open canvas tote slung over his arm, to no avail. "Our idea is that if we can train a real dog perfectly to let us carry her around, then Mrs. Oden will have to say yes. I mean, she'll have to, won't she?"

The dog wriggled to the ground and ran in skittish circles, still not used to so much attention. Mason crouched down and the terrier slid spastically down the hill toward him, smashing its wet nose into the knees of his jeans. He laughed, rubbing its ears with his unbraced hand. "I wouldn't hold my breath, kiddo."

"It'll be better with a basket. I need one so we can practice."

"Well," Nova said, "you might be in luck. We just came from dropping donations at this thrift store, and I spotted a blue gingham dress that might work for your Dorothy costume. I had them put it aside for us, if you want to go back? My bike's there anyway."

Willow clapped her hands. "Is it okay with Mom?"

"She said to go for it, if you want."

"Did she mean it? Or will she feel left out?"

"She even used the halo emoji."

"Sweet!" That was Mom's way of saying thank you.

Nova turned to Mason. "I'll drop you first, and then . . . Shoot. The whole reason I was getting Willow today is because Kelly's putting on this seminar at the rec center. She walked so I could use her car. Which means she can't pick me up."

"I'll just come with," Mason offered. He wasn't even looking at them, so smitten was he with the dog. "I need something to hang on my bare walls anyway—they're giving my mom a complex."

Nova hesitated. Mason didn't seem to notice, but Willow did. So Nova wasn't ready for her to *really* meet this boy. Was she still not sure about him? Or did she like him a lot and not want to jinx it by moving too fast?

"Seriously," Mason said. "I don't mind." Willow smiled to herself. Nova might not have made up her mind, but Mason seemed happy for the excuse to stick around. Even the twitch around his eyes seemed to calm when he looked Nova's way.

Willow ran to retrieve her coat and waved goodbye to her friends.

This was going to be good.

An hour later, they were the proud owners of the gingham dress, a mauled but unopened pack of white ankle socks, a picnic basket with only a couple breaks in the weaving, a trio of framed woodcut prints of running wolves (for Mason's bare walls), and a vintage copper bangle bracelet (for Nova, not to be left out). As they'd made their way through the shop, trying on silly hats, chatting about rotary phones and Polaroids, Willow kept finding herself thinking of this Zen desktop toy in her mom's office, with shiny silver balls hanging from delicate metal threads. If one of the balls was set in motion, another would be drawn to it right away. The only way to keep them apart was for them to remain absolutely still. *Shared energy,* Kelly had explained when Willow asked, and something about attraction, in a vague way that told Willow her mom didn't really understand the toy either.

That was what it was like watching Nova and Mason in the thrift shop. They'd gravitate toward each other again and again, without seeming to realize it. From the outside, the pull was obvious enough to make you curious what made it work—but you didn't need an explanation, really. Willow was just happy to see it. While she never viewed Nova as a third wheel, it hadn't escaped her that Nova had so little that belonged only to her. Like she was reluctant to take up too much space in the world.

Afterward, Mason insisted on treating at the ice cream shop across the street, winking when he said he had money to burn—clearly some inside joke Willow wasn't in on, but remembering Nova's hesitation earlier, she didn't ask. Mason and Willow ordered strawberry hot fudge sundaes, Nova an unsweetened citrus smoothie, and they settled at a metal table tethered to the sidewalk.

"So you know about being onstage, huh?" Willow asked Mason. He looked surprised, like she'd called him out on some big secret. "You talked me out of that blouse you said might be loud against a lavalier mic," she clarified. She didn't mention the guitar picks in his back seat drink caddy, or the way he'd looked longingly at that retro mic—the guy dropped hints like a kid with a hole in his pocket.

"Ah. Well, I used to."

She licked a smear of whipped cream from her knuckles. "But you've forgotten?"

"No," he admitted. "I haven't forgotten."

"What's it feel like? I mean, when you get out there and the auditorium is full? This is my first time."

He skimmed a spoonful of melting vanilla from the side of his dish and took his time swallowing. "Ever ride in the front seat of Diamondback?"

Diamondback had long been the tallest, fastest, sleekest roller coaster at Kings Island—*the* place to be on a Cincinnati summer day.

"Last time I tried, I was an inch too short," she lamented.

Mason looked at Nova. "Have you?"

"I don't think so. I mean, I've ridden it. But the front has a separate line, right?"

"The only one worth standing in!" He turned back to Willow. "Okay, so you crank up that first big hill, real slow, and you're right in the middle of the park, where half the people standing around with their Potato Works fries and funnel cakes are looking up at you. And half of *those* people are too chicken shit to get on, and the other half are wishing they were on. But either way, they can't help but watch. There's this energy building—*tick-tick-tick-tick-tick*—with everyone on board getting nervous, everyone on the ground feeling it for you. Then you finally get to the top and the car in front goes over the hill, and then you're vertical, staring straight down at a two-hundred-plus-foot drop. Only the cars behind you haven't caught up yet, so you hang there waiting, and time grinds to a halt."

He paused for effect, and Willow froze, too, spoon midair. Mason was so enthralled with his retelling, they were hanging there with him, three to a seat.

"It's this exhilarating rush of fear," he continued, "but also just a *rush* because you know this will be the most fun thing you do all day, the thing you can't stop talking about until your friends get sick of hearing it." He tilted his bowl, swirling hot fudge around the edges. "That's what it's like. You have to get over that first hill when the curtain goes up—Dorothy has the front seat for sure—but then momentum takes over and if you hang on for the ride, it's the best."

Willow had heard her mom and Nova refer to doula work as their calling, and she didn't doubt they meant it—but they didn't talk about it like *this*.

"Man, I gotta grow an inch," Willow said. "And you gotta ride that, Nova."

Mason raised an eyebrow at Nova: a challenge. "My brother and his wife have season pass cards. We could totally pass for them."

Nova looked surprised. "They live around here?"

"A ways out. Big house in the country. Kids. Dogs. The whole deal."

"Somehow I had the impression you two weren't in touch."

"My mom would never stand for that." Mason glanced at Willow. "You have brothers or sisters?"

She shook her head. "I have Nova, though." She was *like* a way-older sister.

"Even better," he said. Nova smiled self-consciously into her smoothie. "You two should never lose touch, either."

"Never," Willow agreed.

"Whaddaya say?" Mason asked Nova. "Diamondback or bust?"

Nova glanced at his arm, and Willow could tell what she was thinking. Maybe they should ask a doctor. But Nova could see, as Willow could, what this meant to Mason. For him to conquer that hill again, now that he'd thought of it.

All Nova had to do was say yes.

# 22

## *Nova*

As many times as I've been to Mason's house, I've never knocked on the front door. As I make my way up the walk, my insides twist at the sight of the gravel pad along the driveway. Where the Jeep should be.

Even before he was gone, I'd mourned what he could have had here if only he'd wanted to try. The separate rear entrance, the money from the guitar sale, the fact that he had no qualms about sleeping where he worked—how many other artists might he have helped, had he hung out a shingle? But suggestions like that did nothing but convince him I didn't understand. *Why,* he'd pleaded, *couldn't you leave it alone?*

I still can't. I have to see his mother. As I left the police station, a certainty overwhelmed me that I couldn't go home and face Kelly without coming here first. I don't know if I've convinced Officer Dover of my ignorance, nor can I guess how deep Asha might dig, or whether anything will come of any of it. But I need to try to speak with Bonnie again, now that we've both had some time to process the initial shock.

Bonnie is the only one who might still be able to stop all of this from going any further. Maybe if she understands how much I cared for Mason, she'll accept that Parting Your Way did not enable this tragedy.

At the very least, maybe I'll learn something, anything, that can reassure *me*.

I ring the doorbell and step back so that if she looks out, she can see my whole, vulnerable self: not some evil entity, just another heartbroken human. This is not an ambush.

It's an olive branch.

The door opens, and Bonnie stands gripping the knob, moving neither to let me in nor to close it again between us. Her eyes are shadowed with lack of sleep, but she is freshly showered, her hair damp and wavy, her clothes neat.

"Hello, Mrs. Shaylor. I'm sorry to intrude, but I think it's important we talk."

She doesn't register anger, but she doesn't soften, either. "I'm listening."

I glance behind me. A woman is striding by with three beagles on leashes, and waves in a neighborly greeting. The sidewalk is too far away for anyone to hear, but having any kind of audience seems wrong.

"Maybe we should sit down?" I venture.

"Whatever you have to say, you can say it out here." Her foot taps impatiently.

"Okay." I clear my throat. "First, I've met with Officer Dover, more than once. He has everything he's asked for from me."

"I'm in contact with the investigative team. I certainly don't need you to fill me in."

"I didn't think you did, I just—"

"Did you come to pick up your participation trophy for cooperating?"

"Of course not. It just doesn't feel right that I've talked more intimately with the police about Mason than I've had a chance to do with you." I know how carefully I need to choose my words. But if I've left that equally careful conversation with Officer Dover feeling anything, it's that I need to speak my heart here. I owe Mason that much. "When you came to see me, I was so caught off guard . . . I wish I'd handled myself more articulately. If you're not ready to sit back down with me yet, I understand. But any time you are ready, day or night—I'm here, and willing. I need you to know Mason was important to me, and I'm devastated by . . ." I want to say *by his accident*—the only way I can stand to think of it—but I don't want to invite her to correct me. "By this tragedy."

"It's too late for anything you say to make a difference. The damage is done."

I've obviously taken the wrong tack, but I'm still not sure what the right one is.

"I think it could make a lot of difference what we do from here. For instance, Kelly and I had a visit from Asha Park today that was pretty concerning."

"I bet it was."

I take a deep breath. "Mrs. Shaylor, there's been absolutely nothing public about Mason's death yet." I check roughly every few hours. "Is this really how you want his fans to find out he's gone? He deserves better: tributes to his talent, and an outpouring of support. I worry any story Asha writes will put all the focus on what he was going through at the end. He so badly wanted that to be kept private."

"That's A-plus spin right there."

"It's not spin. It's true. Look, you have every right to be angry. I can only imagine how terrible it is for you, not being able to question him or yell at him. There's a lot I'd like to ask him myself. But as far as going public, this isn't just about what anyone thinks of me or you or what happened. It's about Mason and how he deserves to be remembered."

"You're damn right it is. And I think I know best what my son *deserves*." Her face colors, bright and full. Almost as if, in that moment, she realizes that she might not know best. That if she had, maybe we wouldn't be in this position. And that there's nothing she can do about it now. At least nothing, in her own words, that would matter.

"Since you've gone to the trouble to come here," she says, "I'll give you fair warning: I've filed a lawsuit. Malpractice. Even if I can't prove something more sinister went on between Mason and your hack operation, you better believe I'll make an ironclad case that you're negligent. If the police won't make you pay, then I'll make sure no other mother finds herself in the situation I'm facing now."

I blanch. I'd known this was a possibility, but hearing her say it—the thought of what this would do to Kelly, her livelihood, our partnership, our *friendship* . . . it's more than I can bear.

"I wish you wouldn't, Mrs. Shaylor. I know my partner would be willing to sit down with the two of us and see if we can come to some other resolution."

"Your partner?" She laughs. "Sounds like an impartial mediator to me."

I can't get *any* of this right. "Point taken. This doesn't need to involve Kelly at all. I could . . . disassociate from Parting Your Way, and you and I can go from there."

It's a strange panic, being this desperate for her to agree to something I'm this loath to do.

"That would be convenient for Kelly. She made it clear you operate under her umbrella."

"At the edge of her umbrella. Please, can't we try some intermittent step before rushing to a lawsuit? I'll do whatever you ask, whatever it takes."

"Asha said a lawsuit would give the article more weight. Otherwise she wasn't sure they'd give her enough space to get in depth enough to tell Mason's whole story in print."

*Asha said.*

I should have known.

A cough comes from deeper in the house, and Bo appears in the throughway from the kitchen.

"Nova," he says. "I've been thinking of you."

*His brother,* Bonnie had said, that day she stormed our office. *He doesn't know anything more. And when he finds out about this . . .*

Surely she's told him by now. I met Bo only the once, but I glimpsed why Mason found him so formidable.

And didn't exactly hold back in saying so, right then.

Not that I didn't find *both* brothers a bit harsh on each other. Not that I didn't share at least part of an evening with Bo that I genuinely enjoyed.

Bonnie whips around. "You *know* Nova?"

"Don't you?" He doesn't seem to comprehend the incredulity in her gaze. "She was Mason's only friend here, far as I know."

She looks to me, then back to him, then to me again, engaged in some emotional table tennis volley. "I'd hardly call her his friend."

Bo steps closer. His gaze is not on his mother, but on me, and it's full of compassion and sympathy, human reactions Mason didn't think his brother very well capable of. Human reactions I've craved ever since Mason went away, and been utterly unable to seek. I want to throw my arms around Bo and cry. Even if it means apologizing for what I said when I saw him last—even though I'm not entirely sorry. I want to hear his favorite Mason stories, only remembering the good times. I want to mourn Mason with anyone else who loved him, too.

But the opportunity is gone as soon as it presents itself. If Bonnie didn't refer to me by name before now, I suppose Bo wouldn't have any way of knowing that the doula she's rallying against is the woman Mason brought to his party. But he's about to put two and two together, and all of that compassion will fade into something I already have plenty of.

Blame. And the worst part is, maybe I really do deserve it.

I brace for the blow, but before she can speak, Bo shakes his head with sad affection. "Sly fox." He chuckles, wistful. "He said you were just friends. I *knew* that was bullshit."

He says it like I didn't make that bad of a first impression after all.

Bonnie gapes at her son, not in confusion but horror. Maybe if Bo caught it, he'd stop there, ask what's wrong—but he's so intent on saying something to make this better that he has no idea he's making it infinitely worse.

"I've never seen him look at anyone," he tells me, like it's good news, "the way he looked at you."

# 23

*Kelly*

THEN

She found Nova in the usual spot in the corner of the yard, statuesque in a perfect triangle pose. The full circle of the sun hung just above the horizon, and Nova's gauzy pants lent a softness to her silhouette. Kelly slowed on her approach so as not to startle her, calling out only when Nova moved to switch sides.

"Good morning."

Nova glanced over her shoulder and smiled. "Morning. Care to join? Mountain pose?"

This was an inside joke. Kelly swore "mountain pose" was a fancy term for just standing there—and that as such, it was her favorite pose, no offense to Maggie.

Kelly came to stand beside her partner, hands flat against her sides, and inhaled deeply. "Behold, Mount Kelly. Waiting for the right man to come along and climb her."

"Free solo, I hope. If ropes and hooks are involved, I don't want to know."

They both laughed, but then Nova closed her eyes again, and Kelly did the same, and they stood that way, faces to the sun, breathing in the new day together.

Kelly hadn't set out to partner with Nova so closely. It began as a pairing of convenience: Kelly had drummed up more business than she could handle, and Nova—who'd been waitressing by day, studying at night, saving up to move back and be closer to her family—had reached out looking for bedside hours to complete her doula training. Kelly was, quite simply, the only practitioner in town. Both agreed to a trial period sight unseen.

Kelly started out big on boundaries. And maybe she'd have kept them if Nova hadn't been so . . . Nova. She wasn't just good company, her very presence in Kelly's sometimes lonely life was reassuring. And she wasn't just helpful, willing to step in without notice. She was *interesting.* Though she asked questions constantly, she never seemed like a student—more like someone who Kelly could learn from in turn. Kelly had never once seen Nova shy away from anything hard. If anything, she ran toward it.

So it was the night the walls came down. A storm had knocked out the power to the garage, and Nova found Kelly in the kitchen, on the tail end of a stress-cleaning frenzy, crying alone at the table. Nova already knew about the client Kelly lost that morning. But she didn't know about how Willow had overheard the client's grown daughters on the porch and finally registered, at that moment, that "moms die, too." And she didn't know Kelly had handled it terribly, going overboard to reassure Willow that *her* mom wasn't going anywhere.

"Watch a meteorite fall on me tomorrow and make a liar out of me," Kelly cried. Before she knew it, she was confessing her fears—that she was adept at discussing these tough topics with everyone but the person who mattered most. That Willow would have a screwed-up childhood not because of the doula practice on-site, but because of Kelly's inadequacy. That single motherhood would ruin them both.

She'd expected Nova to overcompensate much like she herself had—to say she was sure Kelly had done fine, her best, which was good enough. But Nova didn't say any of that.

Nova said that if the meteorite did fall, she'd be there.

And if it didn't fall? She'd be there then, too.

Nova said that if Kelly needed someone else to count on, she could count on her, and that she wasn't worried about mixing business with their private lives. "Our work is already so personal to me," she'd explained, "I couldn't separate things if I wanted to. Plus, I've been living almost *too* independently, if there is such a thing—you'd do me a favor by giving me someone to worry about other than myself. That's half the reason I became a doula."

Since then, Kelly often thought she had the better end of their deal. In fact, sometimes, in her best mother-daughter moments with Willow, Nova would float into the edges of the room—with them and yet not *of* them—and Kelly would find herself wondering how long any of this would be enough for her partner.

The flip side, of course, was that it made it hard to take issue with Nova when she did, occasionally, step out of bounds. Especially on a morning like this, when Kelly would brace for a serious talk and instead walk head-on into a needed reminder about taking a moment to breathe. For their clients, self-care was important, but for doulas, it was nothing short of a survival skill.

Still, Kelly retained exactly one hard line. The protective one drawn around Willow.

"How's your client load without Wendell?" Kelly asked, starting with the easier of her reasons for trekking out here. Nova bowed her head, and they shared a wordless moment for Glenna's gentle husband. Kelly plopped onto the tree stump that housed Willow's fairy garden, and Nova doubled over to stretch. "Got a call about a late-stage case— they'd probably only need you for a week, tops. Intense, but on a set schedule."

"What's the case?"

"Sandwich generation stuff. Both caregivers have already missed a ton of work for their special-needs child, and their bosses are over it. Hospice set Grandpa up in the living room, and turns out the poor kid is terrified to go anywhere near. Parents have staggered their schedules, but they want someone to help cover evenings, four to eight, until he passes."

Nova straightened and rested her hands on her hips. "What about Grandpa?"

"Pancreatic cancer, end of a rapid decline. Mostly sleeps."

"I should be able to do that. My others are more flexible."

"Thanks. Those are my main hours with Willow . . ."

"I got you."

Kelly hesitated. "Speaking of Willow. I owe you for that thrift store trip."

"Forget it, it was less than twenty bucks."

"I don't mean money. I mean—thanks."

"My pleasure."

"She said Mason went with you two?"

Nova's face fell. "I never intended that, Kel. They've been trying to find him an alternative to these nasty corticosteroids, and the new scrip was giving him blurred vision. I couldn't let him drive home, and couldn't be late to pick up Willow. I was stuck—but I know how you feel about having her around clients. If it helps, I don't think she realized he was one."

Kelly didn't know why she'd expected more of a fight—*You do realize Willow is growing up? How long can you sustain these rules?* Or, *If you want me to chauffer your kid, beggars can't be choosers.* She must be projecting her own insecurities. Again.

"I thought maybe you'd forgotten," she admitted.

"Forgotten not to bring clients around Willow? Or forgotten Mason was a client?"

Kelly raised an eyebrow. "Surely there's no danger of that?"

Nova's eyes slid sideways. "Course not."

"Well, I've noticed Willow noticing him anyway." Kelly sighed.

"Thought it would be a few years before I'd need to have that talk warning her off musicians."

Nova gave a soft laugh. "One is never too young for that talk. Or too old."

There was that sideways look again. Kelly had been puzzled by how smitten her daughter seemed with surly, standoffish Mason. Until it dawned on her Willow might not be the only one.

"How is he?" Kelly asked.

"Struggling. But in healthy, necessary ways, I think."

"What's it been, six weeks? Seven?" Nova nodded absently. "I'm surprised he's around so much—he seemed so unsure at the start. What's the exact prognosis, anyway?"

But Nova's eyes stayed on the horizon, miles away. "That's the rare client we say we want, right? The person who comes to us with plenty of time left?" She smiled sadly. "It's taken some getting used to that Mason seems to have nothing but."

They did hold up time as a gold standard. But it also presented certain potential dangers.

Kelly gestured around them. "Maybe he could benefit from implementing a daily ritual."

"I've hinted that he might join me one day, before sunrise. Suffice it to say he isn't a morning person."

"By himself, I mean." Kelly wasn't sure why this suddenly struck her as vital. Clients weren't discouraged from learning by example from their doulas, or from forming close bonds with them. "Maybe his case would be a good one to bring to the consult group."

Nova toed the ground with her bare foot. They both leaned on the consult group when a client pushed them out of their comfort zone—in some respects, doulas were more like general practitioners, often fielding questions that fell under someone else's specialty. But now that Kelly had said this aloud, it felt touchy, like accusing Nova of not being able to handle Mason. Which wasn't what she'd meant. If only everything surrounding this case wasn't still vague.

Including Nova herself.

"You know whose case I might take first?" Nova mused. "Glenna's."

It hadn't escaped Kelly that every time she asked Nova about Mason, the discussion took some other turn. Away. But what could she do but follow? Nova didn't ask for help often. "Why? Is she going downhill without Wendell?"

"Actually, now that she's not consumed with chemo and taking care of him, she's keeping busier than ever. Meeting friends for brunch, knitting hats for the maternity ward. She's also gone hog-wild labeling every single thing in her house with who she wants to inherit it."

"Then what's the problem?"

"I've never faced a situation where it's going to be *all* on me when she goes. She has literally no family to involve. It's me or a stranger to serve as executor of her will. And everything else."

That *was* blurring some lines. Kelly shifted into mentor mode. "Okay. You know you have to sidestep anything that could be construed as funeral directing without a license?"

"I do know. She's prepaid a funeral director to handle the cremation and interment, which at least helps define the split. She wants a memorial service off-site, but her ashes will be in the columbarium with Wendell. I just don't want to do anything that could be seen as a conflict of interest—I already told her I can't charge a fee for running herd on any of that after she's gone. Which of course made her say never mind, she couldn't ask me to."

"That *would* set a precedent you wouldn't want for other clients." Kelly didn't point out that a theme was developing here. Still, it was hard to object to a partner this selfless. Even if it created an uncomfortable amount of gray area. "Maybe it's better you don't."

Nova nodded. "Better for me. But how can I say no to Glenna? There's no one else. She's donating almost everything. And I don't mind doing it for free—money isn't my concern here."

"What if some relative comes out of the woodwork?"

"She's putting all of it in writing and having me cosign, with a notary. That she's appointing me, that I've agreed voluntarily, that my paid duties end on the day of her death. I even made her promise not to leave me anything, even small. It wouldn't look right."

Kelly knew this breed of anxieties well: They'd overtaken her back at the nursing home whenever residents entrusted her with anything of value. A message. A memory. One day her supervisor had found her crying in the kitchen and offered such warm reassurance: *If they could see the way you're moved by this, they'd know they chose the right person to trust.* The same so clearly applied to Nova, Kelly's own worries again began to ease. The same doula simply could not be this conscientious about Glenna and lose her head over Mason. Could she?

"The will is straightforward? Clear instructions for the memorial and all the rest?"

Nova nodded. "It's just more intimidating than I anticipated."

Kelly considered this: the widow biding her time; the brooding young loner. "Well, maybe we should get the group's take on both. That doesn't sound so different from Mason."

"Mason and I haven't gotten that far yet. And he has family. They're just—complicated."

"All the more reason to sort that out sooner than later." Kelly had been bitten many times by complicated families. Every time she vowed *never again.* And every time she was reminded that simplicity is harder to find than one might think.

"I know you're right, but I'm still reluctant to push too hard. He's in pain and dealing with big, fast lifestyle changes. But we're making small strides toward acceptance."

Kelly had to admit that sounded better than she'd been prepared to hear. "If he's on a loose timeline, maybe he could connect with a therapist."

"Maybe," Nova agreed. "He hasn't been receptive when I suggest any-thing along those lines, but . . . He opens up more if we're working on a project or going for a drive. It *is* working: He did one letting-go rit-ual, and at least acknowledged this cycle of resentment he's stuck in."

Nova smiled as if remembering an especially lovely breakthrough, and the fondness Kelly saw there made her—reluctantly—glad for

Mason. Why was she so uptight about this? Mason was exactly the sort of client doulas existed to serve, and exactly the sort of client Kelly herself could not manage. If any doula could help him, it was Nova. And if Willow bore witness to some of that . . . Was that so bad?

"Half the battle is Mason needing someone to respect what this is like for him," Nova went on. "Without imposing their ideas on how he should be handling it. But I *think* he's starting to see that the time he has left can be something other than completely awful. When we're a little further along maybe I will bring it to the group. We're just not quite there yet."

Kelly wanted to know more. But she had to admit, her curiosity stemmed less from a professional place than from this softness she'd seen in her partner—and in Willow, too. This sense of Nova holding back was not new. Nova was tight-lipped about her pre-doula life, aside from an occasional entertaining story. But never had this made Kelly uncomfortable.

Until, perhaps, now.

She couldn't put her finger on why, though. Kelly liked her check-lists and her client demographic fine, and she certainly wasn't aiming to start doing . . . whatever it was that Nova did differently.

So she resisted the urge to press. Because, at the end of the day, though she was drawn to Mason's story?

She was glad figuring him out was someone else's problem.

# 24

## *Nova*

### THEN

"You sure we can pass for your brother and his wife?" Mason slips me the Gold Pass as we file through the metal detector, nodding at the security guards stationed between the ticket counters and the turnstiles at the entrance of Kings Island.

"They barely look at the picture when they scan you in."

I don't want to risk spoiling his unusually buoyant mood, but the real issue seems obvious. "But what if they recognize *you*?"

I admit it: I broke down and googled Mason after we sold the guitar. The speculation about where he'd disappeared to wasn't quite as pronounced as I'd been led to believe—but it's hard to say for sure with so many search results to dig through.

So many.

A staggering number of tour dates and appearances, nonstop, big and small, coast to coast, years' worth. Four albums with independent labels; a bunch of eclectic podcast appearances; a short but glowing review in *Rolling Stone;* a sea of think pieces on why this guy wasn't bigger when he was slaying absolutely everywhere, the consensus being that no one knew what to make of him, but to quote one blogger, "They'd better figure it out"; a line of merch bearing the words *Sunbeams and Moonshine,* some with the tagline "Sons of bitches got me!" Then the press releases announcing his big breakout record deal, over a year ago. His last performance a couple months later; his engagements thereafter "postponed indefinitely."

The whole thing made me feel like I'd already ridden this roller coaster with Mason. At least, to a point. His live album seemed the logical place to start listening, but I made myself stop halfway through.

Turns out the only thing sadder than watching Mason struggle is listening to him play.

He grins at me sideways. "The biggest perk of my downfall? No one recognizes me anymore." I squint back at him. Sure, he's grown the facial hair and let his style go, but his build is the same. Plus, everyone knows it's his hometown.

"They look at me like I remind them of me," he says more quietly, answering a question I haven't asked. And I believe him then. I've been on the receiving end of those looks—ironically, from the people who knew me best. He jostles my arm playfully. "Have you seriously never used a fake ID? Wouldn't have taken you for a worrywart."

"I'm not. I just don't mind paying admission. I'm selective about the places I get kicked out of."

"We're not dodging admission, we're dodging the ten o'clock rush." He points to a sign boasting early ride times exclusively for pass holders. "On a gorgeous day like today, that front seat line's gonna be insane."

He has me there. Cincinnatians take the massive amusement park in our backyard for granted, but the place is a major destination for Midwestern road trippers. If you're a local, you do your best to avoid them, which means timing visits when it looks like rain, or on days when something else big is happening in town. Or now: When it's newly opened for the season, and kids' weekends are spoken for by soccer and tee-ball and scout camping trips, and a morning like this is a rare treat: translucent blue sky, low humidity, gardens in bloom. As we approach the entrance pavilion, the fountains on the other side sparkle with sunlight, and the Eiffel Tower beyond beckons with its elevator lift into the sky.

I glance down at my pass. "I've always liked the name Sara."

"And I've always loathed the name Bo. But whatcha gonna do?"

Our timing is perfect. The loudspeakers blare musical fanfare, the milling crowd actually cheers as the gates open for the day, and Mason's right: We're admitted without issue. We beeline past the shops of International Street, hugging ourselves as a brisk wind showers us with mist from the fountains, and head toward the rear of the park where the Diamondback awaits.

If Mason feels conflicted about buckling in for this self-described simulation of the life he's missing, he doesn't let on. But I can't help thinking back to what Kelly said earlier about daily rituals and how one might work for Mason. Even if he could board the front seat of the Diamondback every morning, I bet the luster would wear off, as it does for every regular who finds themselves less and less enthralled by the old favorite rides and more and more annoyed by the convoluted parking and rowdy teens.

No, we're not here for the ritual, even if we are re-creating a moment Mason knows well enough to close his eyes and describe sound by sound, turn by turn.

We're here for the thrill.

We duck under the maze of railings that will hold a long queue later, and high-five: Only four pairs of riders are ahead of us for the front seat.

"Nice maneuvering, Bo."

"Likewise, Sara. You scared?"

"Who, me?" I take in the massive metal mountain looming ahead of the gate. Diamondback is—well, as Mason told Willow, it's all about getting past that first hill, and then the worst is over. Or the best. Diamondback is like a cartoon squiggle of a snake, climbing and plunging into the woods behind the park three times in quick succession before

making the sideways turn to come back. I don't love the idea of dan-
gling over the first drop, but I'm not afraid of coasters in general. I'm
not big on heights, but I adore speed, so it's a take-the-bad-with-the-
good scenario. "Bring it on."

The empty train chugs to a stop in front of us, and I eye the front
car, seeing instantly what Mason was waxing poetic about. As far as
front seats go, there's not much between them and the track: The
yellow-scaled nose that helps give Diamondback its name comes barely
waist high to the first row, the sides are open air, and the passenger
restraints extend from the floor in unobtrusive T-shapes. The view is
panoramic, even from here.

"Sorry, folks, slight delay from a power surge earlier," the ride at-
tendant announces, not bothering with the intercom. "One more test
cycle, and we'll board the first group." The line behind us is growing
by the minute, and there's a bit of grumbling in the rear.

"I have to say, this is the most excited I've been about waking up
early in months," Mason says, leaning on the metal railing behind us.
"Thanks for being game."

I catch his smile, and it hitches itself to mine, pulling me along for
the ride. "You call nine o'clock early?" I tease, knowing that he does.
We find reasons to text on the regular now—though maybe that's the
wrong word, since *text* is conspicuously absent. He'll send a sunset emoji,
and I'll look out my window to find a brilliant pink sky. I'll reply at daybreak with a smiling sun, and he'll respond hours later with closed eyes
and Zs. I dismiss each quiet worry that it's too much, for either of us: How
could it be too much, when it's so little? I like the wordlessness of it.

The way I catch myself humming.

"Let me rephrase. It's the most excited I've been about waking up.
Period."

Another empty train appears, and the day's first riders file on.

*The most excited I've been about waking up.* Put that way, it sounds more
transformative—like maybe he'd started from somewhere more dire
than I realized.

But I relate to this, too. On multi-levels. I woke up today excited that Mason was excited. Now, though, my nerves rattle as the front seat riders begin to roll. One of them looks thrilled. The other has clearly been talked into this.

"Is Bo short for something?" I ask, needing to make conversation, keep my mind off. "Reminds me of *Days of Our Lives*."

"Yes and no. It's not a nickname, but it's short for Bonnie. When he was born, my mom had complications and was out of it for a while. It fell to my dad to name him, and at the time he was scared she might not make it, so he named him after her."

"Are you named after your dad, then?"

"In keeping with tradition, I got his first two letters. But at least they didn't stop there and name me *Ma*."

I laugh. "What was your dad's name?"

"Matthew. Everyone called him Matty."

He looks so at ease divulging this information, I decide to chance it. "Do you think you and Bo are both most like the parent you're named for?"

"Maybe. To hear my mom tell it, you'd never know my dad and I left for entirely different kinds of tours." He raises an eyebrow. "You're one to be asking about unusual names."

"True. My sister had wished on a star for a baby sister, so . . ."

"Seriously?"

"My parents found it adorable. But I think she was just in the mood for a sister that day, the way you might wish for a cheeseburger or a donut. Before long, she was more in the mood for something else. But there I was."

"Well," he says, "I'm never not in the mood for a cheeseburger or a donut."

"Well," I echo, weirdly touched. "Thanks."

Our turn comes up then, and I glance back as we board. The line behind us is long, the park now open to the public. I buckle my lap belt, and the attendants *thud thud thud* our lap restraints down the line, bored already with their day. Then we're off, straight up the steepest, highest incline with no preamble.

Below the track, Kings Island stretches beneath us in the sun, spinning and sparkling and sending up bursts of distant happy squeals.
I've had my share of new adventures these last years, but this is the best
kind of basic, like being a kid again. Mason drums his fingers on the
lap bar, and I push my sunglasses tight on my nose, give my ponytail a
tug, and press my head back into the seat.

Up, up, up, and as we inch over the crest of the hill, Mason calls,
"Here we go!" and *God,* he wasn't kidding—it can't be a right-angle
drop, but it sure looks like it, and I squeeze my eyes shut for a second,
until the rest of the train catches up. And then . . .

We grind to a halt.

My eyes fly open, and a collective gasp goes up behind us, followed
by a chorus of sarcastic yells—"Hell no!" "We're gonna die!" "No f-ing
way!"—amid more run-of-the-mill screams. Mason is the calmest, a de-
jected: "Story of my life."

We all fall silent, waiting to see if this sticks. Literally. I sneak a look
over my shoulder, but all I can see is the pair of teenage boys directly
behind us, laughing nervously, and the tops of the two heads behind
them. All the other cars are on the other side of the hill, and we're dan-
gling here alone.

"Look," Mason says. "The Racer stopped, too, there near the bottom."

"So did the Beast," one of the teenagers says. It's midway uphill, a
less terrifying spot.

"Think it's another power surge?" I ask, trying to sound normal. The
way I'd sound if I were not suspended hundreds of feet up a sleek red
track, with nothing but a lap bar between me and the ground. But my
voice has jumped an octave, giving me away.

"Bet so." Mason looks up from the park. At me. "You *are* scared."

"I am now." I'm clinging to the bar, looking left, right, anywhere
but down, and all at once, my right hand is encased in warmth.
Warmth that's trying but failing to extract it from its death grip. I
look down to confirm that Mason's hand is over mine—not teasing

me, but reassuring me. He gives up trying to hold it and simply curls his fingers around my knuckles.

"It's all good," he says. "It's a helluva story for Willow, right?"

I'll grant him that. There's this thing Willow does when she's freaked out by a story, rolling the bottom of her shirt and biting down on it. It's funny, and cute, and the thought is just enough incentive to get one tiny percentage of my mind to stop hyperventilating.

That, and Mason's hand. It's rubbing mine in this soothing motion that's sort of working, too.

"What scenario do you think we're bracing for?" I ask. Inside my sneakers, my toes grip the inside panel, for all the good that will do. "Or, uh, hoping for?"

The PA system crackles, and all I catch is "power . . . working to . . . restore." A groan goes up from the train behind us, but I'd rather be any of them, on the incline, looking up at the sky. That wind we noticed by the fountains picks up again, and I shiver in my damp sweatshirt as the whole arch we're sitting atop begins to sway, quieting everyone down quick. We hold our collective breaths, and I've never felt so connected to a whole train of people I can't even see.

"Well," Mason says, "we could start up again any second and, uh, plunge down. Which *is* what we came to do."

"The classic way down," I agree. We both pause, as if saying this aloud might be enough to bring it on. "Although I did expect to be able to anticipate when that would happen."

"Of course, there's also the classic *roll backward.*"

"Ah yes." I swallow hard. "I can't say I've experienced that, but I can visualize how it would go. Third option please."

We turn in unison toward the stairs that run parallel to the track. A glorified fire escape. The top step is a full car's length behind us, to our right.

"They evacuate us." Now even Mason sounds uncertain. I can't imagine how they'd lift our lap restraints at this angle, let alone pull us out. I try to press back from the bar on my own, and gravity barely lets me.

He shrugs. "I should've known better than to ride this with a premature death specialist."

"Ha ha."

"You have to admit this is taking my concert metaphor to an extreme." Beneath my terror, some sadness for Mason stirs, realizing how right he is. "If this is some kind of death doula test, I think you're required by law to tell me."

"Trust me, if it were, I'd figure out a way to do it without me on here."

The guys behind us are cataloguing which rides are functioning. Most of Planet Snoopy, stopped. Shake, Rattle & Roll, stopped. Wind-Seeker, running.

"This wouldn't be bad doula training, actually. Like a final test." Another puff of wind: another dizzying sway of the track. "Doula graduates," he intones. "You are now ready to accompany clients to the gates of death. But first, to prove your worth once and for all, you yourself must face a death-defying drop."

He's just reaching for banter at this point—to give us something, anything else to focus on. But I wish he'd pick something different.

"Brilliant marketing, if you think about it," he goes on. "The doula who defied death."

"Stop." I don't so much say the word as it just . . . slips out. I try to pull my hand away, but Mason holds his firmly over mine. Like he's actually worried what will happen if I let go, in a way that has nothing to do with the heights.

"Hey," he says, kindly. "I was joking."

"It's fine," I say, though to my chagrin, I don't sound fine. I sound like I feel: frightened. And not only because we're stuck. "Just please stop."

My face burns as he looks at me. Really looks at me. There are so few people I've let see my vulnerable side, and even then, only glimpses. Talking to Kelly this morning, I had logical defenses for every line that's blurred around Mason. But the truth is, I can't explain them all.

The truth is, I'm not sure I want to.

When he speaks again, his voice is quiet. "You've already had your test, haven't you?"

The guys behind us haven't tired of their game. Stunt coaster, running. Eiffel tower and carousel: hard to tell.

"There is no test."

"Not for all doulas. Not for Kelly. But for you." He's not teasing anymore. "That's what makes you so good, isn't it?"

I won't be baited with a compliment. I decided long ago this story would stay off-limits, the only place that not even a client—especially not a client—could get me to go. But only now do I realize the extent to which this had nothing to do with them, and everything to do with me.

"Please," he says softly. "Will you tell me about it?" And this close to the sky, it's almost more like a prayer than a request. Like he *needs* the answer. Like just hearing it will help him.

And who knows, maybe it will.

Maybe I can find a way to make sure it will.

"If we make it down in one piece, I'll tell you—on one condition."

"Okay, riders!" The PA system shrieks with feedback, obnoxiously louder this time. "We need a minute to get the other train into the station, and then let's get you going again. Be prepared for the ride to resume motion. Thanks for your patience and hang onto your hats."

Mason clears his throat. "One condition, huh?"

"The forgiveness exercise. Two names: Someone you need to seek forgiveness from, and someone you need to grant forgiveness to. Promise to do it, and I'll answer anything."

For a second, I almost hope he won't agree. But he grins, like he never cared about resisting forgiveness anyway: "Deal." And I know I won't live to regret this.

Or I will. But if Mason's making progress, I'll live with that regret.

The ride shudders forward toward its plunge, and we take one big breath together, waiting.

One way or another, when this is over, things between us will never be the same.

# 25

## *Nova*

### BEFORE THEN

By the time my cancer showed up on any screen, it was good and ready to show up on every screen. Not a single blood test or imaging scan came back clean, to the point that ordering them almost became a game where the objective was to find someplace the cancer *wasn't*.

No dice.

It was everywhere.

*You feel fine?* they asked, incredulous. Not one specialist, but a team of them, huddled in the hospital room where they'd admitted me for the round-the-clock frenzy of lab-ordered scrutiny. *No headaches, nausea, stomach or back pains? No nagging cough, night sweats, increased urination, blood in stool? No poor appetite, weight loss, fatigue?*

In other words: What have you been ignoring?

The first time I met Kelly, much later, she said that doctors haven't been properly trained to accept that some patients are inevitably going to die under their care. No matter how old or miserably sick you are, a death, in their eyes, is a failure—a black mar on their record. That's how I felt that day: like they needed to explain me away. Like this must be my fault.

In that moment, I bought in. I actually lamented the fact that I was asymptomatic, that no discomfort had sent me running in sooner. That I'd gone for a physical simply for the "healthy living" discount my insurance company offered and mistaken that morning follow-up appointment for the start of an ordinary day. For about forty-eight hours after my diagnosis, I looked on in a shocked daze as my parents cried and my boyfriend, Drew, looked shiftily around our shared apartment, trying to hide his panic. He and I both knew our relationship wasn't up to this, which begged the question of why we were in it in the first place.

I'd been presented with two choices, both of them terrible.

Option one, do nothing and expect to be calling palliative care in six months or fewer. Admit the twenty-ninth birthday I'd recently celebrated would be my last. With this option, words like "succumb," "defeat," and "quality of life" were bandied about, each volley draining another shade of warm color from my parents' drawn expressions.

Not an option for them, I could already tell.

Option two, fight like hell—and feel like hell. Not to save my life, but to extend it. Certain tumors were problematically inoperable, but I could theoretically recover from a handful of more doable surgeries while relinquishing my body to aggressive chemotherapy and a cocktail of clinical trial drugs. This course of action was more of a tease—if my circulating tumor cell clusters were responsive, I might see a few years of my thirties, provided I was willing to spend half (or more) of that time left undergoing torture. If they *weren't* responsive to treatment— and there was a fifty-fifty chance that would be the case—I might be looking at even less time than inaction would buy me. And a guaranteed prognosis of being too miserable to enjoy any of it.

It didn't take long for me to look up stories of what others had endured and decide:

Not an option for me. Which brought us to an impasse.

When I really thought about it, when I pictured what it would mean to attack my body with poison, to waste away before my eyes, I realized how crazy it was to be cursing the fact that I felt good. True, earlier symptoms might have saved my life, but it was too late for that now.

And in the meantime?

*I felt perfectly fine.*

If the illusion of health was all I had, shouldn't I be grateful for it? Especially since it might disappear tomorrow? Any day now, I could wake up feeling very, very bad, and have a new normal. Never good again. Never myself again.

"I've been reading up on what to say when a loved one is diagnosed with terminal illness," Drew told me late that night, when I found him in the dark kitchen, sitting alone in the blue glow of his laptop screen. "What not to say, actually," he added, his grin sheepish as I slid into the chair across from him. I didn't need to see the list to know he'd already said all the wrong things.

"It doesn't matter what you say." I wasn't trying to be unkind—all I'd meant was that talk wouldn't change my situation. But it came out like *he* was the thing I was dismissing.

Before I could backpedal, he nodded, resolutely. "They've done studies," he offered. "The number one regret of patients who are . . . counting down . . ." He wavered, clearing his throat. "They wish they'd had the courage to live the life they've always felt they were meant to live. To live bigger, really go for it, you know?" We both looked around at the shadows of our decidedly uncourageous apartment. An affordable, practical box miles from the walkable, historic neighborhood we'd really wanted. The value-priced microfiber couch had more in common with my wardrobe and my hairstyle and, hell, the contents of our fridge than I wanted to admit. We had an actual swear jar of coins on the counter, though why we were trying to break the habit I don't even recall. I think it was more about saving up for a trip, any trip, though later, when I took the thing to a coin counter it would amount to only $37.52.

We'd met at the paper, where my ill-advised detour as a barista had

me self-consciously starting at entry-level years after college, and Drew
was a sportswriter who liked the job mainly as an excuse to watch an
exorbitant quantity of games. Workplace flirtation was hot when we
ended up shirtless in the copy closet after hours. But when we made
that relationship real and took it home with us, one day I woke up and
realized it had become the romantic equivalent of those foam cubi-
cles we'd once distracted each other from. And not just because we
couldn't stop talking about insipid office politics, even when we were
supposed to be having fun—all of it ruthless, from Asha's rising star-
dom to the waves of impending layoffs. It seemed a hassle to break up,
though, when we'd still have to see each other every day.

"I don't want to be part of that regret for you," Drew said finally,
into the silence.

"I'll make sure everyone knows I did the breaking up," I said. "You
won't be that asshole who dumped his girlfriend with cancer."

We did hold each other, we did cry. But his sadness didn't mask his
relief.

I left him with almost everything, pretending not to read his hints
that he had no desire to live surrounded by reminders of a dead woman.
My problems were bigger.

My parents got quiet when I told them my decision. Before they
could argue, I asked who might want to come along on a cross-country
road trip. That distracted them. Was this a good idea, to be so far from
the hospital? It was a great idea, I assured them. Also, I was going no
matter what. Then it turned to, how many vacation days could they justify now, when they might need paid time off to care for me later? Retirement was still a ways off, a fact that only enhanced how premature
my situation was. It was decided that Mom would take off two weeks,
and Dad, nobly hiding his disappointment, would keep his boss happy.
They'd need *someone's* employer to be understanding down the road.

Eight thousand miles we put on my car. It was supposed to be for
me, but I think it turned out to be more for Mom. We had a lot of Moments with a capital *M*. The kind that already feel like memories as
they're happening.

And she'd be the only one who'd get to keep them for very long.

My sister lived out of state, and had toddlers, babies, a houseful of five, but she flew out to join us for a weekend in Vegas. I cashed out my retirement funds and paid for everything. You can't take it with you, right? I left big tips at every restaurant, in every hotel room. Saw states I'd never seen before, posed for hundreds of pictures, which I'd catch Mom scrolling through between stops, tears welling in her eyes.

And I read.

Before we left, I'd loaded a backpack with every book I could find on the cleanest diets, natural remedies, and lifestyle choices for cancer patients. Not because I had any delusion of curing myself, but because I wanted to hang onto this *feeling fine* stage for as long as I could. I eliminated refined sugars, stopped at roadside stands for organic produce, raided natural stores for superfoods every time we rolled through a sizable town. Started up mega doses of herbal supplements that made Mom wring her hands and frown. "What harm could they possibly do, when I'm already like this?" I finally asked her, and she laid off after that. By the time we got home, I felt even better, if you can believe it.

She waited until we were back in the house I'd grown up in before mounting her offensive.

Please would I try treatment? Clinical trials were by definition unproven. The doctors couldn't be sure that they couldn't buy me more time. Think how much growing my nephews and niece would do in the next few years. Maybe the surgeries or some immunotherapies would get me in good enough shape to make the road trip an annual thing, to go with Dad next time.

They staged an intervention as a united front. My sister came in for that, too. They didn't understand my choice was *not* synonymous with giving up. Not at all.

*There's nothing more we can do,* doctors always tell the most dire patients. But there was so much more *I* could do. So much I hadn't done with the years I'd squandered, undriven, letting things happen instead of making them happen, always waiting for . . . what? Some sign of the direction I was supposed to take? This was the only sign I was going to get.

I couldn't make my family see, and I couldn't stay. That hurt them the worst, I know, when I left on my own. *How could you?* they cried, and I had no answer other than: *How could I not?* I didn't like feeling bad about my choice, but it wouldn't feel better to prioritize their wishes over mine. I promised to text updates and pictures every day, and to phone every Sunday night, like I had in college. I promised to come straight back when I started to feel *not good.*

The road trip had been more of an all-you-can-eat buffet: cover as much ground as I could, in as little time as I could, without being too discriminating. You freeze-frame the national parks, the places you saw in a movie once, the postcard lookouts, but all the highways and motels in between blend together. I'd had my fill of the journey; now I wanted to enjoy the destination. There was no big, outlandish goal, no pilgrimage across Europe or safari in Zimbabwe, not even a stretch of the Appalachian Trail. What seemed most novel to me was merely the chance to stop and stay for a while in one of the many, many places I'd been driving right by with a wistful sigh my entire life.

Short-term, furnished rentals became my new best friends. There's something pure and beautiful about fully occupying someone else's space for a time. In place of standard-issue hotel comforters, I found handmade quilts. In place of mini fridges, I had full kitchens, complete with those wonderful odd collections of coffee mugs people amass. While strangers were on business transfers out of the country, or visiting their long-distance boyfriend, or writing a dissertation at a presidential library, I paid to sleep in their beds, to experiment with paleo recipes on their stoves, to feed their betta fish or their outdoor cat. I stared at their ceilings in the night and hoped I was paying it forward by funding their travels, by being here rather than in some anonymous room, though they'd never know anything about the woman who'd come and gone, soon to be gone for good.

I went to places I'd always thought I might like to live and stayed until I felt done. A month in Nashville, two in Gulf Shores. Six weeks in St. Augustine, six days in Amelia Island. Winter in Savannah, then spring on Edisto Island, and over into the Blue Ridge Mountains. I tried not to count how much they added up to. *Counting down,* Drew had called it. I didn't want to do that.

I learned that grabbing a seasonal service job is the best way to feel like a local pretty much anywhere. You'd think waiting tables in a seafood joint was a crummy way to spend one of the only days you have left, but not if it's on a pier, with a 360-degree view of the water. And not if you end up with friends, places to be, and things to do that you'd never find otherwise—an invite onto a fishing boat, tickets to a pop-up concert, a staff bonfire after hours in a private cove. You end up having real conversations with people who think you remind them of someone, or who want to know why the blueberry cobbler went away, and lament that the menu had to revolve around what the tourists ordered, and not what the regulars liked. Everyone knew tourists didn't have any sense.

I was starting to agree.

With the exception of my food intake—easier to regulate when I wasn't eating out—I did what I wanted, when I wanted. I also got vigilant about sleeping, but it didn't have to be at night—eight hours in the day worked fine, too.

My first casual hookup appealed solely because he was so not Drew. He offered me a ride on his motorcycle, then agreed to help me buy one, then made love to me up against the seat, rubbery and hot.

When I wasn't worried about long-term consequences, the short-term was a hell of a lot more fun. I spent money I didn't have on things I didn't need. I took dares just for show; I took bribes just for kicks; I blew off my breakfast shift to befriend the old man who flew a different kite from his collection every morning on the beach. I broke the buddy rule and swam alone—beyond the breaking waves, literally bathing in moonlight. You might call my freest moments reckless, and you might be right. All I know is, those moments where my heart or my body or my sanity was on the line? Those were the moments I felt most alive. Each small survival compounded into a confidence I'd never had before. I was shedding a skin that had always been too tight, and once the top layer was off, I realized how many there were to peel back—a new one, if you wanted, every single day. If you want to live like you're dying, I recommend living like you've just been born. Like the world is new and fascinating and yours to explore and there's no *maybe later,* only today.

Here's what I know now: that patients who have the biggest shift toward embracing life reap the most health benefits from that mind-over-matter transformation. A positive attitude is great no matter what, but I didn't shift there from neutral. I'd practically been living in reverse, actively doing things I disliked, choosing a relationship and a job that I always knew in my gut were not just baseline, not just settling, but counter to the direction I'd wanted to go.

Here's what I've realized I don't know: How to throw yourself into life with that level of abandon once you're told that the end is no longer imminent.

Radical remission, they call it. Ask around, and every oncologist has at least one firsthand account, but they keep them quiet—it's no use fueling unrealistic expectations. Besides, science can't explain it. *Why me? What did I do right? Or was I even in control at all?*

There are theories, and then there's this truth: A nothing-to-lose attitude is harder to maintain once you have something to lose again.

And what then, when the only thing you've really gotten good at is preparing yourself to die?

# 26

*Kelly*

NOW

In the hours after Nova was called back to the police station, Kelly had tried to calm herself with plausible explanations for the words that wouldn't stop circling through her head.

*As far as I knew, she was dead.*

"What do you mean?" Kelly had asked Asha, unable to hide her shock. "Why would you think that?"

The reporter had demurred, fluttering her fingers. "Clearly I misunderstood. You know, nosy as we journalists are, we make a point of respecting the privacy of people in our personal lives. Otherwise all our boundaries would crumble."

Kelly had let it go; best to ask Nova herself. Only later—after the terrible scene in Nova's office—did it occur to her that Asha's slip-up may have been anything but accidental. Or that Asha had mentioned boundaries to falsely imply she heeded them.

Of course Kelly didn't know, couldn't know, everything about Nova, but she knew the important stuff. She knew, for example, that when Nova texted to say she was detouring to Bonnie Shaylor's on her way home, her intentions were good. Hopeful. Courageous even—though Kelly wished she had more confidence that Nova would succeed. So Kelly went through the motions, knowing that when Nova did return, she'd appreciate that Kelly had set a place for her at the dinner table—a show of good faith that this worrisome mess of a day was not as insurmountable as it may seem. Even if that show was a bit skeptical, too. As Kelly had blended sauce for the veggie stir fry, she'd watched the garlic and chili flakes swirl as if a better theory might be among them.

Sure, Nova had made no secret of hating that newspaper beat—but faking her own death as a way out seemed over the top. Maybe she'd been so impassioned about leaving to turn over a new leaf, she'd spoken in hyperbole on her exit from the newsroom: *"By this time next month, Nova Huston as you all know her will be dead and buried."* Or maybe it was a case of mistaken identity. Or one of those comically wrong rumors, like a game of telephone. "Oh, did you say Nova was *assisting the dying*? Goodness, I heard someone *witnessed her dying*!"

Nova did come home then, and Willow was there, pulling egg rolls from the air fryer with long marble chopsticks, so Kelly merely carried the tray of oolong to the table and the three sat down to a tense meal. They battered Willow with so many questions about her day, the poor kid barely touched her sticky rice. She seemed about to call them out when Kelly offered to let her take the computer tablet up to her room—selectively "forgetting" Willow was still grounded from that and every other device.

Only after Willow bounded up the stairs, tablet and fortune cookies in hand, did Kelly and Nova carry their tea tray to the couch and begin to really, finally talk.

Only then did Kelly find out how far all her explanations had been from the truth. That Asha had assumed Nova was dead because by all accounts, Nova was supposed to be.

Kelly felt, in a word, dumbfounded.

A nicer word than the one she kept pushing from her mind: *betrayed*.

"I don't understand why you didn't tell me any of this before."

"The thing is," Nova began again, "I don't like saying aloud that I'm better now, because I don't know if that's true. When no one knows why your cancer left, or where it went, it doesn't take much stretching to imagine it coming right back."

"Wouldn't you think if anyone could understand living with that, it would be me?"

"Absolutely." Nova looked earnest. Maybe it was unfair to think she'd owed Kelly the whole truth? Even as it directly pertained to the nature of the work they'd partnered in? "But being around people who knew what I was up against wasn't only hard for me, it was *bad* for me. Freeing myself from all those questions and expectations seemed to be what worked. I never acknowledged the cancer aloud except on my weekly check-ins with my parents—and then I'd need to take long walks and deep breaths afterward, to reset. I was terrified being back with anyone who occupied that mental space with me would lead my physical self to follow."

"Why move back to Cincinnati, then? Your folks haven't exactly stopped stressing you out."

Nova sighed, looking every bit like a woman who agreed she had no business being here at all. "When I got the clean bill of health, my mom sobbed. I mean, sobbed. She had a hard time with me going away, and the only way she got through it was by me promising to come back when I started to feel as sick as I actually was. In some weird way, she'd actually been looking forward to that, which was . . . a hard thing to know." Nova cleared her throat. "Mason had a similar struggle with his mom. He and I both knew our parents acted from love, but understanding that and being okay with it are two different things."

Kelly nodded, slowly. "What made you go back to the doctor to get rechecked?"

"She did. I had made peace living with uncertainty. But she *had* to know why all the things the doctors told us to brace for hadn't happened. I held her off as long as I could. I'd never gotten an oncologist anywhere else, so she made an appointment with the one who'd diagnosed me, and I drove back for it."

Kelly couldn't help but think how out of place everything about this conversation seemed. Most of all, Nova herself. If a stranger walked into the room right now, they'd never guess someone was recounting a life-saving miracle.

The sense of foreboding was too strong.

"From my parents' standpoint, I was out there working odd jobs and living on a shoestring because I had no future to plan for, no practical matters to take care of. So Mom's immediate response, right in the hospital, is she's sobbing and saying, *Oh, you can come home. Thank God, thank God, you can come home.* And I didn't have the heart to say I didn't want to. I didn't have the heart to say anything. My sister had come, and the whole family is hugging and crying and the doctors are speechless, looking like they want to redo the tests to make sure their equipment isn't *all* broken. And I'm just sitting there, waiting for the happy feeling. I was relieved, but also terrified—not of death, but of life. Which scared me more than anything. Like, what's wrong with me? Who finds out they're not dying anymore and isn't jumping for joy?"

"You were in shock." The shock phase was one they'd trained to help clients and their families through. Even if it did usually come from *bad* news.

Then again, Nova should know all that. Nova had studied and practiced and lived to know all that.

"Sure. But it wasn't just that. The last thing I wanted was to go back to who I'd been. But it was like my permission had been revoked to keep on living in this way that had been making me so much happier. It felt irresponsible to keep choosing the unstable path, and selfish to disappoint my mom, and—I don't know, all this negativity flooded in and all I could think was, *be careful what you wish for.*"

That was it. Why this whole thing felt wrong. And not entirely unrelated to Mason. Kelly braced for the question she couldn't get around asking.

"Were you—thinking of hurting yourself?"

Nova looked like she couldn't decide whether to hug Kelly or to crawl behind the couch and hide. Clearly no one else had ever asked this.

It stood to reason no one else had known enough to.

"It was more like I wished I was still sick. Which felt like spitting in the face of every person in that ward who wasn't as lucky. Not to mention my family. I hated myself for all of it."

"You mentioned permission. But no one needs someone else's okay to live a certain way."

"I know. Or I should know. But—I can't overstate how big of a change my life had undergone when I thought it was my last hurrah. I didn't know how to maintain that lifestyle without all the justifications behind it. That's what my family's support and understanding hinged on. Nobody would have dreamed of me carrying on the same way, other than me."

Kelly watched her friend as she spoke, trying to place her in this new context. Finding out about this unknown side of Nova was one thing. Under different circumstances, Kelly would have been touched that Nova had finally opened up, and they'd have cried together. After all, what end-of-life doula—what decent person of any kind—would judge someone for their handling of something so intimately terrible and wonderful and otherworldly?

But finding out like this? When Nova had no choice but to tell her because some awful reporter *investigating them* had strolled in with a blinking neon example of how maybe Kelly didn't know her partner so well after all?

Kelly loathed feeling ill-prepared and off kilter on a normal day; now, when she most needed her strong, professional legs to stand on, she found it difficult not to resent this. She could sympathize with Nova's reasons for keeping her past quiet. But that didn't make this all okay. Especially now that it was tangled up with their present crisis.

"Do you think you related to Mason on more than the mom stuff?" she asked finally.

"I know I did."

Kelly put her empty cup back on the tray. *The tea's been spilled, all right,* she thought wryly. Someone had to clean it up.

"Remember in QPR training, how they talked about 'perfect storms' of emotional stress? Like an unwanted move, loss of a job . . ." Kelly's voice faltered. Nova was no stranger to perfect storms. It was Kelly who'd been oblivious to them all. "Is there any chance you related so strongly to Mason in those areas, you didn't read them as warning signs?"

Nova shook her head. "No. I related to them *as* warning signs. Which is why I focused on regaining and maintaining hope, like we're supposed to."

That was the textbook approach, and Kelly rarely advocated going off book. Still, maybe the best way to encourage Nova to be more open was to stop polishing over the holes in her own veneer, too.

"But let's be real," Kelly said, taking a chance. Leveling in a way she almost never did—even with herself. "No doula sits through that program without thinking, *How the hell do you give a terminally ill person sufficient hope? Hope for what—a painless death, an easy goodbye?*"

Nova responded with a sad, curious smile, and Kelly felt instantly, overwhelmingly foolish. Nova herself had had hope under those circumstances, somehow. Either that, or she'd learned to hope for something . . . different.

"This will be the only time I ask," Kelly said. "Did you honestly believe Mason to be terminal?"

She could almost convince herself that Nova didn't hesitate.

Almost.

"I did."

Kelly nodded. She didn't think Nova was lying.

But she also couldn't bring herself to ask if Nova had believed it to the end.

Or if she still believed it now.

# 27

## *Mason*

"When you say no one else knows this . . . not even Kelly?" They'd found an out-of-the-way spot near the pirate ship ride, a bench along a manufactured stream. Coffee for Mason, bottled water for Nova, even though it cost just as much. He felt like a dolt for only now understanding why.

"Not even Kelly. I can't stress how much I do not want to be defined by this story."

The ship's bow rose above the young trees shading them, as it had periodically for the past hour, and they were showered again with a chorus of delighted screams.

He didn't want to question her. Not when she'd entrusted him, so thoroughly and unexpectedly, with this bombshell of a story. "I wouldn't want that, either." He hesitated, because that was just it: *She'd trusted him.* "It just—seems like a pretty big part of who you are. Especially given your choice of work."

"Well, unfortunately, we don't get to choose how other people define us. We can't say: Here's this big thing about me but don't let it change how you see me." Her eyes drifted to his arm, then back to his face. "As you know."

She had him there. In fact, she had him pretty much everywhere. Some last piece of his picture of Nova had clicked into place, and everything made more sense. No wonder they understood each other so well. The way the rug could come out. The panic of having no purpose, no passion. The shame of people knowing, and of people not knowing. The all-sided heartbreak of a family that misunderstands.

How many times had he put his foot in his mouth, before they got stuck on that stupid, wonderful ride today? Before he'd unwittingly joked about her defying death for the sake of clever marketing? *Ugh.* And why wasn't she holding his track record of ignorance against him?

"Then why tell me?" he dared to ask.

"You didn't leave me much choice."

He rewound those moments they'd spent suspended above the park. Mostly, he'd been trying to keep her calm—an unfamiliar reversal from their usual M.O. "Didn't I?"

She tried to feign offense, but there it was: a smile. She looked relieved. Maybe she'd worried he'd react badly, make her regret telling him. "It seemed important," she rephrased.

He wanted to tell her that it was. That he wished he'd known all along—although if he had, he'd have never stayed Nova's client. He'd have figured he'd come to the wrong place.

And he'd have been wrong.

The truth was, Mason felt sorry for Kelly—for anyone who was lucky enough to know Nova but who didn't know this. He understood why she needed to keep it close. But you'd have to be crazy not to want to listen. Not to want to know her all the way through.

"I get the permission thing," he heard himself saying. "My guitar was mine."

He searched her eyes and realized that whatever she'd been expecting, it wasn't simple compassion. As far as she was concerned, she'd just confessed to a dying man that she'd beaten the odds he never would. "Your permission to . . . live on your own terms?"

He shrugged. "I never thought of it that way until this moment. But it was—maybe too much so. People could call me out as a lousy boyfriend or son or brother or friend, but nobody ever wondered at the reason for it all. Nobody ever questioned whether I had a drive that was worth chasing at the expense of everything else. Weirdly, that went without saying."

"And now," she finished for him, "you can't chase it anymore."

He wanted to say more. Wanted to ask how Nova had kept her heart open to the world—and the people in it—when she'd thought they could have no future together. He supposed those goodbyes would have been easier for Nova than for the people on the other end. But now, Nova *was* the person on the other end—yet still she didn't flinch. This seemed, in a word, astounding.

"For what it's worth," she said, "I don't think you're a lousy friend."

Their eyes locked, two people wholly uncomfortable with this level of vulnerability, and hers were so damn clear. Like whatever she saw through them must be in complete focus. He wasn't sure if this made him want to be sharper, or if this strange mixture of urges—to apologize, to thank her, to better explain—signaled something else.

"This from the woman who just cornered me into a forgiveness exercise," he joked. She burst into a warm laugh, and he tilted his face toward the sun. "Would you believe that's not the only deal I had to make today? Bo made it clear these Gold Passes would cost me."

"Well, you can't expect to get stuck on Diamondback for *free*. That's top dollar."

"Good point. Maybe I could call the deal off."

"Of course, Bo's not really responsible for the wind, or the power grid . . ."

"Shh."

She laughed again. "What was the deal?"

"He guilted me into a thing. At his house, next Saturday."

"A Gold Pass for a party invite? Talk about quid pro quo." Seeing the dread on Mason's face, her smile faded. "Sorry," she said. "That was insensitive. I haven't even met your brother."

"Want to?" He didn't plan to ask, but suddenly—yes. Nova would make it bearable. Nova made everything bearable. "Come with me, I mean?"

She hesitated. Or maybe, time seemed to move more slowly because his heart was beating faster.

"Not as my doula," he hastened to add. "I could use a friend along."

"If you want. Sure." She sounded normal. Casually agreeable. Nothing in her tone should have set off these old pre-show jitters.

It must just be this moment. He knew she didn't want this to change the way he saw her, but he couldn't stop thinking: *I'm so glad you're still here. At all. With me.*

"Nova?"

"Yeah?"

*I'm so glad you're okay.*

"I'm . . . glad you told me."

She smiled, oblivious that what he really wanted to say remained caught in his throat.

# 28

## *Diana*

**THEN**

Diana knew it was petty to be this mad at Nova over something as basic as a missed family dinner. So what if Diana had spent days hunting recipes that conformed to her daughter's baffling litany of self-imposed dietary restrictions? So what if she'd invested hours bringing it all together: rinsing and soaking "ancient grains" she'd only recently heard of, roasting wild-caught king salmon that cost a small fortune, chopping organic root vegetables she wasn't sure she could even digest, and preparing an entirely separate meal of more recognizable food for the grandkids? And so what if Nova hadn't managed to inform them she wouldn't be occupying her seat at the table, while Diana's older daughter and unfailingly polite son-in-law filled the awkward silence with cheerful banter? *Amelia, did you tell Nana about the songs for your kindergarten graduation? Poor Jonah's tee-ball team can't catch a break, nearly every game has been rained out. But Joey scored two goals last weekend—in a total downpour!*

Diana was only half listening. The dinner was just so damn representative of everything.

What were mere wasted hours, after all, compared to the three years she'd spent researching medical treatments Nova refused to consider? Or the thousands of dollars spent refurbishing the guest suite Nova declined to spend even one night in? Or the dozens of texts and voicemails that went unreturned?

None of it was about the time or the money or even the effort. But oh, how exhausting, having one's overtures of love and support rebuffed because they weren't the right kind.

"May we be excused?" Joey asked. The adults were through all three courses, stalling to see if Nova might appear for dessert. To his younger brother and sister, the seven-year-old was kingpin, and without waiting for a response all three kids fled, thundering down the stairs to the basement game room.

Diana didn't mind—she'd have all weekend with them. Lori was the real reason for this dinner. She was tagging along with Joe to his conference in Lexington, making a long weekend of it to hit the bourbon trail. Cincinnati was en route from Michigan, and Diana talked them into dropping the kids here rather than leaving them with the in-laws, Michiganders who babysat all the time. Dinner was the pit stop, but Lori and Joe still had a ninety-minute drive ahead of them.

"Mom?" Lori leaned across the table to refill Diana's wineglass. "You're doing that thing again."

Diana sighed. It wasn't that she didn't know she was doing *that thing* no one wanted her to do: letting her annoyance with Nova show. Failing to suppress it, the way everyone else seemed to. Apparently whether her annoyance was justified had no bearing on whether *that thing* was acceptable. But asking Diana to stop was akin to asking her to stop being Nova's mother.

Which she would never do.

No matter how badly Nova seemed to want her to.

"Why is it always me?" she mused aloud. "Why are none of you accusing Nova of *doing that thing again*?" They were a family of shorthand.

Diana should not have to spell out how Nova's *thing* wasn't about being inconsiderate or late. It was about leaving them no choice but to worry, then acting surprised when they did. Even now, cold rain pattered the windows in the dark, slick night, and Nova's only method of transportation involved neither windshield nor roof.

"I'm sure she got caught up at work," Tom said, for the tenth time, patting his wife's hand. This time, he added: "We should all be used to waiting on Nova by now."

Lori and Joe chuckled good-naturedly, but Diana bristled, pulling her hand away. She didn't want to get used to it: She wanted it to finally, at last, stop.

Twenty-seven years she'd waited for Nova to wake up and take control of her life. Or was it twenty-nine? The newspaper job had been a half-assed step, but at least Diana's waiting had turned hopeful then, up until the whole mess of it screeched to a halt.

Two horrible days, she'd waited for test results at Nova's side—days that felt longer than all those years put together.

Thirty months, then, of praying their very lives might *slow down*: biding time until the next phone call confirming that, for now, Nova remained okay. Bracing for the opposite: the news that would bring all the waiting to its heartbreaking end.

The news that, when it did come, took the form of not a *time's up* but a reset of the clock.

The news that should have marked a new beginning.

And yet here she was, waiting still. Waiting ever since. Another year. Another day. Another hour. For Nova to jump at the chance to see her sister and niece and nephews for the first time since the holidays. For Nova to meet her mother's eyes and smile her real smile.

For Nova to *really* come back, in all the ways Diana had grown to fear she never would.

"Is it such a fault," Diana said icily, "that I can't be so laissez-faire about time? We've all seen how fast and irreversibly everything can change. How we shouldn't ever take each other for granted. So I'm not going to apologize for wanting Nova to be here. And I'm not going to apologize for wanting Nova to *want* to be here. I have been trying my best."

She gestured at the remnants of the dinner none of them had particularly enjoyed, satisfied that their startled faces also looked a bit conciliatory. She was doing that thing again, all right, and she'd keep on doing it until Nova gave her something better to do.

"And *who*," she went on, "stays on a cancer-killing diet even after all their cancer has been killed, unless you're some kind of sadist? I mean, *cabbage*, for crying out loud?"

The front door flung open and Nova burst in, shedding water droplets like a shaking Labrador. She was clad in a space-age silver all-weather jumpsuit, tugging at the zipper, calling, "Sorry. So sorry!" and when she dropped it to the doormat and shook her boots loose from the slimy wet fabric, Diana could only stare. The entire front of Nova's street clothes beneath—pale pink button-down, khaki pants— was covered with ugly bright orange splatters.

"Oh my," Lori cried, hurrying to hug her sister. The men pushed back their chairs and stood, half-smiling. Diana tried to look as if she hadn't been yelling about cabbage.

"I wanted to stop home and change, but I worried I'd miss you completely." Nova returned Lori's hug at arm's length, careful not to get too close with her messy clothes. Or her mascara-smudged cheeks. Or her dripping hair.

Diana was supposed to look at Nova and feel joy. See joy. It was the bargain she'd made with God, to keep her youngest daughter walking among them. Don't get her wrong, Diana was grateful to still have Nova in any form. And yet Nova did not exude joy.

Nova could not seem to resist surrounding herself with the opposite.

"Did a *client* do that?" Lori asked. "Is that a spill, or—" Diana's stomach turned. Surely Nova knew better than to arrive covered in . . . client biproduct.

"A client's grandson. And if by *spill*, you mean, *throw SpaghettiOs in a tantrum, yes.*"

"That right there." Lori pointed triumphantly, shooting a smile at Joe. "That is what we're taking a vacation from." She caught Diana's frown. "Thanks again, Mom. Dad."

"At least I get paid for it," Nova joked. Or tried to joke. She normally made an exaggerated point of how enthralled she was with her rewarding new doula life, but she looked neither enthralled nor rewarded at the moment. She looked tired, and worry tugged at Diana's sleeve.

"They're keeping you late to babysit now, on top of everything?" The words escaped Diana's mouth before she could stop them. It was a strange pick as far as low blows go. They all knew Diana would much rather Nova babysit then pursue her career in *everything*.

Nova sighed. "No. The child is struggling with what's happening, and his mom asked me to try to talk to him, and her husband got stuck at the office, and I didn't think things would . . . spiral as long as they did."

Well. If Diana could relate to anything, it was a spiral. When Nova was diagnosed, they'd actually had a period of closeness, both dropping everything for that mother-daughter trip in a way they never had before or since. Even later, when Nova forwent treatment, Diana tried to accept this wasn't about her. To set her own feelings aside. Not that she didn't understand what her daughter was chasing—Diana, too, had shared those perfect weeks on the open road, when life had been stripped down to the simple, the beautiful. But even then, she'd thought, *felt*, that the things they already had—decades of love—were a far stronger pull than the things they had yet to discover.

She'd never reconcile how Nova had done all the rest. Taking off, not looking back. Not reporting the bear—the *actual mama bear, with cubs*—living under the deck of her Airbnb because she "didn't want anyone to bother them." Sleeping alone at rest areas—and maybe worse, not sleeping alone. Bedding a man old enough to be her father and then "balancing the sex scale" with a conquest who was barely legal.

Lori, a notoriously awful secret keeper, had told Diana that last bit as if both she and Nova considered it a boast-worthy achievement. As if all this behavior signified really living, when all Diana saw was a lost grasp on standards and integrity and consequences and things that were supposed to matter. When Lori said maybe they didn't matter anymore—"maybe they *shouldn't* matter anymore, circumstances being what they were"—Diana couldn't accept that, any more than she could accept her daughter spending those days anywhere other than with her family.

Circumstances being what they were.

It would have been one thing if Nova were off pursuing lifelong dreams, but Nova had never been driven by high ambitious goals. She seemed to instead be looking for any excuse not to stay with the people who had loved her fiercely all along, who would be lost without her.

Who already were.

"I can't believe they didn't offer you a clean shirt." Diana was belaboring the point, but couldn't seem to stop.

"It's fine," Nova said levelly. "People don't think clearly during a week like they're having. Besides, they won't be my clients long."

A weighty silence fell over the room as everyone tried *not* to absorb what that meant. Diana had asked Nova once: How can you talk so lightly about people dying? Like it's nothing? *Of course it's not nothing,* Nova had replied. *It's as miraculous and life-altering as birth—but we talk about that "lightly" all the time. In fact, we rub strangers' bellies and ask intrusive personal questions—"like it's nothing."*

"There's a great quinoa salad here, kiddo," Tom cut in. "Probably as good cold, if you're hungry?" Nova nodded her thanks and slid into her seat as Tom passed the bowl.

"I'll get dessert for the rest of us," Diana announced, swiftly clearing the plates.

"Where are the kids?" Nova asked, taking a bite straight off the serving spoon. "They can't pass up dessert."

Joe frowned, looking at his watch. "Actually, we'd better take ours to go. Sorry, Lori, but I have that breakfast speaker tomorrow." He turned to Nova, more apologetically than was warranted. "Maybe we could catch you on the way back? Bring you a souvenir?"

Nova's eyes caught the candlelight, shining. "You know what? If Woodford has those special Derby bottles, will you bring me one?"

"I'd have to check if that's organic," he teased.

"For a friend," she clarified. "I'll pay you back."

"I'll pack up the dessert, then. Give you sisters a minute to chat." Diana made for the kitchen, hoping no one had noticed her blinking back tears. So much for the whole family together around the table. Fun Auntie Nova would stick around long enough to rile up the kids, and guaranteed they wouldn't see her for the rest of the weekend. Behind her, Joe asked Tom if he might have a peek at the Reds score, and the men headed to the living room.

Diana dropped the dishes onto the counter and leaned against the kitchen wall. What she wanted to do? Honestly? Was call bullshit. On everyone who talked about this journey of Nova's like it was so inspiring. On everyone, herself included, who'd assumed the journey was over the day the diagnosis was reversed. If Nova's story was life affirming, then why had Nova not had her fill of death? And if she'd won her so-called battle, then why did Diana feel as though she'd lost her anyway? Why did she look back at her own past self and want to shake her every time she judged the "old" Nova's passive approach to life as lazy? Why was there nothing she wanted to scream louder than "Be careful what you wish for!"—because once Nova started taking action, things might go quickly off course?

"Are you dating a jockey?" she heard Lori tease.

Nova's laugh floated in from the dining room. "As a general rule, I like to weigh less than guys I date."

"A horse owner? A bookie? A racing *aficionado*?"

"I'm not dating anyone."

"The look on your face when you requested that bourbon says otherwise."

"If I had a look, it's just that a friend turned me onto bourbon recently. Two friends actually."

"One of whom is male and good-looking and into the Derby?"

"*Lori.*"

"Fine, don't tell me." Diana found herself smiling along at Lori's teasing, though she'd been too caught up in her indignation to notice any smitten sign from Nova herself. Lori was six years older than Nova, and as such had a pseudo-maternal read on her younger sister. She'd been Nova's latchkey babysitter, spending her teenage years protesting that she had better things to do than drag Nova along to the movies or the mall. But Diana remembered the awkward quiet in the house after Lori had left for college. The way Nova shuffled along without her at first.

And what it had meant to all of them when the two finally became more like friends, adults on equal footing at last, when push came to shove. Nova's diagnosis being the push.

"I've actually kind of gotten into bourbon, too," Lori was telling Nova. "We may be the only people on our distillery tour who did a bunch of tasting in preparation for the tastings."

"There's a bunch down in Tennessee, too," Nova said. "What about a sisters' trip? We could do Nashville, Knoxville—I've been itching to get away."

"I don't know how soon I could swing it, but yeah."

"Want to look at your calendar? I could plan around whenever you want."

"It sounds great, Nov, but we had to pull strings just to do this, and it's half for Joe's work. I don't know if I can drop everything for another road trip anytime soon."

"Come on," Nova coaxed. "Joe can handle them. Tonight was my fault, but we haven't done anything just us since Vegas. And Mom was there."

"It's their first season in sports—I don't like missing games. But hey, you could come up? They'd love it. They are always asking to see more of you. There's so much more we could be doing without having to get away, you know? Vegas was different."

"Right." Nova's voice sounded funny. "So, we only plan trips when one of us is dying?"

Lori shot back: Something about that being unfair. But Diana felt stricken. Any mother could recognize sibling spite. This sounded like genuine hurt. *Almost* wistful.

Was it possible part of Nova missed the way things used to be, too?

Whenever Diana caught herself thinking fondly about any aspect of that devastating time, self-loathing consumed her, thinking of those messed-up parents who poison their own kids for attention and sympathy.

And yet. Some of their best moments—as mother and daughter and as sisters—had been when they didn't think they had many more of those moments left. With the threat gone, they should have an infinite supply of that happiness stretching out in front of them. Instead they had this: strained table talk where no one seemed able to please anyone else.

"Only you could decline my invites to Michigan *all the time* and then get mad about this idea you literally just had off the top of your head." Somehow Lori managed to sound gentle even while bickering. She certainly hadn't gotten that from Diana—but now Diana found herself wondering if both sisters had a point. Nova *had* started this whole thing not by dodging overtures, but with her own invitation. She hadn't meant it as a test of Lori's stretched-thin priorities.

Was it possible for people who shared real love to misunderstand each other's intentions so thoroughly? Diana found the possibility heartening and terrifying at the same time.

"Anyway, you'll understand where I'm coming from when you have a family," Lori went on. "Which, you're thirty-three. You know there's no reason you can't get on that now, right?"

"And double the people throwing pasta at me? Sign me up."

"Auntie Nova!" The trio of kids bounced in. "You had a food fight?"

"It was very one-sided," Nova deadpanned, and Diana heard their happy squeals as their aunt pulled them in for hugs. "I do not recommend it."

"My friend Abby got sent to Miss Paula's office for throwing Goldfish," Amelia said seriously. "She didn't commend it neither."

Nova laughed, and Diana didn't know how her daughter didn't see, right there for the taking—everything she was still, somehow, missing out on.

# 29

*Nova*

THEN

⌣

All day, I've been on the brink of calling up Mason to bail on Bo's party, with mixed feelings: that I hate to leave him on his own—he seemed almost heartbreakingly relieved when I agreed to go. That if I'm honest, I'd be just as disappointed—because I've been looking forward to tonight way more than I probably should. That maybe, given the latter, having fate intervene and leave me no choice is for the best.

For Mason and me, I mean. Not for poor Mr. Timson.

I really thought today was it for him—his breathing increasingly irregular and slow—but he's hung on long enough for hospice to come and go again, a mean insurance limit when we'd all prefer they stay. His daughter, Mia, is so nervous she's making *me* nervous, asking the same questions over and over about what to do in the event of this or that. But as I'm about to pick up my phone, Mr. Timson's eyes flutter open. He motions for ice chips and then for Mia to sit. As they lace their fingers together and begin whispering, it becomes obvious: This is all she needs. Just her dad—her conscious, familiar dad inside this shell—one more time.

Her husband sees it, too. He calls me into the kitchen, thanks me profusely, and says they'd prefer to be alone after all. And I'm glad, not just because Mason won't have to face his dreaded plans tonight alone, but because of what a gift this is. For Mia and her father.

I get home late and am horrified when Mason pulls in just as I do. Ever since I took on the Timsons, I seem to arrive everywhere a mess: late, unshowered, unready. I'm not sure if their sad chaos is rubbing off on me, or if it's me who's been *that* distracted. I guess I'm not used to so many . . . feelings.

Since the day I spontaneously bared my soul, things are different between Mason and me. He reacted with such tenderness—and without judgment of my decisions, only concern that I was really okay with them. Which made me . . . more okay. If I'm honest, the most okay I've felt in a while.

I don't look it, though.

"Oh no," I call out. "I'm late, and you're early."

"We have time," he calls back. "Actually, this works out. My manager just called."

"You have a manager still?" I wheel my bike under the overhang and head toward him.

"Technically. Dex. He's been kind of unreachable, recording with one of his big-shot clients on this crazy remote island. I think the South Pacific is some opposite time zone? Not that I've been trying to reach him." From the set of his jaw, I get the sense the call got kind of heated.

"So what's up?"

Mason frowns. "We'd agreed to donate a one-on-one video consult to this charity auction for music education funding. It was forever ago, before my surgery, and we forgot all about it, but the charity did not."

"So you have to . . . consult with somebody?"

"Apparently the request got a little lost in transit, and the winner paid a lot of money to hole up in his garage with his equipment and wait indefinitely. *Let me ask you this,* Dex says. *Can you do it right now? Thirty minutes of coaching you could do in your sleep.*"

I get the feeling I'd appreciate this impersonation more if I'd met this Dex character.

"*Can* you?" I ask. Isn't a manager's job to get Mason out of this kind of thing? Will this aspiring artist or whoever be expecting him to demonstrate techniques? What if Mason has to admit, before he's ready, that he can no longer play? What a crummy way for the rest of his fans to find out, when one of them goes public demanding his money back.

"It's just some high school kid with a rich daddy," Mason mutters. "Can I use your office while you get cleaned up?"

I give him a once-over. And honestly? Mason passes muster on sight. A smart zip-neck pullover, dark jeans, new shoes, a whiff of cologne. If I didn't know he'd dressed to measure up to Bo, I'd think he had a date. When I nod that this plan works fine, he pulls a guitar from his back seat—a spare that clearly lives there, leaving him for once totally, improbably prepared.

"Remember that forgiveness exercise?" I ask as we make our way inside. "Maybe Dex is a candidate."

"I haven't forgotten." He pauses. "Dex and I are good. He's . . . not the way I made him sound. He actually cares more about his smaller clients, but the big ones keep us all in business. He has to fulfill his commitments though. And I guess so do I."

I log him onto my Wi-Fi and go to take a shower, hoping the call doesn't bring back the sullen, angry Mason we've been working to move away from. I'm in maybe ten minutes—long enough to reset my energy, shave my legs, and opt for dry shampoo—and as soon as I shut off the water, I can hear the kid playing. My studio is that small, my walls that thin. And regardless of how much his rich daddy had to do with this call, I can tell right away he's good. The song has the makings of a radio hit—a smooth pop-quality tenor, a catchy, easy melody, and a sound that would polish up nicely outside of the Wi-Fi connection. Mason doesn't interrupt, but the kid stops at the end of a verse, right where the bridge should probably be. I wrap myself in a thick terry towel and inch closer to the door.

"That's all I got, man. It's killing me—I feel like I'm right there. I've been trying to finish this thing for months." The speaking voice sounds much more like the kid Mason called him—less confident and more meager without the accompaniment of his strings. Which, come to think of it, is sort of how Mason seems to feel without his instrument, too.

"Your instincts are spot-on. You are right there," Mason says, and—could this be?—he isn't humoring the kid. He's *excited.* "Let's try backing up, to the structure of the verses. Your phrasing is sick—just outside of what I'd expect, which I love—and you might think that has to be balanced by a more straightforward rhythm, but let's try more syncopated, on the off beats."

He replays the last verse with impressive accuracy by ear, and in his hands it's not so much different as *extra.* A repeated note here, a skipped beat there. I'd never guess playing was physically difficult for him, but then again, it's only thirty seconds.

"Hey," the kid says, and I can hear his smile. "You get it. It's like that's what I meant."

Mason laughs. "It is what you meant. All you. But if you make that change, and maybe switch voicings here, you can incorporate what you had before into the bridge. Kind of like . . ."

He strums a segue, a variation on the original that takes it a few measures further.

"Or maybe . . ."

He tries a faster strum pattern, and all at once, I realize that Mason is in my office playing. Only a bit, sure, but he's doing it. For someone else. He's out of his own head and it's happening and it's beautiful. I crack open the door, clutching my towel. Through the doorway Mason leans into the screen, intent.

"You're a genius," the kid says. "Holy shit, I've been agonizing forever, and you slide in and solve it."

"Eh, sometimes you just need a fresh eye. I got a treasure chest full of half-written songs I stared at too long. You could probably finish one of those for me, too."

"I wish."

"What else you got?" Mason asks, catching my eye. I nod and indicate I'm nowhere near ready yet, then shut it again, my head spinning.

This is not the moment I fully realize the extent of what Mason has lost.

It's the moment I fully realize the extent of what Mason still has.

I want to jump up and down, hug him, climb up on the roof and whoop at the moon. I don't know why this hasn't been obvious to him, too, but surely it will be now? We don't have to waste another second looking for his purpose for the time he has left.

This is it. The most alive I've ever seen him.

I survey the basket of makeup I rarely use, the curling iron collecting dust on its barrel. We're not just going to get through this party—we're going to *celebrate*. And I don't know what Mason has told Bo about who I am, but it won't hurt to look like I haven't spent all day at a cancer patient's bedside. To the muffled sounds of Mason critiquing and laughing and chiming in, I curl my hair, shadow my eyes, even brush quick-dry polish on my nails. Then I slip to the closet and pick out a clingy black tunic I've worn only once, plus leggings, boots, a turquoise necklace I bought in New Mexico. By the time I'm done, I feel more like me than I have in a long while. Ready to match Mason, point by point, wherever the night takes us.

"Seriously, man," the kid is saying when I finally emerge. "What your music has meant to me—it's gotten me through tough times." The pure emotion that this is it, the end of this kid's life-changing call, is so earnest and raw, my own breath catches.

"I'm glad you could connect with it," Mason says.

"Understatement. My twin sister has been in and out of trouble for years, and when I played her 'Shadow of a Doubt,' that's when she agreed to go to rehab. She's not out of the woods yet, but as of now? That song saved her *life*."

"It saved mine, too," Mason says. "Thanks for telling me, man. You take good care."

When I venture into the office doorway, he's standing at the window, looking out at the dark, eyes glassy. They turn on me and instantly clear.

"You clean up pretty nice, Nova Huston."

"So do you, Mason Shaylor."

We grin at each other.

"Ready to go?" he says.

I'm not. "Are we going to talk about that? What you did for that kid . . ."

"Lucky I got someone who knew what he was doing already."

"Whatever, modest mouse. That was amazing. For both of you. That's it—that's what you can still do. You can coach. You can—"

He shakes his head, once—more like a single hard jerk to the left. Away from me.

"Nah, I don't do other people's music."

"Maybe not before, but now—"

"Nova, please. This night is fraught enough having to go to my brother's. Can we leave it?" He holds out his arm, like a gallant gentleman. Like a man whose good mood will leave him if I press. "Let's just go have fun."

A smile twitches at the corner of my mouth. I'll let it go, for now. But not for good. "I thought it wasn't going to be any fun."

"That was before."

"See? The call was a good thing."

He looks at me sideways. "Not that. I mean before I knew you were coming, too."

## MALPRACTICE ALLEGED AGAINST
## POPULAR ALTERNATIVE CARE CENTER
### by Asha Park

Local end-of-life doula business Parting Your Way is facing a malpractice lawsuit in the wake of startling allegations from the family of a former client.

Bonnie Shaylor, 63, of Miamiville has been tight-lipped about the death of her son, Mason Shaylor, a critically acclaimed singer-songwriter who had a cult following for his soulful live performances until he disappeared from the public eye without explanation last year. His mother says a health condition forced him to stop his grueling schedule of year-round touring, but it was a horrific early morning single-vehicle collision that ultimately ended his promising career. The Eastern Township Police Department classifies that incident—involving a ravine overpass on Route 128—as under investigation. The Shaylor family kept funeral services private as they grappled with what Mrs. Shaylor calls an "apparent suicide."

"I know Mason's music meant a lot to people, so I'd hoped to avoid public statements until the police investigation is complete," she says. "However, I cannot in good conscience allow these doulas he'd hired to continue negligent practices unchecked. Waiting even one more day to speak up could be a day too long for another family."

Parting Your Way is a holistic practice run by Kelly Monroe, an eldercare specialist who worked in assisted living before opening her business five years ago. "Many people are familiar with midwives and birth doulas, so that's a good jumping-off point for describing what we do at the other end of life's journey," Monroe says. "We offer care and companionship that supplements the sometimes limited assistance made available to terminal clients through the traditional health care system. If they're looking for hands-on guidance getting their affairs in order, or desiring more bedside hours than palliative care providers can offer, or just hoping to ease the caregiving burden on family, that's where we come in." Indeed, the Parting Your Way website boasts no shortage of glowing testimonials, and last year Monroe expanded, bringing on a doula partner, Nova Huston.

"According to his calendar, Mason met with Nova a minimum of twice a week," Mrs. Shaylor says. "When I looked up her business, my jaw hit the floor. Mason had no terminal illness to my knowledge, and he lived under my roof. If any doctor out there reading this was treating him for something I can find no record of, I'd love to hear about it."

Monroe and Huston declined to answer questions about Shaylor's case, but MTPD Officer Derrick Dover says they are cooperating with their investigation and no charges are currently pending. Monroe referred to allegations of wrongdoing as "unthinkable."

"We meet our clients wherever they are with their end-of-life transition. They steer what they want to get from their doula relationship," Monroe says.

"You can see my problem with *that*," Mrs. Shaylor says, "since I can only conclude that what my son wanted 'to get' was coaching for his impending suicide. If they were honestly too clueless to realize that, well, that's a problem, too."

Monroe cites the growing Death Positive Movement as a cornerstone of her philosophy that the subject of death should not be something we put off discussing until it is upon us. Reciting the cliché about death and taxes being unavoidable, Monroe explains that she regularly consults with non-terminal clients to help guide preparations she says everyone should make to be sure their wishes are honored, and to ease their fear of what happens when we die. However, she says those consults are typically on an as-need basis, and not part of an ongoing care relationship like that between Huston and Mason Shaylor.

Huston, however, brings to her work a unique perspective that not all doulas share, having been diagnosed with terminal cancer in 2015. Huston's mother, Diana, says her daughter is a rare case of what is known as "spontaneous remission," now cancer-free with neither medical intervention nor explanation, and that Huston has already outlived her life expectancy in unfailing health. A former journalist, Huston spent the years after her diagnosis traveling and moving through an assortment of jobs before landing at Parting Your Way in 2018.

"She's a walking miracle," the elder Huston says. "Maybe her clients find inspiration in that."

Huston's office, in an annex building, is a stark addition to the warm and welcoming Parting Your Way center maintained in Monroe's home, where she lives with her elementary school–aged daughter. Monroe explains that the two operate with independent client rosters but share consultation, resources, and referrals.

"I've not met her partner, but I know Kelly Monroe to be a thoughtful, caring practitioner. Locally, she's been at the forefront of this end-of-life doula trend, and whenever a patient expresses an interest, I have no qualms referring them her way," says Angel Seager, director of the Pleasant Bend Senior Facility that employed Monroe from 2004 through 2014. "However, anyone enlisting holistic care should understand those businesses aren't held to the regulatory standards that licensed practitioners are. As the eldercare crisis outgrows what our traditional system can bear, I wouldn't be surprised if we see more cases raising ethical questions that deserve to be addressed on the public stage."

That's where Mrs. Shaylor finds herself, in unchartered territory where she's struggled to find appropriate channels to file her complaints. "I'd urge anyone else in the care of so-called death doulas to reconsider. Think of all that could go wrong: You can never get these days with your loved ones back. If what they're offering sounds too good to be true, it is."

Parting Your Way appears to be the only end-of-life doula practice in the greater Cincinnati area, though the profession is fast growing, complete with rigorous online certification curriculums developed by advisory boards of oncology nurses, spiritual leaders, and elder law attorneys. Though Seager points out that virtually anyone can call themselves an end-of-life doula, both Monroe and Huston are certified.

In her heartbreaking search for answers, Mrs. Shaylor says she plans to pursue legal action to the fullest extent.

# 30

## *Willow*

Unbelievable. The irony was that Mom had clearly let her take the iPad last night just to get her out of her hair. Willow had gone along, gladly: Mom and Nova acted so fake and weird at dinner anyway.

Now, she knew why.

Willow sat calmly while the article spooled from the old printer a page at a time: one, two, three, four.

It wasn't enough to shove this cracked old tablet under their noses and yell, "You lied to me!" Paper would convey the permanence of what they'd done. Paper could be loud. Paper could be crushed between her fists, torn to shreds before their eyes. Paper could be soaked with tears.

Willow was used to her mom stretching the truth to suit her philosophies. But Nova?

Nova was so *what you see is what you get*—with everyone—that Willow had honestly not thought her capable of anything but the unfiltered truth.

Nova had understood that a separate client entrance would never be enough to keep Mom's work separate from their lives. Nova had at least tried to answer Willow's questions, getting that all she wanted was to understand better all these things Mom was convinced the rest of the world had wrong. Nova had quietly stepped in where Mom would not, in ways Mom wasn't even aware of.

Nova had been Willow's friend.

Until now.

To think all this time Willow had been agonizing over how to talk to *them* about Mason. She remembered everything about the last time she saw him: He'd been on his way in to see Nova and stopped to ask her about Toto. "He's still too scared to do what he's supposed to do," Willow had replied, defeated. And he'd said: "I'll tell you a secret, Willow. Everybody's scared." These past couple days, she'd started putting other little details together, started wondering . . . but it was tough to make sense of anything when you were grounded from everything.

If only she hadn't gotten caught sneaking out. She was learning how much you could obsess about those two little words: *if only*. But hey, why would Mom or Nova think that Willow—the other person who *lived here, where they worked*—could help them compare notes and piece together answers, or defend themselves, or at least feel better about *some* aspect of this mess? Why would they bother to do anything but discount her?

*Apparent suicide.*

*Walking miracle.*

Such a lot to absorb, alone in the wee hours in her bed: Maybe Mason's accident happened on purpose. Maybe he'd never been dying. Maybe Nova—the most *alive* person she knew—had been.

*Legal action to the fullest extent.*

Maybe Mom was in bigger trouble than even Maggie had realized. Could they lose the house? Was *malpractice* something you went to jail for? What would happen to Willow? How dare they leave her to learn all of this from a Google Alert. She didn't bother getting dressed for school. Just marched downstairs: messy hair, bare feet, nightgown. Papers in hand.

Mom was at the kitchen table with her back to Willow, speaking quietly into the phone. "Of course you didn't, Angel," she was saying. "Yes, she was quite slick here, too." There was a long pause, where Willow could imagine Mom's kind old boss fretting, walking back her comments from the article, for all the good it would do. Every Christmas Willow went with Mom to volunteer at Pleasant Bend, days of carols and cookies and gift wrapping. She'd learned to wear short sleeves because the heat was kept so high, and to stick near the residents who wore the biggest scowls—they were the most fun to win over.

Would they ever be welcome there again?

"It's kind of you to call. I'm not upset—not with you." Another pause. "I'm confident it's all a misunderstanding that will blow over."

She didn't sound confident. When she hung up, she took off her glasses and dropped her head to the table.

"Why did I have to read about what happened to Mason in the news?"

Mom jumped, hand to her heart. "Willow! You scared me." She pulled out a chair next to her, sighing heavily. "Sit."

Willow didn't sit. "Why did I have to read about what's happening to *you* in the paper?" She began ticking off her fingers. "You said Mason had an accident. You said the police being here was routine. You blew off my questions. The whole time, all this was going on, and you honestly thought you could keep it from me?"

"I've never believed there was anything to these accusations, Willow."

"Is suicide an *accusation*, Mom?"

"Suicide is . . ." Panic flashed on Mom's face. "A very serious, complicated issue. Even for adults to grapple with."

She'd used the same words last year, when she'd had to drop everything for a client on the brink of death from an opioid overdose. The woman had been outside of Mom's client demographic, but she'd also been Mom's hairdresser. Mom had never explained what made addiction or any death *not* involving old people too serious and complex for Willow to grasp. What she'd done was hire Nova, soon after.

"Do you honestly think I don't know what suicide is?" Willow stared at her, hard. "Do you think kids are oblivious to the reasons we're dragged into the auditorium for anti-bullying assemblies? Those speakers are literally begging us not to torment each other to death."

Actually, the speakers never said as much, but everyone heard the horror stories. All it took was one kid with an older sibling for word to get around.

Now, that kid they whispered about would be Willow. She could already picture her friends' breakfast tables. *That girl Willow you talk about . . . Isn't her mom Kelly Monroe?*

Even with the more accepting drama club crowd, no way would their parents want them anywhere near the daughter of that death doula who's being *investigated*.

Mom looked stunned. "Willow, I—I hope you know you can talk to me about anything."

"Untrue. We can talk about stuff you want to give me speeches on. Like why there's nothing weird about what you do. But when I ask anything you'd rather I didn't? Forget it."

"Oh, love, no. I so wish you didn't feel that way. I wish—" She shook her head. "Can we start over?"

"It's too late for that." Willow threw the papers onto the table. "Did you know all this about Nova? Did you both keep it from me?" She couldn't stand the idea of the two of them having long heart-to-hearts about how Nova had stared down death and then deeming Willow too young or dumb to handle it.

Mom didn't answer.

Only then did Willow wonder if the fact that neither of them had known was worse.

"Is this why you two have been weird around each other?" she demanded.

"I wouldn't say we've been weird . . ." The words faded at Willow's withering look.

"It's normal to sit on the porch bad-mouthing her with Maggie?"

"Nobody was *bad-mouthing* anybody. You're eavesdropping on me now?"

"How else am I supposed to find out anything around here? Besides waiting for the news story to be broadcast to the entire world?"

Willow knew she should force herself to slow down, take one question at a time, but the roaring flood of them overtook her.

"What does it mean for *us* if the business is in danger? Our family? And what about Nova—is *she* suicidal? Over Mason, and all this coming out when she clearly didn't want it to?"

"What? Of course not!"

"You talked her *off the roof* the other day."

"That was just Nova being Nova." Mom suddenly looked less sure.

The side door creaked open, and there Nova stood. Her face fell when she saw Willow, the exact opposite of her usual reaction. Nova was never about neutral waves or nods. She always, always lit up at the sight of people she loved. Willow. Mom.

Mason.

Every day since he'd left—even before they'd known he was gone for good—she'd looked a little paler, a little more defeated, a little less *Nova*.

"I always thought you were so brave!" Willow wheeled on Nova before Mom could register her presence. "When I step on the stage at practice and imagine the auditorium full of people, I tell myself, *Be like Nova.* But all this time, you were pushing me to do things you never got up the guts to do until you became this 'walking miracle'?" Nova winced at the words from the article, though her shoulders held their defiantly squared stance. Maybe Nova was mad at her own mom, too. For blabbing to that reporter, sharing a story that wasn't hers to tell.

"That doesn't mean I'm not brave," Nova said, and she looked sad about it, like she didn't *want* to be brave. Willow wondered if Nova could have somehow seen any of this coming. Did cheating death give you a sixth sense about its arrival? "And it definitely doesn't mean you're not brave. You are. I've never claimed it was a good idea for you to be like me."

"You didn't have to *claim* it. You just were wonderful. A wonderful, terrible liar!" Willow was yelling again, but no one moved to stop her.

Which could only mean she was right to be this upset. She basked in the righteousness, trying it on for size. A smug fit.

"I'm sorry, Willow," Nova said.

Three more words Mom would find any excuse not to say, even now. They were powerful. But they weren't enough.

# 31

## *Nova*

NOW

I flinch as Quinn Whitehall flings today's edition of the *Cincinnati Enquirer* on the desk between us, sending up a whoosh of angry air. I should have known Asha wouldn't bury her reporting in the *Business Courier* once she found more to it than just business. What's more surprising is that she published *this* fast. Like she knew she had to stay out ahead, lest Bonnie or Officer Dover or her own damned conscience convince her to stop.

"One of the charming things about visiting my dad is that he still gets an actual paper delivered," Quinn says drily.

I know this. He hovers over it with a magnifying glass, like an Appalachian Sherlock Holmes too stubborn for reading glasses, and when he tires of that, has me read aloud: the sports section, movie reviews, an occasional editorial if he's in the mood to argue. But I honestly did not know, when I retrieved Quinn from the airport before sunup this morning and deposited her at Mr. Whitehall's, that precisely this edition was on its way.

"Quinn." My voice shakes. "I'm horrified. But you know me better than to believe there's anything to this."

"Do I?" Her hands go to her hips. Not two hours ago, the poor woman told me how she'd barely napped on her red-eye flight. She's here on pure adrenaline—which, given the sleepless night I spent replaying my conversations with Bonnie and Kelly, makes two of us. "It's only a crazy coincidence that the day I arrive from two time zones away, the person responsible for my dad's care makes headline news? Forgive me if I feel like I'm missing something."

I suppose it's unwise to admit I feel that way, too. I've scarcely managed to do more than stare at Asha's words, absorbing the naked exposure of our biggest regrets and newest fears, imagining who else might be reading them. With each scroll through the harsh comments from strangers, I have the dizzying sensation that I need to sit down, though I already am.

"I understand. Listen, you've caught me on my way to a meeting to get this sorted." After Willow stalked back to her room this morning, Kelly informed me she'd called an emergency session of our consult group at ten a.m. sharp. Who knows how many members can or will spare the time for us during business hours, but she thinks it's our best shot at sourcing some collective PR and legal advice—while shoring up things with our tightest support network. "Why don't I come see you and your dad afterward, and we'll talk."

Midmorning, my inbox and voice mail are flooded with concerned messages, some friendlier than others. I should get back to them all: clients who have me on retainer, caregivers who've recommended me, hospice workers who see me on rotation, and Asha, who has the gall to blame her editor for the article's "aggressive tone"—but by the way, *would I be interested in a follow-up* that tells more of my side? And my dad.

*Your mother is sorry, but . . . She had no idea that's what the article was about, but . . .*

*But* they want to know. What to say to people. What to tell themselves.

What I might be guilty of.

"Let you get back to damage control? So you can come at me with some scripted statement? Nova, I'm here now. What the hell?"

Quinn is right. What business do I have attending the consult group, when the damage they're trying to control is me? And what's the point of returning other client calls if I can't figure out what to say to the one standing before me?

"If your business is in trouble," she continues, "Dad needs a backup plan. Even if the stuff about that musician isn't true, that article made some points."

I hold up a hand—*okay*—and she plops into the chair opposite my desk. Maybe Kelly won't be livid that I'm missing the meeting . . . maybe she'll be secretly relieved.

"The truth is," I begin. I wonder how long it's been since I've really known how to finish this sentence. Too long, it seems. So I stick to what I know for sure is true.

"I adore your father. I'm so sorry anything has made you question my capabilities, especially now, when you two have only a few days together. This is the last thing that should be clouding your visit. You hired me so you'd worry about him less, not more."

Quinn's shoulders lift, as if I'm easing some burden by arguing her points for her.

"If you want to cut ties, I get it. The only other local doula would be my partner, but I could pass along contacts in palliative care. Let me say this first: I'd never do anything to harm or neglect a client. I pride myself on treating them the way I'd want to be treated in their shoes."

"Because you've been in their shoes?" She's asking, without asking, whether it's true.

"Similar shoes. I'd never claim to be in anyone else's. I've seen how differently they all fit, so I try not to judge."

"Not even Mason Shaylor?"

I shake my head. "Not even now."

"You were surprised to learn . . . what he'd done?"

"Surprised and heartbroken." My voice cracks. I will not cry now. If I start now, I won't be able to stop.

She sighs. "If that's true, then I'm here piling onto a nightmare for you."

"You're here being a good daughter." I know how much she's trusted me with. She wants me to assure her she still can. And for the sake of Kelly and Parting Your Way, I should be falling all over myself to do just that. But I don't seem to have it in me.

She turns her gaze out the window, and we sit in silence for a moment. "Sometimes when we're talking late at night," she says finally, softly, "Dad makes these comments. Like: *This is no way to live, playing golf on a screen.* Does he say things like that to you?" Her eyes fill with tears, still fixed on some distant point.

"No more than anyone else," I promise.

It's little comfort to either of us.

# 32

*Nova*

THEN

"Hold the phone," I say. "Your brother lives *here,* and you're staying with your *mom?*"

Somewhere other than Ohio, you'd call Bo's place a ranch, maybe, or an estate. It's tucked in a rural area north of Cincinnati known for picturesque state parks: Caesar's Creek, Cowan Lake, Fort Ancient. As we rumble toward the gravel patch where a dozen cars are already parked, the floor-to-ceiling windows of Bo and Sara's rustic-luxury A-frame brighten the night, illuminating the glassy surface of his private pond, the paddleboats tied to the sundeck, and the silhouettes of the barn and kennels beyond. Mason had mentioned Sara breeds designer dogs, and fences mark the fields where she must let them run. Beyond the house, a massive bonfire shines bright against the dense woods, with a group clustered around it in a mishmash of camp chairs, Adirondacks, and loungers. A burst of laughter drifts on the cool air.

Mason shrugs, not turning to meet my eyes. "It's my turn to take the mom shift."

"Your words, or Bo's?"

He thrusts the Jeep into park and cuts the engine. "Not mine. But he's not wrong."

"What does your brother do?"

"Partnered early in a contractor business that got big."

"High-end clients?"

He nods. "And lucky breaks. Not that he'd admit it."

To be fair, I think all three of us know about those. I'm not here to be fair, though. Mason specifically asked me not to come as his doula, and the truth is, I was glad. Still, it's a line from doula training that comes to mind now—the one I think of every time someone is dismissive of my own family hang-ups: *Advice is often wrong. Listening is always right.*

So as we grab our chairs and cooler and head across the grass to join the party, I make no judgments. And when Mason introduces me to Bo, I politely thank him for the Gold Pass.

Bo laughs heartily. He's a taller, meatier cut of Mason, and the way his guests all keep turned toward him with anticipation, he'd clearly be the life of this party even if he wasn't hosting. He's got that conventional handsomeness where, if he turned up to lead a renovation in your house, even a happily married, totally sensible adult female would be on the phone in the other room, giggling to her girlfriends.

"Don't thank me," he says. "From what I hear, we made out better *not* being there that day."

"This is true." I smile. "Your place is gorgeous. Bet this land could tell some stories."

"Did Mase tell you how my neighbors found a half-buried moonshine still?" I shake my head, eyes widening. "Complete with a sawed-off shotgun."

Bo goes on about the juicier local history—some rumor about an old brothel house by the river—while we unfold our chairs. "Sara!

Come meet Mason's friend Nova." I squint at the raven-haired, curvy figure sashaying toward us and am momentarily sidelined by disbelief that I actually passed for this woman. Mason was either really confident in the Kings Island gate agents' incompetence, or his view of me is wildly distorted.

"Hey, Nova," she calls. "What a great name." She turns her smile on Mason, and I follow his eyes to the black ball of fur I only now notice her cradling. "Want to hold a puppy? Of course you do." She thrusts a squirming, adorable doodle into his arms. "I'm about to put them away for the night. Everyone else has had their turn."

Mason lowers into his chair and I watch the puppy make itself at home in his lap. "Okay, this is the second time I've seen you loving on a dog. You tempted?"

"Trust me, this dog is out of my price range."

"Surely there's a family discount?" I look to Sara, who smiles nervously in Bo's direction, but he's talking to another guest and doesn't hear. I drop into my chair next to Mason and lower my voice. "You got a better plan for that money you won?"

I'd honestly love to know. It hasn't come up since he treated Willow and me at the ice cream shop. But he just says: "I'll know it when I see it," and hands the puppy back to Sara, who carries him off toward the barn.

It's one of those nights where strangers seem fast friends. Bo holds court, dipping in and out of conversations long enough to call out connections—*Liam was at that football game, too, weren't you, Liam? Sandy's boys are about the same age as yours, Becca.* It's been a while since I've found myself surrounded by people having such easy, laid-back fun, and it's contagious. I know things are rarely as simple as they seem. Still, at this moment, from this vantage—the ring of warmth wrapping around us, hazy stars above, fizz on my tongue, laughter in the air, hell, even designer puppies making the rounds—it's hard to imagine anyone could need to be strong-armed into being here. Who knows, maybe Mason is thinking the same thing—even he seems relaxed. So when Sara says she's headed to the house for snacks, I offer to go along and help.

Before I know it, I'm admiring her aggressively stainless steel kitchen. It's enormous, with two farmhouse sinks, each adjoining a full-sized cooktop. I count three ovens.

"Wow. You must really love to cook."

"I do." Breezing into the pantry, she tosses a couple bags of marsh-mallows onto the granite island behind her. "Mason has a standing invite to our Sunday dinners. He should bring you sometime."

"He does?" I guess I don't hide my surprise, because she laughs a little sadly and sets down a box of graham crackers, stopping to regard me.

"Not that he comes. You know, if they'd leave their mom out of it, the boys would get along fine."

I stop short of asking why, what's the deal. Instead I reach for the tote bag waiting on the counter and start loading up the supplies: wet wipes, paper plates, Hershey's bars. "We haven't met yet," I say care-fully, "so I don't have an impression of her."

She looks impressed. "How have you managed that? He lives there!"

"Catlike stealth."

She laughs, handing me a pack of bamboo skewers and leaning against the counter behind her. "When I first met Bo, I did worry she came across as, you know, *overinvested.*"

This conversation is taking a presumptive tone. Mason introduced me as a friend, but she's assuming I'm his plus one. Still, I can't resist: "But she's not?"

"Oh, no, she totally is." This time, we both laugh. "I used to wonder if she was waiting for someone to actually say the words: *All those years of sacrifice, you did good! You're done, you're free!*"

"Has anyone tried?"

She raises her hand with an exaggerated cringe. "Turns out you could also view overinvestment as a thing you earn."

You know those women who you kind of expect to dislike, even kind of *want* to dislike, but the more you talk to them, the more you basi-cally . . . don't? That's Sara.

"I minded less after I had kids," she went on. "Maybe a part of me kind of got it."

"Can I ask: Wasn't she proud? Of what Mason was out there achieving?"

"She knows every word of every song he's written. Bo does, too. But she hung on those lyrics because at times, she felt that was *all* she had."

"Do you think she views Mason as ungrateful to her?"

"I've never heard her say that. But Bo does. Between us? He might be a bit jealous."

I look around me—at Bo's gorgeous wife, state-of-the-art-kitchen, magazine-worthy portraits of his kids on the walls—and think of what an odd beast jealousy can be.

And of how much I like being taken for someone who matters to Mason as much as he's starting to matter to me.

# 33

## *Mason*

It wasn't that Mason regretted bringing Nova to Bo's. She was the only thing tipping this evening into the enjoyable side of tolerable. The problem, he'd realize later, was that Nova and Bo offset each other in a way that gave Mason the illusion of feeling . . . balanced.

Where the mere sight of Bo riled him up, one look at Nova calmed him down. Where Bo was a person he should want to be close to but instead justified avoiding, Nova was a person he should hold at arm's length but instead rationalized keeping near. Where Nova was painfully willing to sift through everything he'd lost in search of something he could reclaim, Bo was impatiently stuck in a good riddance shrug, annoyed that his brother couldn't cut his losses and get on with things already.

"It's not that I'm unsympathetic," Bo had told him once. "It's that you're wallowing. It's useless, Mase."

*Useless* was a word Bo tended to apply to things he personally did not have use for. A word he had no problem extending to Mason's early musical ambitions, Mason's place in the family, even Mason himself.

A word Mason could not imagine Nova using for much of anything. Certainly never for a person.

Mason would take responsibility in exactly one part of what went wrong: He hadn't accounted for how disarming Nova would be—and not just to Bo. As Bo coaxed Nova to regale them all with their Diamondback story, Mason couldn't stop watching her, trying to recall the last time he'd let himself really know a woman. Marveling that he could guess at what Nova was thinking: For example, the way surprise washed over her face when she caught herself laughing at something Bo said, and on the receiving end of a warm hug from Sara. Like she didn't doubt Mason had good cause to dread this, and thus was waiting for their asshole sides to show.

He'd tried to tell her the most unlikable thing about Bo was how he was with Mason . . . and only Mason. And he'd never said Sara was an asshole. It was just hard to overlook that she'd married one.

Bo's friends were an affable bunch, most of them contractors of some kind, too—a carpenter, stone worker, landscape architect— teasing Mason that he fit in by name if nothing else. There was an age-old camaraderie inherent in gathering around a fire, especially under such a clear sky. Nova and Sara went together to collect fixings for s'mores and came back chatting like old friends. Mason belly laughed at a story about how a dropped nail on a site had ruined someone's day with impeccable timing, right when his new girlfriend showed up with his lunch. The guys started retelling their most embarrassing injuries on the job, but then it wasn't just laughs—honest talk about how a stupid mistake can cost you, put you in your place until you recover.

When Bo first drew his little brother into the conversation, it was almost like he was simply making sure no one felt left out while they talked shop.

Almost.

"Talk about ego checks," Bo said. "At least we're dealing with the ER, where those docs have seen it all and the waiting room is not exactly a public image contest. Try having to go to a sports medicine clinic for a regular guy injury. Right, Mase?"

Nova tensed beside Mason before he registered his own freeze response—but Bo didn't even look their way from his spot a few seats over, where Sara now perched in his lap. He just thumbed his hand in their direction. "Mase and I are in this waiting room surrounded by, like, linebackers. Big men, even the teenagers. And they're all obviously out of commission in a big-man way—casts, walking boots, but even injured, these guys look chiseled out of granite. Like their crutches might not hold them." His audience laughed appreciatively.

"Then there's Mason," Bo went on, "who weighs *maybe* a buck seventy-five soaking wet, the only dude there who doesn't have athletic logos stamped across his T-shirt, pants, socks." He claws his hands out in front of him, elbows bent, like one of those inflatable T. rex costumes. "'Help me, doc, I play too much guitar.'"

The way it went down, Bo's friends probably assumed Bo forgot himself, got carried away with the help of too many beers. He made for a forgivable, even sympathetic antagonist—Mason got that, even as the one being antagonized.

The others missed the key component, though:

Context.

Only two people had that, other than Bo and Mason. Sara, who suddenly became intent on peering off toward the woods. And Nova, whose look of pleasant surprise had been replaced with a distinctly incredulous disappointment. Like it was so obvious this would go over badly, she couldn't fathom how Bo could be this clueless, unless he was this cruel.

Mason had to fight the urge to turn to her and say, "Weird, right?"

The laughter erupted again.

"An ego check, huh?" Mason didn't so much find his voice as it found him. "For which one of us was that?"

"Aw, come on, Mase." Bo tipped back his beer can, found it empty, and dropped it to the ground. "One day you're going to have to be able to laugh about this stuff."

Mason got his point—he did. He and Bo *had* been fish out of water that day. This would make for a funny bit if it weren't so serious.

Or if—maybe—Bo had nudged him to see the humor another night, while chilling in front of a Reds game, just the two of them. No audience.

But he and Bo didn't do *just the two of them*.

"You're right," Mason said. Nova's knee moved ever so slightly to press against his. "I just wish I'd realized it would be so humiliating for you. Not that I could have driven myself, with my limp little musician arms in splints at the time."

Calling out Bo was not unfair. But that didn't make the ensuing silence less awkward.

"Hey." A guy on the ground next to Bo rocked forward, elbows on knees. "I heard about this violinist who had to have brain surgery, and they had her stay awake and play the violin *during the operation* to make sure they weren't damaging her ability to play. I guess they couldn't do that for you?"

Mason smiled tightly. He'd seen that article. He'd watched its glossy edges turn to flame, then to ash in a fire ring smaller than this. Right after he'd doused it with lighter fluid.

"I guess it's unlucky my brain is fine," he said drily. "Kind of hard to play the guitar while they're slicing open your arm."

"Oh. Right."

The barometer plummeted as all eyes averted from Mason. What was he doing? The only sympathy he was inspiring was for Bo—everyone here now pulling for their host to save face. In fact, if Mason didn't want this to become the thing they'd all go home gossiping about, the smart move would've been to let it ride.

He'd spent too much time lately measuring just how far the distance between knowing the smart move and making the smart move could grow.

"It is terrible being in a waiting room you don't belong in." Nova spoke up, clear and strong. "Like, in the ER, everyone is either having a really unlucky day, or they're a dumbass, so it's interesting you feel so at home there, Bo." Mason's mouth twitched with the threat of a smile. *Did she just—?*

"I mean, back when I was sidelined by cancer, I found waiting rooms *so* jarring."

Mason's head snapped toward her, leaving the smile behind.

"There I was, never smoked, followed the rules, never really stuck my neck out for anything, and yet suddenly surrounded by these way more cancery people. You know, the ones who probably asked for it?" She rolled her eyes. "Hilarious, right?"

Mason's mouth hung ajar. She was really laying this story on perfect strangers—the one she hated to tell, the one she'd gone to lengths to keep hidden—to defend him.

"God," Sara said. "Nova, we had no idea."

"Of course you didn't." Her tone remained friendly. "But you know, if you think about it, a linebacker willingly assumes a risk: There's a good chance he's gonna get torn up. Whereas someone who's just happily playing music, oblivious it could be physically taken from him? You got one thing right: He's the one in that waiting room who doesn't deserve to be there. Guess I just never saw it as funny."

Nova got to her feet, hands on hips. "Nice chatting, but I'm hoping Mason could give me the backstage tour to more of this old, beautiful land? I can't resist anything with such great stories behind it."

Bo looked as stunned as Mason felt. Not embarrassed or put off—more like he'd just realized something, too.

"Backstage passes are my specialty." Mason jumped up and fumbled with their chairs. Nova already had the cooler by the handle. "By foot or by Jeep?" he asked.

"That question is an insult to Jeeps."

She reached for his hand as they turned back to where they'd parked. Behind them, the chatter restarted, but he didn't bother to eavesdrop. For the first time since he'd come home, he didn't have to pretend he didn't care what anyone said.

# 34

*Nova*

THEN

From our vantage point at the far edge of Bo's property—where the woods end in a wide, long slope down to a glimmering creek—the sky is a perforated tent, a million pin-dot holes letting pure white light shine through. They make an artful reminder: If you back far enough away from a ball of fire, all that remains is a sparkle. And maybe it was at the heart of it all along. Maybe you just started out too close to see.

Mason had turned the Jeep's headlights down the dirt back road and blown by the party in a cloud of dust. We'd bumped and wound between the trees in silence until the road ran out and he backed us waterfront in a three-point turn. He seemed nimbler around the Jeep in the dark, none of the pained, sluggish movements that marked his days, as he made quick work of removing the roof, folding in the seats, and rolling out mats that fit the truck bed so perfectly they could only be custom. We sprawled on our backs, close but not touching, and looked up.

Up, and away.

Waking with the sun tunes you to the natural rhythms of the world. Staring into the opposite end of the day, I'm usually spent. But now, I can't remember the last time I felt so awake. I didn't stop to think through what it would mean to reveal so much of myself in Mason's defense. But I'm not sorry I did.

It's reassuring: When all the moment required was for me to be my real self, there I was.

"Thanks." Mason's voice, when he breaks the silence at last, holds such emotion it's crackling under the weight. "That was . . . more than was called for."

I swivel my head toward him and find his eyes intent on mine, our faces inches apart. My breath catches.

"Sorry if I—"

He shakes his head, and I leave it. Neither of us is sorry.

"Does it get easier," he asks, "talking about your story?"

"Only to you," I whisper. He slides an arm around me, nesting my head under his chin, and we're engulfed in an intense rush of emotion so warm it seems to have some source beyond us, beyond reach. Like he's pushed wide open a door that we'd both assumed to be locked, but never tried before, though it was right there between us all along. Because what's on the other side is so sought-after, so rare, how could it possibly be a mere handle turn away? How could anyone really just walk on through?

We stay that way a long time, simply occupying this new space, pressed together, not wanting to break the spell. It's funny, things that pop into your head when you know your life is about to change. What I'm thinking is that I can't be Mason's doula anymore. The jig is up: He knows that I'm no wise spirit guide. That I'm as lost as everyone else, probably more so. Which is just as well, because this kind of intimacy is definitely not allowed. I should resign now, should have resigned *by* now, but that would involve conversation, and this—it's beyond words.

When I finally pull back to look at him, he isn't smiling. "I haven't told you how relieved I am," he says, so soft I can barely hear, "that your story has such a happy ending."

"Does it?"

I'm not being facetious or coy. I honestly don't know. Don't even think I've reached the real end yet. I know what he means, though. He means my prognosis. He means I gave him a scare, in the possibility that the doctors might have been right. Might still be proven right.

But he has a prognosis, too.

He tucks my hair behind my ear. He seems about to kiss me.

I seem about to let him.

I close my eyes as our foreheads touch. We both smell of the bonfire, that smoky musk I'd already associated with Mason, and it permeates my heart with an ache that feels like missing him already. I flatten my hand on his chest, firmly enough to stop his lips, molecules away.

"Tell me," I breathe, "you're not really dying."

It's a plea and a prayer and the cruelest possible thing a doula of all people—a source of comfort, of acceptance, of *all is well*—could ever say to a dying man. But I can't keep the words in. I've never so badly, my entire life, wanted anything to be true.

This warmth and this ache and this smell and these stars and this whole night, all of it is much more than affection or desire or understanding. It can only be love, the invisible force defying gravity and logic to pull us this far against all manner of resistance, and we're hanging, suspended at the top of that huge first hill, and I can't stand not knowing if we're about to plunge forward or roll back. If I have to take it one second longer, I'll throw off my harness and jump.

Mason's hands are cradling the back of my head, and tears are in my eyes, and his voice sounds gruff with surrender. Then his lips are on mine, and everything else is lost.

Everything except his words, echoing in my ears.

"I'm not," he'd said, drawing a slow, shaky breath, "really dying."

# 35

## *Kelly*

NOW

Kelly couldn't say which part of her day had been the worst. The publication of Asha's article was the logical low point, but that had come so early, it already seemed years ago. There had been so many new lows since then:

The silent treatment from her fifth grader, who'd slammed herself in her room, refusing to go to school.

The reporters—locally and beyond. There were calls from Nashville, from L.A., from *IndiePulse* and something called *Under the Radar,* even someone claiming to be with *Rolling Stone.* They rang her phone, filled her inbox, spammed her direct messages, even showed up with camera crews, content to broadcast from the curb when she didn't answer the door.

The clients who pulled their business right away. The clients who put her on notice. The clients who called to more supportively ask what on earth was going on.

*Yes, it is sad.* She had a habit of nodding into the room, though of course they couldn't see her through the phone. *No, I don't believe you ever would have crossed paths here . . .* She listened, agreed some more. *No, dragging us through the mud won't bring him back. Yes, we'd gladly be dragged if it would. We feel for his mother. We share her pain.*

"I understand this is upsetting—it is for us, too," Kelly told caller after caller. "What I'd like to ask is for you to hold a space for that uncertainty right now. Our hope is that this will straighten itself out in time, and that no one will make any hasty decisions about their relationship with Parting Your Way until it does."

Some clients sounded genuinely sorry, saying they wished they had the luxury of waiting to see how this played out.

Others simply said they had enough uncertainty in their lives, *thank you very much.*

Most devastating was the provider network she'd spent years building—the people who, regardless of any lawsuit or its eventual outcome, Parting Your Way couldn't exist without.

"What's all this nonsense?" her favorite oncologist gruffed. Kelly always had a good laugh with the patients he sent her way: *He says he doesn't know what goes on here, only that people seem to like it.* A skeptical referral could weirdly be the best kind.

Kelly leveled with him. "I know of exactly one case where public accusations of a woman calling herself an end-of-life doula held water: She was at best an opportunist, at worst a predator, had no training. Any of us could have spotted her miles away."

Doulas weren't oblivious to the havoc a disgruntled family member who materializes after the death could wreak—disputing the client's last wishes, questioning the doula's motives or integrity. When emotions and stakes ran high, throw in a messy signature on a form or a sentimental ring missing from its box, and rational thinking didn't always prevail. Every doula had at least one case that left her shaky, vulnerable, and relieved it was over.

*Clearly unfounded in your case,* the oncologist agreed. *Out of proportion.*

"Let me know when it's blown over, will you? It's a pisser, but I can't send anyone else your way until it does."

It was the network that signaled how deep and wide this could go. How fast.

How powerless she was to stop it.

Not *I'm sorry*, but *it's a pisser*.

Not *screw this, carry on*, but, *let us know when the coast is clear*.

Would the world have cared so much if Mason hadn't been Mason? If the same story had played out with someone whose name didn't carry the intrigue of the fan-favorite musician?

It was tough to say, but didn't really matter. Because it was Mason. And because Kelly cared more than all of them put together.

Kelly had to do something.

But only one person—*one*—from the professional consult group she'd founded had shown up when she'd begged an SOS meeting today.

And that person—she could still hardly believe this—wasn't even Nova.

It was Maggie.

Maggie launched right into her speech. "Here are two women doing the hard, important work of lifting people up—all hours of the night, no matter who calls, you're there, holding their hand, all but literally walking with them 'through the valley of the shadow of death' when no one else will or can. Then along comes some entitled white man playing games, thinking of no one but himself, ruining it for everyone else, and somehow it's your fault? And now you're left to clean up his mess for his mommy and everyone else who can't accept *he* is responsible for doing this fucked-up thing? Patriarchy bullshit is what this is!"

"O-kay," Kelly said slowly. "I'm not sure a feminist rant is warranted right now."

"A feminist rant is always warranted."

That at least made her smile. Kelly collapsed onto the couch of her office suite with a groan. Maggie surveyed the empty room, hands on hips.

"Where's Nova?"

Kelly closed her eyes. "I asked her to be here."

"Wow. And you worried she'd think you were hanging *her* out to dry?"

"Maybe something held her up."

"Something more important than this?"

When Kelly didn't answer, the cushion next to her dipped under Maggie's weight. "Kel? Don't you think it's time to consider maybe Mason's mother is at least partially right? Maybe not about anything nefarious, but that he was never terminal and Nova failed to identify the real issue? If you want a shot at saving yourself here, I don't think Nova can stay on."

"But . . ." Kelly sat up, hugging her knees. She'd been trying so hard *not* to consider this. Was it really worth ruining everything for? "If the police rule his death an accident, this all goes away."

"Is there some indication that's about to happen?"

Kelly sighed.

"I don't have a track record of bad advice. If you'd listened to me about that reporter . . ."

"Don't remind me. And don't get me wrong: I'm angry with Nova. Not just about Mason. Be honest: Is it unfair to think she should've been more up-front about her past when she signed on?"

"No. It's called a lie of omission."

"Was it though? We are talking about private medical history. Who am I to say she didn't have the right to leave it out?"

"But it's relevant to your work. And she should've foreseen that you'd find out some other way and feel betrayed when you did."

"I can't decide if I feel betrayed or just hurt that she didn't trust me enough. Maybe not at first, but at *any* point over the past year. Like our whole friendship was . . . not what I thought."

Maggie's face darkened. "We're not in middle school. Your business is on the line."

Kelly wasn't blind: She knew Maggie never cared for Nova. But maybe it hadn't been driven by jealousy, the way Kelly always assumed. This *wasn't* middle school; maybe Maggie had a better sense about Nova all along.

"But Nova has a stake in Parting Your Way now, too."

"Even if this is cleaned up publicly—say the police do rule accidental death, or Bonnie loses her lawsuit—will you trust Nova again the way you need to?"

Kelly wanted to. Nova had already lost so much. The idea of cutting this last tie . . .

"Parting Your Way is your baby." Maggie sounded so sure. "Imagine if Willow's father showed up out of nowhere, first time in twelve years. Would you let him make all kinds of trouble just because he technically has some claim to her?"

Like hell she would.

That was the thought that stayed with Kelly though the rest of her terrible, lonely day. When evening came and she'd managed to return only a small percentage of her messages, panic overtook her. It was Friday night. She'd have to wait the entire weekend before she could reach anyone else during business hours.

By Monday, misconceptions could have taken firmer hold, spread further. By Monday, it might be too late for damage control. The damage irreparably done.

She stared into her cup of tea, ready to trade it for something stronger.

Then, in walked Nova. She dropped into the chair opposite Kelly's desk, looking sorry.

But not sorry enough.

"You blew off the consult meeting," Kelly said icily.

"I didn't blow it off. A client confronted me—I had to make a judgment call."

"And you couldn't come out here after? Literally all day?"

"I called. You didn't answer. Reporters were outside. I'm here now." It was as good as any explanation—but Kelly realized Maggie was right. From now on, no explanation would seem good enough.

"Client retention seemed the priority," Nova added. "I was at it all day, trying to help."

"You call this helping?"

"Kelly, I know it's been a terrible day. I'm so sorry."

Normally, Kelly would have returned the sentiment, or at least offered Nova the drink she wanted herself. But maybe the sooner they accepted nothing was going back to normal, the better. Their eyes locked, and Nova nodded slowly, somewhere between understanding and disbelief.

"You . . . don't want my help. Anymore."

Kelly didn't answer. Nova blinked several times, fast, and for a second, Kelly thought she might burst into tears, run from the room.

Instead, Nova sat straighter. "You're comfortable with taking on a partner, as long as the partner simplifies your life and never runs into complications of her own? Is that it?"

Kelly's face flushed. How dare she? "They're not *of your own*. Safe to say they're my complications too at this point."

"So that's it, things get complicated and we fall apart? Since for once I can't handle all the messier stuff for you?"

"What's that supposed to mean?"

"I have never heard of another doula picking and choosing like you do. Was there some *selective death* training module I missed? Because if so, sign me up!"

"Unfair, Nova. Sooner or later we all have to face things we don't want to. That doesn't mean I should have to face the consequences of your actions."

"My actions? I took on Mason based on *your* initial assessment. In fact, I didn't even make a determination to take him on—you assigned him to me."

Kelly's gut twisted with the truth of it. But no. They were far past that.

"Maybe if you'd pressed him on filling out those forms," Kelly tried. "If just once, when you didn't know what to do, you stuck with all the resources I gave you instead of making it up as you go."

"Those forms overwhelmed him. And do you know what I told him?

I told him no one wants to do them—even the hospice profession is full of people who have yet to complete their own advance directives. Even people who spend all day confronting death don't want to contemplate their own."

She said this pointedly, and Kelly bristled. What business was it of Nova's whether Kelly had filled out her own directives? Why should Kelly honestly discuss her future with someone who hadn't been honest about her past?

Nova went on: "Besides, if someone wants to argue he hired us to get his ducks in a row, him refusing your 'resources' doesn't fit their theory."

"It doesn't matter what fits. It matters what's all over the internet, ruining our lives!"

Nova shook her head. "You're the one who taught me how toxic it is to want someone to blame for every death. The client's spouse and their secondhand smoke, or the doctor who didn't catch the tumor, or the clients themselves for their lifestyle choices. You call it 'unproductive' and 'unhealthy' for blame to have any place in end of life. Yet here you are coming after me."

"At least I'm honest with my clients about what I'm equipped to handle, and I expect them to be honest with me in turn. I think it's fair for me to expect that much from a partner."

"I wasn't dishonest."

"I can't get past it, Nova. All those late nights we bonded over our calling to do this work, and not once did you mention the truth about yours. I was so real with you. I let you into my business, my home, my family."

Tears pooled in Nova's eyes. "I loved those talks. Keeping that to myself was never about you. I would never have done anything to jeopardize you. This. Willow."

Kelly tried to swallow the lump in her throat, but it was lodged there, where it had been since the day Mrs. Shaylor arrived. Where she suspected it would remain for some time. Being mad at Nova was easier than being this horribly sad.

"I will look back at this year and remember how nice it was, not to be alone in the business, not to be alone in . . ." She drew a deep, shaky breath. *Picking and choosing*, Nova had called it. The words still stung. "But I've let that cloud my judgment. I may have hated all the red tape when I worked at the nursing home, but I understood why it existed. And I can't pretend I didn't know you were never big on guidelines. That much is on me."

Nova's eyes betrayed growing panic not unlike Kelly's own. "Can I have a few days? To pack up and figure out where I'm going to go?" Where *would* she go? But they couldn't turn back now. They'd said too much, yet somehow still not enough.

"Fine. Actually, it might be best to wait until you can escape notice." Kelly didn't relish the thought of photographers catching Nova hauling away boxes, a meme in waiting. *Death of a career.*

"If it's okay, I'd like to say bye to Willow. Maybe even still come see her as Dorothy?"

"That's up to her."

Kelly stayed there long after Nova had gone, in the room where families came to face the inevitable, doing what they all do: wishing for a rewind button, a lost chance to get things right.

Wishing, even now, for more time.

# 36

## *Nova*

### THEN

My eyes snap open into the gray dawn, alert to the soft trills of bird-song.

Gray. Beyond the rails of the Jeep, the world remains all but dark. My eyes fall closed again, relieved. There's still time before the sun.

Even if there weren't, I wouldn't want to move—to wake this man beside me, to leave the delicious luxury of skin-on-skin, limb on limb. And if I don't want to, why feel like I *have* to? Maybe what started as a healthy ritual has morphed into superstition. Maybe, it's driven not only by gratitude but fear—that if I don't greet the daybreak it may not come.

Maybe I've never been as good at any of this as I thought.

But here, this moment—no, this second—with Mason, I don't want to think. Not about the things we said, the line we crossed, or what happens next.

I just want to breathe him, keep him close. Be.

I nestle into the crook of Mason's arm, beneath the layers of blankets he pulled over us in the night. His skin is the smoothest thing about him—not the rough hide he'd have people believe. Even this truck bed beneath us is much more comfortable than I'd imagined when he told me he used to sleep here. Everything cut to fit. His breathing is even but shallow, and I wonder if he's awake. I'm not ready to look. Not ready to—

My phone's ringtone slices through the dawn.

I sit up, holding a blanket to my bare chest as I search out my jacket, feeling for the vibration of the ring in its deep pocket. This will be Mia Timson, confirming her father didn't last the night, and though I'm sad for them, I'm glad to put these clients behind me. As I catch it on the third ring, Mason's hand falls on my back, his fingers tracing a line that could lay me right back down.

That I'd never let myself imagine this physicality with Mason had made it so much more powerful. Like that first cool gust on a stifling day that turns your face toward the wind, letting it blow back your hair and soothe your skin, wondering how you never realized how parched you were, how lovely it is. How now that it's begun you never want it to end.

"Nova? It's Christine."

I blink, clearing the sleep from my eyes. Christine. Not a Timson. The palliative care worker who'd befriended Glenna in caring for Wendell—and when she apologizes for the hour, the words crackle, like she's broken up about something.

Christine doesn't do broken up.

And before she says another word, I know.

She tells me anyway. How Glenna was her first appointment of a very early day—and her knock received no answer. She doesn't patronize me by saying we should be grateful she passed peacefully, in her sleep. We both know. We are. But also we're not. Because fuck that.

"Glenna," I tell Mason. I can't look at him as I hang up, can't take seeing my sadness reflected there. It's not just that Glenna is—was—her lovable, irresistible self. She's also a reminder that we can't not think about what's brought Mason and me together in the first place.

*I'm not really dying,* he said.

I told him to say it. Begged.

Was he just—were we just—pretending?

"Oh no." He sits up, and I let his bare, scarred arms engulf me. Over his shoulder, the sun is rising. If not for Christine's call, I'd be nudging him awake to see it right now, and I would not be thinking of how it's rising without Glenna and Wendell and Emma and too many other clients and friends. I'd be thinking of how many more times it might rise for us, just like this.

"I have to go. Before they take her. I was meant to be there when she . . ." A sob clogs my throat. I can't finish, but I don't have to. Mason knows. Just as he knows that Glenna meant more to me than any business arrangement could cover.

"Of course," he says, the exact right way, not gruff or annoyed or anything but tender. "I'll take you wherever you need to go." When we roll past Bo's house moments later, everything is still—the dew-covered cars of the guests who stayed, the empty chairs encircling the smoldering fire ring, the fields waiting for the barns to open. The whole expanse looks different in the daylight—still lovely, but ordinary enough that I can almost believe I imagined last night: the imperfect introduction to Bo and Sara, and everything right about Mason and I falling, and the sad call that has us rudely leaving too early to say goodbye. *Thanks.* I send the silent message with one last look as we pull away.

*I'll make it up to you.*

I have three days to pull the memorial service together. Being solely responsible for a client's wishes in the absence of family is every bit as overwhelming as I'd feared. Disorienting, too, being so anxious to do exactly right by Glenna, and so alone in the interim, mourning her.

Kelly covers the Timsons, who by that afternoon are planning a funeral, too. I stop by to pay respects and find the family distracted and, having had little time to grow attached to me, unfazed by Kelly taking my place. Their son swings on a red plastic disc beneath a tree in the side yard, the way only a child can on such a day, though maybe everybody should. If only grieving didn't involve so much to *do.* Kelly hugs me tight in their driveway. *This is why we have each other,* she reminds me. Signing the right number of clients is a tricky balance; too few and you can't make a living. Too many and you risk overlap when they need you most. *Focus on Glenna,* she assures me. *I got this.*

Every waking moment, I'm on the phone with the venue, printing poetry cards, sorting belongings earmarked for recipients who will be attending from out of town. You'd think all our planning would make it easy, but so much of this couldn't be done ahead of time, and I worry I won't finish. I take my meals there, cleaning out Glenna's fridge, thawing one of the casseroles from the biddies and laughing out loud at that first inedible bite. I pull long hours, sleeping on her couch.

And when I do? I'm missing Mason. A constant, throbbing ache that intensifies with sleep, when my body curls around the memory of his, and my mind wraps around his last words to me under the stars, before neither of us had any words left at all:

*I'm not really dying.*

It was hardly something I could ask him to clarify as I rushed off to meet the coroner's van. I think of the way Kelly might say, going into a new client consult, "Tell me I don't have to explain inheritance laws again," and I'd obediently recite, "You don't have to explain inheritance laws again," and then we'd both smile wryly, because odds were, she was about to field no fewer than a dozen questions on the subject—but for a moment, it was nice pretending. I consider all the empty things people say that no one can actually deliver: *This will turn out to be a blessing in disguise. The worst won't happen. I'm sure everything will be fine.*

Is it possible—anything more than a crazy wish—he said it because it's true? Because it's been true all along? And if so, what to do with that? As a woman who's heart-to-ground crazy for him, I want to cheer. As a doula who he ostensibly enlisted to help him die, I have questions. Concerns that can't be pushed aside.

But they have to wait. These days belong to Glenna. Mason offered to help, that first morning, but untangling things with him at the same time seemed too much, so I declined, saying I'd catch him on the other side. In the meantime, he sends texts that make me smile: emojis of a campfire, a Jeep, trees. Stars. Part of me wants to break and call him, but the idea of forcing a heavyweight talk that should happen in person—no. The icons he sends are kind and reassuring. That while I might worry about what he said, I don't have to worry if he regrets what we did.

When the doorbell rings, I'm expecting Kelly, who offered to refresh the contents of my hastily packed duffel: a clean change of clothes, plus my dress for the service. I'd joked we were officially like sisters now if I was sending her rooting through my underwear drawer.

But when I open Glenna's door, it's my real sister looking back at me.

Well, not really back at me. She's glancing around the porch like she's expecting the disembodied spirit of its owner to chase her away. Even in the early May afternoon sun.

"Lori?"

"Hey." She holds up a bottle of amber liquid with a racehorse on the label. "I came to drop this by your place, and Kelly told me where to find you."

"Auntie Nova!" I crane my neck to see the three kids making their way up the walk in a row, my black dress draped across all six of their outstretched arms.

"Is it me, or do they look like pallbearers?" I try to joke.

"Sorry, yeah. They were fighting over who got to bring it to you. I couldn't let them carry the bourbon, so . . ."

"Well, thanks. I didn't think I'd get to see you again."

"Can you spare a quick break? Let the kids run around the yard before I pack them in for the long drive home?"

I'm not sure I should let them in, but . . . Lori doesn't look too eager to step inside anyway. "Unlatch the fence and I'll meet you around back."

I carry out ice waters and Lori and I sit on the glider, exactly as Mason and I did the night I brought him here. Amelia cartwheels through the grass while her brothers play like they're trying to copy her, falling to the ground in mock exasperation.

"How was Lexington?"

"Intoxicating. Literally." She smiles at me sideways. "You look sad."

"I just loved the lady who lived here."

Lori nods, unsurprised. "Girl, I know Mom gives you a hard time about this job. I don't mean to sound like her. I think it's great, the way you want to help people. But do you ever worry? That's it's too hard getting so close to your clients? *Love* is a big word."

My eyes fall on the items she's draped on the table next to her. My standard funeral garb. The bag with clean socks and T-shirts. The souvenir I'd requested on a whim. *Do I worry?* I'm not sure whether to laugh or cry. I just want someone to tell me this will all be okay.

And before I know it, I'm telling her everything. Not about Glenna, but Mason.

"I *knew* that bottle was for a guy," she says when I've finished, and I jab my elbow into her ribs. "Ouch. Well, this is stranger than I knew it could get."

"No kidding."

"So we're actually hoping he hired you under false pretenses?"

"I mean, we kind of have to, right?" I pause. "But at the same time, if that is what happened, and if I respect myself here, should I also be . . . mad?"

Lori considers the question. "This came out because you asked him directly. Is this something you've suspected awhile then?"

*Yes. No?* Somewhere along the line, I'd stopped asking direct questions, telling myself things went better when I laid off. But was that the only reason? *Love is a big word,* she'd said.

"I don't know," I say finally.

"Well, it's all messed up. I'm sure he didn't expect things to turn out this way either."

I know he didn't. I've had all these accidental tastes of what it's like to just *be* with Mason. I close my eyes and see him juking through mist skimming off the fountains at Kings Island. Throwing back his head and laughing in the sunshine. Inching his chair closer in the firelight. Lowering his voice so only I can hear, eyes intent on mine.

This doesn't feel like the end. It feels like a beginning. I want more. But should I?

"If we're going to have any kind of shot together—however short or long—I need to get out of doula mode. You know what happens when people try to 'fix' their significant other."

"Yeah. But you're going to need some closure on that side of things first."

"Exactly." I'm thinking out loud in a way I rarely do, and it's nice having a sounding board. "Part of me can't believe I've made it this long without demanding to know what he meant. I think I'm scared to hear the truth. What if it's bad? What if he is dying, or what if he was planning to end things, and yeah, what if he's been misleading me this whole time? What if we really can have a future together, but I can't get past all that?"

Lori falls silent. "If you want to," she says finally, "you will. You're not exactly an open book yourself. We're all still sort of waiting for you to rejoin the family, and you might not be misleading us, but you're withholding." I start to object, but she raises a finger. "If there's one thing I've learned from you, it's to respect the importance of surviving a crisis on your own terms. Which for better or worse sounds like what Mason did."

I don't know what to say. She's right. All I can think to do is hug her tight, so I do, and then the kids are piling on and we're a squirming, squeezing ball of giggling, teary-eyed love bringing this sweet, neglected porch back to life.

I can't remember the last time I've been this sorry to see my family go.

For her memorial service, Glenna chose Withrow Nature Preserve, a small estate dotted with gardens, arbors, gazebos, and short hiking trails. With its brick pathways and historic house for rent, the place is more accustomed to weddings than funerals, which makes it fitting for the way Glenna envisioned this day. I set up inside what was once the living room, empty now of plush furniture, flinging open every door and window to the grounds beyond in peak bloom. The sole, oversized portrait I've been directed to display is a framed candid of Glenna and Wendell at some years-ago backyard party, looking at each other with amused affection. I know she hoped that now, they're together again just this way.

I recognize many guests from Wendell's funeral not two months before. Aging hippies from the music scene, fellow knitters from Glenna's volunteer group, a smattering of her former coworkers who seem shockingly young and healthy by comparison, our hospice friend Christine.

The small crowd clusters in chairs I've arranged around linen-covered tables—no stoic churchlike rows for Glenna. They help themselves to the catered dessert spread, plus coffee and mimosas, displayed with an embroidered placard that hung, until this morning, in Glenna's foyer: *Skip to the good stuff.* Next to that: A napkin-lined basket of Doritos.

I watch the way everyone smiles when they see it. The way no one can take their eyes off the photo up front. There's an open mic for sharing memories, and her playlist—more hopeful than sad. The Grateful Dead's "Scarlet Begonias," Dylan's "Mr. Tambourine Man," Tracy Chapman's melodious rendition of "Stand by Me."

As we're about to get started, in walks Mason.

Even with all the questions careening through my brain, seeing him feels like the reward at the end of this tunnel. He's clean-shaven, hair air drying from the shower, in a charcoal button-down loose at the neck and tucked into jeans that have yet to fade.

And he's looking at me like he wants to pull me aside, too—though maybe not to talk.

Even from across the room, I blush.

Which makes me start to laugh, for the first time all day. Because though I've done my best on my own, *this* is the final thing Glenna really wanted.

"Not a stuffy memorial dressed up like a celebration," she'd scoffed. "An actual party—with laughing and beer runs and, hell, sneaking off to find an empty bedroom."

I'd feigned shock, and she'd pointed a finger at me.

"If no one else will do it," she'd joked, twinkle in her eye, "I guess that leaves you."

## MASON SHAYLOR'S MISSING EULOGY
### By Rich Craigie, *Guitar World* Senior Editor

Discovering Mason Shaylor on tour was like one of those all-time great episodes of *Antiques Roadshow*—a priceless treasure right out in the open, in the possession of people who did not yet fully recognize its worth. Talent like Mason's was something anyone could appreciate, but the technically trained could *revere*. That's how specialized it was, how rare.

You're in good company if you've sought some explanation for why he didn't shoot straight to the top. The answer is so obvious, no one could believe it's that simple: He was doing exactly as he wanted. Taking his sweet time, savoring the fun of getting there.

Ever since the startling news out of Shaylor's hometown that the artist died a week ago in an accident that is still under investigation—one his mother has gone so far as to call an "apparent suicide," though authorities have yet to corroborate—a chorus has emerged from those of us who crossed paths with Shaylor in the music industry, and even those who didn't: Each of us saying we felt like we knew him. The real him.

If you passed Shaylor backstage, your small talk was not about the weather or the crowd, but something memorably specific. A few such topics recalled and shared from artists of note: the satisfying crackle of inhaling a clove cigarette, the perfect pacing-the-floor rhythm of Dolly Parton's "Jolene," a cautionary tale of why one *can* have too many guitar picks, and the perfect font size (18 point) and out-of-sight position (trade secret) for a set list.

Listen—*really* listen—to any of his songs, and you've had a conversation of sorts with him, too. We've all hummed along as he propped the windows open on "Cycle Avenue," as he soaked in "Sunbeams and Moonshine," reminding us "Shadow's Just Another Word for Shade." He was the kind of artist people would run up to, eyes alight, and then realize with a start that they had to introduce themselves. Only they didn't need to, really: The man never met a stranger.

Though the circumstances of his passing remain unknown, the real tragedy might already be plain: that for an artist who was so connected with his community, who poured his soul into every song he wrote and every note he played—whether for twenty people in a dive or twenty-thousand at a festival—his hometown seems the one place where no one knew him. There, he was a legend but also already a ghost walking among them. His family aside, only one other person has any recent account of Shaylor at all:

An end-of-life doula who may know more about both his life and its end, but who isn't talking.

I wonder: Can we honestly blame her? We're all holding our Mason Shaylor stories close, wanting to keep them for ourselves even as we share them.

We can't have it both ways, of course, and neither could Shaylor.

Maybe if he could have, he'd be here today, one way or another.

# 37

## *Nova*

THEN

I wake to the sounds of a guitar, so faint I might be dreaming it. Beside me, my sheets are warm from where Mason slept. From where he should still be sleeping—it's the dead of night. But the sound comes again, clearer now. It must be the guitar he left in my office after his mentor session in our rush off to Bo's. I've liked knowing that piece of him was still here. A reminder, then and now, of how capable he was with that student. How all is not lost, in so many ways.

Whatever he's playing is already my new favorite song.

I slip from beneath the covers, searching the darkness for something to pull on. I find his button-down and hug it closed as I cross to my ajar office door.

Mason is on the floor in the far corner, back against the wall, eyes closed as if in prayer. Beneath his fingers, the strings sound ethereal, mesmerizing—and it's not a song I'm hearing after all. It's patterns of notes, finding their way together. The *basis* of a song, a fantastic earworm of a song, the musical equivalent of the few precious pages a writer hands her most trusted reader and says, "I might have hit on something. See what you think?"

I think: Yes.

I think: I can't wait to hear the rest. *Everyone* will want the rest.

I think: How is it possible that what he's playing sounds exactly like *us*?

I tiptoe over, hoping he won't stop and try to hide what he's been doing. He keeps going until I'm beside him on the floor.

Then, he starts to sing.

His voice rises and falls over the accompaniment without forming words, like you do when you've forgotten the lyrics and are prompting a friend to tell you what a song is called or who it's by. More than a hum, with inflections and feeling, a placeholder where vocals will go.

My tears are falling before I even recognize them. This man is literally still writing songs in his sleep, pain be damned. Some musicians love playing, love creating, so much they'll do it even if no one is listening. Mason loves it so much he'll do it *only* when no one is listening.

But he's doing it for me.

When he stops, we remain motionless, letting the silence surround us.

"Sorry," he says, finally. "I was trying to be quiet."

As if I'd have ever in a million years wanted to sleep through that.

"You were. I never knew a guitar could sound so quiet. Or so beautiful."

He turns to meet my eyes, and a switch flips at the sight of my tears. Not a hardening, but a hesitation.

"It's been in my fingers for days," he says. "Something about waking up here . . . I needed to hear it."

"What's it called?"

"It's not called anything." He tips his face away. "It's not a song. Just a . . . thing."

I'm stuck on *something about waking up here*. Since Drew, I've woken up next to my share of men. They've been my choices, distractions, companions; I've regretted zero of them.

But I have loved only this one.

I nestle into his shoulder, torn between dragging him back to bed and begging him to play it again. "You could call it 'Last Night.'"

Last night *was* an unfinished song, intense and full and lost and found and head-spinning enough to defy logic. I'd returned late from closing out Glenna's memorial to find him waiting for me, and neither of us had said a word. How to do justice to what it was like to be together, finally and again, exhausted yet needing to redefine this space that's been marked for us both by loneliness? A space with a real bed, so much more room than we had in the Jeep. So much more softness. So much more time.

Time: the biggest, most elusive gift anyone can possess or give or share. Under the wrong circumstances, it can be mistaken for a curse. Under the right ones, you can never have enough. We'd fallen asleep clinging to it, not wanting to rush or force or interrupt.

Mason's melody said all of that and more.

"It's still last night," he says. I twist my head from his shoulder and catch the playful twitch of his mouth. I kiss his ear.

"Good news," I murmur.

"Hmm." He doesn't turn, though. "Whenever I hear *last* in a song title, I think *the* last. 'Last Call,' 'Mary Jane's Last Dance' . . ."

"In that case, suggestion withdrawn."

"Last Song," he says softly. "If I did finish it, I could call it 'Last Song.'"

I should let it go, pull him to his feet to follow me back to my pillow, to sleep, to me.

But this feels too important to let go.

"Would it have to be your last, though?"

He blinks, as if trying to suss out what I'm really asking. So am I.

"I may have mentioned once or twice," he says, "I'm not a musician anymore."

Like hell he's not. I don't want to spoil a moment of this night, or morning, or whatever it is. But this isn't just the end stop we both need to my role as his doula. I care for him too much to see him suffer any worse or any longer than he has to.

"You're a songwriter. What else are we doing here in the middle of the night?" I cup a hand over his mangled forearm. "That was so good it made me cry. It was so good, you said yourself you couldn't ignore it anymore. Which seems a lot like . . . us."

That earns me a reluctant smile, and my confidence lifts. "If you can create *just a thing* like that, even when you're telling yourself you can't? Imagine what you could do if you told yourself you could."

"I don't write stuff for other people to play."

Maybe he's not being obstinate. Maybe as someone who isn't an artist, I just don't get it.

I can't help feeling, though, that these months with Mason, he's *made* me get it. What his life was like, why he's lost without it. If he didn't feel I'd understood, would we be here now, with so much more at stake between us? With me staring down the answer right in front of him, and Mason refusing to open his eyes and look?

"It's not how you wanted this to go—it'll be harder and messier and awkward, at least at first. But you can do this: write, sing. Every day it's clearer you're not done unless you want to be. And you don't want to be. It's why you came here in the first place, isn't it?"

He doesn't answer.

"What did you mean, when you said you weren't dying?"

I hold my breath, and it hangs between us: what I've been trying to ask all along. Talking with Lori has helped me realize that I *am* ready to know, that this is what matters, enough to trump everything else. I want so, so badly to hear that we won't have to say goodbye anytime soon. That he can stay here with me and we can figure this out—us, life, the universe—together. That he won't be my client anymore, and maybe never should have been in the first place.

Except I'm so glad he was. Because we needed each other.

Mason has given me what I didn't know I'd been missing: a reason to start each day with something other than greeting the sun just to make a point.

Someone to share the day with.

"What did you mean?" I persist.

He closes his eyes. What I'm asking is wrong. I'm supposed to be helping him come to terms, not pleading with him to fight and find some way to stay. That's exactly the kind of thing people come to me to get away from. Family members who can't help themselves. My mom, for one, and probably Mason's, too. Denial is never stronger than when it comes from love. But even before the night at Bo's, that nagging wonder whether Mason really belonged here never felt like "false hope."

"Mason, I need to know." I take a deep breath, pushing down the fear. "Whatever you have to say, I can take it. Even if . . ." I falter. "I'm not going anywhere."

When he looks up at me, his eyes are . . . not what I expected.

"Is there a rule, about clients falling for their doulas?"

*Falling for their doulas.* Hearing him acknowledge this, I want to throw my arms around his stubborn, sexy shoulders and cry. But there's no mirth in his question. Of course there's a rule, though I always took it as having more to do with discouraging sexual favors as dying wishes. Not a visual I'm about to bring up now.

"I didn't think I needed one."

"The industry standard rule, I mean."

I try to smile. "Neither did the industry." There it is, unspoken:

Only a fool would fall in love with a dying man.

But isn't the reverse equally true? Doesn't the act of dying involve enough impossibly hard goodbyes as it is?

I thought so, back when the dying one was me.

Mason looks too sad, though, for the conversation at hand. I can't tell which one of us he thinks has ruined things. But this isn't ruin.

It's repair.

"You know what is frowned upon?" I take a deep breath. Somebody has to say it. "Treating clients who enroll on false pretenses."

"I didn't." He slides the guitar to the floor. "I'm sorry I danced around your questions at the beginning. But on this matter"—he gestures at the acoustic—"I've been honest. It's not an option for me to get by with this. Writing songs I can't play, teaching other artists things I could do better myself—that's not a guy who's making the best of things. That's a guy who doesn't know when to quit."

His hands clench into fists, and he's picking up steam now, like the argument is familiar, like we've been through all this before. And I get the feeling he has. With himself.

"That," he goes on, "is a guy who can't let go, so he settles for stuff he never wanted just because it files under *music*. Sure, a few people are glad he stuck around, but the overall feeling? From his colleagues, fans, even idols? It's just a lot of head shaking behind his back. A lot of *that's too bad*."

I think back, improbably, to that day in the thrift shop with Willow, where an old Brett Favre jersey hung in the window. *You know why that's here?* Mason had asked me, pointing.

I'd blinked at him blankly. *Because he retired?*

*Because he didn't retire at the top of his game,* he'd corrected me. *Fans would have worn these shirts forever, or framed them. Instead, he had the worst season of his life, a losing record with seven touchdowns fewer than his rookie year, and got fined over a scandal involving dick pics.* His disgust had been fierce, but I'd taken him for—well, a Packers fan.

He winces now and rubs his elbow. "I came here for help walking away from this. And you made me think maybe . . . Maybe I didn't have to walk away alone. Maybe I could go with you. But I don't need advice on how to live my best life as a pathetic shadow of myself. Make no mistake: The day I hang up this guitar is the day I bury Mason Shaylor."

*How* had I not made this leap? I of all people should have known.

Maybe, deep down, I of all people did.

"You have it wrong," I hear myself say.

He looks surprised, but I'm not sure why. He knows I don't capitulate.

"You're not a quarterback, with a team depending on you to keep

throwing touchdowns the way you always have. And no one's suggest-
ing dragging yourself out there and giving shitty performances. We're
talking about designing plays, coaching, commentating—roles that
players grow into all the time. Maybe they'd rather be on the field,
but they accept that's behind them. They're not pathetic shadows—
especially if they're as good as you would be. You're right, though, that
no one wants to see them on the sidelines saying they could have done
it better. If you're going to adapt, you can't have so much pride you get
in your own way."

"I went all in on my music, only to end up here," he growls. "Pride
in what I have to show for it is all I have left. I won't apologize for protecting my work and my reputation."

"I'm not asking you to." I'm not sure how this is turning into such
a vapid argument. It's not one I want to have. But maybe we need to
have it all out, right here, if this is what's holding Mason back. Holding
us back. "Your brother's story about the sports medicine clinic? My
takeaway is that you're *lucky* you aren't an athlete. You're an artist. Your
legacy can't be reduced to stats. You can reinvent yourself. You think
I don't appreciate how much you accomplished? You think I watched
you sell your guitar and never got what it meant to you? Even when I
couldn't figure out why the hell you were here or what you wanted from
me or how to give it to you, I knew Mason Shaylor was someone I could
never turn my back on."

"I'm not Mason Fucking Shaylor anymore."

"Yes you fucking are. I'm not sure you understand why people love
you."

We blink at each other, both of us taking in the weighty word I've
just said aloud. He grimaces, but not unkindly. More like it's taking real
effort not to forget the rest and kiss me.

I wish he would, but he just sits there. So I blab on, trying to regain
my footing.

"So you can't be the total package anymore. You don't need to put
all your gifts together for any one of them to be enough. You don't
think the fans who've saved their Shaylor ticket stubs would pay to hear

*anyone* play a new song you wrote—especially one so good, it lured us both out of bed in the middle of the night? You don't think they'd go crazy to see you take the mic as a special guest or a new lead singer of some other band they like? You are not an all-or-nothing artist, Mason. You're anything you decide to be. And I'm not just talking about music."

Strange, to tell someone how thoroughly wonderful you think he is and have him glare at you like you've done something unforgivable.

"You know there's more to it than *deciding*, Nova." His eyes burn. "You're the total package who doesn't want anyone to know. The death doula who dodged death but is too chicken to say so."

I flinch. It should have been, could have been, the start of something miraculous: this moment when it's clear we see each other this well.

"I don't know why you're acting like this is stuff you don't want to hear, Mason. Isn't the fact that you can still have music *exactly* what you want to hear? Or is it too scary to find a way that doesn't involve marrying your Jeep and staying far away from everything else that's broken in your life?"

"This from the girl who can't imagine her life without the threat of death."

"But I can imagine yours!"

The words roar out of me with a ferocity that startles us both. *And mine,* I want to say, *as long as you are in it.* But I'm crying too hard to speak.

"Look," he says, softer. "You're amazing. If not for you, I'd . . ." He shakes his head, as if to be free of some haunting memory. "But finding one thing you're good at and sticking with it isn't the solution for everyone. Maybe music doesn't make me happy anymore—maybe it makes me miserable. And maybe all this preparation for dying doesn't make you happy, either. Maybe it's just the only thing you know how to do."

It hurts both more and less knowing he might not be wrong. My parents and Lori would certainly agree. When I told Mason my story,

I tried to stay sensitive to his situation by leaving out the strangeness of surviving against the odds. How the new benchmark for everything becomes, *Hey, it could be worse, you could be dying.* How exhausting it is to hear that on a loop—from your mom over dinner, from your old Gulf Shores crew over the phone, from your own brain, which now lectures you over every catty thought, negative reaction, and bad day. How any stakes smaller than life-or-death start to feel invalidated, in-validat*ing.* How you can actually overdose on perspective—too much of a good thing spiraling into shame and self-doubt. And how all of this is a very good problem to have, even when you dare to wish you didn't.

"Maybe you're right," I admit. "Maybe I've just been this fixed point in the sky, living up to my name, burning and burning until I streak myself out. I've had plenty of miserable, hard days doing what I'm sup-posedly good at. Every job has that, every *life* has that—moments where you're on fire, and moments where it's a drag, and nothing feels as sat-isfying as you hoped it would. You know what, though? It all comes back to purpose and passion—things that are damn near impossible to live well without. If it wasn't about that, I wouldn't care what you do. But this is so clearly your joy, someone needs to care enough to say so. You've convinced yourself music is making you miserable, but maybe you're just miserable in the first place. When something's calling to you at all hours, that means something."

I want to say more. That just knowing Mason exists in this solar sys-tem has made me want to be something more solid. A moon, a planet. Something capable, at last, of sustaining life.

But I can't find the words—because the light in his eyes has gone out.

"Well, we've established I can't be your client anymore," he says, with-out bitterness. "Cross me off your books, okay?"

He gets to his feet, and in seconds he's through the open doorway to the bedroom, gathering his clothes from the floor.

"Mason, wait." I scramble after him, panic rising. I hug his button-down to me fiercely, as if he can't possibly leave without it.

"I thought I could do this—all of this—but I can't."

"What does *all of this* mean?"

He doesn't answer. He's fastening his jeans. Pulling on his T-shirt. Grabbing his wallet and keys from my dresser. I go to him, placing my palms over his forearms, the center of his pain. He stops and lets me, standing rigid.

"I thought you'd fire me so we can be together. Not so we can be over."

His hands cup my elbows, and the tremor in his grip travels my nerves, shaking them loose. "Why couldn't you leave it alone?" he whispers, thick and throaty. "Why couldn't you just let me love you? I started to hope that might be enough."

"It is enough. It's all I want." We're both crying now. Next thing I know, he's kissing me, rough and deep and warm and . . .

Then he's not.

He takes a step back. "I'm sorry. I can't. Everything between us is too entwined. You'll end up disappointed, and—and so will I."

"Please," I say lamely. "If you're that set against it, I won't bring any of this up again."

"You will though. Or I will." He strides back to the office and swipes the guitar from the floor, stuffing it into his gig bag. "It's hard enough getting over this myself, without feeling like you're holding onto some secret hope that I'll come around."

"So believing in you is wrong? You want me to love you without believing in you?"

"It's not your fault. I brought this on myself."

He's referring to the song, and oh God, I don't *want* him to be sorry he played it for me, sorry for the most moving moments of my life. But I know he's right: If it happened again—a connection I'd long for until it did—we'd end up right here, running this same circle. Not because of anything I want for or from Mason. Because I can't stand to see him turn his back on one of my favorite people in the world.

"Remember it, will you?" he asks.

"What?" I can barely croak the word.

"The last song."

I want him to stay and *make* me remember. But I know better than to ask.

And as he opens my door into the night, he knows better than to look back again.

# 38

*Nova*

NOW

"Can I come in?"

I stand aside to let Bo through to my office, and we shift awkwardly around each other as he takes in the state of things: half-packed boxes, empty walls. I've been up all night reading the tributes for Mason trending on social media and music outlets, and from the looks of Bo, I'd guess he's done the same. At Bonnie's the other day, he looked about like I remembered him—sadder, sure, but with that same king of the hill vibe. Now, he's less certain, as am I. If one thing has become clearer overnight, it's who Mason belonged to for the best time of his life. Collaborators, cohorts, crowds. They're the ones Mason chose, without a glance back. Is it any wonder? They adored him.

They still do.

"Is it true my mom never met you until . . . after?" He runs a hand through his hair, a gesture so *Mason* it hurts. I nod, and he sighs. "I wish he'd brought you around before. So she could have seen what I saw."

"You and me both."

"You're not going to tell me your relationship was strictly professional, are you?"

I shake my head again, reticent to explain. That all my clients are personal, but I'd never planned to cross that line. That we tried not to. That I'm sorry.

Except I'm not. Even now.

"But you *were* his doula?" He says this with more curiosity than contempt. He seems seconds away from promising to withhold judgment, to call off the dogs if I'll fess up one way or the other: Yes, Mason did come here for all the reasons his family fears. Or no: No way, no how Mason ever thought that way—our talks flew in the face of it.

His is the face of a man who just wants to know.

"It started out that way," I say, as if Mason might've realized he wasn't paying for much more than companionship and un-hired me at some point. I keep coming back to why I never broached this with Mason. The explanation seems purer than anyone's likely to accept: Mason had it in his head that a doula could help him, and I didn't want to poke holes in one of the few beliefs he held onto. He seemed to like our dynamic the way it was, and maybe I did, too.

Maybe he wasn't the only one who was scared to let himself try being any other way.

Bo is staring at me patiently, clearly waiting for more. "He was disconsolate," I elaborate. "Lonely, in pain. Not receptive to the kind of help I was used to giving. All I could do was try to be there for him. The things they're saying about me . . ."

It's not just Bonnie or Asha or Maggie or even Kelly anymore. I've read the comments trailing those tributes to Mason. *Imagine having Mason Shaylor of all people come to you for help,* one fan had written, *and letting him kill himself anyway? No wonder she won't show her face! She should drive off a bridge, too!*

"I'm sorry," Bo says. "I wish I'd put two and two together sooner."

Would it have changed anything if he had? Seeing his face, I feel a twinge of guilt—not for the first time—that I haven't called my own sister. *I'm sure he didn't expect things to turn out this way, either,* she'd reassured me on Glenna's back porch. She was the only person who knew, before, and I'm dreading her finding out the rest. Not only because that would somehow make all this heartbreak and regret seem more real, but because I know she'll feel like the one time I asked her for advice, she steered me wrong. Even though she didn't.

"I thought about reaching out to you," I tell Bo. "The first time your mom came here, she was adamant no one else on her side get involved. Made it seem like you'd blow your stack if you knew. Of course, that was before she opted to go public."

"Blow my stack?" He crosses to the window, looking out over the driveway like he still can't believe either of us is here. "If there's one thing I've never done with my mom, it's that." He turns to face me, eyes ablaze with confusion and grief. "Maybe I should have."

I'm not sure I follow.

"She's gone on this crusade," he continues. "Like it's about protecting Mason—like she can't accept that it's too late for her to do that now. But it's not just about that. It's about saving face. A world in which Mason hired an *end-of-life* doula is a world in which Mason felt his life was so bad it might as well be over. And part of what made it so bad was apparently living back with her. Where she wanted him." His eyes shift to the floor. "Where I left him."

"It wasn't your fault." This may not be the naked truth he's come looking for, but kindness is a good stand-in for most anything.

"I knew exactly how stuck he felt there, and I had the means to set him up somewhere less claustrophobic. I could have even given him one of those dogs he can't resist. But did I?"

"The things I said, the night I met you—it wasn't about showing you up or embarrassing anybody. I just wanted you to see him the way I did."

Bo's gaze circles my office again. "Can we sit?" I lead him through to the apartment, where he joins me at my kitchenette table.

"What can you tell me," he tries again, "about what you think was going on in Mason's brain?"

"It's been torture not having anyone to ask the same thing," I admit. I'm afraid he'll twist this the way Bonnie would, accusing me of having no right to wonder this too late. But the way Bo talked to me right in front of her: *I've never seen him look at anyone the way he looked at you.* I take a deep breath and press on.

"We had an argument. I hadn't heard from him for nearly three weeks leading up to . . . the end. I have no clue what he was thinking during that time."

"What was the argument?"

I need to let go of the idea of keeping this between me and Mason. As badly as I don't want him to be, he's gone. And I'm the definition of having nothing left to lose.

"Well . . . Mason the artist and Mason the person, there was no separating the two."

"Tell me about it."

"So: I realized he still had the ability to compose songs. Don't get me wrong, it was difficult, but he could do an astounding amount without even picking up the guitar."

"He could?" Bo looks as surprised as I'd felt that bleary morning.

I nod. "It seemed obvious to me this was his saving grace—how to keep a foothold in what he loved. But he had this all-or-nothing stance I didn't get. He said if he couldn't perform them, they weren't worth writing. I pushed him on it, and . . . I pushed too hard."

Bo takes a minute to absorb this.

"What can you tell *me*?" I dare to ask. "Did you see him, hear from him? Did your mom say anything about how he spent those three weeks?"

"You say that like it's a long time. When it comes to family not hearing from Mason, three *months* isn't unusual."

Mason had been so present with me since we'd met that the danger of this hadn't struck me.

"Until the past year," I say quietly. "Where you knew right where to find him."

We sit for a few uncomfortable minutes, surrounded by our own mistakes.

"The day my dad shipped out overseas," he says finally, "everyone cried but me. Mase made this scene, clinging to Mom's legs, wailing, and she just kind of stood there, so quiet it took me a minute to realize tears were streaming down her face, too. When she finally looked at me, that kind of snapped her out of it. I was going to miss my dad while he was away, sure, but I wasn't scared. He was this big, invincible guy, and Iraq was this faraway place that seemed more like a movie than anything real. When we found out about the explosion, I felt like an idiot. I saw the footage of the oil fires and tanks and bombs and thought, I'd watched my own father go off to *that* without having the sense to be afraid."

"You might have been the older kid, but you were still a kid."

"Even so, I made up my mind to have more sense. I stepped up to help my mom, which amounted to taking care of Mase. Beyond being latchkey kids—through dinner, past bedtime—I assistant coached his Little League team. Let him drag me to yard sales looking for beat-up amps. I barely dated in high school. Didn't entertain the idea of college. I behaved more like a single parent than a teenager."

"I had this picture of your mom burning it at both ends, handling everything."

"She worked hard. She also lost enormous amounts of time to grief. She didn't lean on me so much as I stepped in. Half the stuff I did, I don't think she even knew."

I hesitate. "I think that has something in common with how Mason spent this year. He's been grieving his career, his lifestyle. The most frustrating thing about grief is when everyone wants you to snap out of it but you can't."

"I guess other people's grief burns me out." A hint of his old bitterness shows through. "I didn't just love Mase like a brother. I loved him like—I won't say a father, but someone who'd had a lot to do with raising him. But when I finally left home, I was so glad to be out of there, and so guilty over feeling that way. It drove me crazy that I couldn't shake feeling this obligation to my family that apparently he was never going to feel. I called him selfish, but he was just living his life."

"Mason said when he came back, you thought it was his turn to take care of your mom."

"By then—with my own kids in the picture—she'd fully realized how much she'd missed out on with us. I think she hoped to make up for lost time. Hard to fault her for that."

"His turn to take care of her," I ask gently, "or her turn to take care of him?"

He looks down at the table.

"I'm not proud of it, okay? It's not like I couldn't see how inconsolable he was. She saw it, too. But finding out he hired you . . . It's easier for her to cast blame on the doula than to admit we failed him."

I've spent a lot of time watching families at their best and worst since I became a doula. But I've never worked out why some relationships manage to skirt right through the rapids, floating on the benefit of the doubt, while others snag on every single rock, turning you sideways, stranding you in the shallows. Maybe it's everybody's fault. Maybe it's nobody's. Maybe it's just the slippery nature of water.

"If it helps to know, Mason was more fixated on how he'd failed himself."

"Blaming his surgeon, you mean."

I shake my head. "Him, too. But . . . I kept trying to prompt him to forgive himself. That's something you have to come around to on your own."

He looks at me strangely. "Do you know Mason actually went to Mom and said he forgave her? Unprompted, the week he died. He said he didn't want to be angry with her anymore. She ended up actually apologizing for being *too happy* he was home."

I'm not sure whether to laugh or cry. In spite of everything, he honored our deal—at least, half of it.

"Did you have something to do with that?"

I swallow hard. "If he offered her forgiveness, she should take it. She shouldn't be railing against herself instead."

Of course, she's mostly railing against me.

"Do you think he was—like, making amends before he . . ."

"I don't know."

He nods. "After you came by Mom's house, I tried to explain you two were close. I even told her you'd been sick: If anyone values life, surely it's someone who's beat cancer. I said everything I could think of to convince her to call that reporter and pull the story. But she wouldn't. I'm sorry."

It's jarring, hearing truths I barely tell anyone come from this virtual stranger's mouth. Still, with him I feel both closer to Mason and less alone. "Thanks anyway." I smile sadly.

Bo stands and crosses to the door, then turns back. "If either of us ever finds out that we missed big signs, that we really blew it?" He swallows hard. "Let's not tell each other, okay?"

There's a backward kind of kindness in it. Even Mason would approve.

# 39

## *Nova*

What was I doing with myself, in those May weeks between the day I last saw Mason and the day Bonnie showed up at my door? Between the gut punch of him leaving, and the gut punch of knowing he was irreversibly gone?

It had been a while since I'd had such an intense feeling of not knowing what to do with myself. It reminded me of my early wave of stockpiling books on cancer-killing diets, of the first time I left town to try freedom on for size. I had a vague sense back then of what I wanted, but not of how to get it, exactly. I did things that felt ridiculous, like actually googling "things to do before you die." I seriously considered any search results that conveyed some sense of irreverent fun or adventure, even though seriously considering anything was missing the point. After reading a blog by a writer who, grappling with mental illness, had hilariously rented sloths and kangaroos just to hang out with them, I got as far as a booking company's website before balking at the price and settling for goat yoga.

Although, nobody really *settles* for goat yoga. Goat yoga is awesome.

Eventually, after a bunch of forced fits and false starts, I'd realized I had to figure out my own way to do crazy or desperate or whatever I was.

So it was after the blowup with Mason. I had to figure out my own way to do heartbroken and longing and sorry but not sorry.

I could say those resulting weeks are a blur, but that might give the wrong impression. I did walk around in an awful fog, but I remember the fog, how it was too thick to see, how it left me stumbling, arms outstretched and grasping at thin air where I hoped Mason would be. How more than anything else, I waited, hoping he would come back.

How I kept on loving him.

Which—to me—meant giving him time. And space.

Time, maybe, to reconsider that I hadn't been entirely wrong about his music, and that if I'd martyred myself on that sword, maybe he should at least pick it up, hold it in his hand.

Space, maybe, to reconsider me.

It seemed such a waste, letting our magic die off just as it began, as unfair and unthinkable as leaving his best songs unwritten. I tried, more than once, to call. I didn't leave messages, figuring he'd delete them unheard. I only wanted to repeat myself anyway: that I didn't want to lose him over this. Over anything.

I grieved Glenna. I arranged pickups for her most precious possessions. I watched the ticking tail of the cat clock on her wall and steeped a cup of tea to her specifications. I imagined us having one more proper Midwestern goodbye, where she'd walk me to the driveway and wave until I was out of sight.

Come to think of it, Glenna would have made a good end-of-life doula herself.

I let Mr. Whitehall coach me through eighteen holes of virtual golf, positioning his recliner so he could correct my form without standing. I marveled at the simple pleasure of teaching someone else about something you love, even if they don't bring to it the same passion you do.

There's always a chance that one day they might.

Carrie—my camp host friend from Kincaid Lake—finally called in that favor from the day I'd taken Mason to sit by the water. There'd been some malfunction, leaving her desperate for a hot shower. We switched places for the night, and Willow—one last hurrah before she'd get angrier with me than I dreamed possible—asked to come along.

From our campsite by the entrance, we dutifully checked campers in, then made rounds in Carrie's golf cart for good measure. We swung in the same hammocks as Mason and I, beneath trees astoundingly thicker and greener. Annoyed fishermen by skipping stones. Burnt marshmallows over the fire. I have never been what people call easy company, but Willow is.

It felt significant, realizing I'd choose being with her over being alone.

I kept on being the Nova whom she and Mason and Glenna and Kelly and everyone else in my newest life knew. I pulled my bike over to help a kid who was skittishly trying to lift a turtle out of the road. I explained that you can't take him back to the side he started on. Once he's made up his mind about a course, he'll keep trying to take it: To make sure he's safe, you have to carry him across, the way he wanted to go. Even if whatever's on the other side—in this case, a soft-serve stand surrounded by concrete tables and weeds, isn't great. You have to let him see for himself.

Maybe humans are more like turtles than we realize. If that's true, we've been cheated out of having protective shells. We're all so vulnerable. No wonder so many of us are scared.

What was Mason really doing with himself, in the three weeks between goodbye and the end? Did he seethe with anger, never wavering? Did he think, after all, of reconsidering? Or did he spend the whole time curled in bed, deep in the end stages of encroaching darkness, thinking of what a failure our months together had been? If I'd swallowed my insistence that *I was right* and *he needed time* and knocked on his door, might I have changed the outcome that easily?

I'd give anything to know.

# 40

*Nova*

Dear Willow,

*By the time you have this envelope torn open, you're probably even angrier: How dare I write to you when I'm right here, when I could knock on your door and face you? It's bad enough I'm not the person you thought—now it turns out I'm a coward, too?*

*If that sounds like an unbelievably cold reversal of everything you and I have between us, it's because it is. Unbelievable, I mean. I'm begging you: Don't believe it.*

*I'm writing this not because I'm afraid to talk to you, but because I know you wouldn't hear me right now. Not while you're still so mad. And that's not because you're a kid, by the way, who still has that amazingly freeing ability to stomp and yell when someone wrongs you, to react without the adult pressure to be "rational" all the time. It's because you have every right to be furious with me.*

*And I have no right to talk you out of it.*

*But before you give up on me, please: Keep this. Crumple it if you want, throw it across the room, but don't put it in the trash. Shove it into a drawer: Come back to it later, when the fury starts to fade. I don't know if that'll be three days from now, or next month, or not until next year, but whenever that day comes, I hope these words might read differently.*

*I won't be across the driveway anymore. But for you, I'll never be more than a call, text, or email away. Every day that your name doesn't light up my phone or inbox, I'll still think of you. That I miss you. That I'm sorry.*

*In my heart, I believe what happened to Mason was an accident. I've learned to live with a lot of uncertainty, but not knowing what really happened to him would be the hardest kind. So I'm choosing to hold onto what I do know, and I hope you'll believe it, too, no matter what else you hear.*

*Mason may have felt like his life was over the first day he came here, but the same was not true on the day he left. To the end, he argued about the possibilities ahead of him, with real fire—not with the resignation of someone who's given up. Fear is something that sometimes, we need to run toward. Mason was still getting up the nerve, but I never once saw him retreat. Every step he took, from the day we met, was forward. Toward me. Toward you and your friends and that silly dog, with a big, genuine smile on his face. Toward a future that looked different than he wanted, but that I have faith he'd have found a way to make bright.*

*If Asha's article made you think anything less, then she has wronged Mason far worse than she could ever wrong me or your mom. You can push back by refusing to believe it. By choosing empathy rather than anger when you think of Mrs. Shaylor, too. By putting that article, not this, in the garbage, and moving on.*

*Two things about your mom: 1) She is doing her best. 2) She loves you more than anything. When your last day on this planet comes, that's all that will matter. And we never know which day that will be. So try, if you can, to let those be all that matters today, too.*

*I'm grateful to you both for letting me be part of your lives for a while. Not a moment of our time together was insincere. My diagnosis didn't make me some guru spouting nonsense I'd never followed before. It only made me less timid and complacent in figuring out how to be me. Every-one makes mistakes; living boldly means your mistakes could be pretty bold. But you shouldn't let that deter you. Don't be like me and have to learn this lesson the hard way.*

*Some people think you can't give the people you care about the benefit of the doubt without being a doormat, a pushover. They're wrong. The hardest, strongest thing you can do is forgive them anew, every day, for their flaws—and forgive yourself, too.*

*I hope when you think of me, it won't be of this mess I've made of things at the end.*

*Even now, when I think of you, I'm happy. I know that you will be okay.*

*Love, Nova*

Nobody answers the door at my parents' house, but beneath the sun-set sky, the lights are on, the garage door propped open for the cat, the muffled sounds of Santana coming from the old stereo within. I walk around the side and find my mom stretched on a palm-print cushioned chaise on the paver patio, glass of white wine in hand, wet washcloth over her eyes.

There's no sign of Dad, and it's rare to see her relaxing alone. When-ever she's without him, she's off to work, shopping, some errand or ap-pointment, book club, or brunch. I stop at the edge of the grass, reticent to disturb her. I should've stopped by more to sit with her, to borrow whatever book she's just read, to give her something to *do* without do-ing anything at all. I guess it's not true that I've learned to live without regrets. I'll miss her, I realize: Miss the person I've been most avoiding since the day I moved back. Miss doing things we never actually did.

"Hey, Mom," I say softly. She whisks the washcloth away, startled. "Headache?"

"No, just puffy eyelids. It's every time I garden these days, like I'm allergic to dirt itself."

We stare at each other across the fading June light, the moment turning awkward as she realizes she's fallen to small talk with someone she's maybe not talking to. I never returned Dad's calls Friday, and Bo's visit did in my Saturday, emotionally speaking. But now, at the close of a quieter Sunday, I'm packed. I've written to Willow and prepared detailed client notes to hand off to Kelly in hopes that enough of them will stay for her to get by. And maybe I shouldn't have saved my parents for the end.

I guess I didn't know how to defend the job they'd never wanted me doing in the first place. I'm still absorbing that in some respects, they may have been right.

"Where's Dad?" I ask.

"Next door. Helping George carry God knows what down to his new basement man cave."

Dad listens to his cardiologist about stuff like red meat. But when it comes to golf with friends and, apparently, moving mini fridges, he gets a little murky. "Should he be doing that?"

She looks at me pointedly. "No one asks my opinion."

I cross to the chaise next to her and sit in the center, leaning over my knees to meet her eyes. "Asha Park did."

"If you'd thought to tell me you were in that kind of trouble, I would've known to keep my mouth shut."

My kneejerk reaction is to say sorry, but then again, she hasn't said it, either. "Do you know if Lori has seen it?" I already know the answer. She would've called.

"She hasn't given me hell yet. So no."

I nod, though this is cold comfort. "I'm not going to stay at Parting Your Way."

"Well, thank God for that. Do you have to give notice, or—?"

"I think Kelly is happy to have me gone as soon as possible."

We both know *happy* isn't the right word.

"You're here to ask for your room back for a while?"

I shake my head. "I'm here to say goodbye."

She blinks. "Are you even allowed to leave? Isn't the investigation ongoing?"

"No one has told me I can't."

She takes a long, slow sip of wine before she answers. "Where is it you're so eager to go, exactly? Or are you just running as far away as you can get? Again?"

"What would you rather I do?" I sit straighter. "I came back to please you and Dad, but nothing I've done since has pleased you. You really want me to stay? The real me, not the version you wish I could be?"

"You know we'd never not let you stay here."

"That's not what I asked."

She sighs, a sound so heavy it's hard to believe it's only air. "This man who they're saying may have killed himself . . ." Her face strains with the effort of turning the question into a complete sentence.

"I was in love with him."

This, she didn't expect. Her hand flies toward me but catches itself midair, retracting to her lips.

"Oh, Nova, I had no idea." Her change in tone is reassuring, but sad. Imagine your parents not even knowing this person had existed, this person who'd occupied your thoughts for months, who'd curled around your heart. Imagine not calling them when you lose him, because it's too long of a story, too big of a mess. Imagine hiding your grief, uncertain if they'd cry with you or think you got exactly what you signed up for, because you can still hear all the times they said: *Why in God's name you'd want to surround yourself with all this death is beyond me.*

Because they *did* say that, the day you found out he died. Even though they didn't know.

"Honey. You're really hurting." Tears fill my eyes, but I keep my head high. Keep breathing. "At Dad's birthday dinner, when you were so distant, that was—?" I nod. "Why on earth didn't you say so?"

I sniff. "We'd had a fight, before—but I still don't think . . . I honestly don't think he . . ." If I'm going to fall apart, better here than at the Shaylors'. Which is where I'm headed next.

I suppose this is my practice run.

"My God. Does his mother know?"

I hesitate. "His brother, Bo, had met me."

A flash of anger. "Then *how* did these accusations get this far? The police, the media?"

"Bo didn't know anything about me being a doula. By the time he realized the person his mom was so fired up about was me, the damage was done. I tried to talk to her myself, but—she wasn't exactly receptive. Can't blame her for that."

She rubs her temples. "No. I can't."

"I'm headed there next. I can't leave without knowing I've tried my hardest to explain as much as I can. Even though I can't explain the things she most wants to know. And I hate that."

My tears spill over, and for a moment, I'm behind a wall of water, wishing it could wash me away. Just when I think maybe I'll dissolve right there, Mom's voice cuts through the rush, strong as stone. "I'm going with you."

"No." I wipe at my eyes.

"Honey, I don't understand what we've done to make you think you need to go through hard things like this alone. We've been frantic all weekend, not knowing how worried we should be, or how we might help. Your father talked me out of banging down your door, but I shouldn't have let him. We try to follow your lead, Nova, but too often that means you shutting us out. Please, let me do this."

I try to picture Mason's mom meeting my own. Would it make me seem more human somehow, or anger her further? And what about me—would I lose my nerve under double the maternal judgment? "How would that look?" I hedge. "A professional, bringing a parent along?"

"It would look like this is not merely professional, but as personal as it gets. It would look like you have someone who cares enough to stand beside you, even when your partner will not. It would look like I recognize this mother is grieving her child, and so am I."

"Mom. I'm right here."

"Hardly. You're leaving. She has something to do with that. As do I." She tears up, and I waver. For years, Mom *has* wanted to be my partner—first in fighting cancer, and then in moving on from it. And I relegated her to one road trip, then pushed her away. Because partnering always

seemed to mean doing things on her terms. But maybe I stopped noticing her trying to accept mine. Or maybe this really is the first time
she's had my back no matter what.

Either way, the least I can do is try letting her.

Before Mom has the car in park outside the Shaylor house, I know this
is not a good time. Bo's car is in the driveway, along with an intimidating black Lincoln Continental I've never seen before. Every light is on;
silhouettes move across the sheer living room curtains. Bonnie has
company, and my first thought is: *I should go.*

But there is no better time, because there is no other time. I've promised myself: One more sunrise here in Ohio—only one. Unless she's
still on bereavement leave, Bonnie's workaday commute will resume in
the morning; it's now or never.

And never isn't an option, for either of us.

Mom and I head up the cracked concrete walk in the same silence that marked our drive. Bo and I already said our goodbyes, but
maybe it's good he's here. Maybe he'll step in, encourage Bonnie one
more time to hear me out. Maybe Sara is with him. Maybe—

The front door opens, flooding the porch with yellow light. We
freeze on the bottom step, like we've been caught sneaking up rather
than about to knock.

The man filling the doorway could not look more out of place as
the tired house sags around him: dark suit tailored from iridescent fabric, lavender button-down, silver bolo tie. My eyes travel downward.
Purple leopard-print loafers.

Bonnie comes into view behind him, smiling in a way I've never had
a chance to see. It falls at the sight of me, but no flash of anger takes
its place. Instead, she points in my direction, looking almost—eager?

"This is Nova." The words explode out of her with a force I can't
identify. Mom's hand falls on my shoulder, meant to be reassuring. It
would be, if not for her shaking.

I brace for them to charge at us, but the bespoke man's hand goes instead to his heart.

"Nova?" He says my name softly, as if beholding some miraculous creature. I try to place him: a musician? A bona fide music journalist from some glossy magazine?

"You conjured her!" I hear Bo before I see him, clapping the shiny suit on the shoulder. Everything about this is out of place. Bo looks . . . triumphant. "You read those verses aloud, and here she is. I knew it was a powerful song, but damn."

Verses. *Song.*

One last miniscule seed of hope stirs inside me.

"*Mason* conjured her," the suit corrects him. He steps onto the porch gallantly. "I'm Dex Marion, Mason's manager. And you, Nova Huston, have saved me a phone call."

# 41

## *Dex*

Dex was trying to keep his composure, because goddamn it, he should've been here sooner. He'd promised Shaylor, last time they spoke: *This is gonna be huge. This is gonna be great. You'll be reborn*—holy shit, he'd had the audacity to use that of all words.

It had been the right one, though. Reborn as an artist, was what he'd meant. And Shaylor was nothing if not an artist—literally. Could not find a way to function without his music. The past year had proven that. The past year, in fact, had drilled such a raw, tender hole in Dex's own heart, he'd ended up making pie-in-the-sky promises on that call, the kind of promises that as a personal policy, Dex Marion did not make. That's what set him apart from flashier managers, the guys who wanted you to just trust them, sign now and figure out the rest later. The guys who'd make no mention of the industry's volatile, senseless state of being until after a great album tanked, after a good-on-paper tour failed. Dex was honest maybe to a fault: *I think you are special. I will do everything in my power to make the world agree. I cannot ven-*

ture a guess at some grand end result, because *I* am not a goddamn fortune-teller, and *you* don't want to know how much beyond-anyone's-control bullshit is involved in the success of a single song, let alone an album, an artist, and in Mason's case, a whole next-level playing field of talent and soul and drive that rarely coexisted in the same body.

Dex needed Shaylor to hear him on that last call, though. Needed him to keep hold of hope, just a little longer. He'd known what it took for Shaylor to pick up the phone and hunt him down, known how close to the brink Shaylor had been for too long, known exactly how fast that brink itself could change, in the mere space of a routine sound check. Like no one before or since—and Dex could say this with absolute authority: *no one before or since*—Shaylor had fought to live on that line, had goddamn kicked and clawed and climbed to the point, a short year ago, where he'd stood at last on the verge of more than he'd ever wanted. And to the point, every day since, where he'd teetered a toe nudge away from tumbling into that bottomless crevasse nobody comes back from, even if they change their mind midair.

In the end, Dex had promised Shaylor because he knew it mattered, but more than that, he'd promised Shaylor because for the first time in his gorgeous panoramic mess of a management career, he'd been sure.

He'd been *right.*

But he hadn't been in time.

Now, he was here with these sad, beautiful people because he owed them this much: a face-to-face telling of this sad, beautiful story. He hadn't even gotten to the best part and already they were looking at him like he was the second coming. Not that they struck him as a religious bunch, not that he was qualified to speak on the subject himself. But if the hand of God was called for where faith had been shattered, this was the place.

"I'm sorry for your loss," he said to Nova, once she and her mother settled uneasily on the couch nearest the door. There was something about this young woman, this *death doula,* he couldn't look away from.

An energy that was somehow both defiant and resigned, so like Shay-lor it was all he could do not to throw his arms around her.

"I'm sorry, too," Nova said, looking sideways at Shaylor's poor mother like she was ready to make a break for it if need be. On the love seat across the room, Bonnie's eyes stayed on her fingernails as she tapped them in fidgety patterns.

Bo had done the talking so far. Bonnie had done the crying.

"As I was telling Bonnie and Bo, I came as soon as I heard about Shay—about Mason. And I'm truly sorry I heard the way I did, and not sooner. When I say I was off the grid, I'm not talking about some mountain cabin with spotty cell service."

Nova nodded. "South Pacific, was it? Private recording studio?"

Dex stole a look at Bo, who looked both impressed and chagrined. There it was, already: Mason had told Nova more about Dex than he'd told his own family.

"That's right. I wouldn't have dialed back in at all, except I had one project that couldn't wait. A hot new songbook I'd promised to hand sell."

She nodded again, politely, and turned once more toward Bonnie, more purposefully this time. "Mrs. Shaylor, I'm sorry to have inter-rupted such an important visit. I was hoping we could try one more time to talk. Soon. Maybe I could come back in the morning?"

Bonnie didn't lift her head, but said one soft, unmistakable word: "No." Then another: "Stay."

Nova's eyes darted to Bo, who nodded toward Dex. "He's talking about Mason."

"Mason?" Her tone matched the way Dex was feeling at the odd task of delivering the best news under the worst circumstances. "You were shopping new songs by Mason?"

His chest puffed, in spite of himself. "To my great relief and delight. And I'd been going crazy trying to get back in touch with him. I told myself he'd gone back into creator mode, but in retrospect, I should have known something was wrong."

"New songs by Mason," she repeated, slowly. Taking in what this meant. For Mason and everyone rooting for him.

"So you didn't know? That he was writing again?" Bonnie fixed Nova in her skeptical gaze, the first time she'd spoken more than one syllable. Everyone watched, waited. Nova's own mother sat a little straighter.

Nova shook her head. "I knew he could. I'd heard snippets, when he thought no one was listening, and he was so—" She grappled for the words. "He swore he didn't want to anymore, but it was like he couldn't help it. I tried to encourage him, but I pushed too hard, and the worst part was, I lost him over it."

They'd all lost him, of course, though not in the way she meant.

Dex wondered if Nova had yet gone to do the unthinkable thing he felt compelled to do—in some way that was more reluctant, darker, than *wanting* to do it. To follow the route Mason must have taken, on his way to God knows where. To stand at the edge of a small, unassuming bridge and look down at the innocent ground below, searching out signs of impact—a broken shard of taillight, an indentation in the ground. To stare into that abyss, while life went on in the whoosh and glow of lazy night traffic, and to weep. To weep at last, and to say to himself, over and over, *goddamn, Shaylor.*

He supposed that was what people meant by closure. It felt gruesome and wrong to go and yet somehow disrespectful not to take the opportunity, when he may never be here again.

If Nova could resist that, then good for her. She was the professional, after all. But she didn't look at ease with the dearly departed now.

She looked wrecked.

"You didn't push too hard," Bo told Nova. "Apparently you pushed just right."

"I still don't understand—" She turned her wide eyes back to Dex. "You said a *book* of songs? Like, on paper?"

"Paper and audio. The demos are a little rough. From what I understand, he recorded twenty, thirty seconds of guitar at a time and then patched them together and laid the vocals over. Last time we talked, he was bathing his arms in ice. I told him, 'Shaylor, you could have found someone to book a studio with you and play these, take direction—everyone knows a songwriter's demo is just the gist'—but you can guess how that went over."

A knowing laugh rippled around the room, and Dex found his eyes on that dark back hallway. Bonnie had shown him earlier where it all must have gone down, where the closet of that back bedroom was lined with squares of egg crate foam, poor man's soundproofing stapled—stapled!—right into the drywall, the floor lined with pillows, the microphone jury-rigged with duct tape and zip ties. Bonnie swore she hadn't heard a thing. She couldn't even fathom how Mason afforded the software and what little recording equipment he did have, though the receipts were there on the dresser. He'd paid cash.

Meticulous to the end—that was Shaylor. Even if you had to know what to look for in order to see it—and come to think of it, that was Shaylor, too. Not that he never lost control, but never without good reason. Shaylor was the only client whose bill for a trashed hotel room Dex had ever paid. Dex would've torn the pictures from the walls himself, had he known the surgeon would make that of all phone calls on that of all days. He'd have run the curtains through the same shredder the record label was at that moment using on Shaylor's newly inked contract.

Dex had thought back to that mess as he'd taken in what Shaylor's bedroom might look like to someone who didn't know better. The bowls of water, wet towels, ice packs long since thawed. The bottles of pain relievers and creams. The pile of discarded hand braces, bands, and wraps. The trash can spilling over with broken strings, energy bar wrappers, and tall Styrofoam cups with lids stained from gas station coffee.

No torn paper. No overt evidence of any lyric or tablature attempts, let alone their success. Dex looked anyway, though Shaylor had told him how he'd done it all on the laptop, dictating as much as he could. When Dex asked for the computer, Bonnie explained it had been in the Jeep, and too badly burned to recover any data. What the hell kind of injustice was that, the goddamn suicide note in the glove box outliving every last scrap of melody on that machine?

Nova smiled sheepishly at Dex. "The demos turned out good enough, though?"

He wanted to laugh at the way she said those words—good enough—because there was Shaylor again. The mark of his artistry: A hyper-awareness that *good enough* was not enough.

Except for when it was.

"He could have tapped them out on a xylophone and they'd have done the job. If anyone but Mason tried to claim they'd written that many brilliant songs in a couple short weeks, I wouldn't believe it. It was like someone had fixed the knob to finally twist on an old faucet, and he didn't trust that the water would flow again if he turned it off to rest."

He looked meaningfully at Nova, leaving no doubt *she* was that someone. The things these people had accused her of, had put her through. They should have known better. Mason didn't do one-sided. They shouldn't have needed Dex here to confirm what anyone could see—that she loved Mason still.

"I'm here," he continued, "on the cusp of the biggest bidding war for raw material I've seen. We've got chart-toppers offering creative col-laboration, the whole nine. Would have been a dream come true."

"Would have been," Nova's mother broke the spell, her words clipped. Defensive. No—deflective. "But the bids were too slow? You think things would've ended differently if he'd known? Because it sounds to me like my daughter did some good here. Surely no one's still holding her responsible then?"

Nova looked at her with a guarded emotion Dex might describe as *gratitude adjacent.* There was an odd energy between the two, difficult to pinpoint even for Dex, who saw his share of mother-daughter duos. In his office, they ranged from codependent, the parents waving the red flags of their overinvestment like matadors, to skeptical at best, where the tougher-sell parent would seek, and thus find, some reason to say *I told you so,* and the insulted child would refuse to admit any-thing could be too good to be true.

"Let me ask you this," Dex began, and Nova looked at him like she'd seen a ghost. But she put out a hand to stop him.

"Mom," she said gently, "this isn't about me. And Dex? I can't tell you how happy I am to hear this. But all the bidding wars in the world could never make up for losing him."

Dex smiled—not the Pan Am smile he'd given Bonnie and Bo earlier. The one he used in those client meetings, when he wanted things to work. Flags—red and white alike—be damned.

"Couldn't agree more," he said. "But you were wrong to say you'd lost or failed him over this. There's one song in particular I want you to hear. It's called 'The Next Thing You Know.' I've already played it for the family—I was headed to the car for the rest when you got here, but before I do, let's take another listen?"

He looked to Bonnie for her okay, not that he needed it. You had to know how to deal with wounded pride, and sure enough, Bonnie nodded, looking like she wanted to say more. She'd worn that look ever since Nova walked in—the awkward anticipation of owing an apology to someone. There was so much here to sort out, and Dex would do his part. He'd handle the press, the fans, too, free up Bonnie to speak to the police and make things right with the people in this room. But there was no longer any question of which way the cards would fall.

Thank goodness for that.

Thank *Mason* for that.

Though really, they should all be thanking Nova.

Dex hit play on the Bluetooth Bose hooked to his phone, loud and clear for a speaker so small. He didn't anticipate what he saw in Nova as the first sounds of guitar filled the room, but maybe he should have: recognition. A hint of a smile—perhaps a memory. But as soon as the lyrics began, she froze, spellbound, straining not to miss a word. That's when he understood:

The music she'd heard before, but not the vocals.

And for the first time ever in a Mason Shaylor song, extraordinary as that guitar may sound, the words mattered more.

### The Next Thing You Know

*I wrote this note*
*Carried it in my pocket*
*Slept with it under my pillow*
*Put a copy in the glove box*
*For proof of registration*
*Paid all my fees, nothing left to do but wait*
*Looking for the right time to say goodbye*

*Then you came up*
*With your death-defiant eyes*
*Looking right at me, seeing right through me*
*Daring me not to go and die*

*The next thing you know*
*It can wait until tomorrow*
*The next thing you know*
*We're talkin' 'bout the sunrise*
*The next thing you know*
*I'm counting the days up, not down*
*'Cause we'll be back together*
*The next thing you know*

*Funny thing about the sky*
*New stars light up all the time*
*A nova flares bright out of nowhere one night*
*And catches your paper on fire*

*I'm gonna keep it*
*'Cause it's hard to believe I wrote it*
*'Cause it's hard to believe I forgot to care*
*I need the reminder there*
*That you made me want to see*
*The next thing you know*

*The next thing you know*
*I can't wait until tomorrow*
*The next thing you know*
*I'll meet you at the sunrise*
*The next thing you know*
*We're counting the days up, not down*
*'Cause we'll hold up together*
*The next thing you know*

*Your work here is done but we're just getting started*
*'Cause I may not need you but boy do I want you*
*I'll be on my knees, let me love on you please*
*The next thing you know*

*I'm never gonna wanna leave you*
*The next thing you know*

# 42

## *Nova*

By the time I leave my parents', it's late. I'd stayed while Mom told Dad all about how Bonnie apologized for jumping to the wrong conclusions, and how I'd told her no apology was necessary. Mom repeated this like I was gracious, but that's bare minimum grace in my book.

Truly listening to another person is one of the greatest gifts we can give. I understand why Bonnie didn't think me worthy of that audience before. *Exonerated,* Mom called me. And maybe I am. But I'm not *absolved*—and I said so to the Shaylors. There's still plenty I wish I'd done differently—but I hope it won't haunt me anymore. Hope it won't haunt them, either.

Dex let me leave with a printed copy of the songbook. Maybe he sensed that the song with my name was a fraction of the meaning it held for me. The folkish twang of "Sure Bet"—in which Mason remembered every horse name we'd bantered about that day. The nostalgia of "Hammock Blues," *wishin' this lake was a gulf or a sea / wishin' your tree would move closer to me.* "The View from the Floor"—which can only be about the *middle of the night breakdown, middle of the night showdown, middle of the night slowdown* that, unbeknownst to me, convinced him to pick himself up.

The only audio Dex would part with was "The Next Thing You Know," for my ears only—and it's the only one I need, for now. Even if no one outside that room tonight ever knows this rough version exists, it will be the one all my sensory memories return to when the rest of the world hears it through some other voice, played on some other guitar.

It'll never be close to the same, coming from anyone else.

I never did argue Mason wasn't right about that.

If Mason had to go when he did, how he did, the song was the best kind of goodbye. Never mind that he couldn't have spelled out his defense of me more clearly, down to the note in the glove box—those lyrics held so much more: a thank you, a promise for the future. It leaves me devastated anew by the loss, what might have been.

But I can sing along to the beauty of it, still. Whenever I'm ready, whenever I need him, the song will be there. The last thing Mason ever did was make sure of that. I want to believe what he wrote, take him at his word, and everyone else does, too. So we're going to try.

What really happened next, I guess we'll never know.

"Kelly has to give you your job back now," Mom said, turning to me once she finished recapping for Dad. I wasn't sure if tonight had given her a new respect for my job, or if this was just code for *now you can stay.* "Right?"

I shook my head. "I won't ask her to. I'm not sure Kelly and I could come back from this." Whether I'd even want to feels up for grabs. If the most rewarding thing I've done as a doula is to fall for a client who was there under false pretenses, possibly I should find better pretenses myself.

"Well, now," Dad said, at last. "This Dex character sounds pretty slick. He must be old hat at turning bad PR around. You know I admire you doing things on your own terms, but why not let him help you set things right, this once?"

"I intend to." Dex seems sure I won't have to answer to this again—

not to Asha, maybe not even to the police. But even with my head spinning and teary and overwhelmed by the song and Bonnie's turnaround and my parents' relief and everything else, I'm not deluded enough to believe he can fix everything. What's happened between Kelly and me is a lot deeper than her doubting my instincts or mistrusting my judgment—in part, because she wasn't entirely wrong to do so. "But," I continued, "that doesn't mean staying here is the right call."

Mom looked so wrecked I could only feel ashamed. "Sitting in that living room tonight . . ." She took a shaky breath. "I didn't like how much I related to the hasty judgments Bonnie Shaylor had made. I don't want to ever feel that way again. Most important, I don't want to make *you* feel that way again."

"It's not like your objections to me doing this job weren't understandable," I conceded.

"They're still understandable," Mom said, and Dad elbowed her. "But," she went on, "it's clear that you're good at this work, and that it's been important to your own healing, too. If we'd been more supportive, you wouldn't have felt so alone. I want to do better, no matter what you decide from here. If you'll forgive me."

"Us," Dad corrected, putting an arm around her.

I fought a mixed-up urge to laugh. I'd waited so long to hear those words, but now that they'd come, I wasn't even sure I'd wanted to be a doula anymore.

"Of course I forgive you," I said. Only then did I realize how much I needed to follow my own advice on this topic especially. "Forgive me back? I know I haven't made this easy."

The irony is that on paper, I'm prepared to die now. But in practice?

I'm prepared to live.

※

The truth is, as I pull into my—Kelly's—driveway at last, exhausted and spent, nothing feels right to me anymore. Not even leaving, after the events of tonight, though I'm struggling to put my finger on why.

Wasn't closure what I was after? And didn't I get more of it than I'd dared expect? I'll need time alone to sort myself out. To shut the door behind me for one last night in the little room I've called home, collapse on the bed, and cry for everything and everyone I'm about to put behind me.

In the end, my parents and I didn't say goodbye yet. Dad is going with me in the morning to buy a car or truck, something that can carry more of my life with me. I know this much: I'm ready to have something worth carrying again.

Kelly's kitchen light is on, so I slip my copy of the songbook through the mail slot in the door. Dad made a scan of the pages for me—*for us, too,* he boasted. Much as I'd love to keep the hard copy, it's more important that Kelly see it. Willow, too. Peace of mind should never wait until morning if you can help it.

Watching for the sun to peek over our slice of the horizon one last time, I know I'll miss this curl of muddy river in the distance, this bench and these birds and those trees they call home. I'll miss knowing my little surrogate family is snug in the house behind me, waiting for me to come claim a cup of tea, help with a last-minute homework check, compare itineraries for the day. And I'll miss something I never thought I would: knowing what I'm going to do with myself.

The last ritual feels at once familiar and different, as it should—as it must.

As the sun lifts into view, I close my eyes and stand completely still, honoring all the moments I stood here looking forward to Mason's appointments. How it felt to realize I was *counting the days up, not down*— that Mason had given me back that feeling of wishing and longing and thanking the stars for as many days ahead as we could possibly get. The feeling that if I'm honest, I hadn't had since my diagnosis disappeared.

The more I've read over the song he wrote for me—for us—the more I've realized how much of it I could have written myself. Maybe I should have told Bonnie and Bo and even my parents last night that everything Mason gave me credit for, he'd done right back for me. But it seemed too much to pile on. I didn't want to scare them, that I have to do it without him now.

It's scary enough for me.

For the first time in my second chance at life, I really, *really* want to take it.

# 43

## *Willow*

Willow huddled next to her mom on the bottom stair to Nova's studio, hugging a basket of sugar-crusted muffins, breathing in the most reassuring smell she knew. Whenever her mom was most stressed, Willow would wake to the scent of these baking in the middle of the night, and in the morning, somehow, everything would be okay. Like Mom had worked out the science of her troubles in the recipe's steps, or the batter itself had coaxed a solution to rise as it baked.

That's what Willow needed today. For everything to be okay.

They watched, quiet and still, as Nova made her way back from her hidden corner of the yard, so lost in thought she didn't notice them until she was almost upon them.

"Oh," Nova said, stopping short. "Hi."

"Hi," they replied in unison. Next to Willow, her mom fidgeted with the songbook she was holding.

"Can we come up?" Mom asked after a beat.

Nova glanced at Willow. She could tell what Nova was thinking: that Kelly never wanted to discuss anything of substance in her daughter's earshot. And that maybe they had things of substance left to say. She couldn't know that Kelly had woken Willow early, sliding the lyrics to "The Next Thing You Know" onto her pillow. Urging her to read them—and if she was up to it, to get dressed and come along.

"Please," Mom said, putting an arm around Willow. "We should talk. All of us."

Willow smiled in spite of herself: It felt good, being included at last, even if things were still . . . unresolved. She'd been shedding anger like a virus for days, and was slimmed down now, spent. Nova looked from mother to daughter and seemed to relax a little.

"Okay."

Inside, it was jarring seeing Nova's studio ready to be rid of her. How few boxes it took to hold her belongings—Willow remembered helping Nova unload them, making shy small talk, breaking them down to lay flat beneath the bed. Now, with a little packing tape, everything was back the way it came.

Everything but them.

Would the next tenant be another doula partner, or just a source of rent money? Would she be invited in, like Nova, for meatless Monday dinners and Scrabble nights? Or would Mom keep her at arm's length, Nova's whole tenure transformed so easily from a godsend to a cautionary tale?

Willow didn't want another tenant. And judging from the stricken look on Mom's face, she didn't really, either. But after the way they'd both failed Nova, maybe they deserved one.

Willow set the muffins in the center of the tiny rectangular table, where she'd often sat with her script, running lines with Nova or sketching in the margins: tornadoes, winding roads. She felt suddenly nervous as Nova slid over a counter stool, perching at an awkward height while they took the more suitable chairs. Kelly dropped the songbook onto the well-loved wooden surface, and they all stared at it. The logical place to start.

Nova cleared her throat. "You shouldn't have any more trouble from Bonnie Shaylor. She'll withdraw her complaints against Parting Your

Way. Mason's manager, Dex Marion, is going with her to the police station first thing today."

She paused, but they could only blink at her, processing: Yes, these lyrics were the clear-cut answer they seemed. But *where* had they come from? Nova pressed on, calm. "Dex was out of the country, busy working with another band—and shopping these, totally oblivious as to why Mason wasn't returning his calls. In light of what's written here and his own account of their last conversations, he hopes to speed the police to make a public ruling of accidental death. But even if the investigation stays open, he'll issue a statement saying new information has come to light and the family is satisfied no one—including Mason—was at fault. He also promised to ensure Asha writes a sequel to her little opus. I can't say everything will go away overnight, but it will go away. I made certain everyone involved appreciates the importance of that."

"All that from a song," Willow marveled.

"It's quite a song," Kelly said.

Nova nodded. "It is."

Willow's wide eyes fixed on her mom. Was she really just going to say, *Well, thanks for clearing that up,* and let Nova go? Worse, would she start lecturing—that Nova never should have put herself in this position, where she'd dodged a bullet only because she and Mason had fallen in love . . . which, by the way, Nova also shouldn't have done? Would she go on pretending none of this was her problem, even though she'd been there the whole time, looking the other way? Willow had so much to say. So much she should have already said, if only anyone had been listening. But first, she needed to hear her mom.

Mom leaned in. "From a doula standpoint, want to know what those lyrics said to me?"

Nova bit her lip, shooting another sidelong glance at Willow, lest Mom forget she was there. "That we need a better process for recognizing clients having suicidal thoughts?"

Mom looked surprised. "No. I mean, yes: I do. Your process seems fine. What I was going to say is: You didn't recognize Mason as suicidal because from the day he met you, it wasn't true." She took a deep breath. "My only question is how I didn't recognize how close to the brink you could get, too."

Willow held very, very still.

Nova looked about to deny it, but then . . . shrugged. "We're so close to death every day," she said. "We stand on the brink for a living. If there was a difference with me, that masked it. Like I wanted it to."

"I read your letter," Willow blurted out. "I didn't rip it up like you worried." If they wouldn't fix this, she would. She could. She'd been waiting for the chance, and now . . .

Nova met her eyes. "I'm still so sorry I put your mom and you in this position. I hope I really did get you out of it." She stood, signaling not much left to say, but Willow didn't move.

Neither did Mom.

"I'm not here for your apology, Nova," Mom said, sitting straighter. "I'm here for mine."

"You don't owe me—" Nova started to say, but Mom shook her head.

"I know we've been fast friends. But the truth is, from the day you arrived, you've made me nervous." She said this fondly, like a compliment.

"Thanks?" Nova tried.

Mom gave a little laugh. "Yeah. Mentoring you, you asked questions that never would've occurred to me, which forced me to find answers that wouldn't have occurred to me. We might have both written our own rulebooks, but off paper? You practice by instinct. I only give seminars about instincts."

Nova shook her head. "I don't know anyone less afraid than you to take a client's hand at the end, Kelly. You've done it way more than me. Literally hundreds of times more."

"But I don't throw caution to the wind the way you do. And I'm not talking about leaving your helmet off or smoking with Glenna." Mom pointed at Willow. "You didn't hear that."

For an instant, Nova actually looked frightened. "How did you—"

Mom waved her away. "I'm talking about letting yourself get close enough to your clients to do those things. Even the ones getting the rawest deal. You never did doula work from a place of fear—even though, as it turns out, you were the one with the biggest reason to be afraid. The one who could have *been* a client."

Willow found herself really thinking, for the first time, about why her mom had named this business *Parting Your Way*. Was it about ending things on your terms, or ending things on good terms? These were not, Willow understood now, the same thing. And the last goodbye you ever said wasn't always the most important one. There were so many little goodbyes in between.

"The things you said on Friday . . . they were all true," Mom confessed. "I've avoided anything that made me think too hard about my own mortality. Anything I didn't want to have to discuss with my daughter. Any emotions I didn't want to feel." She reached over and ruffled Willow's hair, even as tears sprung to her eyes. "I even framed our partnership in fear. I left the hardest cases to the newest doula—and yes, there were logistical reasons, but let's call them what they were: excuses. And then, when your roughest case got rougher? Not only did I not shield you from blame, but I doubted you myself. And then to find out that you used to be a little more like me, before?"

Nova was teary now, too. "I was never like you, Kel. You might work by the book, but you love that book. I was a sleepwalker. Meek, passive, numb—and even after, all I did differently was promise myself that no matter how bad I messed things up"—they both laughed, wryly, sniffling—"I wouldn't sleepwalk again. I'd march or run or stand in mountain pose or walk backward, as long as I had purpose. That's what you gave me when you made me your partner. Purpose. So don't give me that whole student-becomes-the-mentor bit, okay?"

This was what Mom called "having a moment." Willow watched her and Nova smiling through their tears and could almost convince herself this would be enough to make things right, no matter what happened next. But it wasn't enough. Because it wasn't everything.

It had not occurred to them that all of this was anyone's fault but their own.

But as Willow had struggled to piece things together all by herself

during this terrible, cryptic, heartbreaking week, it had more than occurred to her.

It had not left her alone.

"You have to stay!" Willow erupted, before she lost her nerve.

Both women flinched, like they'd almost forgotten she was there.
Willow stomped her foot beneath the table. She had to go through
with this. She'd even figured out how to say that line. *There's no place like
home.* And the thing was . . . it did hold up.

Even when you got caught trying to sneak out late at night, even
when you were grounded, even when you told yourself that if no one
asked what you thought, they didn't deserve to know . . . Not only did
it hold up, but this was Nova's home, too.

"When Mom first showed me that song, it seemed like happier
news—all I could think was, *thank goodness he didn't kill himself. Thank
goodness.*" Willow's voice shook. "But now that it's sinking in, I'm sad all
over again. Almost sadder. Because he wanted to live, and he didn't
get to. He wanted to stick around and love you, and *you* didn't get to."

"It is hard," Nova admitted. "I thought it would be enough to know
that all signs point to an accident, but I still find myself wondering
what happened. Maybe it's better not knowing. But if I stay here, I don't
think I'll ever be able to stop imagining."

"If you knew, would you stay?" Willow looked anxiously from Mom
to Nova and back. This was so backward: All she'd wanted was to pull
the people she loved closer. And now look.

"Why do I get the vibe," Mom asked slowly, "this is not a hypothetical question?"

"Please don't be mad," Willow pleaded—not with Mom, but Nova.
"I didn't put it together at first. They told me *truck,* not Jeep. I mean,
who doesn't know the difference? Plus I was grounded, so I could hardly
ask them anything—I had *no* downtime at tech rehearsals, I'm in every
scene. But maybe if I hadn't gotten caught, if I'd been there that night,
too . . ."

"Who's *they?*"

It all sounded so juvenile. She'd just wanted to make the show so epic that no way could the fab four fade. They'd thought they were so clever. Travis had dirt on his older sister. She owed him, and he cashed in on a late-night ride along. The plan seemed innocent enough: She was meeting her high school friends for a bonfire by the creek; the kids needed someplace they could test run in the dark, like onstage, without anyone's parents pulling the plug. *Fine.* His sister had rolled her eyes. *But if you guys get in trouble, I don't know you.*

Willow took a deep breath. And launched into a story about a lion, a scarecrow, and a tin man skipping down the yellow brick road.

# 44

## *Mason*

Mason still didn't know how he'd done it—how he'd moved through the out-of-body experience of the past few weeks and found himself here, out on the other side, his anger and heartbreak transformed to clarity, his output soaring, his faith in himself and his art and the world restored.

Here's what he did know: that Nova's voice had been in his ears, the way she'd sounded that last night—soft and reverent and barely restraining excitement—when she'd only wanted him to give her something to sing along to. That he'd never been much of a computer guy, but he was about to become one, no matter how clumsy these early stages felt—because while this first attempt had taken the form of a near-manic state that barely numbed his pain, the most valuable thing he'd learned was that it didn't have to be this way.

*He* didn't have to be this way.

Songwriting software had never appealed. He'd taken it for a robotic stand-in for the most human process he'd ever known—but man, had tech come far enough to prove him wrong. This was no coded copy:

It was a conduit, one no botched surgery could short-circuit. Imagine his delight to rediscover that fourth dimension he'd lost—where the laws of physics twisted and his heart migrated to his fingertips. The musicality of it could be translated into malleable digital fragments, if he only found the patience to try. Recording interfaces with production modes—multitrack sequencers, samplers, chord progression editors, hair-trigger technology that could let you be *more* of a perfectionist asshole about your compression and reverb and never would he be caught dead using one of those rhyme generators, but still. He took a learn-as-you-go approach.

And he had much more to learn. Much further to go.

Not that all was set right—not yet. But for the first time, and just in time, enough would be enough.

The best and most surprising part of that feeling—that exhale of relief, freeing him at last—wasn't just about the demos he'd sent Dex. It wasn't even about the fact that his phone had rung back precisely thirty-seven minutes later, exactly the length of time required for Dex to play everything through nonstop. *You're back, baby!* Dex cheered, and Mason wanted to yell, *You're damn right I am,* or maybe, *I never really left,* but he no longer knew which was true. Never had he felt both so changed and yet so glad to again feel at home in his own skin. Possibly he hadn't gotten back to anything at all, but pushed past it, to a place where he knew at last what he wanted. Where he might not be able to see where he was going, but at least his legs still worked.

He'd squinted into his future and gotten a good look at the once insurmountable boulder blocking his path. At the thing Nova had been banging her head against right up until that last night, when she'd looked so dumbfounded that Mason couldn't just step around it. And finally, he'd seen: that the obstacle was no rock but only him, arms crossed and ears plugged, planted smack in the center of his own damn way.

He refused to believe he'd lost her for good. On the floor of his closet, with his feet flat on the ground and his back against the wall, he'd done the thing she'd been most insistent he do.

He'd forgiven himself. No more crying, no more yelling. Just a good long self-talk, trying out the assurances he'd heard plenty of times from other people, but never once believed.

*You didn't have any way of knowing how it would turn out. Overuse injuries this severe are freakishly rare—and even if you could do it over, would you honestly do it differently? Would you stop to rest knowing what you'd be missing, knowing there were no guarantees?*

*Easing up might have helped. Or not. The nerves could have flared right back up the second you resumed playing. And you'd never have gotten as far as you did. Never even known that you could.*

He was surprised to find that somehow, at last, he meant every word. He watched in amazement as the stone of his stubbornness rolled aside, and every other thing that had been stopped up behind that boulder shook loose. The music. The vision. The love.

The *love*.

Nova had been right—about the songwriting, sure, but infinitely more. His mind was so like his arm—he hadn't known the damage he was doing until it overtook him. He'd forgotten the way to forge ahead to his big, horizon goals *was* to stop and notice what was around him, to watch the man with the bottle of moonshine, to find the poetry in an empty parking lot, and to let his brain write the music while he drove. He'd never been one to wait until he got where he was going to get started.

What he wanted to do now—*all* he wanted to do now—was fall down at Nova's door. But he didn't deserve the chance yet, not quite. Their forgiveness deal had called for only two names, but Nova had taken it easy on him.

If Mason was back to stay, Bo needed to know the boundaries, too. No more muscle jokes. No more grudges. No more deadlines on his grief or pain. Just—no more. In turn, Mason would step up and stop acting like a one-man show. He was ready to lay it down now, and he thought that after meeting Nova, Bo was ready to hear it. That unfamiliar chastised look in his eyes at the bonfire—she'd helped Bo start to understand. Mason would finish.

Seeing Bo *could* wait, but seeing Nova could not. Not an hour longer than necessary. So he'd yank his brother out of bed in the middle of the night if it meant he'd be done in time to beg Nova's forgiveness in that corner of her yard where she began every day greeting the sun.

He headed out in the dark, a man possessed, though he'd barely slept for days. He'd been asleep for months before this; he wasn't tired, but more awake than he'd been in too long, and Nova had been right about that, too. How the sharp edge of doing something you maybe shouldn't could carve you into a more interesting shape. One that might seem hard at first, until you held it in your fingers and realized it had so very many edges, the combined effect was rather smooth.

He didn't turn on the radio, preferring the silence. He did take down the top, preferring the stars. He forewent the highway for his old favorites, the back roads. They were mostly empty, hazy in the streetlights' glow. He used to love this time of night, until he'd taken to avoiding all the things he loved. It had been a night like this, in fact, when he'd found himself pulling into that dive to "celebrate" the one-year anniversary of signing that record deal. He'd hunkered down with a whiskey double, wondering how many it would take . . . and overheard the conversation about death doulas. The one that led him to do the most nonsensical and yet smartest thing he'd done since his life fell apart.

He'd gone to a death doula to say goodbye. And somehow, she'd saved his life instead.

He saw the kids in the road with plenty of time to stop. Three of them, backs to him, arms linked, doing some skip-dance down the center of the street, poised to go over the little concrete overpass ahead. He slowed, thinking how their silhouettes looked like an album cover, so incongruous—and what they hell *were* they doing out here in the dark? They glanced back in unison when they heard the Jeep coming, and—they looked familiar. Vaguely, and then he put it together: *The Wizard of Oz*. The kids from the day he'd ridden with Nova to pick up Willow. He half wished Willow was with them—as good an excuse as any to turn around right now and take her home to Kelly. And Nova.

They were on the sidewalk now, safely out of the way, and he picked up speed again, keeping his eye on the kids, just in case.

It was the dog he didn't see. Not until it leapt from the basket and landed square in the center of the bridge, running right toward him.

Toto. The rescue pup they'd wanted to take onstage, though it wasn't allowed. Not unless they could convince the grown-ups the dog could cooperate. Mason got it, then: They were out here practicing. Training.

Innocent kids. Stupid dog.

Braking wouldn't cut it. He yanked at the steering wheel—or meant to. His brain gave the command, but his dominant arm seemed unplugged from his body. He stared at it in horror, waiting for it to engage, but it didn't.

Couldn't.

He'd swerved out of the way in plenty of time. Swerving back was the trouble.

Later, Willow's friends would wonder at the way he'd driven straight off the side. After they'd screamed, clutching each other, peering in horror over the edge, they'd argued over what they'd seen. He'd had time to correct the swerve, but didn't—did that mean he *meant* to jump the barrier, to start that midair roll? Or had something gone wrong with his car?

The sirens would come right away. A police patrol nearby had heard—the crash, it turned out, but not them. In their shock, they'd panicked. They were supposed to be home in bed. They'd been expressly told *not* to attempt this with the dog, which was why they were here in secret. They'd be grounded forever, maybe even kicked out of the play. And besides, what could they tell the police that would be useful? They were as baffled as anyone. They would tell no one.

Only Dorothy. Who'd been intercepted on her way out that night. Lucky for her.

After Willow's tearful report, going hand in hand with Kelly and Nova to meet Bonnie and Dex at the police station, crash investigators would check again for any sign of mechanical failure that might align with this order of events, but find none. Speculation would touch on other explanations: that he might've been half asleep or seen something the kids didn't.

It was Nova who said what they were all thinking: Maybe his condition had proven fatal after all. But they'd never know for sure.

In the last seconds that his tires kept contact with the pavement, Mason didn't have time for much. But he realized what he'd done, for the first and certainly last time: He'd failed to account for his shitty reflexes, the sluggish muscles that refused to move if he didn't ask nicely, the constant numbness and throbbing dull pain that had dominated every thought, that he'd just spent two and a half weeks pushing to the brink and apparently over it. All that unpleasant, life-ruining hyperawareness had left his mind, in the one moment he'd needed to remember.

He marveled, as the ground rushed to meet him, that he'd finally achieved the last impossible thing he'd come to Nova wanting: to forget all about his injury.

To replace it in his mind, and in his heart, with better things.

# 45

*Nova*

LATER

In the end, I stayed.

Stayed an end-of-life doula.

Stayed an honorary member of Kelly and Willow's family.

Stayed in Cincinnati, closer to my own—and not just geographically.

Stayed in contact with Asha, even, who apparently had a conscience after all. One that pulled strings to offer me my own weekly column, where I answer reader questions. Her pitch? Maybe those of us who have a long way to go need a death doula's advice most of all.

*Live to Tell,* it's called.

We have so much business now, Kelly is looking to take on a third partner.

It's not going to be Maggie.

Dad helped me trade the bike for a Jeep. I still get almost as much wind in my face, still race through the open air with a freedom and defiance I love. It's a little safer this way—but not too safe.

I like to take the top off and drive out to someplace with a nice, wide view of the sky. I climb into the back, stretch out my legs, and breathe deep.

I don't need music on to feel closer to Mason there.

And it's one of my favorite places to never miss a sunrise.

# Acknowledgments

Every one of my books begins feeling like a far-flung dream. None of them would become reality without my agent, Barbara Poelle: Thank you, for believing in me and my work, then and now, for knowing exactly when to offer to carry a heavy weight, and for all the turduckens, rat kings, and PJ pants that add up to make you one of my favorite people.

Alexandra Sehulster, your insightful editorial suggestions have once again improved upon this story immeasurably: Thank you, for makir every step in the process a true collaboration and a joy.

I'm so fortunate to be publishing a fifth novel with such warm support from the team at St. Martin's Press: Endless gratitude to Jennifer Enderlin, Katie Bassel, Alexis Neuville, Brant Janeway, Mara Delgado-Sanchez, the pros at Macmillan Audio, and all the hardworking colleagues who've had a hand in bringing my books to the world.

I was two-thirds through the first draft of this novel when the pandemic shutdowns began, and the whole context of end-of-life doulas, their calling, and their work changed seemingly overnight. Even as an observer, writing about connection at the end of life, knowing so many people were taking their last breaths alone, proved more difficult than I could ever have imagined. My heart goes out to all the doulas who found themselves in the helpless position of being unable to meet their clients in person, to the patients who found themselves without immediate access to family, dear friends, and doulas in their most difficult hours, and to all the first responders and medical workers who so courageously stepped up to fill those shoes and more.

My sincere hope as we move forward is that the value of palliative care has become clearer than ever, and that the system expands support and recognition of their efforts to meet the needs of future clients in ever more accessible, affordable, accepted, and meaningful ways.

When I landed on the idea of writing about a death doula, one of the first and best things I did was to become a regular listener of the *Ask a Death Doula* podcast by Doulagivers founder Suzanne B. O'Brien, R.N. With her background as a hospice and oncology nurse—and her groundbreaking initiatives to train, grow, and connect both new and established end-of-life doulas—O'Brien is a compassionate and well-informed host who generously gives listeners invaluable insights to consider, no matter what challenges they're facing (or not yet facing) in their lives. Her Doulagivers webinars, many of which are free and accessible to the public, offer a more in-depth look at the doula approach and a wonderful starting point for anyone interested in learning more.

Dr. Karen Wyatt's *End-of-Life University* podcast proved another fantastic resource for patients, caregivers, novelists (ahem), and everyday people looking to be more thoughtful in how they view the end of life—and make peace with tough goodbyes of all kinds. Her episodes early in the covid crisis were especially enlightening, and her insights on goodbye rituals helped inspire Mason's parting with his beloved Gibson.

Closer to home, Cincinnati-based end-of-life doula and A Ray of Hope founder Rev. Dr. Kristy A. Meineke-Brandabur, Ph.D., responded kindly and patiently to my inquiries, answering emails, graciously making time for an interview, and sharing helpful examples of the types of paperwork new clients may receive.

None of my characters are in any way based on any of the above individuals, and as a fiction writer I've taken creative liberties for the sake of the story and its characters. Any perceived errors or stretches of the imagination are mine alone.

Several nonfiction books were instrumental in better understanding some of this novel's more difficult subject matter: *Radical Remission: Surviving Cancer Against All Odds* by Kelly A. Turner, Ph.D. (which helped inform Nova's backstory, as well as some of her favorite client exercises), *Maybe You Should Talk to Someone* by Lori Gottlieb, *When Breath Becomes Air* by Paul Kalanithi, and *Being Mortal: Medicine and What Matters in the End* by Atul Gawande. In the absence of many other novels featuring death doulas, I also found meaningful inspiration in works of fiction focusing on those who bear witness at the other end of life's journey, including *Midwives* by Chris Bohjalian, *The Secrets of Midwives* by Sally Hepworth, and *The Midwife's Confession* by Diane Chamberlain.

I'm grateful to The Clermont County Public Library for hosting a free public QPR training that not only provided valuable insight to this novelist, but a valuable resource to the entire community. The QPR Institute's *Question, Persuade, Refer* method is designed to help every one of us prevent suicide. Learn more at qprinstitute.com. If you are having thoughts of suicide, please don't struggle alone. Reach out to the National Suicide Prevention Lifeline at 1-800-273-TALK.

Sonja Yoerg and Katrina Kittle, your expert reads of an early draft provided valuable feedback as well as a much-needed gut check. Sonja, I've said it before and I'll say it again: I'd have paid good money for those line notes! Your background in psychology makes for such wise direction, and you always make me laugh—the *best* kind of support. Katrina, your eye on sensitive subject matter is a true gift, and I'm grateful for your friendship in writing and in life.

Special thanks to Mike Heffron, whose musician's eye on Mason's key scenes proved invaluable: Thank you, for your willingness to make the time to read, and for applying your expertise to such thoughtful suggestions. And to my original and forever boss, Jack Heffron, for calling in the favor on my behalf: I owe you one! But then again, I owe you a lot.

During such an isolating year, friendship became a lifeline for my creative process. My colleagues at Career Authors, *Writer's Digest*, Tall Poppy Writers, and Fiction Writers Co-op make me feel like I still have coworkers in all the best ways. I'm grateful to the Dayton power trio of Sharon Short, Kristina McBride, and Katrina (already mentioned) for our text chains, email threads, and meetups; to Heather Webb, for being so good-humored and smart about all things writing and publishing, and to Abbey and Lauren for totally un-writing-related sanity checks and late-night laughs from six (or more) feet away.

Glenna Fisher: I'm cheering for you and your beautiful way with words. Thank you, for so much kindness and support, and for letting me borrow your name.

To Joseph-Beth Booksellers and Penguin Bookshop: Big gratitude for keeping a hometown girl's titles front and center, and for always being such lovely launch hosts.

To all the book clubs who've selected my titles for your discussions, and especially those who've invited me to visit with you over wine, laughs, and/or Zoom: Your enthusiasm means more than I can say. Thank you, for making everything more fun! (Interested in getting your own book club in on the action? Simply visit the contact page of my website, jessicastrawser.com.)

Astute readers from the Cincinnati area may notice some minor liberties taken for the sake of the story: Though many of the story's settings are real, Parting Your Way is in an imagined composite town on the far east of the city, outside the 275 loop. Kincaid Lake State Park, where Nova takes Mason on a March day, typically doesn't open its campground for the season until April 1, though many other Kentucky state parks offer year-round camping. And no, I've never been stuck atop Diamondback—though I've seen it happen.

Saving the best for last, my family: Holly and Michael Yerega, Evan and Courtney and my beautiful niece; Aunt Lindy and Uncle Bob; Susan Hayden and the whole Pittsburgh crew: Thanks to all of you for a lifetime of encouragement and love. Terry and Martha and all of the

Strawsers: I'm so lucky to have married into the best kind of second family.

Scott and the kids: You all walk the world carrying my heart. I'm so lucky to share my best days in this universe with you three. Ain't no mountain high enough.